A HEART ONCE BROKEN

# JERRY S. EICHER

HARVEST HOUSE PUBLISHERS
EUGENE, OREGON

All Scripture quotations are taken from the King James Version of the Bible.

*Cover by Garborg Design Works, Savage, Minnesota*

*Cover photos © Chris Garborg; Bigstock*

This is a work of fiction. Names, characters, places, and incidents are products of the author's imagination or are used fictitiously. Any resemblance to actual persons, living or dead, is entirely coincidental.

**A HEART ONCE BROKEN**
Copyright © 2016 Jerry S. Eicher
Published by Harvest House Publishers
Eugene, Oregon 97402
www.harvesthousepublishers.com

Library of Congress Cataloging-in-Publication Data
Eicher, Jerry S.
A heart once broken / Jerry S. Eicher.
    pages ; cm. — (St. Lawrence County Amish)
ISBN 978-0-7369-6587-3 (pbk.)
ISBN 978-0-7369-6588-0 (eBook)
1. Amish—Fiction. 2. Mate selection—Fiction. 3. Man-woman relationships—Fiction. I. Title.
PS3605.I34H43 2016
813'.6—dc23

                                                      2015016852

**Printed in the United States of America**

        16 17 18 19 20 21 22 23 24 / LB-KBD / 10 9 8 7 6 5 4 3 2 1

# Chapter One

Lydia Troyer smoothed the wrinkles in her dress with a quick brush of her hand as she watched Ezra Wagler's buggy pull into Deacon Schrock's lane on Kelley Road. Now Ezra would put his horse, Midnight, in the barn and join the other St. Lawrence County Amish young people with the work at hand.

They had all gathered on this Friday evening to help clean the house and yard of the recently arrived deacon and his *frau*, Ruth Ann, who had both just joined the community. After their tiring move from Holmes County, Ohio, the couple appeared happy and had settled easily into the North Country in upstate New York.

Lydia gave her dress another quick brush and glanced at the barn door, hoping to catch Ezra's attention as he joined the young workers. A minute later and still no Ezra, Lydia looked across the yard to where her cousin Sandra Troyer was on her knees in the garden, pulling weeds with several of the other girls. Lydia allowed a smile to creep across her face. Tonight she had the advantage over Sandra. Her brush-cutting assignment wouldn't leave smudges on her dress or dark streaks on her hands. Sandra, too, was looking at the barn door for the same reason she was. As were a few of the other young girls with similar aspirations.

That was one of the things so maddening about Ezra, besides his handsome *goot* looks. He was the young man many of the community girls set their *kapps* for…though everyone knew she and her cousin Sandra had the inside track. The two had vied for Ezra's attentions ever since they finished their *rumspringa* days—about the same time Ezra and his family joined the community.

The rivalry of the two cousins had begun in their school days, long before Ezra had arrived. Even as rivals, they had managed to stay steadfast friends, though lately things had become a little grim. What had begun as a healthy competition—such as who could get the most 100s in school—had turned into something more serious after their *rumspringa* convinced both of them to be baptized and settle into Amish life. The cousins had wasted no time making their interest in the newcomer known. And Ezra, seeming to enjoy the attention, was obviously in no hurry to choose between the two cousins.

"Maddening!" Lydia muttered aloud.

"I know," Rosemary said from a few feet away. "These weeds are stubborn as all get-out." Lydia took another whack with her hoe as she gave Rosemary a smile. Thankfully the younger girl couldn't read her thoughts.

Though Lydia's rivalry with Sandra descended to low depths at times, neither she nor Sandra seemed able to back off. On this point they were equally determined. Whoever won Ezra's hand in marriage would have won the most important competition between the two girls.

For this contest they were evenly matched indeed. Both Sandra and Lydia had decent looks—among the best in the St. Lawrence County Amish community. Lydia had heard whispered more than once by one of the younger girls in frustration, "Those pretty Troyer cousins!"

Lydia stood up straighter as she caught sight of Ezra's smiling face. He walked her way, but then he glanced across the barnyard to where Sandra was working and waved toward her. Sandra waved back, but stayed on her knees. Lydia grinned as Sandra tried in desperation to tuck a few loose strands of hair under her *kapp* with one hand. The attempt, no doubt, left further smudges of dirt on Sandra's face.

Ezra hollered something toward Sandra she couldn't understand. Sandra appeared to smile and hollered something back as Ezra moved closer. Lydia could see the girls near Sandra giggle at this exchange between the two. After a few words, Ezra moved on, walking toward Lydia.

"Looks like you get your chance now," Rosemary said with a wicked smile. "When are Sandra and you going to settle this matter?"

Lydia didn't answer. There wasn't anything to say. Ezra would choose soon. He would have to. She so wanted to win this competition. It had always been difficult to tell who would gain the upper hand, whether Sandra or herself. Back in their school days Sandra would have the best average grade one week, and the next week Lydia would be ahead. But with this contest, someone would be left heartbroken. That would hurt worse than any defeat they'd suffered at school.

Lydia rallied her emotions as Ezra drew near.

"Hi there, Ezra," Rosemary chirped before Lydia could speak. "We've been needing a man on this fencerow for some time."

Lydia gave Ezra a sly smile, but remained quiet now that Rosemary had spoken up first. She used a low-key approach. Sandra, on the other hand, could chatter a hundred miles a minute when she had the opportunity.

"Well, then. It looks like I've come to the right place," Ezra said with a chuckle.

Lydia gave Ezra an admiring look. "You should be able to handle the rest of this fencerow all by yourself then."

"Oh no," Ezra protested. "I wouldn't want to lose the company of two such pretty females. Please stay."

Rosemary gave a sly grin. "Your sugar tongue will get you nowhere with me, you know."

Ezra grinned. "A man's gotta try, doesn't he?"

Lydia joined in their laughter. That was what she loved about Ezra. He could joke and laugh with any of the young people and make everyone feel special and appreciated.

Rosemary handed her hoe to Ezra. "Here, I'll go get another one."

"Thanks," Ezra replied, seemingly pleased with the offer.

Lydia worked on a tall thistle as Rosemary hurried away. This gave her a few moments alone with Ezra. Giving him a quick glance, she said, "You look handsome tonight. Did your *mamm* make that new shirt for you?"

Ezra grinned and said, "*Yah*. Thanks for the compliment. Now I can relax for the rest of the evening knowing everything's fine. There's nothing like arriving at a gathering and finding out your *mamm* forgot to sew a seam."

"You're *mamm* wouldn't do that," she chided. "She's among the best seamstresses in the community."

"*Yah*, I was teasing." Ezra whacked away at the weeds again before he looked up to say, "I heard there was another new family moving into the community. Have you met them?"

"No." Lydia busied herself with a stubborn root.

"The oldest boy is around our age, I was told." Ezra gave Lydia a quick glance. "His name's Clyde Helmuth. He's the boy right over there—the one with the pitchfork."

Lydia looked toward where Ezra had motioned with his chin. There was indeed a new boy near the barn. She had been too wrapped up in Ezra to notice. His straw hat cast shadows on his face, but he looked handsome enough.

"I imagine you girls will have him matched up with someone before long," Ezra teased.

Lydia teased back by saying, "Maybe so. Maybe it'll be me. I seem to be available." She gave the weeds in front of her another wallop.

"Surely you wouldn't fall for a strange man so quickly," Ezra scolded.

"Maybe I would and maybe I wouldn't," Lydia said. "And who knows. My cousin Sandra might fall for him."

"Are you wishing she would?" Ezra's eyes twinkled. He was on to her now.

"*Yah*," Lydia admitted. She knew she might as well say the truth. "That might help you make up your mind."

Ezra grinned from ear to ear. "Maybe it would and maybe it wouldn't," he teased back.

Ezra was still grinning when Rosemary returned with her new hoe. She gave them both a quick look and said, "Is something funny going on that you want to share with me?"

"No," Ezra said, teasing again. "We thought maybe you got hung up talking with the new fellow over by the barn. Young and handsome Clyde Helmuth?"

Rosemary colored a little. "Clyde who?"

Ezra laughed. "I can go tell him you're available."

"No need," Rosemary snapped. "He already knows that. Clyde and I go way back. Our families have been friends for years…before his family moved here."

Ezra's tone softened. "I didn't know that. Did something happen between the two of you?"

The look on Rosemary's face was enough of an answer, but she still said, "I used to date him, but we broke up."

"I'm sorry to hear that." Lydia reached over to give Rosemary a quick squeeze on the arm. "I had no idea."

Rosemary shrugged. "Most people don't know. It was only for a few dates. Clyde felt like the relationship wasn't what he wanted."

"There will be someone for you, I'm sure," Ezra encouraged her.

"I can see why your heart is still attached to the man," Lydia whispered to Rosemary, loud enough for Ezra to hear. "He's quite handsome."

"*Yah*." Rosemary bit her lip and attacked a thick weed with her hoe.

Ezra gathered up an armful of thornbushes and headed toward the garden where Sandra was working. Lydia tried to keep busy and not pay attention to what Ezra was doing. The burn pile was near the garden's edge, and Lydia was sure Ezra would stop to speak with Sandra.

Lydia turned her attention to Rosemary. "Is it hard for you, then? With Clyde now living right here in the community?"

"No, it's fine." Rosemary put on a brave face. "I have to get over him, that's all. And I will. He and his *daett* just moved here after his *mamm* died. He's carrying a heavy load now."

"Oh, I'm sorry to hear that," Lydia said.

Rosemary paused with her hoe in one hand. "And as for me, you or Ezra don't need to feel bad. It's not as though I want another chance with Clyde. That's clearly in the past."

Lydia didn't respond, and the girls turned their attention to their work. Their tools rose and fell in unison as they attacked the thornbushes. The simple peace and camaraderie of their shared disappointments was comfort enough for the moment. But before long, both of them glanced toward the garden where Sandra and Ezra were engaged in a lively conversation.

"See what I mean?" Lydia muttered. "It's maddening."

Rosemary choked back a laugh. "*Yah*, I see what you mean. So that's what you were muttering about earlier. I thought it was the weeds."

"Maybe it *is* a weed," Lydia said, but she knew it was the bitterness in her heart speaking. The truth was, she loved Ezra.

# Chapter Two

The following Saturday evening, Lydia ran to the front window of the Troyers' living room and peeked through the drapes. A buggy had rolled into the drive a few moments earlier, and Lydia watched as the lengthy form of Deacon Schrock climbed out. The deacon tied his horse to the hitching post, but he made no move to go any farther. Rather, the deacon stood beside his horse with clasped hands. Lydia pulled back from the window. Did Bishop Henry already have the deacon busy on church work—even though he'd only recently arrived in the community? That was possible, but what anyone in the family could have done to provoke a visit from the deacon was beyond her. All of her older brothers and sisters were married. The deacon would visit their homes if there was a problem, and she certainly hadn't disobeyed the *ordnung*. Her younger sisters, Emma and Rhoda, were still in their *rumspringa* time. They would be gone for the evening in thirty minutes or so, but they weren't subject to the deacon's jurisdiction. Unless her sisters had brought embarrassment to the community. She should check with her sisters more often, Lydia told herself. Maybe the two were up to something that had aroused the community's concern. Everyone kept close tabs on the young people in the North Country.

*Rumspringa* in St. Lawrence County wasn't quite the loose affair it was in other Amish communities. All of the families had made sacrifices to move this far upstate in New York, and they didn't want the problems from the old community to follow them. Lydia hesitated but looked past the drapes again. *Daett* had just come out of the barn. She watched as he walked up to the buggy and shook hands with Deacon Schrock. The two were soon deep in conversation. Did Deacon Schrock want something with *Daett* after all?

Lydia ducked behind the drapes again. Come to think of it, *Daett* had seemed distracted lately and so had *Mamm*. But what could *Daett* have done wrong? Lydia peeked out and saw *Daett* and Deacon Schrock still talking beside the buggy. The deacon's visit must have involved some other member of the family. She dropped the drape's edge from her fingertips and walked toward the kitchen, where Emma and Rhoda were busy at work with supper preparations. Neither of them looked up—which wasn't necessarily a sign of innocence. Her sisters always rushed through the supper preparations on a Saturday night so they could leave sooner for their weekend's taste of the world's freedom.

"What have you two been up to?" Lydia demanded. "The deacon's here."

The girls acted as if they hadn't heard. Emma hummed a worldly tune she must have learned from her *Englisha* friends. If *Mamm* had been in the kitchen, Emma would have quit this nonsense at once. But Lydia was too soon out of her own *rumspringa* to complain about an *Englisha* tune being hummed. At least she'd had the decency not to bring anything from the world into the house.

Lydia sighed and glanced toward the living room window again. Maybe one of her sisters had hidden a radio upstairs and had let the fact slip at the Sunday evening hymn singing. That could provoke a visit from the deacon. There would be no discipline for her sisters, but *Mamm* and *Daett's* reputation would suffer if they failed to keep control of their children's *rumspringa* time. The parents were expected to draw the lines clearly between the world and their home. Nothing but trouble would come from such a situation, and trouble was something Lydia didn't need right now. Everything needed to be in order at the Troyer's house so Ezra Wagler would have no excuse to choose Cousin Sandra over her. After all, Ezra came from a well-thought-of family, and his parents would see to it that Ezra chose a *frau* who would uphold the family's tradition as faithful Amish church members.

Lydia tried again in a louder voice. "Why else would the deacon be here if you're not up to no good?"

Emma ceased her humming long enough to say, "I don't know and I don't care."

"That's not a decent attitude," Lydia scolded. "Sounds like the deacon should speak with you while he's here anyway."

Rhoda added her two cents. "That's why I'm in no hurry for church membership. And you wouldn't have been either if you didn't have Ezra Wagler on the brain."

Emma and Rhoda giggled and high-fived each other. That was another thing they wouldn't have dared to do with *Mamm* around.

Lydia exploded. "I didn't join the church for Ezra's sake, and don't do that silly gesture in the house."

"You used to act just like this yourself," Emma shot back. "So don't go all high-and-mighty on us."

"At least I had enough sense to leave that *Englisha* stuff out there," Lydia snapped. "If you two get too silly, you'll never make your way back into the faith."

"Maybe we don't want to," Emma said with a glare. "Look how we work ourselves to the bone when a little electricity in the house would save so much labor. Benny Coon's sister, Avery, had us in her house for a party last weekend, and you should have seen all the fancy things she has. Even the clothes dryer is inside the house and runs on electricity."

"You should be ashamed of yourselves with such talk!" Lydia said, trying to keep the tension out of her voice. "You're supposed to taste the things of the world and get them out of your system, not get used to them or bring them home with you."

"Speak for yourself." Rhoda gave Lydia a rebellious look. "Be thankful we made supper so you can work on that new dress to impress Ezra Wagler with tomorrow."

Lydia winced but kept the confidence in her voice. "*Yah*, and maybe I'll be sewing his shirts soon—if the two of you don't destroy the family's reputation first."

The two girls were silent, and Lydia refrained from any further protest. Where was *Mamm*? Without *Mamm* around, Lydia always seemed to stoop to silly arguments with her younger sisters. If her two older sisters, Lucy and Betty, were still at home instead of married, they'd know how to handle Emma and Rhoda. Lucy was wise beyond her years and a true asset to the family's standing in the community. And Betty had married Bishop Henry's son, Lonnie. Lydia could never match the reputations of her older sisters, but that didn't mean she had to descend to Emma and Rhoda's level.

"I'm going to find *Mamm*," Lydia mumbled. The two girls giggled as Lydia walked off. Clearly Emma and Rhoda thought they held the high ground. *More like the low ground,* Lydia told herself. But she had other concerns at the moment. Why was Deacon Schrock there? That question still wasn't answered. Her sisters acted too confident. They obviously hadn't done anything wrong—at least that they knew of.

Lydia peeked out of the living room window again as she passed. *Daett* had his head bowed, and Deacon Schrock appeared to be in the middle of a lecture. Could *Daett* have done something wrong after all? Fear stabbed at Lydia. But what could that be? *Daett* didn't bend the *ordnung* in any way, and both of her parents gave the community their full support. Betty couldn't have married Bishop Henry's son under any other circumstances.

Lydia opened the stair door and glanced up the steps. Only silence greeted her, so *Mamm* must have finished the Saturday cleaning and was no longer upstairs. Had *Mamm* gone outside? Maybe she was in the garden? But that was unlike her on a Saturday evening. Lydia closed the door but paused to listen. She had heard something—a faint sob coming from the first-floor bedroom. Lydia held her breath as she tiptoed in that direction. Did *Mamm* know why Deacon Schrock was there?

The bedroom door was ajar, and Lydia entered to find *Mamm* seated on the edge of the bed, her face in her hands.

"*Mamm*, what's wrong?" Lydia sat down beside her.

"We're ruined," *Mamm* whispered.

"Ruined?" Lydia tried to breathe. "Why are we ruined?"

"We just are. That's why Deacon Schrock is here." *Mamm* stifled a sob.

Lydia gripped *Mamm*'s arm. "How can we be ruined?"

*Mamm* stared blankly across the room. "*Daett* made some bad business investments and all our savings are gone. He still owes much more than we can ever pay back." *Mamm* placed her head back in her hands, but the sobs had ceased.

"But *Mamm*." Lydia slipped her arm around *Mamm*'s shoulder. "Deacon Schrock is here to help in our time of trouble. You mustn't let this shame overcome you. Others in the community have had financial problems. It's not like this is—"

*Mamm* stopped Lydia with a shake of her head. "Deacon Schrock isn't here to help, not after *Daett* tells him everything."

"There's shame, *yah*," Lydia allowed. "But you shouldn't take this so hard. Money isn't everything. You know this."

*Mamm* lifted her face and sat up straight on the bed. "The shame is too great. *Daett* is telling the deacon because he must. I didn't want him to, but I know that's not possible. Not if we're to get support from the church, which we must. We can't go bankrupt. That would bring an even greater shame on the community."

"I still don't understand," Lydia said. "But then what do I know about money?"

"Thank the Lord you don't," *Mamm* whispered. "I have learned so many things the past few weeks that I think my hair must have all turned white."

Lydia glanced over at *Mamm*'s hair. "Your hair is not white," she said as she reached over to hug *Mamm*. "It will turn out okay, I'm sure."

*Mamm* didn't look convinced as she got up from the bed, wiped her eyes, and headed toward the kitchen with Lydia following her. Thankfully Emma had begun to hum the Sunday morning praise song by the time they walked in, and *Mamm* joined in the supper preparations as if nothing was wrong.

Lydia returned to working on the new dress she had started that morning. She focused on the pieces of cloth as the foot-pedaled sewing machine hummed under her. Emma and Rhoda had been correct about her interest in Ezra. Her failure to keep Ezra's attention at the youth gathering this week troubled her more than her family's financial problems. Ezra couldn't go on forever in his undecided state. If she wore a new dress this Sunday at the services, it might push him in her direction. Of course, Sandra likely had the same idea. They thought alike in most areas—maddeningly so.

The sewing machine hummed again. This competition was so silly and beneath both of them, Lydia told herself. Maybe the seriousness of Deacon Schrock's visit would stop some of this foolishness. Sandra would certainly find out about her family's problems—eventually, at least. Maybe she should have a talk with Sandra on Sunday to settle the matter of Ezra between them. But how would they do such a thing? They had never been able to settle even the simplest matter before. Now their competition involved love. You couldn't divide a man's heart, or your own, for that matter. They both couldn't marry Ezra, so one of them would have to back down. But who? She wasn't ready to give in, and she was sure the same was true of Sandra. They both wanted Ezra's hand in marriage. A King Solomon was needed to decide between them, but King Solomon had long ago passed from the earth.

Behind Lydia, Emma and Rhoda burst out of the kitchen and raced upstairs. Moments later they came back with carry-on bags in their hands.

"Have fun tonight working on that dress," Emma chirped. "'Cause we're sure going to have fun!"

"Behave yourselves," Lydia chided, but both of them were already out the door. Her sisters had some nerve to set out in their open buggy right in front of Deacon Schrock. She would have waited until Deacon Schrock had left before dashing outside, broadcasting her intentions for the evening. Not that Deacon Schrock disapproved of a *rumspringa* time, but a little discretion was called for. That was a lesson her younger sisters had obviously failed to learn. Lydia laid down the dress with a sigh. She would finish after supper when things had calmed down. Whatever the extent of the problem *Daett* was discussing with Deacon Schrock, his mood wouldn't be improved by his two youngest daughters spiritedly bursting out of the house to set out for a night on the town.

Lydia peeked out of the drapes again. Sure enough, *Daett* still stood with his head bowed as Deacon Schrock glared in the direction of her sisters. *Daett* made no effort to help Emma and Rhoda as they giggled and hitched Archer, the oldest driving horse, to the open buggy. Emma and Rhoda soon climbed in and drove off, without a backward glance.

# Chapter Three

On Sunday Sandra Troyer stood with the long line of single girls near the kitchen doorway. Bishop Henry had walked in the front door moments earlier, and the church service was about to begin. Sandra smiled across the room to where the unmarried men were seated. Ezra Wagler returned her smile at once. He appeared extra handsome in his black suit pants and vest this morning. She had noticed Ezra in his new suit several Sundays ago at the fall communion.

Ezra's *mamm* had a firm conviction on how her men should be dressed, and a new suit every year was on her list of family traditions. Today, Ezra's suit had lost none of its shine. And neither had Ezra. *Yah*, she would marry the man someday, Sandra vowed. And why couldn't she? The competition with Lydia had always been a fifty-fifty chance, but she would try her best. Her very best!

Sandra gave Ezra another warm smile as she took her seat with the other girls. Not a crease was out of place on her dark green dress, which she had sewn together yesterday. She had taken extra care this morning on the way to church. Mark, her older brother, had expected her to help hitch his driving horse, Dixie, to the buggy, and she had obliged him. Thankfully Dixie wasn't like some horses who shed hair for no reason, and Sandra's shawl had served as protection on the drive to church.

"You look pretty this morning," Mark had commented.

"Thanks. I'm surprised you noticed," Sandra answered.

"You don't have to wear a new dress every Sunday," Mark grumbled. "You're *goot*-looking enough in your own right."

She had beamed at him. "This Sunday is important."

Mark appeared befuddled, but asked no further questions about why this Sunday was special. But it was. Something big would happen today. How she knew, she wasn't certain. Maybe the humiliation she had suffered last week at the youth workday with her hands all dirt-smeared and her face streaked with mud brought on the feeling.

On the bright side, Ezra hadn't seemed to mind. He had been as friendly as ever, and had spent more time with her than with Lydia, who worked all evening on a fencerow with Rosemary. Maybe her time had arrived, and Ezra would make up his mind.

And even if he didn't, Ezra deserved extra smiles for his consideration last week, and she had given them to him this morning. Ezra had seen her at her worst, and now Ezra was seeing her at her best. The only fly in the ointment was that Lydia must have had the same idea.

As Sandra made herself comfortable on the hard bench, she noticed Lydia sitting half a bench down in a new dark blue dress that appeared as beautiful and well-made as hers. Which wasn't a surprise. They were well-matched in most things. She had the sunny disposition and the gift of gab, while Lydia had the hidden graces, as *Mamm* said. Sandra was impatient, but Lydia seemed to take Ezra's indecision in stride.

Maybe this afternoon Ezra would ask to take her home from the hymn singing tonight. Sandra clasped and unclasped her hands as the service began. Maybe this final competition with Lydia would even be solved by evening. Lydia would be disappointed, but that couldn't be helped. She, Sandra, was the best match for Ezra. They were the perfect couple. Totally perfect!

Sandra tried to catch Ezra's gaze again, but he was lost in the sea of men seated across the room. Not until she stood at the conclusion of the service did Ezra's smile find hers again. Ezra had smiled at her first this time, Sandra assured herself. *Yah*, something special would happen today. She took a deep breath as the group of girls entered the crowded kitchen, where everyone chattered as they received their assignments on where to help with lunch.

Sandra slipped up to Bishop Henry's *frau*, Lena, and whispered, "I'll take the unmarried men's table."

Lena smiled but didn't object. She handed Sandra two peanut butter bowls. "That should get you started."

"Thanks." Sandra gave Lena a quick smile.

Her interest in Ezra wasn't shameful, Sandra assured herself. Nor was her offer to serve the unmarried men's table. This would give her a chance to speak with Ezra—and the other unmarried men. It couldn't hurt if Ezra was reminded that she had other chances, even if she didn't take them. The newcomer, Clyde from Holmes County, was handsome enough. His *daett* was a widower and had recently moved into the community. Clyde had sent glances her way several times already—glances she had ignored.

Sandra held the peanut butter bowls high as several smaller children looked up hungrily.

"Go find where your *daett's* sitting." Sandra paused long enough to whisper to them. "He might take you with him to the first table." Several of them scurried off to follow Sandra's suggestion.

The unmarried men's table was set up in the back bedroom, and

Sandra paused near the door when Bishop Henry's voice called for the first prayer. She bowed her head along with everyone else. When the "Amen" came, Sandra bounced into the room. Several of the men looked up, and one hollered out, "Howdy there, Sandra. At least we have a server today. I thought they'd forgotten about us."

"You know no one forgets about you, James," Sandra teased back. "And they wouldn't leave a table full of such handsome young men to suffer hunger."

Laughter filled the table, and Ezra looked up with a twinkle in his eye. "And to think that we have one of the prettiest girls to serve our table. What an honor."

"That's sweet of you to say." Sandra beamed in Ezra's direction.

Loud throat-clearing came from several of the men, and protests of, "Please do your courting tonight after the hymn singing."

Sandra joined in the laughter. "Don't eat too much while I'm gone," she chided. "I'll be right back."

Two other girls came into the bedroom when Sandra stepped through the doorway. Thankfully Lydia wasn't among them. Lydia wasn't bold like Sandra was, but Lydia had other charms that she had no compunction to deploy. Likely Lydia would try to sneak out early once Ezra went out to hitch up his horse and engage him in conversation—all under some innocent pretext, of course. They both had their different ways to attract Ezra's attentions. But surely Ezra would soon see that Sandra's way was the best. She would make the man happy as his *frau*. And even before that, she was sure they would be the bubbliest couple in the community—if only Ezra could be brought to his senses. Surely he enjoyed her conversation and light banter. Wasn't that a *goot* enough reason to see more of each other? What better way to spend this winter's cold Sunday evenings than to gather around the pot-bellied stove in the living room of their place on Madrid Road and play backgammon and

Monopoly? Ezra was *goot* at all those board games. She had played with him often enough at the youth gatherings to know. And once married they could laugh and tell each other stories as their *kinner* grew up around them.

Sandra hurried past the married men's table on her way back to the kitchen, but a low whisper stopped her. Sandra turned to see her *daett* motioning for her to come closer. As she approached and bent over with a warm smile, he whispered, "Get your *mamm*. Tell her I have to leave for home right now."

Sandra stood up and stared at *daett*. His face appeared pale under his lengthy beard and his hands were shaking. "*Daett*, what's wrong?" Sandra reached down to hold his arm.

He attempted to smile. "I'd best be going home. I don't feel well."

*But this is unthinkable,* Sandra almost said, but caught herself.

*Daett* must have read her thoughts. "I know," he said. He dropped his fork and groaned. "The meal isn't done, but I must go home."

Several other men must have overheard the conversation and now turned toward *Daett* with concerned looks. *Daett* groaned again and held onto the edge of the table with both hands. Sandra left them to hurry over to the women's table. *Mamm* was in the middle of a conversation with Lena, Bishop Henry's *frau*.

Sandra interrupted. "*Mamm*, you must come. *Daett* is ill."

Alarm filled *Mamm's* face. "*Acht!*" she exclaimed. "We should have stayed home today. Emil hasn't been feeling well all morning."

"Is it something serious?" Lena glanced back across the room toward the men's table, where at least five men had gathered around *Daett*. "You had best go, Edna." Lena prodded *Mamm* with her hand.

*Mamm* stood and hurried toward *Daett* with Sandra following, but *Mamm* was quickly swallowed from sight amongst the gathered circle of men. As Sandra waited a hand came around her shoulder, and Lydia's voice whispered in Sandra's ear. "What's going on?"

"*Daett* is sick. We need to go home," Sandra said.

"We should pray," Lydia said firmly.

Sandra lowered her head and listened to Lydia's whispered prayer. She couldn't understand the words, but thankfulness and peace crept over her. They might be rivals in everything from schoolwork to boyfriends, but when trouble showed up, they were still cousins who lived on the same road and stood by each other.

Sandra slipped her hand around Lydia's shoulder and pulled her close. Lydia finished her prayer and met Sandra's glance with a soft smile. "My *daett* has some problems too. The deacon stopped by to talk with him last night about financial things, but they wouldn't tell me the details."

Sandra nodded. They understood each other well. This was how it always had been. She leaned over to whisper, "You have a nice dress on this morning. It looks *goot*."

"And so do you," Lydia whispered back.

Sandra smiled but the smile faded seconds later. The circle of men around *Daett* had parted to reveal his form lying on the bench, supported on each side by three of the men. *Mamm* was on her knees in front of him, with *Daett*'s head cupped in both of her hands.

"Move back, everyone," someone ordered. "Emil needs air."

Bishop Henry hurried to the front door and swung it open. He grabbed a hat off the floor and fanned the room. The other men lifted *Daett*, and the bench was pulled out from under him.

"Someone bring a blanket," the same voice ordered. A blanket appeared at once from the bedroom and was slid under *Daett*. The men lowered him to the floor.

Sandra stared. *Daett* was more than a little ill. This was serious. Lydia's hand tightened on Sandra's arm, which only made things worse. Lydia had come to the same conclusion.

"Someone should call for the *Englisha* doctor," the authoritative man's voice spoke again.

Bishop Henry hesitated only a moment before he motioned to one of the younger men. Mose Graber hurried out the open front door and ran once he was in the yard.

Sandra tried to move closer, but Lydia held her back. "You can't do anything."

"But I want to see," Sandra protested.

Lydia hesitated, before they both moved closer. *Daett* lay still on the blanket with *Mamm* weeping beside him. Sandra and Lydia knelt down to join them. Tears stung Sandra's eyes as she clung to *Mamm*'s arm.

"I'm afraid he's gone," *Mamm* sobbed.

"Gone!" Sandra tried to get her mind around the thought. *Daett* was dead? But how could that be? He had been alive this morning. She had spoken with him only moments ago.

"Move back," the man's voice ordered again, and several men retreated to allow Lena and several other women through. They stood beside *Mamm*, praying silently.

Sandra felt a numbness creep over her. This was so strange and so sudden. Surely this wasn't true. She looked up to see Ezra's face among the gathered men. His features were drawn with concern. Only moments before they had laughed together and joked while *Daett* had been near death's door. The meal wasn't over, but no one would have any appetite after this. Not if one of their own had died in front of their eyes. The tears trickled down Sandra's face, and she made no attempt to wipe them away.

Bishop Henry spoke now. "We had best move him outside. Maybe that will help." But the effort was useless, Sandra knew—as did all the others. Still, the men obeyed and gathered up the blanket.

Sandra followed *Mamm* with Lydia beside her. Once outside, the men laid down the blanket and they all knelt to pray and wait.

The usual Sunday afternoon noises had begun in the house behind them. The children had to be fed. Life had to go on. But would life ever be the same again for Sandra's family? She tried not to think as flashing lights filled the driveway, and the paramedics took over. *Mamm* left with the ambulance, and Sandra stood unmoving as she watched the lights drive away. Could *Daett* be resuscitated? Sandra seemed to remember stories of men and women who had been dead, but had been brought back by paramedics. Maybe that could happen with *Daett*.

"I'm coming over this afternoon and staying with you this evening," Lydia whispered in Sandra's ear.

Sandra didn't protest, and the two hugged each other. She could use Lydia's presence in the house as they mourned this awful tragedy—if indeed *Daett* had passed from this life.

Sandra had known something would happen today, but not this! Not *Daett's* death!

# Chapter Four

Three days later, Sandra stood beside the open grave as *Daett's* casket was lowered slowly into the ground. *Mamm* wept silently with Lydia's *mamm*, Mary, a step behind her. Sandra's married brothers and sisters, along with their spouses, huddled on either side of them. Lydia had come up to slip her arm around *Mamm's* shoulder during the short graveside service, but *Mamm* had now moved forward to stand alone, so Lydia moved up to stand beside Sandra.

With bowed heads they all waited as the last song was sung. Bishop Henry led the prayer with a tremble in his voice. "Now unto the most High God, the maker of heaven and earth, we lift our hearts today in sorrow and beseech His mercy and grace upon the soul of our departed brother. Be with us as we mourn our great loss, and surrender our own hearts to Your will. Bless the families who are left behind. Comfort them with Your presence. Let us all find peace in the perfection of Your will. Let no bitterness arise in our hearts as we ache and weep. Give us…"

Sandra grasped Lydia's hand as Bishop Henry's prayer continued. She didn't let go even after Bishop Henry said, "Amen," or when the dirt was being thrown on the casket. Not until the mound reached the level of the ground did *Mamm* move back to Sandra, who met her with a long embrace. Sandra's brother, Mark, still stood at the gravesite with his head bowed. He would grieve for a long time, Sandra knew. As the last son in the Troyer household still at home, Mark had been close to *Daett*.

"We must go on with the Lord's help," *Mamm* whispered. "We all must be strong for what lies ahead."

"*Yah*," Sandra agreed. But there seemed to be more to *Mamm's* words than was readily apparent. Since *Daett* had passed on Sunday, there had been little time for private conversations. The whole extended family ached with sorrow.

"Come." Lydia pulled on Sandra's arm and led her back to the buggies parked along the graveyard fence. *Mamm* followed and passed them silently to climb in the front of the Troyers' surrey. "Do you want me to ride with you?" Lydia offered.

Sandra shook her head. "Mark will take us home. I'll see you back at the house for the meal."

"Okay." Lydia let go of Sandra's arm.

Sandra climbed in the buggy and Mark joined them moments later, taking the reins with both hands, his face grim. *I should have taken Lydia up on her offer,* Sandra told herself. Lydia's presence would have been a comfort at least. But she needed to move on. Helping hands were there for a short time, but what about later? *Mamm* was Sandra's biggest concern.

Sandra leaned forward on the buggy seat to touch *Mamm's* shoulder and asked, "Are you okay?"

"The Lord will be with us," *Mamm* responded.

Sandra sighed and settled back into the seat. *Mamm* was putting on a *goot* front, but the pain still cut deep. This wasn't the time to ask, but she wondered what *Mamm* saw in their future. But as she hesitated, Mark beat her to the question. "Jonas and Noah said there's a family meeting right after the meal. What is that about, *Mamm*? Do you know something we don't?"

*Mamm*'s lips pressed themselves into a straight line. "We'd best wait until there's plenty of time to speak of this."

"I want to know." Mark was insistent. "There's something been bothering you these last days—more than *Daett*'s passing."

"I'm still grieving for your *daett*, dear," *Mamm* said in a quiet voice. "Let me have a few more hours before we speak of the future."

Mark fell silent, but he didn't appear happy. *What could be the problem?* Sandra wondered. Surely there wasn't another sorrow that lay ahead for them?

Mark turned around to look at Sandra. "Do you know?"

"Of course not," Sandra said. "*Mamm* wouldn't tell me what she hasn't told you."

Mark nodded and appeared satisfied.

Silence fell in the buggy, broken only by the steady beat of horses' hooves as the long line of buggies made their way back to the Troyers' home. The community women would have a large supper prepared once they arrived. Sandra didn't have an appetite, but most everyone else would be hungry. As supper was served, visitors and family would have a chance for one last conversation. Afterwards they would express their condolences again. The locals would drive home tonight, while the visitors from Holmes County would set out on the long drive home tomorrow. Some of them wouldn't arrive until the late evening hours, but they would all awaken the next morning to a whole new world.

For the Troyer family, *Daett* would be gone, and Mark would be in charge of the farm. He was a year older than Sandra, and should already have found a girlfriend, but he hadn't. Would this change things? Now Mark might be more intent on finding a girl and settling down. No *dawdy haus* had been built yet, and now there wouldn't be one—unless she missed her guess. *Daett* had never been well-off financially, and Mark certainly couldn't afford the expense with *Daett* gone. So what was to become of *Mamm* and her if Mark married? Sandra ran through the options, as the horses' hooves beat the pavement. Maybe Mark would have mercy on them, and they could live in the basement for a few years. That wasn't ideal, of course, and the situation wouldn't be tolerated long by Mark's future *frau*. All Amish women wanted to have a home they could call their own, and raise their *kinner* in peace without in-laws underfoot.

Sandra stared out of the buggy door and thought of Ezra. He had stayed out of sight the past few days, which was proper during a time of grief. Ezra had compassion for her and would find some way to express his feelings soon enough. On her part, she would gather herself together in the next weeks and show Ezra that nothing had changed between them. Lydia wouldn't press on with a relationship with Ezra until Sandra was also ready to pursue him again. Lydia wanted Ezra's attentions badly, but she wasn't underhanded. They would grieve together, as cousins should. She had her *daett*'s passing to mourn, and Lydia her uncle's death. Nothing needed to be said. They both would know when the time had come to renew their pursuit of Ezra.

Sandra focused on the family farmhouse as Mark slowed the buggy and they bounced into the barnyard. The field behind the house was filled with buggies, but an opening had been left for the immediate family to access the property and buildings. After Mark parked, Sandra climbed down to wait for *Mamm*. Mark would have to unhitch by himself. She needed to walk with *Mamm* up to the house, and Mark seemed to understand. His look was kind when they walked past him. Mark would be tender with *Mamm* in the weeks ahead. And Sandra would do her part—but a man's touch was what *Mamm* needed most. Her older brothers might help out with occasional visits, but they had families of their own to care for.

Sandra paused when she heard rapid footsteps behind them. It was Bishop Henry's *frau*, Lena, hurrying to catch up with them. A look of gratefulness filled *Mamm*'s face as they continued toward the house. The whole community had rallied their support, but that was how things were done. *Mamm* would have done the same if this had been anyone else's tragedy.

Sandra stepped ahead to hold open the front door, and Lena entered arm in arm with *Mamm*. Once inside, Lena led *Mamm* to the couch, and helped her sit. Then she said, "You stay right here. I'll get you a plate."

"I don't think I can eat a bite," *Mamm* said.

Lena disappeared toward the kitchen without a protest. Life must go on, which was a lesson everyone was taught. Even in sorrow the point wasn't forgotten. Sandra wasn't hungry either but knew she had better fix herself a plate and eat, hungry or not.

Sandra spooned small portions on her plate and returned to the living room, where *Mamm* was nibbling on a small sandwich.

Women passed Sandra as she sat down to eat. A few stopped to whisper short words of encouragement before they moved on.

"We'll be praying for you and your family."

"Be strong now, Sandra—for your *mamm*'s sake."

"The Lord gives and He takes away. Remember that."

Sandra nodded and tried to smile, but her smile felt worn-out after three days of greeting visitors and family. She finished her plate of food, and as the crowd began to thin out, she moved over next to *Mamm* to hear the good-byes. People had chores at home and had to leave. They came up one by one to give their final condolences as they left. A few of the uncles and aunts also came closer to stand with them.

*Mamm*'s sister Martha, who had driven up from the old community in Holmes County, held *Mamm* for a long time. Martha whispered after she let go, "I'm so sorry for your loss, Edna. I've said this a lot since we came, but our thoughts will be with you in the months ahead. I know these things don't heal quickly."

"Thanks for coming. It means a lot to me," Mamm said, giving Martha another hug.

"You make it *goot*, now." Charles, Martha's husband, shook hands solemnly with *Mamm*. "We're leaving now, and will be on the road at four in the morning, I'm thinking."

"The Lord go with you." *Mamm* tried to smile through her tears.

*Daett*'s brother Richard and his *frau*, Mae, were next in line. *Mamm* shook hands with Jim and said, "Your brother was greatly loved, Jim. He was a *goot* husband to me."

"Our hearts are with you," Richard replied through tears of his own.

Mae gave *Mamm* a long hug and whispered, "We'll be thinking of you."

"Thanks for coming," Mamm told them again.

Sandra's gaze lingered on her relatives until they were outside on the front lawn. Her older siblings stood by the buggies to say their final good-byes to the families, but she would stay with *Mamm* who now stood and moved to the living room window to watch the buggies leave. When the last one pulled out of the driveway, *Mamm* found her way back to the couch.

"Tell the family to come in," *Mamm* ordered, her voice weak. "It's time."

Sandra opened the front door, but she didn't have to call. The children had already been sent off to play, and the adults were on their way in. Sandra stepped aside and held the door open. After they were all seated, she closed the front door and found a chair by the stove. They were an even dozen in all, scattered around the room and in homes in three states. All of them were married except Mark and herself.

*Mamm*'s voice finally broke the silence. "I guess the time has come to speak with all of you about another tragedy in our family. I'm not saying this to place more sorrow on any of you, but because you are my family. The truth is that *Daett* was in serious financial trouble before he passed. In fact, the shock of his loss may have been what brought on his death for all I know." *Mamm* paused to wipe her eyes. "It certainly couldn't have helped."

No one said anything for a moment. Finally Jonas asked, "Would this have anything to do with what the community is talking about, this financial scandal in which several of the men around here were involved?"

"I suppose so." *Mamm*'s voice was even. "Emil never said if anyone else was involved."

Noah spoke up. "I'm sure he knew. These rip-offs depend on someone believing someone else who's already involved. I hear this was one of those schemes where investors receive excessive amounts of interest each month, but the funds in reality come from other people paying in down the line. Eventually the plan falls in on itself when new people stop investing, or too many people draw their original money out."

"So *Daett* was involved in that," Mark muttered. "I should have guessed."

*Mamm* didn't say anything because she didn't know much more about finances than Sandra did. But her brothers obviously understood.

"How badly was *Daett* in debt?" Jonas asked.

*Mamm* looked away before she answered. "I think all of our savings and also all of the money he could borrow on the place."

"*Mamm!*" This exclamation came from Mark. "Was it that bad? Then how am I supposed to take the place over?"

"I don't know," *Mamm* said. "Maybe your brothers have suggestions. You know I don't know anything about money."

This conversation would not turn out well, Sandra knew. She only had to look at her brothers' grim faces to know that.

# Chapter Five

The following week Rosemary Beiler brought her buggy to a stop near the outer edge of the feed store parking lot in the small town of Heuvelton. She climbed down to tie the family's driving horse, Buster, to a light post. Two of the other spots where a horse could be tied were already taken. Fortunately both buggies appeared familiar. She could use help from an Amish man later with her purchase. She didn't normally shop here, but *Daett* wanted a bag of fertilizer and her brothers were busy with fieldwork.

"Rosemary can swing by the feed mill after she goes to the bulk food store," *Mamm* had offered.

*Daett* had grunted and written several numbers out on a piece of paper. "Give this to the front desk, and they'll get what I want. And put the bag in the back of the open buggy," *Daett* had added. "The front is a little small and you could tear the bag."

Rosemary hadn't said anything. The implications were clear. *Daett* figured she would carry the fertilizer out to the buggy by herself—a large bag, from the sound of it. She could ask for help at the front counter if help wasn't readily available from one of the Amish men. She'd prefer aid from someone familiar to her, though, unless

one of those men was Clyde Helmuth. She was still touchy about
Clyde since the man had rejected her. It wasn't right to feel this way,
but she couldn't help herself. Clyde's words had cut deep. *"You and
your family have the ways of the world in your hearts, Rosemary. Some
people just do, and you are one of them. So good night. I won't be seeing you
again."* She could still hear him saying the words at their front door.

What Clyde had meant wasn't difficult to figure out, even if the
accusation was false. *Yah,* her *Daett* had once entertained plans to
join a more liberal Amish church in the old community at Holmes
County. They had attended the services a few times until *Daett* had
reconsidered and repented. But that had happened years ago when
she was a small girl. Everyone in the old community had forgotten,
but not Clyde and his family. They remembered, and now Clyde
had moved here with his *daett.* Few things were feared in the North
Country like people who had liberal leanings. That was the reason the community in St. Lawrence County had been founded in
the first place—to get away from such temptations. No one would
appreciate community members who brought such liberal notions
with them.

Would Clyde drop words to the others about her family's past?
Some of the community people might already know, but if they
did, no one had mentioned anything. Or they thought *Daett* had
sufficiently repented. Lydia and her cousin Sandra had always been
friendly toward Rosemary and went out of their way to make her
feel welcome. She was accepted as part of the community and
needed nothing to stir up old affairs. Help from an *Englisha* man
with a fertilizer bag was innocent enough. Most of the community
would understand that, but she wasn't about to take the chance. If
there were no Amish men inside the feed store, she would carry the
bag by herself all the way across the parking lot. Let the *Englisha* people think what they wished.

Rosemary gave Buster a pat on his neck and checked the tie rope again. "I'll be right back," she told the horse.

Buster whinnied as if he understood. She wanted nothing of the *Englisha* world, regardless of what thoughts *Daett* might have had in the past. And, besides, *Daett* no longer had such thoughts, she was sure. Why would *Daett* have moved all the way to St. Lawrence County in upstate New York if he hadn't wanted a fresh start away from old temptations? Clyde had no right to trouble her here, and hopefully he wouldn't.

Rosemary looked more closely at the two buggies. One was Bishop Henry's buggy. He was older, and if the bishop was inside, she wouldn't ask him for help. Bishop Henry had grown feeble in his old age, which he more than made up for in spiritual strength. The other buggy belonged to Ezra Wagler. She was certain of it now that she looked closer, and surely Ezra would come to her aid. He was polite enough at the youth gatherings, even when he gave most of his attentions to one of the Troyer cousins.

She needed a husband, Rosemary reminded herself, as she lingered near Buster and gathered her courage for the walk to the feed mill's front door. But she hadn't dared to show any interest in a man since Clyde. Nor had any unmarried man paid her more than a passing glance—which was likely her own fault. She didn't give off friendly vibes when it came to men, but it was just the way she was. She couldn't make herself do something that seemed so unnatural to her. She would just have to leave it all to God. As would Lydia and Sandra in their competition for Ezra.

"Dear Lord, help me, and help Lydia and Sandra also to find happiness," Rosemary whispered toward the heavens.

The Troyer cousins had also experienced deep wounds lately. Sandra's *daett* had died, and now there was news spread about the community that both Lydia's and Sandra's *daetts* had been

involved in a scandal that had left their families penniless and
deep in debt.

Sandra's *daett* had likely died of a heart attack over the stress
caused by his financial losses. At least Rosemary's *daett*, David, had
claimed that was the reason for Emil Troyer's passing, and he was
probably right. Before the funeral the whispers around the community had been that Bishop Henry planned to have any man involved
in the scandal make a confession in church—or worse. That could
mean excommunication, which was normally used as correction for
the worst infractions; and on this matter the community had been
greatly shamed. There had been an article in the *St. Lawrence Plain-
dealer* last week about the uncovered scheme. But there was no more
talk of excommunication as punishment for Ben Troyer or anyone
else. The death of Emil had been sufficient rebuke from the Lord,
Bishop Henry said, and *Daett* claimed that most of the community
agreed. Rosemary shivered. Clyde could say what he wished, but at
least her *daett* hadn't been involved in such a thing.

Lydia and Sandra hadn't paid Ezra much attention since the
death of Sandra's *daett*. Ezra had spoken with the cousins at the
youth gathering like normal this week, but both Lydia and Sandra
had responded to his condolences with dropped gazes and short
replies. But soon the two would come out of their self-imposed
mourning. Rosemary wondered, did she dare give Ezra attention in
the meantime? Ezra was here at the feed mill. The thought sent shivers down her back. She didn't have a chance against either Lydia or
Sandra, and besides, both of the cousins were her friends. One didn't
undercut friends, even if she didn't have the slightest chance of win-
ning Ezra's hand. And no doubt Ezra would smile at her clumsiness,
and that would be the end of the matter.

"Hi," Rosemary chirped to the *Englisha* man who stood at the
front door of the feed store.

He was busy with another customer, and only gave Rosemary a passing glance.

"Hi," Rosemary chirped again as she arrived at the counter.

The *Englisha* lady behind the cash register looked up with a smile. "Can I get anything for you?"

"My *daett* wants a bag of fertilizer." Rosemary handed over the paper with the numbers written on it. "This is supposed to mean something, I guess."

The lady chuckled. "It sure does. Just one bag?"

"*Yah*," Rosemary managed.

The cash register rang, and the lady said, "That'll be $12.50, young lady."

Rosemary handed over the twenty-dollar bill *Daett* had given her and collected the change.

The lady handed Rosemary the receipt and motioned with her head. "The boys in the back will help you load, dear."

"Thank you," Rosemary whispered.

She knew an *Englisha* man who worked at the store could load her buggy in a decent manner, but she wanted to find Ezra. She hadn't thought of that before, but an opportunity like this might not arise again. She wouldn't dare be this bold at the youth gatherings, at least not in front of Sandra and Lydia. Here, it didn't matter. She wasn't being disloyal, because nothing could come of a few words spoken to Ezra.

Rosemary took a deep breath and peeked down several of the aisles. Ezra wasn't there. She tried another aisle with no more success. She then made her way toward the back of the feed mill, where she stopped short at the sight of Bishop Henry and Ezra deep in conversation near a stack of feed bags.

What should she do now? Wait? Interrupt them? Before she could make up her mind, Bishop Henry called out, "Well, if it isn't

Rosemary Beiler. What are you up to today, shopping in a feed mill? Did you get lost?"

Rosemary tried to smile. "*Daett* wanted a bag of fertilizer, and *Mamm* had me coming to town anyway." Rosemary waved the receipt in the air.

Ezra appeared friendly enough, but he didn't say anything. Bishop Henry glanced between the two of them and cleared his throat. "Maybe I'd best be getting myself on home, then. And thanks for your counsel, Ezra."

The bishop touched his hat and left. Rosemary tried to breathe. Ezra had given the bishop counsel? Likely this was about the financial scandal that affected the two Troyer families.

Rosemary put on her best smile. "Ezra, could you carry a bag of fertilizer to the buggy for me?"

"Sure," he said, but he seemed distracted. Ezra reached for the receipt and glanced at it. "How's your *daett* doing?" he asked.

"Okay, I guess."

"Thank the Lord your *daett* wasn't involved in what the Troyers got themselves into." Ezra stepped around the corner to hand the receipt to one of the *Englisha* men and finished his thought when he came back. "Their poor families are left at the mercy of the church now."

"I suppose so," Rosemary agreed. "Lydia and Sandra are my friends, although we haven't spoken about this too much. Those things can hurt a lot."

"That they do," Ezra allowed. "I thought both men would have had more sense than to fall for something like that."

"Your *daett* is a *goot* businessman," Rosemary said. She wasn't used to being this close to Ezra alone, and if her heart didn't quiet its race soon, she'd surely pass out on the spot.

Ezra gave Rosemary a kind look. "Your family may not have much, but at least they didn't do something foolish. I've tried to speak a few words of comfort to Lydia and Sandra, but they're quite brokenhearted right now, which is understandable. I don't hold any of this against them."

"*Yah*, it is sad," Rosemary said. "This is a very hard time for them, and especially for Sandra with her *daett*'s death."

"Come." Ezra motioned with his hand. "They should have the bag ready by now."

Rosemary followed him, stealing a brief glimpse of his handsome face when Ezra looked the other way.

"There's our bag of fertilizer," Ezra announced as they approached the back dock. He hoisted the bag on his shoulder and set off across the parking lot without a backward glance.

Rosemary hurried to keep up with Ezra's long steps, and called after him, "You can put the bag in the back."

Ezra braced himself on the side of the open buggy with one hand, then easily lowered the bag with the other. Rosemary forced herself to move closer.

"Thank you." She smiled up at Ezra. "That was nice of you."

Ezra chuckled. "Glad to help, Rosemary. You have a *goot* day now."

She wanted to call after him, and say something…but what? It was all so useless. And she was wrong to act like this anyway.

Rosemary watched Ezra's back for a few moments before she untied Buster and climbed in the buggy. As Rosemary drove out of the parking lot, Ezra waved from the dock and Rosemary waved back. At least Ezra noticed her enough to wave good-bye.

That was a small comfort.

# Chapter Six

Lydia wasn't sure what to do. Sandra had told her at a youth gathering last night that both of her sisters had been with two *Englisha* boys at a rock concert in Canton the weekend before.

On Friday evening, when she found Emma and Rhoda alone in the kitchen washing dishes, she decided she needed to confront them.

As she entered the kitchen, she didn't beat around the bush. "What do you two think you're doing by seeing *Englisha* boys?" Lydia demanded.

Both Emma and Rhoda continued to work and ignored her.

Lydia didn't dare raise her voice. *Mamm* and *Daett* were in the living room, and she didn't want them to overhear this conversation. *Mamm* probably wouldn't say anything, but *rumspringa* or not, this behavior couldn't be *goot* for the family's reputation—especially coupled with the financial disaster *Daett* had already brought on them.

"We're not doing anything anyone else isn't," Rhoda finally offered.

"So who paid for you to attend this rock concert?" Lydia tried to keep her voice even.

Both sisters continued with their work but said nothing.

"Rock concerts are expensive," Lydia continued. "And you were with *Englisha* boys."

"Oh, come on, Lydia. You dated *Englisha* boys yourself during your *rumspringa*. Remember Rudy?" Emma shot back. "So don't condemn us. We're supposed to try out the world during our *rumspringa*."

A denial was useless, Lydia thought. Her sisters knew that many of the Amish girls went out with *Englisha* boys during their *rumspringa* time. But they also should know that those girls paid their own way. Otherwise obligations were incurred, which was the problem. And as for Rudy...well, she had hoped her sisters had forgotten about her dates with Rudy.

"See, she's dumbstruck." Rhoda rubbed the words in. "So don't lecture us, Lydia. There's enough trouble here at home already."

"If you mean our financial situation," Lydia said, "that's still no reason to accept money from *Englisha* boys. They'll expect payment of some kind."

Emma and Rhoda glanced at each other and shrugged.

Lydia didn't hide her horror. "So they already have!"

"I can give out kisses for a rock concert," Rhoda snapped. "That's all we've done, or plan to do."

Lydia sighed. "Will you at least think about our family? Our reputation can be rebuilt, even with what *Daett* has done, but the way you two are acting doesn't help."

"We'll behave ourselves," they said together. "We promise."

Lydia comforted herself, glad that at least her sisters sounded more willing than they had earlier.

"We're good girls," Rhoda added.

Lydia didn't protest as she placed the last of the dirty dishes on the counter and left for the living room.

*Mamm* looked up with a sorrowful face when Lydia walked in. She asked Lydia, "Is something wrong between you and the girls? I thought I heard arguing."

"Just trying to give some advice." Lydia kept her voice lighthearted.

*Mamm* wasn't fooled, though. She chided, "We're all going through some hard times right now, Lydia. Give your sisters some slack."

*You don't know what you're saying,* Lydia almost said, but she tried to smile instead. *Mamm* was doing the best she could.

"I'm awful sorry about our state of affairs," *Daett* said from his rocker. He appeared to have aged some twenty years in the past few weeks.

"We'll make it somehow," Lydia mumbled, then gathered her courage and spoke louder. "Isn't there some way you could give the girls money for their weekends? I think the *Englisha* boys are paying for some expensive items. I don't think that's right."

*Daett's* face grew even longer. "We barely have money for food, Lydia. The church is helping out, so we certainly can't spare money for *rumspringa.*"

"Then tell the girls they have to stay home," Lydia pled.

"And have them rebel completely?" *Mamm* said.

So that was the reason for her parents' hesitation? *Mamm* must have spoken with both of the girls, who must have threatened to jump the fence permanently if their normal *rumspringa* time was interfered with.

"I hope you see our point of view," *Mamm* said. "I know this is hard for you. It has been for all of us…but things could be worse. We still have *Daett* with us."

Lydia nodded. She didn't disagree with *Mamm*, but she wished her sisters would behave themselves. She had never pulled off such stunts while on her *rumspringa.*

Emma and Rhoda appeared in the kitchen doorway. Emma said, "We're all done with the dishes. Anything else?"

*Mamm* tried to smile. "No, girls. You've done *goot* today. Take off the rest of the evening and relax."

Happy looks crossed their faces, and the sisters raced each other up the stairs.

*Daett* stood up from his rocker to look out the window. "There's a buggy coming in the lane."

"Surely it's not the deacon again!" *Mamm* gasped.

*Daett*'s face fell even as he shook his head. "No, it's Sandra. And she's alone."

"Sandra!" *Mamm* and Lydia said together.

Lydia was at the door in a flash, but paused to gather her thoughts before she rushed out. Why would Sandra make the trip by herself? Was there fresh trouble after everything the family had already been through?

"Go see what she wants," *Mamm* ordered. "And bring her in if there's something we need to know."

Lydia jerked open the front door and was at the hitching post by the time Sandra pulled to a stop.

"*Goot* evening." Lydia tried to catch her breath.

"*Goot* evening," Sandra replied with a grim face.

"What is it?" Lydia demanded. "Not more bad news?"

Sandra offered a weak smile. "No, I just had to get out of the house, and speak with you."

Lydia tied Sandra's horse Dixie to the hitching post while she studied her cousin's face. Did Sandra need comfort because of her *daett*'s death?

Sandra climbed down from the buggy and seemed to hesitate before she asked, "Maybe we could find someplace private to talk? Maybe your room?"

"Of course," Lydia said. "But if it's something my sisters can't hear, upstairs might not be wise. They're sure to eavesdrop."

Sandra winced. "Then maybe the front porch would be better."

Lydia nodded, and they walked together to the porch swing where Sandra sat down with a sigh. "So where do I begin?"

Lydia patted her cousin's arm. "Just take your time."

Sandra stared across the front lawn toward the setting sunset for a moment before she began. "You know that you and I go way back, Lydia, to our school years and even before that. We've always done things together, fun things like competing for the best grades in school, and who could win the most points at prisoner's base. And lately it's been Ezra…" Sandra's voice trailed off.

"*Yah*," Lydia agreed, not sure where this was going.

A tear trickled down Sandra's cheek. "You know we're ruined financially, Lydia. And we have no *daett* to get us back on our feet. Deacon Schrock was over last night for a visit. We'll get some support for a while, but we're also expected to make some choices of our own."

"I'm so sorry." Lydia reached over to touch Sandra's arm.

Sandra whimpered. "Deacon Schrock brought an offer of marriage with him."

"For you?" Lydia gasped and leaned forward. "It can't be!"

Sandra shook her head. "For *Mamm*, but it might as well be for me."

"You had best explain yourself."

Sandra tried to smile. "Deacon Schrock wasn't mean or anything, and he said *Mamm* could refuse if she wished. After all, *Daett* hasn't been gone that long. But it's one of those horrible situations. My brother Mark can't support us for long, and *Daett* mortgaged the farm for much more than it was worth because of that awful investment scheme of his. The place will have to be sold. Mark doesn't want the debt when he can buy a bigger place for a lot less in this down market. And what is *Mamm* to do? At her young age she can't move in with one of her married sisters. So the bottom line is that *Mamm* plans to accept the offer."

Lydia's mind raced. She already knew the answer to her question, but the words still came out in a burst. "It's that new family, isn't it? The widower. Clyde's *daett*, Amos."

"*Yah*." Sandra's voice broke. "That's the one. I've heard he's awful strict. They left the old community in Holmes County because the *ordnung* wasn't kept well enough to suit him. And his son Clyde isn't much better. You already know he dumped Rosemary—and it was all because her *daett* once attended a few church meetings with the New Order Amish. Can you imagine that?"

"Some people are that way," Lydia managed. "But will your *Mamm* be happy with this arrangement?"

Sandra snorted. "Happier than if we starve."

"But that won't happen," Lydia objected. "Deacon Schrock would see to that. He's also helping us for a while, you know."

Sandra sighed. "You still have your *daett*, Lydia. That makes all the difference in the world."

She couldn't argue with that, so she asked, "So what will happen to you?"

"I don't know," Sandra said. "No doubt the wedding will be soon. Amos will call on *Mamm* this Saturday."

"And you will live with them? In the same house with Clyde?"

"See what I mean?" Sandra turned her head sideways. "It's not going to work. We're both too old to adjust, and I can't stand the man. Look what Clyde did to poor Rosemary. The girl's still shaken from her experience with him."

"You're probably right," Lydia agreed. "But I don't know what you can do."

Sandra hesitated for a second. "There *is* something you could do. I hate to ask, but I'm desperate. This would be the biggest thing I've ever asked of you."

"So what is it?"

Sandra could barely get the words out. "Lydia…would you please…let me have a chance at Ezra by myself? Sort of step aside and let me see if I can win him?"

Lydia couldn't hide her astonishment. "You want me to give up my hopes for Ezra?"

Sandra's eyes pled. "I've been hoping he'd choose me…but I know you have a chance too. I know I've never asked for something like this in our relationship. We've always assumed our competition would run its course and there would be a clear winner. But we're grown now, Lydia. My *daett* just died. We have to make adult decisions."

Lydia tried to breathe evenly. "But you know I want Ezra as much as you do."

"Then unless Ezra decides soon, we'll just go around in circles for another ten years," Sandra said. "We're too closely matched this time. Poor Ezra will have his neck in a corkscrew before long."

Lydia laughed in spite of herself. Sandra's description fit to a tee.

"Please?" Sandra pled again.

Lydia took a long breath before she spoke. "But if I ignore Ezra and you don't, that may backfire. You know how men act when they're ignored. Ezra might respond in a way we hadn't planned. You might lose him to me for sure."

Sandra didn't hesitate. "I know that, and I'm willing to take the chance. I'm that desperate."

Lydia looked into Sandra's face. Finally, she spoke. "Okay. It's a deal." She reached over to give Sandra a quick hug. "And our friendship remains intact regardless of how things turn out."

Sandra appeared worried. "You won't feel too badly if I win? Ezra's the best catch in the whole community."

"Oh, I'll cry my eyes out," Lydia admitted. "But one of us has to lose. Perhaps this is for the best."

"You're so kind," Sandra said with tears in her eyes. "I never thought I'd find myself in such a low state. But the thought of living under the same roof as Clyde and having him eye me as a potential *frau* gives me shivers all the way down to my toes."

The two girls got up and walked toward the buggy together. Lydia untied Dixie and held the bridle while Sandra climbed in. With a quick wave, Sandra was off down the lane. Lydia watched the buggy until it was a tiny dot in the distance.

So she had given up Ezra for *goot*. The thought pained her. Should she have agreed to this? But in a way the issue wasn't over at all, and Sandra understood that. Ezra might be driven straight into Lydia's arms.

# Chapter Seven

Lydia ironed the last crease again, before she held up the dark green dress. The effort would have to do. The hour was late and *Mamm* would soon object if she continued to fuss over the dress she planned to wear tomorrow at the service. The effort was useless anyway, but old habits to impress die hard.

Sandra had made *goot* progress with Ezra at the youth gathering this past week, while Lydia had stayed in the background. Ezra hadn't seemed to notice, which hurt more than she wished. How could she simply turn off her affections for a person? Or was the pain from the lack of competition with Sandra? She had never before stood by while Sandra surged on ahead. The thought of allowing her cousin to pursue Ezra alone had seemed grand and noble last week, but something felt terribly wrong now. Lydia took several deep breaths and calmed herself. This would turn out okay—somehow. Even if Sandra succeeded.

Lydia would need to prepare herself to see Sandra and Ezra saying their wedding vows. The sight would be easier if Sandra won fair and square, but she must not think such thoughts now. The truth was, Lydia hoped Ezra would pick up on what the girls were up to, and things would go back to what they had always been.

Lydia flinched when *Mamm* appeared in the kitchen doorway. She quickly hung the dress on a hanger, but *Mamm* still scolded, "It's indecent to spend so much time on dresses, Lydia—especially now that the Lord has laid us so low. We should act like the poverty-stricken people we are. The church is helping us with living expenses. Showing up with fancy dresses at the services isn't fitting."

"But this is a year-old dress," Lydia protested.

*Mamm* didn't back down. "*Yah*, but you can make things look new by fussing with them."

"Yah, *Mamm*." Lydia sighed. "I'll try to do better."

"When did the girls leave?" *Mamm* asked, looking around.

"Right after supper."

*Mamm* settled in her rocker. "I can't keep track of my own dishes these days, let alone my children. I declare there is another large stainless steel bowl around somewhere, but I've looked all over the basement. I wonder if I left it at the last potluck?"

"It's above the shelf near the washer," Lydia said.

"Okay," *Mamm* responded, but she seemed to have lost interest already. "So what do you think about your sisters and their outings? Do you think they're okay?"

"Not really," Lydia replied, but they had been over this ground before.

"*Rumspringa* time," *Mamm* mused, gazing out the living room window. "It's getting more dangerous all the time with the way the world is going. I wish we didn't have to deal with it." *Mamm* attempted a smile.

"I'm taking the dress upstairs," Lydia said as she left. She took the stairs slowly, a step at a time. The image of *Mamm*'s forlorn figure in her rocker was still with her when Lydia entered her bedroom. She opened the closet door and hung the dress inside. Maybe she should dress in sackcloth and ashes tomorrow? Lydia grimaced. She wasn't so low that she would resort to those measures for attention, and she couldn't anyway. *Mamm* and *Daett* wouldn't allow her to leave the house in such an outfit. That would be a truly poverty-stricken state. And there was still much to be thankful for even in their present condition. The help from the community was at least there—humiliating though it was.

Lydia paused to listen before she walked over to the bedroom window. A car had pulled in the lane and was stopping near the front sidewalk. The back doors opened, and Emma and Rhoda spilled out. They stood with their arms aflutter, motioning in all directions at once. Several *Englisha* youth were still inside the car and seemed hesitant to come out. As she looked on, Lydia steadied herself with one hand. What were her sisters up to now? She already knew they hung out with *Englisha* boys, but why bring them here?

Lydia turned away from the window to hurry downstairs. *Mamm* was already on her feet, and her face was pale. "Get *Daett*, he's in the barn," *Mamm* ordered.

"I'm not going past those people, whoever they are," Lydia protested.

*Mamm* clasped and unclasped her hands. "Then what are we to do?"

"We have to act normal." Lydia gathered her emotions. She would be strong even if *Mamm* wasn't.

"Why would Emma and Rhoda do such a thing?" *Mamm*'s voice trembled. "Bringing their *Englisha* friends to our house."

Lydia ignored the question. "We have to speak with them at least, don't you think?"

*Mamm* must have agreed because she followed Lydia to the front door and the two stepped outside together. Beside the car Emma and Rhoda were still chattering away. Their *Englisha* friends had climbed out by now, but they hadn't moved any farther. Clearly

Emma and Rhoda had initiated this event—whatever it was supposed to be.

*Perhaps they're offering a tour of a backward Amish farm?* Lydia suppressed the bitter thought. She called across the lawn, "Hello!"

At least Emma and Rhoda had the decency to appear a little embarrassed as they ushered their friends forward.

Emma made the introductions. "This is *Mamm* and my sister Lydia. And this is Benny Coon and his sister Avery. And Jimmy Emerson and his sister Julie. They wanted to see where we live."

So this *was* the Amish farm tour.

*Mamm* found her voice. "Well, come inside. We don't have much to eat on a Saturday evening, but I can mix up some orange juice."

"*Mamm*, you shouldn't," Rhoda said, but the effort was half-hearted. Clearly her sister wanted these people to feel right at home.

*Mamm* was in charge, Lydia told herself, and she couldn't ask these people to leave. She would have to pretend all was well until she could give her sisters a *goot* chewing out for this stunt. The nerve of the two. They weren't content to cause a scandal in the community, so now they had to bring disgrace right onto her parents' impoverished farm. How would she live this down?

*Mamm* led the way to the house and held open the front door while her sisters ushered their friends inside. Lydia stayed where she was, as if rooted to the ground. Emma and Rhoda wouldn't be content until they had given these *Englisha* people the tour of the whole house. That would include her bedroom, which was a mess at the moment. She couldn't stop them without a scene, but *Daett* could. Lydia unfastened herself and hurried toward the barn to find *Daett* seated on a hay bale with his head in his hands.

"*Daett!*" Lydia called out. "What's wrong? Are you okay?"

*Daett* groaned. "I saw them come in."

At least his voice sounded normal, so he must not be ill, Lydia told herself.

"Can't you stop them?" she asked. "Please?"

*Daett* looked up with a great weariness on his face. "I'm a ruined man, Lydia. I'm sorry you have to see me in this state, but I agree with your *mamm*. If we get strict with Emma and Rhoda, we may only drive them away from the faith. And you know I've already given them plenty of cause for offense with my horrible financial mess."

"But *Daett*…" Lydia began to protest but stopped. *Daett* wasn't going to back down and neither would *Mamm*. They were paralyzed with fear.

Lydia tried another angle. "What about the community? Deacon Schrock will have something to say about this."

*Daett* sighed. "I know this is a difficult time for you, Lydia, but we have to think of what's best for Emma and Rhoda. You and the rest of the children have turned out okay, but we still have the two younger girls to get through their *rumspringa* time."

*I'm not doing so well myself,* Lydia almost said, but *Daett* wasn't worried about her. He feared the fancy *Englisha* world her sisters had brought into the house, even as he tried to keep it out.

Lydia retreated and closed the barn door behind her. She expected *Daett* would call after her with some last-minute advice, but he didn't. She knew he must be very low-spirited to say nothing more to her. He also must be quite worried about Emma and Rhoda. She shared that concern, even as she had different ideas on what should be done. But she was not the head of this household, and that was that.

Lydia tried to sneak in through the washroom door, but *Mamm* called to her from the living room. "Lydia, come here. These people have some questions for you."

*Mamm* didn't sound too downcast. Had her sisters' *Englisha* friends already charmed *Mamm*?

"What questions?" Lydia asked before she entered the living room. It seemed easier that way. Smiling faces greeted her when she appeared. *Mamm* had everyone seated with glasses of orange juice in their hands.

"We'd like to show them the upstairs," Emma gushed. "Can we show your room? Or better yet, why don't you come with us?"

Lydia tried to smile. Since when did Emma ask permission? Her younger sisters went freely in and out of her room whenever they wished. There was more to this request than met the eye.

"Please," Emma begged. "It would mean so much to me."

Lydia gave in. "Okay, if you give me just a moment to straighten things up. But I'm afraid there's not much to see."

"I'm sure it's perfect," Emma said with an evil grin.

"That's what's so amazing," one of the *Englisha* girls said. "Your homes are so simple and yet so refreshing to the eye. I never imagined it would be that way."

Lydia forced a smile as she led the way upstairs. "Emma and Rhoda can show you theirs first," she said at the top of the stairs.

"Contraband to hide," one of the boys teased.

Lydia winced. "Just a little messy." She might as well speak the truth. At least her sisters' room was clean on a Saturday night so they wouldn't be embarrassed. But her sisters already knew that. Surely they weren't trying to embarrass her on purpose? Her sisters wanted her up here for some other reason.

When the door opened into Emma and Rhoda's bedroom, Lydia dashed into her own and quickly tucked the quilt into its proper place. She fluffed the pillow and pushed the drapes back farther so that light flooded the room.

Moments later, Emma called from the hallway. "We're ready. Can we come in?"

Lydia pasted a smile on her face as the door opened. The two boys hung back, but Avery and Julie examined every nook and cranny, even the closet.

"Can I try on one of the dresses?" Julie cooed. "I think this is just my size. Oh, for a picture of me in that dark green one, Avery. Wouldn't I look just darling?"

"Can we?" Avery was a little more timid.

Emma and Rhoda answered together before Lydia could open her mouth. "Of course you can…so out, boys."

"I'm getting out of here too," Lydia told them. No one objected.

Lydia stepped out into the hallway with the two boys. Now what was she supposed to do? She was alone with two strange *Englisha* boys. She should have stayed with the girls. Already their giggles filled the bedroom behind her. Lydia steeled herself and didn't move.

The boy who had been introduced as Benny cleared his throat. "Sorry for the intrusion, Lydia."

Jimmy added his own apology. "Julie has always been impulsive like this."

"We just kind of tagged along for the evening," Benny continued. "It's a brotherly thing."

That wasn't quite true, Lydia figured, but she wasn't going to argue about it.

Jimmy appraised Lydia for a moment. "Can I take a picture?"

"No!" The denial burst out in a gasp. They both appeared puzzled, and Lydia rushed to explain. "I'm sorry. We never take pictures of ourselves. It's awful prideful, and…" She wasn't about to say the rest of the explanation. She knew any picture taken would get around once it landed in *Englisha* hands, and it was hard to tell how many people would end up seeing the photo.

"Prideful?" Benny was still puzzled. "You're a beauty, if I must say so. There's nothing prideful about what God has given."

Deep color rushed into Lydia's face at this plain talk, and she moved into the darker shadows of the hallway.

"I'm sorry if I've offended you," Benny hastened to say. "But I wasn't teasing."

"We don't take picture of ourselves," Lydia said again, as if that settled the matter.

Silence in the hallway was broken by the giggles coming from Lydia's bedroom. She was ready to bolt down the stairs when the bedroom door burst open to reveal both *Englisha* girls attired in Amish dresses.

Benny and Jimmy lifted their phones and bright flashes filled the hallway. Emma and Rhoda placed their arms around Avery and Julie to be included in the picture without the least bit of shame. Lydia moved farther back and after a moment fled downstairs.

"What's wrong?" *Mamm* asked, when Lydia appeared in the doorway.

"They're taking pictures of the girls," Lydia managed before collapsing on the couch. "Right in our house."

*Mamm* whispered a quiet prayer. "Lord, please help us through this difficult time." She should do more than pray, Lydia told herself, but she was too upset. Her sisters had little sense left, it seemed. And yet she couldn't do anything about this, and *Mamm* and *Daett* chose not to. How had things come to this sad state of affairs?

# Chapter Eight

The following Saturday evening Sandra placed the last platter of food on the table. She couldn't postpone the moment any longer. Tonight, Clyde and his *daett*, Amos, had come for supper. At least she had a few more seconds to compose herself before she called everyone into the kitchen. *Mamm* was in the living room with Amos, their voices rising and falling quietly. Clyde was out in the barn with Mark, where he had gone when the two had arrived an hour ago. Why *Mamm* had invited Clyde to come along when his *daett* visited tonight was understandable, but that didn't mean she could tolerate the situation any better.

"We must include Clyde as family if I plan to marry Amos," *Mamm* had told her. But Sandra knew *Mamm* had a deeper reason to include Clyde. *Mamm* hoped to spark a romantic interest between them. From *Mamm*'s point of view, such a match made sense. She also no longer expected that her daughter could win Ezra's hand in marriage.

"You'll never succeed now with Ezra," *Mamm* had said this evening, just before Amos had arrived.

What *now* meant, they both knew. But *Mamm* was wrong. She had to be, just as *Mamm* was wrong about her relationship with

Amos. But Sandra couldn't do anything about that, either. *Mamm* hadn't enjoyed her first dates with Amos. That much was obvious from her pained expression afterward. Yet *Mamm* hadn't denied Amos further visits. And she wouldn't. That was just the way things were. *Mamm* was committed. The least Sandra could do was tolerate Clyde's presence for a few hours if that pleased *Mamm*. After all, if *Mamm* married Amos, they would have to live in the same house, so she might as well practice.

The idea of *Mamm*'s marriage to Amos still chilled her. But *Daett*'s death had changed life dramatically for them, so she couldn't blame *Mamm*. *Daett* couldn't be brought back.

Now if only Ezra would hurry and make up his mind, things might turn out great. But Ezra seemed the same as always. Why the man was so thickheaded was beyond her. She was a perfect match for him and was ready to marry this fall—if only Ezra would come to his senses in time. She would have to double her efforts tomorrow at the service and also at the evening hymn singing. She had to maintain a positive attitude or she'd lose all hope. Once married to Ezra, she'd have to find some way to repay Lydia for stepping back. How, she wasn't sure, but maybe she could help Lydia capture the attentions of some other handsome young man. They weren't that plentiful in the community, but she would do what she could. In the meantime, Lydia understood her cousin's situation.

Sandra pulled herself out of her thoughts to call out, "Supper's ready!"

The voices stopped in the living room, and moments later she heard the front door open and *Mamm*'s voice hollering toward the barn, "Supper, boys!"

Sandra bit her lip. This did sound like a family's supper time, but it wasn't. *Daett* was gone, and Amos couldn't take his place. He never could.

Sandra jumped when Amos walked into the kitchen with a big smile on his face. He greeted her with a cheerful, "It all smells so *goot*, Sandra."

"Thanks," Sandra replied, without an expression. She pointed to an empty chair. "You can sit there."

Amos didn't seem fazed by the cold reception. "You're looking mighty chirpy tonight," he teased.

Sandra ignored him, and thankfully *Mamm* showed up seconds later.

"It's ready," Sandra told *Mamm*. "All you have to do is sit down."

The washroom door slammed behind them, and Mark and Clyde entered noisily. Sandra waited until the two had taken their seats before she sat down herself. She made sure her eyes didn't catch Clyde's.

"Let's pray," *Mamm* said, looking at Amos with a smile.

Amos led out in prayer at once. But that was just the man's way, Sandra told herself. She pushed the bitter thoughts away and bowed her head. Amos could sure pray—that much was clear. He could almost match Bishop Henry's prayers. Or perhaps Amos was just trying to impress *Mamm*. He didn't have to bother, Sandra thought. *Mamm* wasn't impressed with such things. *Mamm* would never have consented to a date with Amos, let alone a marriage proposal, if *Daett* hadn't left them in such dire financial straits.

"Amen," Amos said, and they all lifted their heads.

Sandra leaned over the table to pass the mashed potatoes, followed by the gravy.

Amos took the bowl first to proclaim loudly, "*Goot* eating here, I would say. We have much we can be thankful for, and such Christian hospitality."

"Thank you," *Mamm* whispered with a tear in her eye, which she quickly wiped away with her dress sleeve. Amos didn't seem to notice, as he dished out a huge portion of mashed potatoes. "Not in many months have we seen such eating, have we Clyde?"

Clyde grinned. "Not since sister Clara got married."

"That's my youngest girl," Amos said. "She was the last to leave home, leaving us men alone and forsaken. Clara was almost as *goot*-looking as your Sandra there." Looking pleased with himself, Amos added, "Her husband has a huge farm in the old community."

"That's one reason we left," Clyde said. "Everybody was getting so materialistic."

Amos nodded, sober-faced. "That's true. We came here to seek better spiritual values, and already the Lord is blessing our efforts." He gave *Mamm* a meaningful glance.

*Mamm*'s face colored, but she kept her head down.

Sandra gathered her courage and asked Clyde, "Any prospects for you in the matrimonial field?"

Mark choked on his food, and Clyde seemed speechless at this bold question.

"The Lord will provide," Amos answered for him. "And I'm thinking maybe He has already."

"Oh." Sandra didn't hide her surprise. "I know Clyde used to date Rosemary. Is that on again?"

Clyde shook his head. "She was too worldly...though I know the community here seems to have accepted Rosemary and her family. But we remember the way things used to be."

"You shouldn't hold things her *daett* did against Rosemary," Sandra scolded.

Clyde grimaced. "I suppose that's our choice, don't you think?"

"I guess so," Sandra allowed.

Across the table Mark grinned at this exchange, but didn't say anything.

*You should be on my side,* Sandra wanted to tell him. But there were no sides. Not if Amos planned to marry *Mamm*. The thought sent a stab of pain through her heart. How could *Mamm* move ahead with this plan?

Amos leaned forward to say, "We must all follow the way the Lord opens up before us. I hope you remember that, Sandra."

So now the man was lecturing her. Sandra swallowed hard. "I seek the Lord's will with my whole heart."

Amos smiled and dished out a helping of green beans. "Then we have nothing to worry about." Moments later he added, "This supper is very *goot*, Sandra. You're an excellent cook."

"*Mamm* helped too," Sandra said. *Mamm* should have defended herself, but she obviously wouldn't.

"Like mother, like daughter," Amos said, aglow with happiness. "I expected as much, but you have done well in taking on your *mamm*'s excellent ways."

She should say thank you, but the words were stuck in her mouth.

Amos didn't seem to notice as he announced in a loud voice, "I believe Clyde has something he wishes to say, don't you Clyde?"

"I'm not sure what you mean, *Daett*." Clyde appeared puzzled.

"About what we looked at today." Amos waved his spoon around. "You should tell Sandra."

Clyde hesitated. "Well, it's not a done deal, but I'm looking at a farm of my own. Not that large, but a start, and more acres than I could have bought in the old community with the high land prices there."

"It's a right nice-looking place," Amos said, giving Sandra a sharp look. Sandra looked away. Amos had meant this information for her benefit, but why should she be surprised?

"Clyde's not getting any younger," Amos continued. "He'll be choosing himself a *frau* before long. At least, that's what I've been telling him."

The words were plain enough, and Mark had also noticed. He sent Sandra a bemused glance across the table. What was wrong with Mark? Surely he didn't agree, but Mark obviously liked Clyde. They had been laughing and talking when they came in from the barn.

"What do you say to all this, Sandra?" Amos asked, looking straight at her. "You seem lost in a daze."

Sandra jumped to her feet. "I think we're ready for dessert, that's what. There's pecan pie, and apple pie, and…"

Amos was still smiling when Sandra returned from the counter with the pies. Thankfully he didn't force the subject again. Instead, as the pie was cut and served, Amos engaged *Mamm* in small talk and Mark and Clyde talked about horses. Sandra kept out of both conversations. The evening had already been enough of an embarrassment. Thankfully supper would soon be over, and she could clean the kitchen in peace by herself.

Amos finished his last bite of pecan pie with a loud smack of his lips. "That was some kind of *goot* pie there, Sandra, or did your *mamm* also make those delicious desserts?"

"I made them," Sandra admitted, but offered nothing further.

Amos glanced around. "Let's give thanks then, and we can scatter to what needs doing. Your *mamm* and I have much we must discuss."

*Mamm* appeared pale, and Sandra almost reached over to squeeze *Mamm*'s hand, but she was sure Amos wouldn't appreciate that.

Amos bowed his head again and soon pronounced an "Amen."

The prayer had been much shorter this time, but had been delivered with just as much vim and vigor. Obviously Amos liked to pray out loud.

Sandra waited until *Mamm* had left with Amos for the living room, and Mark and Clyde were on their feet before she moved.

Mark headed for the washroom, but Clyde hollered after him, "I think I'll stay and help Sandra wash dishes."

Mark turned around and chuckled. "Suit yourself," he said. "I'll be in the barn when you're done."

"You're not—" Sandra protested, but Clyde interrupted with, "Oh, *yah*, I am. You can't turn down help with the dishes."

He wasn't as brash as his *daett*, but Clyde would soon get there. She stared at him. "I didn't ask for help."

"That's because you didn't want to embarrass me, but I don't mind helping." Clyde grinned and picked up a few dirty dishes to place them on the counter. "I like being around you. And I know how to wash dishes. We're bachelors, remember."

*What if I don't like being around you?* Sandra almost snapped. She forced herself to smile instead. "Really, Clyde, I appreciate the offer, but I need some time alone this evening."

"But you're alone all the time in this big house with your *mamm*." Clyde looked around as if that made his point. "It's not *goot* for women to live alone. Of course, I know you have no choice right now, and this wasn't planned, but still…"

"You've been here for supper. That's *goot* enough for me." Sandra gave Clyde a bright smile. "And you've seen for yourself. I'm still quite sane, don't you think?"

Clyde laughed. "No argument from me on that, but still, I'd like to help."

Sandra's face fell. She wasn't going to win. "Okay. You can dry the dishes, and I'll have my time alone for the rest of the evening."

Clyde leaned against the counter and watched as Sandra filled the sink basin with hot water. He finally offered, "You know, my *daett* will wed your *mamm* soon."

"I suppose so," Sandra allowed.

"Where are you going to live?"

"Maybe Mark will have his own place by then."

He wouldn't, but she wasn't about to tell Clyde.

"*Daett* says we all could fit in our big house." Clyde shrugged. "But I'll have my own place by then…I hope."

Sandra put on her most cheerful tone. "I guess we'll have to cross that bridge once we get there."

"You know, you're wasting your time with Ezra Wagler," Clyde deadpanned.

"What?" Sandra shot back, scarcely believing his boldness.

Clyde laughed. "Don't act surprised. Your attentions toward Ezra are common knowledge in the community. Yours and your cousin's too. Although lately Lydia seems to have…"

Sandra struggled to keep her voice steady. "I will have you know that none of this is any of your business, Clyde. And Ezra will make his mind up soon without your help."

"I guess we'll have to see about that." Clyde smirked.

A chill ran up Sandra's back as she dipped her hands in the hot water. Did Clyde know something that she didn't?

# Chapter Nine

By twelve thirty the next day, the three-hour Sunday morning service had ended and Sandra was hurrying toward the kitchen. Ezra had been sitting on the third bench with the other unmarried men and out of her view all day. That was how things had gone lately when it came to her attempt to catch Ezra's eye. Somehow she had to turn the tide, Sandra told herself. She didn't want to wait on the unmarried men's table today, but she had little choice if she wanted to speak with Ezra. Unlike the men, the girls had limited options in their pursuit of attention. Sandra cringed at the thought as Lena tugged on her arm. "Did the cat get in the vinegar bottle this morning?"

Sandra forced herself to smile. "I guess I should have added a little honey."

Lena chuckled. "I'm sorry, I shouldn't tease you. Your *daett* hasn't been gone that long, and Sundays must remind you of him."

"*Yah*, they do," Sandra admitted.

"The Lord will be with you," Lena said.

"Thanks for your concern," Sandra whispered, then hurried on to the kitchen. The place was filled with women as usual. Sandra waited a moment until there was a chance to approach the kitchen counter. Deacon Schrock's *frau*, Ruth Ann, was in charge.

"Um…I can take the unmarried men's table," Sandra offered.

"Thank the Lord!" Ruth Ann exclaimed. "Only Rosemary has offered so far. What's wrong with the girls today? Have the unmarried men scared them all off?"

Sandra gave Ruth Ann a shy grin and lowered her head. "I don't know, but I'm up for it."

"Then here." Ruth Ann handed Sandra a tray filled with bowls of peanut butter and red beets.

*Rosemary?* Sandra asked herself as she left the kitchen with the tray. Why would Rosemary offer to serve the unmarried men's table? Rosemary usually ran in the opposite direction when there was a chance to be exposed to the attentions of men. Did Rosemary wish to try for Clyde's attention again? That was a distinct possibility. Wouldn't that be a relief if Rosemary succeeded? Rosemary fit Clyde much better than Sandra did, regardless of Clyde's fears about Rosemary's liberal leanings. How dare Clyde think she would take him over Ezra Wagler, a *goot* dishwasher though he was?

Sandra took a quick glance down the stairwell. The unmarried men's table was set up in the basement, and the steps weren't wide enough for her tray with another person on the way up. The steps were empty at the moment, and Sandra moved down carefully. The men's light banter filled her ears even before Sandra stepped out onto the concrete floor. A quick glance around showed her Rosemary at the other end of the table, apparently the center of the men's attention. The girl was indeed up to something. Sandra stilled the anxiety in her chest and planted a big smile on her face.

Rosemary seemed oblivious to Sandra as her chatter continued. "There, that's my last bowl!" Rosemary proclaimed. "You won't starve until I get back."

"Surely you're not the only pretty face we'll see today?" someone teased.

Rosemary blushed and hurried toward the basement stairs. When she looked up and caught sight of Sandra, Rosemary gasped. Guilt filled her face.

"What are you up to?" Sandra asked, in spite of herself.

Rosemary turned an even deeper red and rushed up the stairs without an answer.

Sandra's thoughts were drowned out by a chorus from the men. "Oh, here we go. We're getting something to eat after all."

"Men!" Sandra muttered loud enough for the whole table to hear. "You are so spoiled!" But the warmth of their welcome flooded through her.

Clyde spoke above the noise. "And we are all such handsome dudes."

Sandra glared at him and unloaded her bowls one at a time. Once she was near Ezra, Sandra paused until he looked up. Sandra gave him her sweetest smile and handed him the last bowl of peanut butter. "Here, this is especially for you."

Ezra grinned. "My, I must be special."

"Not fair!" several boys protested. "This is our table, too, and we get no personal service."

Sandra kept on smiling. The men could tease all they wanted, but she had made her point and Ezra had gotten the message. She felt his gaze following her as she went back up the stairs. *Why can't Ezra just make up his mind?* Sandra asked herself again. Her smile faded when Rosemary met her on the top of the steps with her tray full again, and Sandra held the door open for her. Rosemary still had a tinge of red on her cheeks, so Sandra stopped Rosemary with her free hand. "Just a second. What's going on with you and the men down there?"

Rosemary tried to smile. "I don't know. I just felt like serving today, and…"

Sandra gave Rosemary a steady gaze. "You know that's not all the truth. You're not yourself today. You're…" Sandra let the sentence hang.

Rosemary sputtered. "You don't have to—I mean—it's my personal life, okay?"

"So why are you down there?" Sandra persisted.

Rosemary had blushed bright red again. "Look, I have to go, Sandra. They're waiting."

Sandra removed her hand, but she didn't like this in the least. She watched Rosemary hurry down the steps. But what could Rosemary be up to? This was Rosemary, after all. Sandra knew she ought to be offering help instead of feeling these tinges of jealousy. Rosemary couldn't be after Ezra. That wasn't possible. Ezra had always been perfectly satisfied with the attentions she and Lydia had paid him. He had no other need in his life with two such offers dangling in front of his face.

*So stop your worries,* Sandra told herself. She refilled her tray and this time met Rosemary at the bottom of the basement steps. Rosemary had managed to compose herself and offered a smile. Behind them the men had quieted down, their mouths full of peanut-buttered bread.

"I think with your tray they have all they need," Rosemary said. "But I'll check later."

"Okay." Sandra stepped aside. So Rosemary had now taken charge. That was something new. Fear niggled at her again. Suppose Ezra wasn't safe? A lot had changed in the last few weeks—none of which had bettered her position or Lydia's. But still…Rosemary and Ezra?

Sandra pasted on her brightest smile as she dropped off the bowls. "Coffee's coming up," she chirped. That was something Rosemary had forgotten, so she had the edge at the moment. But what a sorry state of affairs. Was she now competing with Rosemary? It didn't seem possible.

"Hi, Ezra." Sandra whispered near his ear. "I thought you might have gone to sleep."

Ezra chuckled. "With this excellent peanut butter lunch, how can somebody sleep?"

"Just teasing." Sandra moved on but gave Ezra another smile over her shoulder. He grinned back, just like in the days before *Daett* passed. Nothing had changed, Sandra assured herself. Nothing!

Rosemary was nowhere around when Sandra entered the kitchen again. She retrieved two coffeepots from the counter and made her way back downstairs. Most of the men wanted coffee, and Sandra teased them, "Don't you know coffee is for old men?"

Light laugher went around the table.

One of the men asked, "Where did our other server go?"

"If you wouldn't take so much coffee you would only need one," Sandra shot back.

"Next she'll be calling us spoiled again," someone said.

Clyde raised his voice. "I'm sure Sandra can take care of everyone. So go easy on the woman."

The man seated next to Clyde punched him in the ribs. "How come you're going sweet on Sandra all of a sudden?"

Clyde nearly spilled his coffee as laughter filled the basement.

"I have to try my hand at love once in a while," Clyde finally choked out. "And what prettier girl than Sandra Troyer?"

Hoots of laughter greeted the words.

"Men!" Sandra muttered again, glancing at Ezra. He now had a calm smile on his face. But why couldn't the man stick up for her? Sandra moved closer to Ezra to whisper in his ear again. "Can't you say something?"

Ezra appeared puzzled. "They're just teasing. What's wrong with that?"

*You should claim me as your own and be offended,* Sandra wanted to say.

"*Yah,* nothing is wrong with teasing," she said instead, and gave Ezra the best smile she could manage.

Ezra shrugged and turned his attention to his coffee. He took a long slow sip. Something had obviously gone wrong with her plan, but what? Had Lydia been right, and had Ezra seen through their scheme?

Sandra took both empty pots upstairs and deposited them on the counter. Bishop Henry called for the last prayer of thanksgiving, and the room hushed as everyone paused to bow their heads. Once the prayer was over, Rosemary appeared in front of her, all cheerful. "Ready to go down to the basement and clean up?"

"I think I'll get Lydia to help," Sandra replied. She needed reinforcements.

"We can all work together, then. That would be nice," Rosemary chirped.

Sandra found Lydia in a corner of the living room surrounded by a circle of younger girls. She must have hidden out there so no one would ask her to wait on the unmarried men's table.

Lydia looked up when Sandra approached. "*Yah,*" she said, before Sandra spoke.

"I need help cleaning the table in the basement," Sandra said.

"Oh, sure." Lydia didn't hesitate, but she did say on the way down the stairs, "I suppose Ezra's gone."

"Of course!" Sandra couldn't keep the irritation out of her voice. "And I'm getting nowhere. Has Ezra been paying you attention?"

"No, but I wish he would," Lydia snapped.

Sandra snorted. "That goes without saying."

"So you're giving up?" Lydia sounded hopeful.

Sandra lowered her voice as they approached the bottom of the steps. "I was hoping you had some fresh suggestions."

Rosemary greeted them with a smile. "Hi, Lydia. Where have you been hiding out?"

Lydia ignored the question and began gathering up the dishes. "You're awful cheerful today."

"Maybe," Rosemary allowed. "I'm trying to be. I think I've moped around long enough, you know, after Clyde hurt me the way he did."

"You should have let the memory of Clyde go a long time ago," Lydia said.

Sandra bit her lip and kept silent.

"Can I say something to the two of you?" Rosemary asked.

Lydia didn't hesitate. "Sure. Is something wrong?"

Rosemary hung her head for a moment. "No, there's nothing wrong. But both of you have been my friends, so that's why it's so hard to say this, but I don't want hard feelings."

"What is it?" Lydia probed.

"So there *is* something going on," Sandra snapped. "I asked you about this earlier, remember?"

"*Yah*, I remember," Rosemary said. Then she blurted out, "Okay! I'll admit it. I'm trying to capture Ezra's attentions. I can't help myself even if I know it's wrong—and impossible."

Lydia appeared dumbfounded. "You are trying to…Ezra?"

"Please don't be angry with me," Rosemary begged. "Both of you!

I have to try or I can't live with myself, and he's not asking either of you home, even with all the work you've put into him."

"Well, I'll be," Lydia said. "Cast me over the barn roof."

"But this isn't possible." Sandra clutched the edge of the table. "Lydia I can understand, but *you*?"

Rosemary appeared embarrassed. "I know. I'm way out of line, so please forgive me."

Lydia shrugged. "I guess you have a right to try. If Ezra can't make up his mind, maybe this will help."

"But…" Sandra stopped. She couldn't express the desperation rising up inside of her.

Surely Rosemary wouldn't succeed. Ezra wouldn't even notice her…would he? She wasn't about to say such unkind words. Lydia's example was the right one. Rosemary needed encouragement, not harsh emotions. Sandra took a deep breath and managed to say, "Well, I know what it feels like to give Ezra smiles and to have things go nowhere, so if that happens to you, too, don't take it personally."

"The Lord will surely guide us in this." Rosemary's voice trembled.

Lydia reached over to give Rosemary a quick hug. "I never thought you would have enough nerve. But I'm proud of you."

Rosemary colored a little. "I didn't either, and maybe I will only embarrass myself—in fact, I'm sure I will. And you can all laugh real hard when it happens. I wouldn't be angry."

"We won't laugh," Sandra assured Rosemary. This was no longer a laughing matter.

"But you won't be angry with me?" Rosemary asked.

Sandra forced herself to smile. "I'm not getting anywhere with the man, am I?" Then she glanced at Lydia, who shrugged.

# Chapter Ten

On Wednesday morning Rosemary flopped down on the couch with the pile of mail in her hand. She had worked for hours already with *Mamm* and her younger sister Ann on bread and pies. This was her first chance to catch her breath.

"Anything interesting?" *Mamm* called from the kitchen.

"I haven't looked yet," Rosemary answered.

She skimmed the letters first. Mostly there were bills for *Daett*, but one letter was addressed to her. Rosemary held the envelope up to the light. The return address was from the old community in Ohio, but there was no name. The handwriting was clumsy and crude.

"There's a letter for me," Rosemary announced.

*Mamm* appeared in the kitchen doorway. "Did one of the relatives write?"

"I don't know." Rosemary turned the envelope upside down. What if this was from a man? The thought left her weak. Perhaps someone had remembered her from the old community? Surely not.

"Let me see," *Mamm* demanded.

Rosemary handed the letter to *Mamm* and held her breath.

*Mamm* didn't look too long before she said, "You'd better open this in your room, I'm thinking."

Rosemary let her breath out. "But *Mamm*, I had nothing to do with this."

"Such things are in the Lord's timing," *Mamm* said. "You don't have to be ashamed of a man's attentions. Take a few minutes to read the letter, but upstairs please."

Rosemary felt the heat rise up her neck as she obeyed. Halfway up the stairs, Rosemary met Ann on her way down.

"Why are you coming up?" Ann asked. "We have to get back to work. There's still the pie fillings to make and supper after that."

"I'll be right down." Rosemary hid her face with the letter and pressed on. *Mamm* could explain once Ann arrived in the kitchen. She didn't know what to say. A man had written her a letter. Did she even remember him? Likely not. He must be a shy fellow not to place his name on the return address.

Rosemary slipped inside her room and opened the envelope. The single page slipped out. "Dear Rosemary," she began to read. "Greetings in the name of the Lord. I hope this finds you and your family well. We are expecting a hard winter here in Ohio, and I expect things may appear even more bleak in upstate New York. *Daett* said yesterday that the almanac predicts the first snow fall by Thanksgiving."

Rosemary paused to turn the page over. The end of the letter read, "Your hopeful friend, Johnny Mast."

Rosemary took a deep breath. Johnny was the same age she was, with plenty of pimples on his face when she had seen him last. But he might have outgrown them by now.

Rosemary scanned the last paragraph. "I hope you remember me. I certainly remember you, and I have a great faith that the Lord may stir in your heart what has been raised in my own. I have spent much time in prayer about this, Rosemary. Would you consider writing letters to me, and perhaps allowing me to visit you soon in New York? Please let me know of your answer at the soonest possible date."

Rosemary laid the letter down. Johnny Mast? She had nothing against him, but on the other hand, he wasn't Clyde and he certainly wasn't Ezra Wagler. Was there something wrong with her? Did she choose the wrong men? Was Johnny right for her and she was too blind or proud to see it? But if she accepted this offer to write him, there went her chance to gain Ezra's attentions. And that after her brave words to the Troyer cousins on Sunday! Maybe she was proud. Lydia and Sandra hadn't laughed at her plans, but perhaps they should have. One thing was for sure—she couldn't play both Johnny and Ezra at the same time. And Ezra was far from a sure thing, while Johnny was…well, he sounded certain of himself, and she had never had a man interested in her who sounded certain of his feelings. But pimples? Could she stand that, even if they had gone away? Rosemary let the thought float around in her mind. The feeling wasn't *goot*, but that might be her pride speaking.

Rosemary jumped when *Mamm* called up the stairs. "Time for work, dear."

"Coming," Rosemary hollered back. She hid the letter in the bottom of her dresser drawer and hurried downstairs.

"So?" *Mamm* asked when she arrived.

"Johnny Mast," Rosemary deadpanned. "He wants to write and maybe visit soon."

"Oh," *Mamm* said, and fell silent.

Ann giggled. "You'd make a *goot* match with him."

Rosemary winced but said, "I'll have to think about it. That's all I know." She then busied herself with the cherry pie recipe.

*Mamm* joined in with the work but didn't offer any advice,

though she seemed deep in thought. Did *Mamm* have an opinion? Rosemary would have to ask soon, if *Mamm* didn't speak up.

Rosemary found a large bowl and stirred in the ingredients. When *Mamm* still hadn't said anything, Rosemary spoke. "Tell me what you think of Johnny, *Mamm*."

"Ann said it pretty well," *Mamm* allowed. "And I've noticed lately that you've come out of your shell around boys, so perhaps this is all the Lord's timing."

"See, I was right." Ann's face glowed. "*Mamm* agrees with me."

Rosemary didn't answer as she continued to stir. Thoughts from the past drifted through her mind. Clyde's face looked down on her with a smile that first evening he'd taken her home from the hymn singing in his buggy. Johnny couldn't match that emotion. Of that she was sure. But Johnny wouldn't have to. Much as she had hoped Clyde's love was the real thing, it hadn't been. Clyde had dumped her with harsh words on his lips. Why he had even taken her home in the first place she never would understand. Johnny wouldn't act that way.

*Mamm*'s voice broke through Rosemary's thoughts. "Remember what I told you after Clyde? Life has its bumps, but things eventually turn out the way they are supposed to."

"You must have been reading my thoughts," Rosemary managed.

"Why doesn't someone read my thoughts?" Ann asked with a grimace.

"You have your own special place in our hearts," *Mamm* assured her.

"Thank you," Rosemary and Ann said together.

Her parents did the best they knew how, Rosemary told herself. But she had never explained to *Mamm* exactly why Clyde had cut off their relationship. *Daett* no longer attended the liberal meetings, and blaming *Daett* wouldn't have done any *goot*. And Ezra healed her heart exactly where Clyde had left the broken pieces. So how could she turn her back on hope that was so real?

"Pray about it," *Mamm* said, cutting into Rosemary's thoughts and making her jump again.

"She's a dreamer," Ann said.

*And dreamers sometimes dream, right?* Rosemary almost said, but pressed her lips together instead.

How had she dreamed this dream? Ever since she had spoken with Ezra at the feed mill the idea had grown and taken root—wrong though the desire was. But in the meantime she couldn't say *yah* to Johnny. She just couldn't. Not with her heart set on Ezra. She'd have to tell Johnny not to write any more letters.

"Do you want to say what you're thinking?" *Mamm* asked.

Rosemary gave Ann a quick glance. "With her around?"

"That's not fair," Ann protested.

"Maybe you can find something to do in the basement." *Mamm* gave Ann a warm smile. "Or there's still some vegetables left to bring in. You could check and see what you can find for supper. Maybe a few radishes, carrots, celery, and lettuce. Then you can clean them in the sink downstairs."

Ann frowned, but left without further objection.

*Mamm* turned to Rosemary when the basement door closed. "Okay," she said. "We're alone now, and I hope you're thinking the right thing."

"I can't accept Johnny's offer." Rosemary felt the color rush into her face. "My heart is set on someone else."

The question grew on *Mamm*'s face. "Why didn't I know about this man? And has he given you any indication that he cares about you?"

Rosemary looked away. "No, but he's like that. He doesn't make up his mind easily."

"And who is this man you think you have a chance with?"

Rosemary met her mother's sharp gaze. "Ezra Wagler."

"Ezra!" *Mamm* exclaimed. "What has gotten into you, Rosemary?"

Rosemary stumbled over the words. "I...I feel like trying, I guess. I want to ride in his buggy, *Mamm*. I want Ezra to bring me home on a date. I want the joy of loving him."

*Mamm* grimaced. "You know this is your imagination running wild, Rosemary. Ezra is not the man for you."

"Maybe not," Rosemary allowed. "But even if this is just a dream, I can't let it go. And what if Ezra does care for me? What if Ezra plans to ask me home soon on a Sunday evening? I've done my part. I've shown him my intentions every chance I've had."

"I don't need to know more." *Mamm* held up her hand. "If you feel like that, then don't give Johnny a positive answer. On that I agree with you." *Mamm*'s voice was firm. "Now, enough of this discussion. We have to get these pies in the oven, and supper made."

"Thanks for not scolding me too badly about Ezra," Rosemary said. "I do feel much better. It's as if...well, like I'm no longer alone."

A smile crept across *Mamm*'s face. "Your heart does lead you into lonely places at times, Rosemary."

"Better lonely than broken," Rosemary muttered.

*Mamm* didn't seem to hear as she opened the oven door and waved away the cloud of heat with her apron. With the way cleared, *Mamm* slipped the pies inside.

She would write a real nice letter to Johnny, Rosemary decided. She would tell him that she appreciated his attentions. There was no reason for harsh words. "Dear Johnny," she would write. "I received your letter and feel honored that you would think of me. And I do remember you from our time in Ohio. I appreciate your offer to exchange letters with a possible visit sometime in the future. I have spoken with *Mamm* about what you asked, and I've decided it would be best if I declined your offer. But thanks for the consideration. I hope you are successful in your journey in life and in your search for that special someone the Lord has prepared for you.

"Sincerely, Rosemary Beiler."

She would remember the words until she had time to write them down after supper. The face of Ezra Wagler floated in front of her vision, and Rosemary hugged herself. *What if*…but she must not daydream right now. She must wait, and pray with all of her might. Surely the Lord would not put such desires for a man's attentions in her heart only to snatch them away again.

# Chapter Eleven

Aweek later, Lydia hurried as she washed the supper dishes. Behind her, Emma cleared the last of the table with a flourish, while Rhoda stood ready at the drainer with her dishcloth, grabbing each dish while the water still dripped. They rushed because Sandra and her *mamm* were coming to visit, but that was no excuse for how Rhoda was wiping dishes tonight.

"Your cloth will soon be sopping wet if you don't let the dishes air-dry for a few minutes first," Lydia warned.

"We're in a hurry, aren't we?" Rhoda shot back.

"True," Lydia allowed. "But that's never an excuse for sloppy work."

Rhoda didn't answer, but she shook the next dish a few times. Lydia gave her sister a quick smile. She had to mind her attitude around her sisters. It wasn't her place to interfere with Emma and Rhoda's training. That was *Mamm* and *Daett*'s duty. But since the family's financial disaster, *Daett* didn't seem to have enough energy for his daily work, let alone the strength to guide the high spirits of his two youngest teenage daughters. Lydia tried not to think about the situation too much, but disaster would strike soon if something wasn't done. Emma and Rhoda were growing bolder every day, to the point of openly flaunting their *Englisha* friends on the weekends. All four of them had stopped by the house again on Saturday night, and *Daett* had said nothing. *Mamm* hadn't appeared pleased, but she wouldn't interfere with her daughters' plans on her own. Not on such a touchy subject. One thing was for sure—none of the older children had dared to bring *Englisha* friends onto the homeplace in their *rumspringa* time. She certainly hadn't. Not even once, let alone twice.

Lydia washed another plate and made sure it was clean before placing it on the strainer. While she had been lost in thought, Rhoda and Emma had vanished down the basement stairs. Lydia's thoughts drifted again. Emma and Rhoda weren't the only ones who were acting different lately. Much had changed in the lives of the extended Troyer family. There was no question about that. Sandra and her *mamm* had been affected greatly by their financial tragedy and the death of Emil. How strange that Aunt Edna planned to remarry so soon. There must be pressures on Aunt Edna she couldn't even imagine.

"I think *Mamm*'s still *fahuddled* with *Daett*'s passing," Sandra had told her at the last Sunday service. "Amos has even offered to pay for the wedding," Sandra had added, with horror in her voice.

But they were all confused in one way or another. What else could explain the strange agreement she had with Sandra about Ezra? Or with how Ezra was acting lately? He was paying less and less attention to either of them at the community gatherings. Ezra could at least pay attention to Sandra when she served the unmarried men's table at the services. But Ezra hadn't done so this past Sunday. Were both she and Sandra losing Ezra? She could stand it if Ezra ended up with Sandra. That had always been a possibility. But his ending up with someone else would be a difficult pill to swallow.

Who was it that was capturing Ezra's interest? Was it Rosemary?

That just didn't seem possible. Yet Rosemary was following through on her announced pursuit of Ezra. Rosemary had made sure she was the first girl to serve the unmarried men's table on Sunday—right in front of Sandra. The whole thing seemed preposterous. Lydia simply could not imagine Rosemary as Ezra's *frau*.

No, some other girl likely had caught Ezra's attentions—someone neither of them knew. Maybe that was why Ezra had delayed all these months. For all they knew, he might have already written to a girl in the old community and begun a writing relationship with her.

Lydia sighed as the basement door banged open and Emma and Rhoda reappeared. They giggled at the sight of her. Lydia ignored them. Neither of the girls would admit to the mischief they had been up to, even if she asked. And maybe Emma and Rhoda had found comic relief from the heaviness hanging over the Troyer household.

Rhoda grabbed the dishcloth and giggled again.

Lydia waited a moment before she asked, "What's so funny?"

"Emma should tell you," Rhoda smirked. "It's her boyfriend."

"He's *not* my boyfriend," Emma shot back. "He's just a friend, and he's interested in speaking with Lydia."

Lydia stopped with a dinner plate in her hand. "He wants to talk to me?"

"*Yah*." Emma struggled to keep a straight face. "Benny wants to speak to you about something. I told him I'd tell you, since you don't exactly talk to him."

"I don't talk to Benny for a *goot* reason," Lydia retorted. "You shouldn't have any of them on the homeplace."

Emma ignored Lydia's comment. "You should consider what he has to say. Benny's a nice man."

Lydia hesitated. "So, has Benny told you why he wants to talk to me?" She pulled the plug on the dishwater.

"I'll tell Benny you'd be glad to speak with him. That's the only way you're going to find out." Rhoda grinned in triumph.

"You both are impossible," Lydia snapped as she moved away from the sink.

Emma's voice stopped her. "So, what exactly did you do in your *rumspringa* time?"

Lydia kept her voice low. "I did the usual. Nothing like what you two are doing—bringing *Englisha* boyfriends into the house."

Emma raised her eyebrows. "That's not what Benny says. And he should know. His cousin is Rudy Coon, who we all remember was the *Englisha* boy you were interested in during your *rumspringa*."

Lydia's chest tightened as she gathered her thoughts. "That was all a long time ago. And isn't that what *rumspringa* is for? You're supposed to experiment with the *Englisha* world."

"That's just what we've been saying to you," Rhoda said.

Lydia sighed. "You're both pushing the limit, okay? I'm the only one in the family who will speak up and confront you about the way you behave…and now you want to hold up my past as evidence to justify what you're doing."

"We're just trying to help," Emma protested, a twinkle in her eye. "From the way Benny talks, it sounds like you had quite a relationship with Rudy. And from what Benny says, Rudy hasn't forgotten you, Lydia. I'm just trying to help. I think you should speak with Benny."

"There's been enough said on this," Lydia replied. She didn't wait for an answer but dashed out of the kitchen.

*Mamm* was in the living room with *Daett*, and they both looked up with surprise at Lydia. "What's the rush?" *Mamm* asked.

Lydia forced a smile. "Sorry. No rush. When Sandra and her *mamm* get here, I'll be upstairs."

"Okay." *Mamm* still appeared puzzled.

Lydia left quickly, and thankfully *Mamm* didn't notice her flushed neck. The mention that Rudy had not forgotten her hit harder than she would have expected. So much for her own resolutions, her baptismal vows to leave all the vestiges of the *Englisha* life behind.

Lydia comforted herself as she hurried into her bedroom and closed the door. This was only a moment of weakness. A glance in the mirror showed that the flush had spread into her whole face. Lydia rubbed her cheeks with both hands. Not since those long ago weekends of her *rumspringa* had she heard his name mentioned. *Rudy!* She had banished the word from her mind and heart.

But Rudy was no secret, Lydia reminded herself. Sandra knew about him. They had both dated *Englisha* men at the time. At least their competitive spirit had not invested in the same man, just the same activity. Sandra had never told her details of the men she had dated, and neither had she shared details about Rudy. That had been her secret—how much she had fallen in love with the man. She had immediately broken off the relationship, after the evening when Rudy had coaxed a kiss out of her. Her first kiss!

She had known that evening that Rudy could no longer be a part of her life. Not if she wanted to return to the community. Sandra hadn't been able to figure out why she was no longer interested in *Englisha* men, but Sandra had followed her lead. Likely Sandra had never been all that interested to begin with. For once life had given her something that was hers alone. Sandra was the one who should have fallen for an *Englisha* man, but she hadn't. Lydia had.

She had been thankful at the time that Sandra hadn't fallen in love. Sandra might not have been able to resist the temptation to jump the fence. But the truth was, Lydia had been tempted. That's why Rudy had to quickly become part of her past. And he had.

Lydia rubbed her cheeks again. Thankfully Sandra and her

*mamm* hadn't arrived yet. The blush on her cheeks would be gone before long. Lydia made a face in the mirror. There was nothing to worry about. Didn't the memory of past loves bring a flush to the cheeks? Perhaps, but she hadn't expected Rudy's name to have this effect on her. Not after all this time. She must bring her emotions under better control. She must!

Unless, of course, she was still in love with the man. The thought blazed in Lydia's mind for a moment. She gasped. Lydia stared at the wide-eyed girl in the mirror. So was this why she had given in so easily to Sandra's request that she back off her pursuit of Ezra? Did her heart know something she didn't?

Lydia paced the floor. This was all so wrong and unnecessary. She was in no danger. She didn't love Rudy any longer. Rudy couldn't arrive in the community and snatch her away. Nor could the kiss they had shared place her in any danger. Not even if Emma and Rhoda found out. Of course, they would take her kiss as justification for what they were doing, but everyone knew that kisses often happened in *rumspringa* time.

Lydia focused on the mirror again. Emma and Rhoda would return to the community eventually, as she had returned. She would think about that instead. *Yah*, that's what she would do. Lydia pulled herself away from the mirror as footsteps came up the stairs, stopping in front of her bedroom door, silence filling the hallway.

Lydia jerked open the bedroom door. Emma and Rhoda nearly fell into the room from where they had been leaning forward, their ears against the door frame.

"Serves you right," Lydia said.

Both of her sisters smiled sweetly. "Tell us the rest of the story," Emma cooed. "Your face was almost on fire when you left the kitchen in a huff."

"No!" Lydia retorted.

"Please," Rhoda begged. "Tell us what happened?"

Lydia glared at them for a moment. "Well…I suppose it's better if you hear it from me, but still…"

"Did you kiss the man?" Emma's face was aglow.

"That's none of your business," Lydia snapped.

"You know we're going to ask Benny, who will ask Rudy, who will tell us," Rhoda gloated.

"Besides, maybe if you tell us the sordid details we won't make the same mistakes you did," Emma added.

Lydia stifled a bitter laugh. "That trick won't work on me." With that, Lydia closed the bedroom door in their faces, and stood against the frame until footsteps went toward her sisters' bedroom.

*That was probably unnecessary,* Lydia told herself. Emma and Rhoda would discover most of her indiscretions soon enough. She should have told them herself. But she had wanted that memory to remain buried in the past. Well buried!

# Chapter Twelve

Some thirty minutes later, Lydia was standing on the front porch waiting as the form of a buggy appeared in the distance. This would be Sandra and Edna, Lydia assured herself. Emma and Rhoda were still upstairs, so she wouldn't have to face them until Sandra and her *mamm* had left. She had no doubt that Emma and Rhoda would pester her again about her past with Rudy. This time she would handle herself better. She'd smile and act as if nothing had happened—which was true. Nothing *had* happened. She had survived her *rumspringa* with only a kiss, and that was just fine.

If Emma and Rhoda persisted, she'd turn this into a lecture for them. She'd remind them how danger lurked out there in the *Englisha* world, and if this could happen to her, Emma and Rhoda should take fair warning. Not that her sisters would be persuaded, but she could try.

Lydia smiled and waved as the buggy pulled in the driveway. Sandra leaned out of the buggy to wave back, and Lydia hurried across the lawn to wait beside the barn. Sandra pulled Dixie up with a flourish.

"Whee! What a ride!" Edna exclaimed as she climbed down. "This is too much for my old bones—and a *goot* evening to you, Lydia."

"*Goot* evening," Lydia replied.

"At least *Mamm* can still laugh at my antics," Sandra said, once Edna was headed for the house and out of earshot. "Myself, I could just bawl the whole day long over what's happened to us."

"I'm so sorry." Lydia slipped an arm around Sandra's shoulder. "Does your *mamm* really have to do this? I mean…wed the man? This soon?"

Sandra shrugged. "*Mamm* seems to think so, and I suppose she's right. We can't make it on our own."

"But there must be some other way," Lydia insisted.

Sandra tied Dixie to the hitching post before she answered. "Remember this, Lydia. Deacon Schrock is behind the plan, and we're receiving support from the community. *Mamm* would have a hard time saying no. And besides, it's not as though love is a great concern when you're older. Other things become more important, I suppose. Things like the community's approval and whether we get to eat. We have to be practical."

"I'm so sorry," Lydia repeated.

"Let's think about something more cheerful," Sandra chirped. "I don't want to spend all evening down in the dumps."

"Well, there's Ezra," Lydia offered. "Maybe he'll come to his senses soon and show you some attention."

Sandra groaned. "I'm at my wit's end with the man. And Clyde isn't backing down on his professed affections for me. If only I could get Ezra to take me home on a date."

"You just have to keep telling Clyde no," Lydia said.

Sandra snorted. "It's not so easy. Believe me, Lydia, I've tried. Clyde tried to ask me home for a date the other evening when he was visiting with his *daett*, and I all but told him no. I can't wait much longer for Ezra to make a move. Mark can't put me up for long after *Mamm*'s wedding. I'm sure he wants to wed himself by the end of next year. After that, I can't depend on him for a place to stay, and I'm *not* moving in with *Mamm*. Not after all this, Lydia. What am I supposed to do?"

Lydia's mind spun as Sandra rushed on. "Clyde's *daett* is behind all this. Clyde's not smart enough to figure the financial condition I'm in or that I'll have no place to stay. Not on his own. His *daett*'s fingers are touching everything now that *Mamm* plans to wed the man."

Lydia reached over to squeeze her cousin's hand. "You do have a problem. But we must pray and see what doors the Lord opens."

Sandra glanced toward the heavens. "If only I had such faith. Not that I'm faithless, but when you're right in the middle of a situation, it's so hard! There's no light at the end of this tunnel, so all my lectures to myself about trusting the Lord go out the window. I make commitments, but they soon fade away. I suppose I could get a job, but I've never worked in those *Englisha* places, or one of those little shops some of our people have. I can quilt, but that's not enough to support myself."

"You shouldn't be so hard on yourself." Lydia linked her arm with Sandra's. "These are troubled times we are going through. But get through we will!"

Sandra glanced at Lydia. "How do you take it so well? You're so courageous. You agreed to leave Ezra alone for me. That couldn't have been easy. Oh, Lydia, I'm so scared. It's never been like this before."

"We just have to have faith," Lydia repeated, almost trying to convince herself.

A pleased expression suddenly crept across Sandra's face. "There is one *goot* thing that will come out of *Mamm*'s wedding. I'll get to make a solid move in Ezra's direction. *Mamm* has agreed to ask Ezra if he'll be a table waiter with me. Isn't that just *wunderbah*? With a whole uninterrupted day with Ezra, maybe I can finally make some progress."

"I hope so." Lydia forced cheerfulness into her voice. "I suppose Ezra will understand, even though he knows that wedding match-ups don't mean anything."

"That's true," Sandra allowed, but her smile hadn't faded. "I'll just have to work all the harder to make sure Ezra has a special day. I, of course, will have the time of my life. Are you sure you won't be jealous, Lydia?"

"I'll be okay." Lydia let go of Sandra's arm and motioned toward the house. "Let's go inside. It's chilly out here."

As they made their way toward the house, Sandra began again. "Lydia, tell me honestly. What do you think of my chances with Ezra?"

"I honestly don't know. I hope it works out for you to wed Ezra."

"Lydia, are you sure you don't want back in the chase?" Sandra asked.

"No, not now anyway."

"What do you mean 'not now'?"

"Well, for one thing, there's Rosemary in the hunt too."

"Is that all? I think Ezra would choose either one of us over Rosemary."

Lydia hesitated, then said, "Well, to be truthful, no—that's not all. We've never really kept secrets from each other."

"So what is it?" Sandra asked with some excitement in her voice.

"Do you remember Rudy…from our *rumspringa* days?"

"*Yah*, but that was a long time ago. I'd almost forgotten him."

"So had I…or so I thought." Lydia grimaced. "The truth is, I think I was quite in love with him. That was the reason I decided to end our *rumspringa* early and you followed."

"*Yah*." Sandra fell silent for a second, then added, "But you made the right choice, whatever the reasons, and I was done with *Englisha* boys anyway. So what has that got to do with anything now?"

"Emma and Rhoda are friends with Rudy's cousin. They think Rudy may still have feelings for me."

"Well, for what it's worth, I kind of liked Rudy," Sandra said. "Of course, now that you joined the church, Rudy is out of the question for you."

"*Yah*," Lydia groaned. "Whoever would've thought we'd end up like this? Poverty-stricken and out of options with men—the both of us."

Sandra laughed. "We're laid low to the ground by the hand of the Lord Himself, that's clear enough."

"If it came right down to it, would you marry Clyde if it was for the best?" Lydia asked.

Sandra sighed. "I can't see how. There are times when I think I'll live in Mark's barn or his henhouse, or sleep outdoors in a tent before I give in to Clyde like *Mamm* did to Amos. How could I ever be happy with anyone after my heart was set on Ezra? And yet..." Sandra let the words hang. "Maybe I am like *Mamm*. I don't know sometimes."

Lydia studied the ground at Sandra's feet. Not so long ago they had both been so certain of where they were headed, but perhaps they had been bouncing off of each other. Once that point of reference was gone...

"You're mighty serious," Sandra said. "You're scaring me, Lydia."

Lydia tried to laugh. "We'll be okay."

How could she put her thoughts into words? The relationship she had fashioned with Sandra over so many years was firm and solid. They *would* be okay. This was a deep valley, but valleys always led to mountaintops…eventually. She would gather her courage for the climb. That was a more worthwhile endeavor than worrying over things that might never happen.

"Come." Sandra took Lydia's arm to lead the way up the porch. "Here we are chattering away, and *Mamm* probably has everything planned for the wedding by now."

"I imagine," Lydia agreed. "And we should help."

Sandra let go of Lydia's arm, and Lydia opened the front door. *Mamm* and Edna were indeed seated on the couch with notebooks on their laps.

*Mamm* looked up with a smile. "All caught up with the news, are we?"

Sandra nodded. "I suppose so. At least our hearts are comforted a little."

Edna's voice trembled. "I can say one thing for sure. I'm so glad I have my sister-in-law and you, Lydia, during this hard time. You don't know how much this means to me and to Sandra, of course."

"We wouldn't have it any other way," *Mamm* said.

Edna wiped her eyes. "Maybe the sun will come out soon in our lives."

"I know we haven't been through the same valley you have," *Mamm* assured her. "So cry on our shoulders all you want. We'll try to understand, but only the Lord can fully comfort hearts."

"I hate these moments," Sandra whispered. "I like life to be orderly and expected, not full of events that ooze and run in different directions."

Everyone laughed because that sounded so unlike Sandra. Once the laughter had quieted, *Mamm* asked, "Where on earth did you hear something morbid like that, Sandra?"

"I remembered it from my *rumspringa* days." Sandra chuckled.

"One of the *Englisha* girls said that one evening when her boyfriend had ended their relationship. It sort of spilled out right now, I guess."

"What made you think of those awful days?" Edna asked.

"Lydia and I…" Sandra stopped. "Let's say the subject came up."

Thankfully, Edna turned her attention back to *Mamm*. "So, that takes care of the cooks, and…"

Lydia leaned toward Sandra and whispered, "Thanks for covering for me. I really didn't want the conversation to go there."

Sandra whispered back, "We'll make it through this time hand in hand. And here's to my great success with Ezra. So help me, Lord."

Lydia tried to laugh, but the sound died in her throat. This was serious business, and they both knew it.

For the next hour, the four of them plotted out the wedding arrangements. Who would do what, and when it would be done. Finally, Edna gathered up her notebook and pens. "Well, Sandra, I think we'd best be going."

Lydia smiled and hurried to open the front door for them. Sandra walked out with her *mamm* in tow and gave a little wave as she crossed the lawn. Lydia's *mamm* came up to stand beside her until Sandra and Edna had driven their buggy out of the lane.

"That poor woman," *Mamm* muttered. "I can't imagine having to marry so soon after losing a husband. The Lord knows I couldn't do it—that's all I can say."

"Edna seems to be taking it well," Lydia said.

"Better than I would." *Mamm* turned to go inside. "The truth is, she mourns Emil more than she worries about her future with Amos."

Lydia continued to follow the speck of the buggy as it faded into the distance. A strange feeling crept over her, as if something else also had drifted from sight.

"How is Sandra doing?" *Mamm* asked when they were back inside.

Lydia jumped. "Okay, I guess. She's worried, of course, about what will happen once Edna and Amos marry." Lydia pasted on a smile. "But Sandra's keeping up her spirits."

What else was she to say? Sandra had kept her secrets tonight, so she shouldn't spill all of Sandra's worries.

"We can pray for them," *Mamm* said, seemingly lost in her thoughts. "Now I'm going to join your *daett* for some much-needed sleep. I suggest you go to bed yourself and tell Emma and Rhoda it's bedtime, even if they are on their *rumspringa*."

"I'll do that," Lydia said, then slipped up the stairs.

Her sisters' room was dark when she arrived at the top of the landing. Lydia shrugged and went straight to her bedroom door. For once, Emma and Rhoda had retired at a decent time. She prepared for the night and slipped under the quilt, but sleep didn't come for a long time.

# Chapter Thirteen

The next two weeks until *Mamm*'s wedding day passed quickly. Sandra woke before dawn and climbed out of bed to peek past the bedroom window drapes. The stars twinkled overhead in a clear night sky. To Sandra, that didn't seem right. *There should be a storm raging outside by all rights,* Sandra told herself. A storm would have better reflected her feelings about what was about to happen.

*Mamm*, on the other hand, had accepted her lot quite well. She already looked at Amos with deference and had obeyed his slightest wish while they awaited this day. Which was understandable in a way. Amos had paid for all the expenses, but *Mamm*'s acceptance of him seemed to go deeper. *Mamm* had made a place in her heart for Amos, and today he would become her husband. The Troyers' home would contain only Mark and her tonight.

At the Helmuth home *Mamm* would be alone with Amos for two weeks, while Clyde would catch a ride back to the old community in Ohio for a visit with relatives. *Mamm* was already adjusting well to her new life. There was no question about that.

Sandra was the one who couldn't change. She pushed the thought out of her mind. Today could be the last chance to reach Ezra. She had to make the most of it.

Sandra turned away from the window and lit the kerosene lamp. By its flickering light she changed into an everyday dress. There was breakfast to prepare. Only after the table had been cleaned and the dishes washed could she change into her wedding clothes— including a new dress in a color she would not have chosen. Amos had made the choice for the table waiters.

*Mamm*'s voice had been firm. "That's what Amos wants."

That sentence would likely be on *Mamm*'s lips for the rest of her life. The thought was bitter, and Sandra grimaced. She must learn to like her new stepfather, difficult as that was, even if the drab blue dress she would wear today wasn't anything like what a Troyer would have chosen.

The happy days when she and Lydia had competed with each other over who could wear the best new Sunday outfit, seemed years ago. Those days were long gone. Today, though, they would be equals again on one point. Lydia would have on a new dress made from the identical blue material.

Things might go so much easier after today, if Ezra would come to his senses and ask her home on a date. She could live at Amos's place with *Mamm*, and Clyde wouldn't bother her if everyone knew she was dating the handsome Ezra Wagler. Ezra would drive her home every Sunday evening, and they could plan their wedding for the end of next year at the latest.

It was a dream, she knew, but dreams were made to catch, Sandra told herself. She took a deep breath. She could do this, and it would all be worth it. Ezra wasn't like Amos or Clyde. She could talk sense to Ezra. He would listen to a woman's wishes when she planned her wedding day. Ezra wasn't impossible like Amos. Not in the least.

Sandra left her bedroom and went downstairs with the kerosene lamp in one hand. Amos was already in the living room when she stepped out of the stairwell. He looked up from the couch with a big grin on his face. "*Goot* morning, Sandra."

"When did you get here?" Sandra snapped.

"You're a sleepyhead." Amos's grin grew wider. "I drove in thirty minutes ago. I figured we couldn't leave anything to chance on your *Mamm*'s wedding day."

*You just want to run everything,* Sandra almost said, but she held her tongue.

"I'll fix breakfast," Sandra said instead. "*Mamm* shouldn't be working this morning."

"That's sounds *goot* to me," Amos agreed. "But I doubt if you'll talk Edna out of going above and beyond her duties. She's a godly woman, Sandra."

*Unlike me?* Sandra clamped her mouth shut before the words came out, then hurried off to the kitchen.

"Clyde will be here soon," Amos called after her.

Sandra ignored him to greet *Mamm* with a soft, "You shouldn't be in here on your wedding morning, *Mamm*. I can make breakfast."

*Mamm* looked up with a weary smile. "Amos came early and he's hungry."

"I can take over now," Sandra insisted.

"And what am I supposed to do?" *Mamm* asked. "Talk with Amos? We already have our plans made for the day."

"He shouldn't even be here," Sandra whispered.

*Mamm* shook her head. "Sandra, I know this is all a little unusual, but we must trust the Lord knows what's best."

"Oh, *Mamm*!" Sandra wrapped her in a tight hug. "How did this all happen?"

"Life is in the Lord's hands and we must trust Him," *Mamm* repeated. "Amos has a *goot* heart. He's had pity on me and my situation. What more can I ask?"

*To not marry the man!* The protest died on Sandra's lips. She must not make *Mamm*'s wedding worse than it already was. *Mamm* needed her support and comfort.

"Amos will take care of you too." *Mamm* laid her hand on Sandra's arm. "And you can come live with us in a few weeks."

Sandra pulled away. "Please, *Mamm*. I still have my heart set on Ezra Wagler."

*Mamm* reached up to touch Sandra's face. "Amos says your spirit needs taming, and I'm thinking that maybe he's right."

*The man knows nothing about me!* Sandra managed to keep the sharp retort quiet.

But a sorrowful look still crossed *Mamm*'s face. "Amos knows of your unwanted pursuit of Ezra—or rather, yours and Lydia's."

Sandra smiled. "The whole community knows, *Mamm*. And Lydia's not involved anymore."

"Amos still disapproves," *Mamm* said.

"So what?" The words burst out of Sandra's mouth this time.

"I heard that," Amos called from the living room. "You shouldn't speak to your *mamm* with such strong words."

At least Amos hadn't heard the preceding comment. Sandra shut her mouth again and busied herself with the bacon pan on the stove. Let Amos and *Mamm* think what they wished, but she would continue pursuing Ezra—especially today. *Mamm* should be on her side, instead of Amos's. The lack of support from her *mamm* hurt.

Silence settled between them until a buggy came into the driveway. Sandra stayed in the kitchen while *Mamm* went to answer the front door.

"*Goot* morning," *Mamm*'s cheerful voice called out.

"And *goot* morning to you, *Mamm*," Clyde answered.

Sandra jerked her head up. Clyde had dared to call *her mamm*,

*Mamm.* Even before the marriage vows were said. And Amos had invited Clyde over for breakfast. The nerve of both of them!

Sandra gave the bacon in the pan a quick shake, and bacon grease spilled on the counter. Black smoke poured from the oven top. Now she had that mess to clean up, and Clyde would no doubt walk in at any moment. He was bold enough. But Sandra jumped when *Mamm* instead appeared at her side. "What happened, dear? You seem as nervous as I am."

Sandra ignored the question.

"I'll clean it up before Amos sees," *Mamm* ordered. "Go get Mark up. We have to eat before anyone else arrives."

*Then call up the stairs,* Sandra almost said, but *Mamm* had never called up the stairs to awaken them in the morning. That had been *Daett*'s job. A pain shot through Sandra, but she managed to whisper, "I'll be right back, then."

"*Goot* morning to you," Clyde sang out when Sandra went through the living room.

She didn't answer, hurrying upstairs with the kerosene lamp in one hand. From the looks of things, Clyde would disturb her all day. He was also a table waiter and had been paired with his cousin from Ohio. Why Clyde had chosen his cousin *Mamm* hadn't explained, but perhaps Clyde wanted to make sure no one thought he had a girlfriend. Clyde was serious about Sandra. There was no question about that. Which was all the more reason she must move Ezra off his no-action position and *soon.* Even today.

Sandra stopped to knock on Mark's bedroom door. "Time to get up, sleepyhead. Breakfast is ready."

"Come in," Mark answered. "I want to speak with you."

Sandra cracked open the door and held the kerosene lamp off to the side. Mark had propped himself up on one elbow with *Mamm*'s Texas Star quilt draped over himself.

"What is it?" Sandra asked.

Mark squinted in the low light. "You know that today changes everything for us."

"*Yah*." Sandra took a deep breath. "You don't have to remind me."

Mark regarded Sandra with one eye closed. "I hate to be the breaker of bad news, but you should know that Amos and Clyde have been quite plain in their opinions about how you and Lydia act or used to act around Ezra."

"Ezra always enjoyed our attentions." Sandra stood up straight. "And we haven't done anything wrong."

Mark swung his legs out on the floor. "Maybe so, but things are different now. I'm afraid you aren't adjusting."

Sandra glared at her brother. "How can you just accept Amos and Clyde like that? They've waltzed into our lives and taken over."

"They've helped us when no one else could," Mark chided. "You know the church can't go on supporting us the way they have been. Not for months and months. And I have my own life to live. You should be grateful, Sandra, instead of sharpening that tongue of yours on Clyde and Amos."

"And I suppose my heart has no say in the matter," Sandra snapped.

Mark glared back. "The heart of a woman can change to fit the circumstances. I'm letting you know, Sandra, that I'm not supporting you once I marry. I plan to find another farm soon and move out on my own. When that happens I'll barely be able to make it financially for myself and my new *frau*—let alone for you."

"You have to have some patience, Mark." Sandra softened her tone in spite of the panic welling up inside of her.

"Of course, I'll be patient." A look of tenderness crossed Mark's face. "But things are what they are. And I think you respect me enough to remember what I said. You can't live off of me after the wedding when I can't afford it."

Sandra shifted the lamp to her other hand. "Then I'll get a job. I'll clean. I'll cook for people. Something!"

Mark didn't look impressed. "That's harder than you think. And you can't stay forever at my place after I'm wed—even if you have a job. I'm just making that clear so you have time to plan ahead." Mark tilted his head. "And just in case you think Amos is completely heartless, he has offered to support you while you continue to live with me—that is, if you and Clyde are making your wedding plans in the meantime."

Sandra tried to speak but choked and fled. She wanted to scream and hear the sound echo through the whole house. Not since she had been a five-year-old had she given in to a temper tantrum. That time *Daett* had taken her out behind the woodshed for a spanking. She could still see the disapproval in his face and the disappointment in his voice. There had been no more meltdowns since. Mature people didn't have such reactions to life's events. And what if *Daett* was looking down today from the other side? She must control herself.

But, oh, if only *Daett* were here! He would be on her side. *Daett* wouldn't want her to marry Clyde. *Daett* wouldn't want her to follow *Mamm*'s example and marry for convenience rather than love. Sandra paused at the top of the stair landing. Surely *Daett* wouldn't object if she tried again to win Ezra's affections. *Daett* would give her support. She had to believe he would. She had to keep up her courage.

Sandra held the lamp high and tiptoed down the stairs. She wiped the tears away and pasted on a bright smile before she stepped out of the stairwell.

# Chapter Fourteen

An hour later, Sandra was dressed in her drab blue dress trying to think of anything but her dull attire. Outside the buggies were pouring into the driveway. This was a small wedding by Amish standards—or was supposed to be—but Amos had invited more people at the last minute.

"But Amos!" *Mamm* had exclaimed. "We only have so much food."

Amos had chuckled. "Perhaps the bishop can pray for the multiplication of the bread and pecan pies. Didn't Jesus look kindly on wedding feasts?"

*Mamm* had closed her mouth and said no more. The man had more nerve than a fox in a dozen henhouses. How did Amos dare joke about a miracle on *Mamm*'s wedding day? There should be sackcloth and ashes with *Daett*'s memory still fresh in their minds and hearts.

Sandra pushed her anger away and focused on the line of buggies. Ezra was her concern. He must receive a proper welcome so their day could get off to a decent start. So far this morning Amos and Clyde had done nothing but spoil things, but that would turn around when Ezra arrived. She was certain of that.

"Hi, Sandra," Clyde spoke softly beside Sandra, making her jump. "I think we can still switch things around between Ezra and me. I think Ezra would get along great with my cousin Lavina."

Sandra ignored Clyde.

"You don't have to be so snobbish," Clyde said.

Sandra gave Clyde a glare and hurried outside. Maybe Ezra's buggy was in the line by now. If not, she would find something she could do until he arrived. Maybe a last-minute check on the table setting in the barn where the guests would eat.

Bishop Henry and Lena passed Sandra on the sidewalk and called out to her, "*Goot* morning, Sandra. What a beautiful day the Lord has given us for a wedding."

"*Yah*, He has," Sandra said as she continued to glance down the line of buggies. Ezra still wasn't there. Had he gotten cold feet? Did the thought of even a short time spent with her scare him off? Sandra's feelings sank. How things had changed, and so quickly. But surely Ezra would be here soon. They had spoken about the wedding at the last youth gathering. Ezra had seemed cheerful enough about the wedding, so she must not despair.

Sandra murmured "*Goot* morning" to several other people she passed before she entered the hushed stillness of the barn. The cobwebs had been swept clean from the beams last week, and checked again yesterday. But now one hung right over the corner table. Where had it come from?

"Busy spiders!" Sandra exclaimed. Where was a broom? Had they left one somewhere in the barn?

"I'll take care of that," Clyde's voice said from right behind her.

She whirled around. "Where did you come from?"

Clyde chuckled. "You wouldn't talk to me in the house, but I see the change of setting has helped. I was hoping for that."

"I'm not talking to you here, either," Sandra snapped.

Clyde laughed and walked up to sweep the cobwebs away with his black wool hat. Sandra hurried out before Clyde could say anything else. Would the man follow her around all day? It certainly seemed so. If Clyde acted like this she'd never get anywhere with Ezra.

Sandra slowed her pace when she noticed Ezra's buggy in front of her. She stopped and waited until the buggy door opened and Ezra's black hat appeared.

"*Goot* morning," Sandra sang out. After all she had been through this morning, the words poured out. "Am I glad to see you, Ezra! Can you believe that Amos and Clyde showed up for breakfast this morning? On a wedding day!"

Ezra's grin was crooked. "Maybe I should have come earlier myself."

"You wouldn't do that." Sandra gave him a bright smile as she helped Ezra unhitch his horse from the buggy.

"Well, I'm here now," Ezra said.

Concern filled Sandra's face. "Was there trouble on the farm? Is that why you're late?"

Ezra nodded. "The cows were out. We have a fence jumper, but we thought we had everything shipshape. Still, she must have found a hole again last night. They were all in the cornfield and we had to run them out. Thankfully the harvest is in. They could only tear up the field."

"That's terrible," Sandra sympathized. "Seems like there's always one of those in every herd. Not that I'm much of a farmer's daughter, but *Daett* always claimed so." Sandra unfastened the last strap and Ezra led his horse forward while she held the shafts.

Ezra walked the horse into the barn while Sandra waited.

"Don't forget to come inside for the service," Clyde said from a few feet away.

Sandra gasped and Clyde hurried on before she could respond. Her face was still flushed, she was sure, when Ezra returned from the barn.

Sandra smiled her brightest. Hopefully Ezra would think she was glad to see him—which she was. Ezra was the only center of sanity at the moment.

Ezra returned Sandra's smile. "Ready to go inside?"

"*Yah.*" Sandra dropped her gaze as Ezra led the way toward the house. Sandra stayed close by his side the whole way. Let Clyde get a *goot* look at the quality couple they were, Sandra told herself, and perhaps he'd lose his foolish ideas about the two of them.

When they entered the house Bishop Henry had already taken his place on the front bench and the other ministers had gathered around him. Sandra led the way to the special benches for the table waiters. The two lines were set up near the front with easy access to the kitchen. That way they could leave right after the ceremony and not have to wade through the crowd.

Lydia was already seated on the second bench with her cousin Enos Troyer, and Clyde had found his cousin Lavina from Ohio. The girl appeared radiant and happy.

When Clyde grinned at Sandra, she quickly looked away. Thankfully Ezra didn't notice the inappropriate attention Clyde had paid her. But Ezra wasn't noticing much. That was the problem. Panic niggled at Sandra. She would have to break through his indifference. But how? Should she wrap her arms around Ezra's neck and profess her deep devotion for him?

No, that wouldn't work with Ezra or any Amish man. They liked to arrive at a decision on their own. She had no objection if only they would make up their minds. And in Ezra's case—choose her.

Sandra stilled her thoughts as the room filled with guests and she and Ezra took their seats. She leaned closer to Ezra and whispered, "Sorry about our drab dresses, but Amos picked out the cloth."

"Oh!" Ezra appeared surprised. He glanced at Sandra's dress. "I guess he does run a tight ship."

"Just letting you know it wasn't *Mamm*," Sandra whispered back.

"Your beauty, as well as Lydia's, makes up the difference," Ezra teased.

Sandra pressed her lips together. That wasn't the response she had hoped for, even though it was nice to hear. Ezra was supposed to have forgotten about Lydia, but he obviously still saw them as the same person.

Sandra willed her racing heart to slow. Someone gave out a song number and Sandra concentrated on the singing. She must not imagine things. Ezra had acted perfectly normal this morning, and if he still thought Lydia was beautiful, that only reflected well on herself. So there!

Sandra sang vigorously, and Ezra whispered from the bench beside her. "Happy that your *Mamm* is marrying today?"

Sandra faked a smile and sang even louder. Ezra would have to think what he wanted. Maybe she had finally made an impression on him. How that would translate into a request for a date, she wasn't sure. But anything was better than this gray existence where Ezra smiled and did nothing.

On the second line of the song, Bishop Henry rose slowly to his feet and led the line of ministers upstairs. Amos stood to follow them with *Mamm* beside him, and the two fell in line behind the ministers. The singing continued for another twenty minutes until Amos and *Mamm* returned.

The ministers had instructed them for the same length of time a young couple usually stayed upstairs. Amos and *Mamm* knew as much about marriage as any of the ministers did, but likely the ministers had spent their time in wishing the couple well. Or in talking about the problems inherent in a second marriage—such as feuding children. That's what Clyde and she were—only worse. Clyde wanted to marry her.

Sandra glanced down at Ezra's arm pressed against her dress. On impulse she slipped her fingers into his hand. He smiled and didn't seem to mind. They rarely had opportunities for such intimacies. Here one had presented itself, and she was not about to pass up the chance. Maybe Ezra would see how pleasant things would be if she saw him every Sunday evening, and they could hold hands together on the couch.

Ten minutes later Bishop Henry reappeared at the stair door with the other ministers behind him, and Sandra let go of Ezra's hand. The singing stopped and moments later the preaching began. *Mamm* listened to each word with rapt attention. Maybe *Mamm* thought she needed fresh instructions as she faced life again with a man. Sandra knew she herself would need more than preaching in order to live with Amos. She would need a lightning bolt from heaven to keep her on the straight and narrow. But *Mamm* was obviously more saintly.

Bishop Henry rose to his feet at eleven o'clock for the main sermon. A smile flitted on his face as the bishop addressed *Mamm* and Amos.

"We have come now to this hour when the two of you will promise your lives to each other for better or worse. You will now walk together in the will and blessing of the Lord. I know that both of you are older and wiser for this marriage. At least one would hope so." Bishop Henry paused for a chuckle. "I wonder sometimes how wise I am when I see childishness and ingratitude in my attitude toward

Lena. But I trust you will both allow the Lord's spirit to guide you in your walk together through life. I know my heart is gladdened today. Especially after the sorrow we experienced recently with Brother Emil's passing. But we will think of happiness today and of the joy Brother Emil must be experiencing with the Lord."

*Mamm* wiped away a tear and Bishop Henry hurried on with his sermon. From the look on his face Bishop Henry wished he hadn't brought up *Daett*'s name. The minutes ticked on and Bishop Henry wrapped up his sermon at a quarter to twelve. "Now if our brother and sister, Amos and Edna, are still willing to enter into the holy state of matrimony, please come forward."

Amos stood to his feet and *Mamm* followed him. *Mamm*'s dress was of a slightly lighter blue color, but still drab. Sandra hadn't thought of how *Mamm* appeared until now. Amos could have chosen a nicer color. The bitterness raced through Sandra. She struggled to push the thought away. *Mamm* was beautiful even with the touch of sorrow that filled her face. With a calm voice *Mamm* said her vows with Amos.

"And now I pronounce you man and wife, in the name of the God of Abraham, Isaac, and Jacob," Bishop Henry said. *Mamm* tried to smile, but the effort failed. Amos practically glowed, though, and Sandra's bitter thoughts came back.

They were still there when Amos and *Mamm* took their seats again and the last song was sung. The long line of table waiters stood to their feet and moved toward the kitchen. Sandra tried to breathe evenly. Her anger toward Amos still hadn't subsided.

Sandra caught sight of the satchel strap that had fallen into the aisle only a moment before her foot caught it. With a cry she sprawled forward into the kitchen, ending up on the floor with a loud crash. The pain in her foot was so intense she couldn't pull in a full breath. Ezra had grasped her arm, but too late. His attention was now fixed on the chair that had tipped sideways and lodged in the ankle of her boot.

"Hold still until I can get the chair out," Ezra whispered.

Hot flashes filled Sandra's face and neck as she clutched the leg of the kitchen table. This was what happened when bitterness and anger entered the heart. The Lord had rebuked her severely for her transgression, and shamed her in front of the whole community. Sandra moaned and looked up as several of the table waiter girls' faces peered down at her. *Mamm's* anxious face soon appeared as she knelt beside Sandra.

*Mamm* repeated Ezra's words. "Hold still."

Sandra almost cried out as Ezra gently moved the chair.

"Is it broken?" Horror tinged *Mamm's* voice. "Surely not! Oh, Sandra!"

"No, it's not broken." Sandra gritted her teeth. She was not about to destroy her day with Ezra. No, not for anything! Not after they had barely begun to enjoy each other's presence. Why did she have to fall over a satchel strap like a klutz and wrap her foot in a chair?

"Come." Ezra offered his hand, and Sandra gripped his arm with both hands. She groaned as Ezra helped her up. Sandra stood with both hands on the table's edge.

"Try your foot." Ezra smiled encouragingly. "Maybe it's just wrenched."

Sandra applied pressure to the floor and cried out.

"You must go into the doctor's office in Canton and have this x-rayed," *Mamm* ordered. "Mark can take you."

"But I have to wait on tables," Sandra wailed. "I *want* to wait on tables."

"You're not suffering because of me." *Mamm* was firm. "And you can't work on that foot anyway."

"You had best listen to your *mamm*," Amos spoke up loudly. Sandra wilted. She couldn't defy the man in public. He was her *daett* now.

"It'll be for the best." Ezra squeezed Sandra's arm, trying to comfort her.

"But who will wait on the tables with you?" Sandra tried again.

"We'll find someone to fill in," *Mamm* said. "Now, let's get you out to the buggy. And here's Clyde already with a pair of crutches for you."

How Clyde had known they had a set in the basement was beyond her. From the grin on his face Clyde didn't seem troubled over her misfortune. Likely he was thrilled to get her away from Ezra. Oh, why had everything conspired to thwart her plans? Was she doomed to failure with victory right at her fingertips?

*Mamm* pressed the crutches into Sandra's hands. "Try these. *Daett* used them last year when he sprained his foot."

The crutches fit, and Sandra moaned as a path was opened in front of her. With short hobbles she worked her way through the living room. Ezra stayed on one side of her and *Mamm* on the other as they went down the front steps. Someone had run ahead to prepare Mark's buggy, and it was waiting at the end of the walk. *Mamm* helped Sandra up into the buggy while Ezra held her arm. Mark jumped into the other side and grabbed the reins.

"It's not an emergency, you know," Sandra grumbled.

"*Yah*, it is." Ezra peered up into the buggy. "I'm so sorry this happened, but maybe you can be back for the evening service."

Sandra squeezed back the tears. A lot of *goot* that would do. Ezra would have been with another girl for hours by then. Some girl other than her.

"We'll be thinking of you," Ezra said before he stepped back from the buggy.

Mark jiggled the reins, and they were off down the lane.

Her day was ruined, and so were her chances with Ezra. She would never get another opportunity like this. Not ever again.

"Don't feel too bad," Mark said. "You'll be better in a few weeks. A cast is the worst that will happen—if that."

Sandra didn't say anything as she let the tears flow freely.

# Chapter Fifteen

Rosemary stood beside Lydia among the shocked group of girls, several of whom were still staring down the road as the last of the buggy with Sandra and Mark inside disappeared from sight.

Lydia leaned closer to whisper. "Did this have to happen to *Sandra*? And after the tragedy with her *daett*. The poor thing."

"I know," Rosemary agreed. "I felt so helpless. I couldn't even get close enough to comfort her."

Not that Rosemary would have been much of a comfort. Sandra was in enough agony with her injured foot without the reminder that Rosemary had set her *kapp* for Ezra. She had hung back while Ezra had stayed faithfully by Sandra's side, right up until Sandra had been lifted into Mark's buggy.

Rosemary turned to look as Amos walked across the lawn and whispered in Deacon Schrock's ear. The deacon soon waved his hand around for attention and hollered, "Please, everybody. We all know this has been unnerving, but Sandra will be okay. Accidents like this happen and it won't stop the wedding meal. So if you will please find your way out to the barn the food will be served as planned. And Amos wants to thank all of you for coming."

The crowd began to move and Lydia sighed. "I suppose I'd best go find my cousin Enos. Looks like we'll have to work harder to make up for the lost time, and we're short one girl now."

The shortage would be at Ezra's table, Rosemary thought, as Lydia hurried toward the barn. Did she dare volunteer to help him? She didn't have a dress ready to match the other table waiters, and such positions were by invitation only. What had gotten into her to imagine such a thing? The thought took her breath away. No doubt Ezra could find some relative to work with him.

Rosemary groaned. How she wanted to work with Ezra today. How badly! And how disloyal this would be to Sandra on her *mamm*'s wedding day, but she couldn't help herself. Rosemary moved toward the house along with several of the other girls. That was the proper direction for her, Rosemary told herself. But she paused when one of the girls hurried out of the barn and called to her, "Lydia wants you, Rosemary."

Was she to work with Ezra? But that wasn't possible. With unsteady steps Rosemary pressed through the crowd and found Lydia in the barn.

"Hurry up," Lydia said. "Edna wants you to help Ezra."

"Ezra!" Rosemary tried to breathe. "But why me? What about you?"

"Just be thankful," Lydia said with a smile. "Edna agreed at once, and it's her wedding. I'd fill in, but I'm paired with Enos already."

Rosemary blushed like a summer rose, she was sure, and no one around had any idea why. Well, they would soon. Ezra was standing off to the corner of the barn with a worried look on his face. Apparently no one had told him who would work with him.

Lydia took Rosemary's hand and led her up to Ezra. "Ezra, Edna wants Rosemary to work with you in Sandra's place. Is that okay?"

"Of course!" Ezra's face lit up. "I couldn't think of anyone better to take her place."

Rosemary's face flamed even more.

Lydia gave them both a sharp sideways glance. "I'm going now. Don't spill anything, Rosemary."

Lydia knew of her clumsiness, but right now Rosemary didn't care. All she could see was Ezra's handsome face right beside her and his smile fixed on her. Ezra stepped closer to whisper, "I meant every word I said. Now, come." Ezra took Rosemary's hand and they headed across the barn to where the makeshift kitchen was concealed behind a thick white curtain.

Rosemary was sure she was floating. Never had Ezra held her hand. Of course, there hadn't been a reason to, but there wasn't a real reason now. Still, she mustn't read too much into the gesture. Ezra must have simply noticed her discomfort and wanted to place her at ease so they could work together.

Ezra stopped in front of the wall where a list was posted. "This is our schedule," Ezra said. "We have the corner table. And there's Bishop Henry ready to lead out in prayer right now. Looks like we're just in time." Ezra grinned as they bowed their heads together.

Rosemary opened her eyes before the prayer was completed to peek at Ezra. He had his eyes tightly shut, and she dropped her gaze at once. How could she be so shameless? And yet, she might never have another afternoon with Ezra. Somehow she had to make the most of this moment. Maybe she could touch Ezra's hand again when he wouldn't notice. But that would never do. She might easily pass out! How could she ever repay Lydia for this kindness? Lydia didn't have to pick her, but she had.

"Amen." Bishop Henry's voice rang through the whole barn as he concluded the prayer.

Ezra reached over to squeeze Rosemary's hand. "Are you ready?"

"I guess." Rosemary tried to stay upright. "Did you say we have the corner table?"

Ezra looked down cheerfully. "Yep, let's go."

The corner table! Rosemary's head spun as she followed Ezra. The words hadn't registered the first time Ezra spoke them. The corner table was the place of honor. Everyone would notice her. Rosemary steadied herself and kept walking beside Ezra.

Ezra paused in front of the long table where the cooks had laid out the food. He gathered up several plates and muttered, "Corner table, here we come."

Several of the women hurried toward them and one scolded, "Not that plate, Ezra. Take the smaller one. And remember that Sandra—oh, *yah*, I forgot for a moment. Remember that Rosemary goes first."

Ezra pretended to scowl. "I'll remember."

"I'm so sorry about Sandra," Rosemary managed. Several of the cooks nodded. She wasn't to blame for this situation, Rosemary reminded herself.

Ezra waited with his hands full until Rosemary filled her own. If the sauce spilled on her arm and burned all the way through the skin, she would not wince. Maybe the pain would wake her up from this stupor and she could gain control of herself.

Ezra hung back as Rosemary forced her feet forward. The aisle seemed to stretch out for miles to where Edna and Amos sat at the corner table, their witnesses on either side of them. Rosemary pasted on a smile and forged on. She didn't dare glance at the dishes. Sandra had tripped in the house over a satchel strap, but Rosemary could stumble on her own two feet if she wasn't careful.

Edna gave Rosemary a warm smile as she set down the first plate. "Thanks for helping out, dear. You're such a blessing."

"I'm so sorry about Sandra," Rosemary replied. "Have you heard anything yet?"

She knew Edna hadn't, but she couldn't think of anything else to say.

"Sandra will be fine," Amos said. "And looks like you made out pretty *goot*. You must admit that Ezra's quite a handsome young man."

Rosemary's face flamed again. Amos sure didn't beat around the bush. Thankfully Ezra covered for her. "You look quite handsome yourself today, Amos. Congratulations on your wedding day."

"Thank you." Amos glowed. "I'm not so *goot*-looking, but Edna's beauty here drifts over on me."

The men laughed at the joke and Edna turned a little red herself. "Now shush, Amos," Edna ordered. "We'll see if you still have compliments for me by this time next year."

Amos didn't hesitate. "Oh, I will. I'm certain I will."

Rosemary slipped away as everyone laughed again. Thankfully Ezra stayed right behind her. Ezra still chuckled when they arrived back in the kitchen. "Right jolly fellow that Amos is. Not too many men could have their new *frau* laughing so soon after she lost her first husband."

"I'm glad they're happy," Rosemary said.

But what really overjoyed her was the fact that Ezra was still by her side. Ezra even smiled at her as they filled their hands with plates again. Rosemary turned and headed back towards the corner table. When they arrived, Amos and Edna were deep in conversation but glanced up briefly. Edna's face was still flushed during what must have been a sweet conversation.

Rosemary's mind drifted to the future. What would it be like to have a conversation with Ezra right after saying the wedding vows with him? The thought left her dizzy, and Rosemary tried to focus on the faces around her. Lydia and her cousin Enos had the table at the other end of the barn. Lydia noticed Rosemary's glance and waved. Rosemary waved back.

"You're doing very well today," Ezra said when they paused to catch their breath.

"You're just saying so," Rosemary said.

"You've said that twice now," he scolded. "I mean what I say."

"Thanks." Rosemary tried to smile. "I'm trying, and I'm grateful for the opportunity to work with you." There, she had said the words.

Ezra appeared pleased, but no doubt he was used to such compliments. Didn't both of the Troyer cousins shower him with attention?

"You undersell yourself," Ezra said, as if he read Rosemary's thoughts. "You shouldn't, you know."

"Stop saying such things," Rosemary responded, her gaze on the floor. "You're embarrassing me."

Ezra chuckled. "Get used to it. You're old enough to hear such true things about yourself."

Rosemary gave him a quick glance. "I'll try." Now she had turned bright red again.

Ezra's chuckle grew deeper. "And you have plenty of spunk."

"Do you like spunk?" Rosemary asked without thinking. "I'm sorry, Ezra. I had no right to ask such a bold question."

Ezra laughed. "There's nothing to be sorry for. I love the way you are. You have nerve, for one thing. You'll go places. As they say, the early bird gets the worm."

"So now I'm a bird?" Rosemary pretended to frown.

"A *pretty* bird." Ezra's eyes twinkled.

"Ezra, don't," Rosemary said, wishing he'd say it again.

Ezra smiled and whispered, "Come, Rosemary, it's time to serve dessert."

He said her name with such tenderness that Rosemary had to look away. Soon she would cry if he didn't stop. Rosemary gathered her emotions and led the way back to the cooks' table where she and Ezra loaded their arms with desserts and headed back to the corner table.

As they approached, Amos glanced up to say, "Thanks again for filling in, Rosemary. We couldn't have eaten this well without you."

Rosemary kept her gaze on the food trays. Amos's praise was unwarranted, but she couldn't find the strength to protest at the moment.

"Thanks from both of us," Edna added. "You've helped make our day so meaningful."

Rosemary smiled her thanks for the compliment and hurried back to the cooks' table with Ezra in tow.

For the next hour, there wasn't much to do but wait and help where it was needed. Then Bishop Henry led in the last prayer of thanks for the meal and people began to get up from the table and approach the corner table to leave their congratulations.

Lydia appeared from across the barn and hurried toward the two of them. "Sandra's back and she's in a cast," she announced. "It was a fractured bone, the doctor said."

"I'd best see to her, then," Ezra said. "Of course, there's nothing I can do, but hopefully she'll feel well enough to sit at the table tonight at the hymn singing."

"*Yah,* I'm sure she'll be there," Lydia said.

Ezra turned to Rosemary with a tender smile. "I hope you find a handsome fellow to take you to the table tonight. I'd take you myself, but I'm already committed."

"I understand." Rosemary tried to breathe evenly. "Thanks for the sweet time today."

Lydia glanced at her sharply, but Rosemary gazed deep into

Ezra's eyes. Was the delight as deeply written on his face as it was on hers? Ezra only nodded and turned to leave. She would treasure these past hours, Rosemary told herself, for years and years and years.

She looked around but the crowd had thinned, and Lydia and Ezra were gone. Rosemary squared her shoulders and headed toward the cooks' table again. They needed help to clean up, she was sure. That was work that fitted her well. Quite well indeed.

# Chapter Sixteen

On Thanksgiving morning Lydia stepped out of the darkened stairwell to listen for a moment. There was a light on in the kitchen, so Lydia peeked around the doorway. Emma and Rhoda had been up for some time from the look of things. Now they were busy fixing breakfast and giggling while conversing in whispers. The two had nothing but silliness to offer of late, with their *rumspringa* pranks and their *Englisha* friends who hung around almost every weekend. At least a surprise breakfast for the family was a change of pace for the two, and for the better.

Lydia stepped into the kitchen, and both girls looked up with guilt on their faces.

"*Goot* morning," Lydia greeted them.

Neither of them answered, but busied themselves with their breakfast tasks. Both girls were careful to keep their backs turned toward her, which seemed strange to Lydia. Why they should feel guilty for making a surprise breakfast was beyond her.

"I'm going outside since you have breakfast under control," Lydia said. "And thanks for the nice surprise."

Their guilty looks only increased, but the two covered them up by scurrying even faster around the kitchen.

*Oh well*, Lydia told herself. She couldn't figure her sisters out right now. But she had time for a short stroll before breakfast was ready and the activities of the day descended upon the Troyer household. They had the final turkey dinner preparation to complete before noon rolled around. Lydia sighed and opened the front door to step outside onto the porch. She took a deep breath as the cool breeze blew over her face. Only the brightest stars still twinkled in the sky, and even those were dimmed as dawn broke the horizon.

The Thanksgiving season was upon them. Aunt Edna and Sandra would be over for dinner to celebrate, along with Amos and Clyde.

*Poor Sandra,* Lydia thought, as she walked past the barn and out to the pasture gate. So many things had conspired lately to adversely affect Sandra's life. Lydia gazed across the pasture where the horses were profiled against the dawning sky.

Sandra had pinned so much hope on her serving with Ezra at Aunt Edna's wedding. But that had all come to nothing when Sandra injured her foot. The tibia fracture hadn't been the day's worst development. Ezra's enjoyable time spent with Rosemary had taken that prize. How could Ezra place his affections on Rosemary? Lydia had played her own part in the day's affair by asking Rosemary to take Sandra's place, but her heart still throbbed with the question.

Sandra hadn't wanted to speak to Lydia about Ezra since that humiliating tumble at the wedding. At the evening supper, Sandra had chattered away like usual, with her foot propped up on a chair. Ezra had hovered at Sandra's side, while the older people served the young folks. But a sadness that went deeper than physical pain had never been far from Sandra's face.

Rosemary, on the other hand, had practically glowed all evening. A visiting young man from Ohio, John Miller, had been coupled with Rosemary for the evening by the two afternoon wedding matchmakers, but Rosemary's happiness hadn't come from the attentions John Miller had paid her. That had come from Ezra.

Lydia turned to look toward the main road as an *Englisha* car slowed on the highway. Moments later the vehicle turned into the Troyer driveway, its headlights sweeping the barn. Lydia maneuvered herself behind the edge of the building in the dawn darkness. Who would be here at this time of the morning, and on Thanksgiving Day? Fear gripped Lydia until the car came to a stop and several young people spilled out. Lydia recognized the voices at once. They were those of Emma and Rhoda's *Englisha* friends. Had her two sisters invited their friends in for breakfast? That would explain why her sisters had been up so early and working so hard. How naïve she had been. No wonder her sisters had appeared guilty. *Mamm* and *Daett* would be pushed to the limit of their endurance with this imposition.

Lydia sighed. The truth was that *Mamm* and *Daett* still had set no limit on what they would tolerate from Emma and Rhoda. So she would have to accept this surprise visit with what grace she could muster. Surely her sisters' *Englisha* friends would be gone by the time Aunt Edna and Sandra arrived. If not, a really uncomfortable situation would begin. Amos would not look kindly on *Englisha* friends who were brought in on Thanksgiving Day.

Lydia peeked around the edge of the barn as the front door slammed and both Emma and Rhoda raced across the lawn to greet their friends. They hugged Avery and Julie while subdued giggles filled the dawn air. Lydia noticed there were three males standing beside the car. Lydia drew a long breath. Either Avery and Julie had invited someone besides Benny and Jimmy, or her sisters had. She should have been more suspicious of her sisters' activities this morning. Nothing they did was innocent anymore.

"Lydia!" Emma called out. "Where are you? Can you hear me?"

Lydia pushed a stray hair under her *kapp* before she stepped around the edge of the barn. The early rays of sunlight crept over the horizon behind her, illuminating the car. The three men turned in her direction and squinted into the sun.

At once, Lydia caught her breath. *Rudy!* Emma and Rhoda had invited Rudy to breakfast—Rudy from the past! The man she had once loved. His face was as handsome as ever, starkly outlined in the morning light. He looked like he hadn't aged since she had seen him last. And kissed him! The memory ran all the way through her. The memory she wanted to forget.

Lydia gathered herself together. The nerve of her sisters! This was what happened when *Mamm* and *Daett* refused to discipline their daughters. She didn't want to see Rudy or have him in the house. She certainly didn't want to remember the love she used to feel for him. She was through with her wild *rumspringa* life, and her sisters had no right to bring this up again. At least Emma and Rhoda could have given her a warning.

Should she run behind the barn again? No, she had been seen now. The men were still shielding their eyes, but her face must be visible to them. Lydia lifted her head and marched forward. Her sisters' foolishness would not overwhelm her. She would show Emma and Rhoda how a decent girl conducted herself.

Lydia greeted the three men. "*Goot* morning."

"Good morning," three male voices answered together.

Emma and Rhoda cleared their throats, but at least they didn't giggle.

"Surprise!" Emma finally sang out, a nervous quiver in her voice. "Breakfast is almost ready."

"I sure appreciate this," said Rudy in a deep voice. "It's a great honor to receive an invitation to Thanksgiving breakfast at the Troyers' home." Memories of that voice sent tingles up and down Lydia's back.

"We're glad you could come," Rhoda gushed. "Lydia has been wanting to see you again for some time, Rudy."

Lydia choked, but she couldn't shout out in protest. Oh, those sisters. How could they do this to her?

After an awkward silence, Emma took Lydia's hand. "Come on, Lydia. You look like you've seen a ghost."

"Maybe I have," Lydia mumbled.

Rudy stepped closer. "I'm sorry to have startled you. I assumed these sisters of yours told you I was coming."

"No, they didn't," Lydia managed. "Nor did they tell us about breakfast."

"It's okay," Emma interrupted. "*Mamm* and *Daett* don't care, so why should Lydia care?"

Lydia finally found her voice. "Maybe I could speak with Rudy alone."

"Of course," Emma chirped. She took Avery's hand and bounced off toward the house. Rhoda followed with Benny and Jimmy in tow.

"It's been a while, Lydia," Rudy said, once the others were out of earshot.

Lydia didn't look at him, lost in her own thoughts. *Mamm* had to be up by now with all the racket in the house, but her sisters would try to smooth things over.

"I've missed you," Rudy said, when Lydia still hadn't answered.

"You know things aren't the same, Rudy." Lydia glanced up at him.

A look of sorrow crossed his face. "I know. But isn't that what they say? Time changes all of us, and no one can go home again."

"But I am home." Lydia kept her voice steady. "This is my home, and these are my people."

"Come." Rudy motioned toward the pasture gate. "Will you walk with me?"

Lydia shrugged. She couldn't exactly refuse, nor did she want to. That was the worst part about this.

"I'm sorry about the abrupt reappearance," Rudy continued. "Benny told me about the connection he had with your sisters, and I couldn't pass up the opportunity to see you again. Not with so much from the past still between us."

"You know it can't be like it was, Rudy," Lydia whispered. "We've been over this before. I'm an Amish girl through and through."

His hand reached for hers, and Lydia felt the familiar touch linger on her fingers. She dropped her gaze. "We shouldn't, Rudy. We've changed."

He let go to lean against the fence. "That's what I've told myself, but here I am. I can't forget you, Lydia. God knows I've tried. I've dated other girls, but there's no one like you."

"Stop it, please," Lydia begged.

"Are you dating someone?"

"No," she answered. Lydia could feel his gaze on her face.

"See, what does that say?" Rudy's voice rumbled.

Lydia didn't hesitate. "That we still haven't found the right one."

Rudy laughed, his voice rich in the morning stillness. "Don't you realize you just made my point?"

"I didn't mean it like that," Lydia protested.

"Come," he said again and smiled. "Will this gate open?"

Lydia lifted the leather strap off the post. "You're not much of a farm boy," she teased.

"No, I'm not," he admitted.

Lydia closed the gate behind them, and together they walked slowly toward the horses who now lifted their heads to watch the couple approach. The past came into focus again. All those evenings she had spent with Rudy in town. All those times they had gone to his place for snacks. She had sampled TV programs and movies while seated on the couch in his den.

Rudy's fingers reached for her again, and Lydia held them for a moment. This was a familiar gesture from the past and one she used to enjoy immensely, but now...Lydia dropped Rudy's hand.

"They'll see us from the house," Lydia whispered.

Rudy seemed to understand, but moments later he asked, "So you would hold my hand otherwise? If no one could see?"

"You ask too many questions," Lydia said, but her face betrayed her. Streaks of heat ran up her neck. Who would have thought she would feel so comfortable again around Rudy? It was almost as if she had come home...only Rudy wasn't home. He was an *Englisha* man and forbidden to her, and yet resistance seemed too much and too cruel. Here was Rudy—with his warm presence, his beautiful laugh, and his handsome face—as if no time had passed at all.

"I don't know what's wrong with me," Lydia said into the silence. "I don't know why I'm out here with you in the pasture."

"Come," Rudy said once more, his voice gentle. "We'd better get back to the house. I didn't mean to startle you like this."

Lydia followed him through the gate and across the lawn. This was the first time in a long time she had followed a man's lead. With Ezra, she had always been the one trying to capture his attentions. With Rudy she felt lifted up and held by light hands. Her whole body seemed to drift toward the house. Rudy smiled at her, but he didn't say anything. *This can't go on,* Lydia told herself. She must get out of this situation.

Rudy broke through Lydia's thoughts. "Here we are."

"Breakfast is waiting," Lydia said, but she kept her head down so he couldn't see her face. She would cry if she looked at him right now.

# Chapter Seventeen

Lydia tried to smile as the chatter at the breakfast table rose and fell around her. She still couldn't understand how this had happened. Here she was with Rudy again, and at her parents' home. It was an impossible contradiction. Lydia ate slowly and willed the tension to leave her body. If she could get up and help with the food, she'd feel better, but Emma and Rhoda were in charge. They had told her to sit beside Rudy, and they wouldn't even allow *Mamm* to help them. For the past twenty minutes the sisters had made sure that everyone's plate was kept filled with pancakes and eggs. She hadn't known her sisters could be so diligent or plan a meal so well. Only the bacon was in low supply, and *Daett* had the last piece on his plate, though there was plenty of ham left.

*Daett* appeared relaxed, as if this was an ordinary event that happened every day. From the look on her face, *Mamm* wasn't too comfortable with Emma and Rhoda's breakfast stunt. She also seemed to have noticed Lydia's discomfort. *Mamm* likely attributed her nervousness to the five young *Englisha* people seated around the table. If *Mamm* only knew that Rudy was the real problem. Thankfully breakfast was almost over, and Rudy hadn't tried to talk to her any more since they had come into the house. He seemed content to chat with the others, but surely that wouldn't last. Not if she knew Rudy.

Rudy had kept *Daett* relaxed all through the meal with easy conversation. He asked *Daett*, "So what's the weather going to do for the rest of the week, Mr. Troyer?"

*Daett* chuckled. "I thought the *Englisha* forecasters had that all figured out."

Rudy grinned as he helped himself to another pancake. "I don't know about that. I think your cows know better than our meteorologists."

*Daett* roared with laughter. She hadn't seen *Daett* this relaxed since all the financial trouble had broken out.

"These pancakes are something good," Rudy said to Emma before he turned back to *Daett*. "I suppose our forecasters don't know anything more than farmers do. The weather doesn't exactly follow what men say."

*Daett* looked pleased as he agreed. "That's for sure. Men have taken too much on themselves in this modern age. The Lord is still in charge, and He likes to remind us of that every once in a while."

Rudy nodded and smiled. The man had charmed *Daett*. If Rudy were Ezra, she had no doubts about what she would do. She would surely open her heart wide. She could almost imagine how that would feel. Abandoning her pursuit of Ezra's attentions would be followed by joy deep in her heart. It had happened before with Rudy when she was in her *rumspringa*. She had lost herself in Rudy's arms and in his kiss that one time. But that was then and this was now.

Lydia pinched herself as her face flamed. The man was seated right beside her, and the memory of his kiss was completely indecent. She must gain control of herself.

Lydia focused on *Daett*'s face. Maybe she could find sanity there.

Why did everything conspire to remind her of what could never be? She couldn't love Rudy again. That was crazy, so what made her heart race and her hands turn cold? Rudy was merely a dream born of her *rumspringa* years that was not meant to be.

"Has everyone had enough?" Emma chirped.

A chorus of voices answered. "It was delicious, thank you."

Rudy added, "And this was a great honor to have breakfast here on Thanksgiving Day, Mr. Troyer. I'd say that's on my list of things I'm thankful for today."

"We all have much we can be thankful for," *Daett* said, but his face darkened. "I would not wish to bring up our troubles on Thanksgiving morning."

Rudy was all attention. "I wasn't aware of recent trouble in your family."

Rhoda spoke up. "Can we talk of something else?"

*Mamm* sat up straight. "Rudy, my sister Edna lost her husband recently but has now remarried. So we both sorrow and rejoice, and we're glad that Emma and Rhoda invited their friends to join us this morning."

"That's right," *Daett* said. "We're thankful even in our sorrow. Now, shall we give thanks for the meal? Then the ladies can clean up the kitchen."

They all bowed their heads as *Daett* led out in a short prayer of thanksgiving.

Rudy said, "Amen," right along with *Daett*, and *Daett* appeared pleased. What had come over her parents? Rudy was charming, but this didn't seem to explain everything. She would have to ask *Mamm* once everyone was gone.

Rudy had risen to his feet and now suggested, "Why don't we help with the dishes, guys?"

*Mamm* gasped. "But no…"

Rudy silenced *Mamm* with an upraised hand. "I've washed dishes for my mother, so I know how. This can be our way of saying thank you for your hospitality."

"Suits us fine," Benny and Jimmy said together.

*Daett* grinned. "Count me out, but sounds like you men have everything under control. I'm out to the harness shop until the noon company arrives."

"You have company for noon? And you had us for breakfast?" Rudy sounded horrified.

"Oh, that's okay," *Mamm* assured him. "The girls will help us get ready, and my sister is bringing some of the food."

"You shouldn't have done this," Rudy protested, but *Mamm* had already followed *Daett* into the living room. Lydia could hear their low voices rising and falling as they spoke, but neither of them sounded upset. She wanted to flee to her room upstairs, but that wouldn't be *goot* manners now that *Daett* and *Mamm* had welcomed these visitors into their home.

"Okay, let's get to it!" Emma declared, as she began to run water in the sink.

Lydia cleared her throat and said, "There's no way we can all work in here. Maybe the boys should leave after all."

"And spoil all the fun?" Rhoda gave Lydia a glare. "We'll make a dish line. That'll work just fine."

Life wasn't all fun and games, Lydia thought, but she remained silent. What was the use?

Rudy touched Lydia's arm and glanced at the others. "I have a better idea. Why don't Lydia and I step outside? We'll take a walk in the garden or something. We have lots of catching up to do."

Avery glared at him. "I thought you said you washed dishes. Now you're the one who skips out?"

"Okay, I'll tell you what." Rudy held his head high. "I'll wash dishes and Lydia can dry. But once the table is cleared I want all of you out."

"Dictator," Avery snapped, but she appeared pleased. Emma and Rhoda absolutely glowed. Not only would they get out of work, but their plan to have Lydia spend time with Rudy had succeeded—and in the most innocent of settings. Even *Mamm* and *Daett* wouldn't complain if Rudy washed dishes with her in the kitchen.

There was a flurry of activity and Lydia fell into a daze by the counter. Emma shoved a dishcloth in her hands, and whispered, "Wake up, silly. He's not going to eat you."

That wasn't the problem, Lydia thought. The temptation to reevaluate her relationship with Rudy was before her, and this time together wouldn't help.

Near the sink Emma beamed at Rudy. "There you are, handsome. Water's all ready, hot on this side, and rinse water over there, and plenty of it. Soap's even added. Do you think you can handle that?"

Rudy grinned and dipped his hands in the hot water and began washing the first plate carefully. Lydia watched his hands move with slow grace. When he finished with the plate, he dipped it in the rinse water.

"I'll do that." Lydia reached for the plate and their fingers brushed. Behind Lydia the washroom door slammed as her sisters and their friends left.

Rudy smiled. "You're still as beautiful as ever, Lydia."

Lydia ignored the comment. "Nothing has changed, you know. We can't continue to see each other. I told you that a long time ago."

"But we can try again. You want to, don't you?"

Lydia still didn't look at him.

"Don't lie to me, Lydia. Tell me the truth."

"What difference does it make?" Lydia wiped the second plate dry and kept her gaze away from him.

"Doesn't love always triumph?"

Lydia pressed back a tear. "Would you quit it, Rudy? Do you know how hard this is for me? You know I loved you once, and let's leave it at that."

"I haven't forgotten." His hand dripped soapy water as he touched Lydia's arm.

Lydia didn't pull back, but she remained silent.

"Your father seems to approve of me." Rudy glanced toward the living room. "And I think he's a decent man."

Lydia jerked her head up to face him. "You know nothing about us, Rudy. Nothing! *Daett* doesn't know about our past, and let's leave it like that. My Aunt Edna is coming soon, and if her new husband finds all of you here, there will be more explanations necessary than *Daett* can ever make. And what I ask myself is this. Why am I in the kitchen with you? That's the biggest question of all."

"No, it isn't." Rudy protested and reached for the bacon pan. "Whether you still like me is the biggest question."

Lydia looked away.

Long moments later Rudy touched Lydia's arm again. The water ran in rivulets across the linoleum floor as his voice pled, "Please, Lydia. There has to be some way. All this time, I haven't forgotten you, and you obviously haven't forgotten me. Don't close your heart to me, Lydia. That's all I ask. As to how this would work, I don't know. But we can figure it out. I want to see you again. I want to talk with you, and I want what we used to have. We belong together, Lydia. I can't help it if we were raised differently. I can't control events that placed our religions worlds apart. But I love you, Lydia. Don't run from me this time. Please."

Lydia tried to breathe. The road lay open before her. Where it would lead was unforeseeable, impossible. It couldn't work, but the temptation pulled on her heart. She couldn't deny that.

Lydia met Rudy's intense gaze. "I loved you once, it's true, but…"

Rudy silenced her with an upraised finger. "Shh…say nothing more. Just give me some time, Lydia, okay?"

"Rudy, I can't say yes. I just can't." Lydia felt more tears starting to run down her cheeks. "You'd better go now. Please."

Rudy looked deeply at Lydia, then pulled his hands from the dishwater. He handed Lydia the final plate. "Okay, I'll go," he said. "But just until we meet again."

Lydia waited in a daze as he left through the washroom door. A few moments later *Mamm* came into the kitchen. In the distance she heard the cheerful voices of Emma, Rhoda, and their friends laughing. Then the sound of a car starting up and pulling out of the lane.

"Why did you allow this?" Lydia asked *Mamm*.

*Mamm* came closer to wrap her arms around Lydia's shoulders for a hug, then let go to sit on a kitchen chair. "*Yah*, I suppose this shouldn't have happened, but we've decided to go easy on Emma and Rhoda. We don't want to drive them off. Not after all the other tragedies we've suffered lately. Your two younger sisters are different. They take a gentler touch."

"And you think this is the way to avoid having them leave?" Lydia whispered.

*Mamm* sighed. "We can only try, Lydia, and do the best we can. The Lord can't ask more of us than that."

"But what about me, *Mamm*?" Lydia asked.

*Mamm* rose to her feet, and the two clung to each other as the stillness of the house crept over them.

"You'll be okay," *Mamm* said. "I've never worried about you. You'll make it through this."

# Chapter Eighteen

C an't you hurry?" Sandra asked Mark as Dixie's hooves beat steadily on the pavement in the morning stillness. She propped her cast against the buggy's dashboard. "I want to get to Aunt Mary's place quickly. This thing hurts."

Mark didn't answer as he kept the reins taut in his hands.

"Sorry," Sandra muttered a few moments later. "I could have gotten the dishes done sooner, I suppose. I know you were ready for some time."

Mark still didn't say anything, but she didn't want to quarrel with him on Thanksgiving Day. Things were tense enough at the house with her half-crippled efforts at housekeeping.

*Mamm* had offered them a place to stay until the cast came off, but Sandra wouldn't consider it. Not with Clyde in the house. Not with all the hints Clyde continued to drop about a relationship between the two of them.

How Mark put up with her, she wasn't sure. Likely because her stay in the house wouldn't be for much longer. Mark had taken Deacon Schrock's daughter, Marie, home on Sunday night again. The two seemed to like each other, and Deacon Schrock understood the

Troyer family's situation. He likely wouldn't object if Mark wanted to wed Marie by next fall.

Sandra shifted on the buggy seat. She wanted to present a cheerful attitude for Thanksgiving Day instead of these dark thoughts, and not just because they would be at Aunt Mary's place before long. She wanted to be cheerful for Mark's sake, and for her own sanity. Darkness didn't sit well with her.

"I'm a little uptight myself, so I don't blame you," Mark finally said, glancing at Sandra. "And I know that cast slows you down."

Sandra breathed in deeply. "Thanks. I know I'm grouchy and hard to live with lately."

"You do try," Mark allowed.

He obviously also wanted peace on Thanksgiving Day. She gave Mark a smile and said, "I'm so looking forward to this meal. No one cooks like Aunt Mary. It will sure make up for my awful cooking of late."

Mark grinned. "I'm not complaining. And I do have some *goot* news. I found a place yesterday for us to rent on Johnson Road. It's small, but it will have to do for now."

Sandra sat up straight on the buggy seat. "So you're giving up the homeplace?" She had known this moment would arrive, but the shock was still intense.

"I don't have a choice." Mark sounded irritated again. "I wasn't the one who became involved in that dumb Ponzi scheme."

Sandra glanced at her brother and lowered her voice. "I know, but *Daett*'s gone now, and you'd best be careful how you speak."

"It's still the truth," Mark grumbled. "And we're left to pick up the pieces."

*And pieces they are*, Sandra told herself. But she didn't repeat the thought out loud. Mark already knew. And she didn't want to think about *Mamm*'s awful wedding day when she had fractured her tibia.

All because of *Daett*. The shame and regret burned inside of her. She hadn't been to any youth gatherings since then. What was the use? Ezra had been kind to her after she came back from the doctor's office. He had even held her hand at supper time, but the glow on Ezra's face didn't come from the time he had spent with her. She had been a complete failure.

She hadn't charmed Ezra on *Mamm*'s wedding day. Instead, Ezra's attentions had moved on. She hadn't failed to notice his repeated smiles in Rosemary's direction that evening. Even when Rosemary was with another man and she was with him.

"I'm sorry about Ezra," Mark said, as if reading her thoughts.

Sandra tried to focus. Did she dare ask the question? She really wanted to know, but Mark might not speak the whole truth. Still… Sandra looked away and asked, "Is Ezra still showing Rosemary attention at the youth gatherings?"

Mark hesitated, then said, "Let me put it this way. You probably should start accepting Clyde's attentions directed to you."

"Has he taken her home from the hymn singing?" Sandra kept her gaze on the road ahead.

"Not yet."

"Is he going to?" Sandra looked at him.

"How would I know?" Mark sounded irritated again. "I don't understand that man's mind, but he's not going to ask you."

"How do you know?" Sandra shot back. "Maybe you're wrong."

Mark laughed now. "There's not a chance in the world, so why don't you let Clyde take you home? He's nice enough, and you could wed about the same time Marie and I say our vows."

"Because I can't stand him!" Sandra snapped. Her spirits sank again.

"Look." Mark shrugged. "I know you don't always think I know what I'm talking about, but *Mamm*'s happy with Amos. *Yah*, he's a little overbearing, but he's *goot* for *Mamm*. Clyde would be equally *goot* for you."

Sandra sniffed, but Mark continued. "Okay, you don't like Amos. But would you have wanted *Mamm* to struggle along on her own, always short on money, having to depend on church aid? I know the family would have tried to help, but none of us is that well off. *Mamm* deserves a better life than that. And you know eventually someone would have come along, someone not as decent as Amos. *Mamm* was going to remarry, and some of the older Amish bachelors can be a pill and a half. Think about Willis Stoll, for example," Mark chuckled. "He can't keep his pants together in one piece without safety pins. And I saw him looking at *Mamm* before Amos stepped in."

"He does need a *frau*," Sandra got in edgewise.

"So you would want Willis for a stepfather instead of Amos?"

"No, but what does this have to do with Clyde?"

"Clyde's Amos's son," Mark said. "Isn't that enough of an explanation?"

Sandra didn't protest. Mark wouldn't change his mind, but she didn't plan to change hers. Not unless she had to. She kept her voice firm. "I'll take a job. I might even move back to the old community in Ohio. Someone will have work I can do, perhaps in one of the Amish hardware stores or at an *Englisha* outfit."

Mark gave her a long look. "You know my opinion about that."

"So why wouldn't it work? Other single women do it." Sandra glared at him.

Mark sighed. "And they usually stay with family. That's not going to work with our family. *Mamm*'s the only one who will take you in without hesitation. And do you want to live with ill feelings toward the in-laws? And I can't have you around once I'm wed to Marie. I can't put Marie through that. She deserves a married life with just the two of us in the house."

"I'm not asking you to do that," Sandra assured him. "And I won't be a burden to others. But what about Lydia? Aunt Mary would take me in."

Mark didn't say anything, so she had finally hit pay dirt. A great happiness rushed through her for the first time in weeks. "Why haven't I thought of that before?"

"I don't know," Mark allowed. "But I do hate to see you say no to Clyde. That's still a mistake."

"That's why no one saw this choice," Sandra said. "You were all too busy pushing Clyde and me together."

Mark slowed the buggy for the Troyers' driveway. "You'd make a *goot* match with Clyde, Sandra. I'm just saying. You need someone to care for you."

Sandra bit her lip as the buggy bounced to a stop beside the barn. The front door of the house burst open, and Lydia came toward them at a fast pace until she reached Sandra's side of the buggy.

"Oh, you're a sight for sore eyes," Sandra cooed. "Mark was tormenting me all the way over with horrible visions of who I'm supposed to marry."

Lydia ignored the comment and studied Sandra's cast instead. "Which leg goes out first?"

Sandra chuckled. "I don't think I have it figured out. I haven't been in a buggy since the wedding."

"I know. We've missed you at the youth gatherings," Lydia said. "But let's get you out of here so we can talk."

With an energetic jump Sandra was on the buggy step, and with Lydia's hand on one arm and a crutch in the other, she soon made it to the ground.

"Is Clyde here yet?" Mark called out.

Lydia shook her head and kept her hand on Sandra's arm as they worked their way toward the front porch.

"How do you get around at home with the cooking and cleaning?" Lydia asked.

Sandra sighed. "*Mamm* comes over to wash on Mondays, and she bakes some things. But the rest of the time I get by with a knee walker in the kitchen. Mark's a *goot* sport too."

"I feel so sorry for you," Lydia said as she helped Sandra with the stairs and guided her to a chair on the front porch.

"Don't you need to help with dinner?" Sandra asked.

"No. Emma and Rhoda have their penance coming for a stunt they pulled this morning. *Mamm* has them both in the kitchen working hard, and your *mamm* should be here before long."

"Stunt?" The interest showed on Sandra face. "I knew I needed to come over here to cheer myself up."

"Don't encourage them," Lydia said. "It's been a rough morning, and you can't imagine the half."

"Really? What happened?"

"It's Thanksgiving Day," Lydia said. "I'm trying to stay thankful, but I can see no blessing in what has happened so far this morning."

"You had best tell me." Sandra reached for Lydia's hand.

Lydia paused to look around. "Emma and Rhoda made an early breakfast for their *Englisha* friends. They brought Rudy along."

"Rudy!" Sandra's mind spun. "But that's all in the past."

Lydia didn't look at her. "That's what I thought."

Sandra searched for words. "But that's not possible. You're a church member now, so that's the end of the story."

"I know," Lydia deadpanned. "But Rudy wouldn't take no for an answer. He thinks something can work out between us again."

"So you spoke at length with him…about…*love*?" Sandra didn't try to hide the tremor in her voice. "Lydia, how could you?"

Lydia hung her head. "It just happened, and I couldn't figure out why *Mamm* or *Daett* didn't stop it. I mean, we walked out to the pasture together when he arrived, and we washed dishes together after breakfast."

Sandra leaned forward to fan herself, even as the wind moved briskly across the front porch. "Wow. And I thought I had troubles. But why did your parents say nothing? That's the first question."

"They're trying to go soft on Emma and Rhoda."

"But *Englisha* friends in the house? How could they?"

Lydia shrugged. "It happened."

Sandra looked down the lane as Amos and *Mamm* pulled in the driveway with Clyde's buggy behind them. "Lydia, you have to put a stop to this! At once!"

"I will…and I did. But you can't tell anyone, not even your *mamm*."

"I won't," Sandra promised. "But tell me. You wouldn't…you couldn't…"

"Jump the fence?" Lydia managed to laugh. "I don't think so."

Sandra groaned and gripped the side of her chair. "And here I was going to ask your *mamm* if she would take me in after Mark is wed."

"You won't want to do that," Lydia said. "*Mamm* and *Daett* will get themselves in trouble with the church soon, if I don't miss my guess. My sisters aren't stopping this kind of nonsense, and my parents seem incapable of doing anything about it."

"What is to become of us?" Sandra whispered.

Lydia laughed out loud. "I guess we could move in together somewhere."

Sandra began to speak, but *Mamm* called across the lawn. "*Goot* morning, girls. How are you both doing?"

"Just fine." Lydia smiled and rose to her feet as her Aunt Edna hurried up the walk toward them.

Sandra stayed frozen to her seat. She couldn't have moved even if her foot had been free of its cast.

# Chapter Nineteen

Sandra joined in the laughter around the table as Aunt Mary's Thanksgiving dinner progressed. The prayer had been said and the turkey had been cut. The potatoes and gravy were still steaming after being passed around the table. The men had their plates piled high with food.

Across the table Lydia still had a hint of sorrow on her face, but the rest of the family appeared to have not a concern in the world. Had Sandra heard Lydia correctly that her parents tolerated *Englisha* friends in their house and that Lydia herself might consider resuming her relationship with Rudy? This seemed so impossible, almost like a dream. How had things come to this point?

Her thoughts were interrupted when Clyde leaned across the table to whisper, "How's your leg healing?"

"Okay, I guess," Sandra said, trying to be civil on Thanksgiving.

"Have you been back to the doctor lately?" Clyde asked.

Sandra wanted to ignore him, but she knew that would create its own scene. She forced herself to answer, "No, but everything should be okay until the cast comes off."

"How long yet?" Clyde continued.

"I don't remember exactly," Sandra said. "It's written down at home on my doctor's file."

Clyde grinned. "My, aren't we privileged? You have your own doctor's file."

Sandra glared at him. "It's a little folder and it keeps me organized."

"I was just teasing." Clyde's eyes twinkled as he spoke.

The man wanted to get under her skin, and she had allowed him to. Sandra concentrated on the food on her plate.

Amos's voice soon boomed, "I think Mary has outdone herself this morning, and Lydia too. This is excellent, excellent eating."

Lydia's *mamm* colored and protested at once. "You don't have to say that, Amos. I'm sure Edna can match anything I've made today. But thank you for the compliment."

"You're right about Edna. She's already fattened me since the wedding," Amos declared with a firm pat on his stomach. "All this *goot* eating has me working night and day to shed the pounds."

Sandra kept her head down as the conversation continued around the table. Lydia's *daett* soon cleared his throat and announced, "Since it's Thanksgiving Day, and the meal is almost over, maybe we should go around the table and share why our hearts are lifted up in thanks to the Lord."

"That's a great idea!" Amos boomed. "And I don't have to look far for that answer. My dear Edna, who is by my side this very moment, has brought great joy and gladness to my heart. The happiness I feel is unlike anything I've experienced in a very long time. My walk these past years had been a lonely one, and I thought at times the road would never end. But the Lord has seen fit to bring Edna's love to me, and for that I am very thankful indeed." Amos choked a bit, but managed to end with, "That's all I have to say."

"I would have expected nothing else," Lydia's *daett* chimed in. "Edna's sister, my Mary, has been a great blessing to my life. Even in this dark time we're going through, she has been a light by my side. I'm very thankful for her and I know that the road ahead may still lead us through troubled waters, but I'll always encourage my heart with the knowledge that we had this lovely Thanksgiving today, together with our family."

"Don't be so gloomy about things," Amos said. "We'll stand with you and try to help out where we can. I'm sure Deacon Schrock will have the church give the support that's needed."

Lydia's *daett* wasn't speaking entirely of financial difficulties, Sandra told herself. So Lydia had been correct; her parents had grown soft on Emma and Rhoda. Chills ran up and down Sandra's back.

"And how about you, dear?" Amos asked Edna.

Sandra jumped in her chair and focused on *Mamm*, who looked up at Amos with a warm smile. "You know I'm thankful for you, Amos. You have a very kind heart."

"Oh, come on," Emma said. "Only young people are supposed to say mushy things like that."

"Well, I mean them," Edna said, wiping a tear from her eye.

Sandra was sure she was going to sink right through the floor with embarrassment. *Mamm* wouldn't lie about her feelings, but neither did she have to make such a public display, even if she had fallen in love with Amos—if that was even possible so soon.

Lydia's *daett* gave Emma a stern look. "It's not only young people who enjoy each other's company, Emma. We're all thankful for the Lord's *goot* gift to Amos and Aunt Edna, and marriage is from the Lord. Don't you forget."

"That it is," Amos echoed, as the thanksgiving continued around the table.

"I'm thankful for three daughters still at home," Aunt Mary declared. "I know I'll treasure each moment with them until they fly the nest."

"And we're thankful for an understanding *mamm* and *daett*," Emma said, as Rhoda nodded beside her. "This is a bit of a confession, but we had a surprise breakfast for our *Englisha* friends this morning, to which *Mamm* and *Daett* didn't object."

Lydia was hiding her face, but her *mamm* and *daett* were smiling.

Amos spoke again. "A special thanks, then, to parents who understand. The Lord be praised. That is how we will keep the next generation in the faith. I give thanks that I have married into such an understanding family."

Lydia's *daett* cleared his throat. "Maybe we should explain things. Emma and Rhoda had—"

Aunt Mary interrupted with a punch to his side. "You don't have to tell all our family secrets."

Laughter went around the table again. Then Amos said, "Well, we all have capers in the house, I suppose." He then turned to Sandra. "We haven't heard yet from you, Sandra. What have you to give thanks for?"

Sandra's mind whirled. She had to think of something, but what? The table had quieted and everyone turned in her direction, so Sandra rushed the words out. "For Lydia. I'm thankful for our friendship, all the way through our growing up years, and the things we've been through together. I've been blessed."

"Well said." Amos gave Lydia a quick glance. "And do you want to add something?"

Lydia didn't hesitate. "I have always felt the same way about Sandra. She's like a sister to me. I'm very thankful for her. I will always remember her."

"You make it sound as if it's all in the past," Amos said, but then he quickly turned to Mark and Clyde.

Sandra focused on Mark as he began to speak. "I'm thankful for what you have brought to our family, Amos. And for my new friendship with Clyde. The hand of the Lord has definitely been with us these past months, despite our tragedies."

Clyde piped up. "I agree. Let that also be my official thanks. And for my acquaintance with Sandra, of course—which I hope will lead to many blessings."

Sandra felt herself turning all sorts of colors as laughter filled the table again. Clearly Clyde had no qualms about making his affection known right here at the Thanksgiving table.

Clyde winked at Sandra, who returned a glare. Amos noticed and laughed. "I'd say these two are off to a *goot* start already. Young love is a beautiful thing to watch unfold."

"You sound awful confident of yourself," Lydia's *daett* said. "Is this a settled matter already? I didn't know."

Amos didn't respond for a moment, then said, "Let's say we have high hopes." And the laughter rippled again.

Lydia's *daett* was grinning from ear to ear. "That is *goot* to hear, but enough of this talk of love. Shall we give thanks now? Maybe you would lead out, Amos."

"Certainly." Amos looked quite pleased with himself. "Let us bow our heads."

Sandra listened as Amos launched into his prayer. He sounded sincere enough. Maybe she had misjudged the man? Would *Mamm* be so deceived? Not likely. And *Mamm* wouldn't fake her affections for Amos. Sandra pressed back the tears as Amos pronounced "Amen."

*Mamm* and Aunt Mary got up at once and began clearing the table. The men pushed their chairs back to stretch their arms into the air.

"I reckon we have a sleepy afternoon in front of us," Amos chuckled. "I should go outside and run around the barn to work off all this extra food."

"The rocking chair is calling me," Lydia's *daett* said. "Running around the barn will have to wait."

The two laughed but didn't move away from the table.

Sandra struggled to get her crutches under her, and Clyde hurried over to help. She wanted to shove him away, but gave in.

"I have to get to the kitchen," Sandra told him.

"You're doing nothing of the sort," Aunt Mary said. "It's warm outside and you can go sit on the front porch. The sunshine will help heal your leg."

She couldn't argue with that, so she gave in with a reluctant, "Okay."

Clyde stayed right by her side on the way out the front door and helped Sandra settle in her chair before seating himself in the empty chair beside her.

"Can I stay for a few moments?" he asked. "I'd like to talk with you."

What choice did she have? She didn't like the man, but events had spiraled out of control. Perhaps this is what *Mamm* had felt the first time Deacon Schrock had brought up the subject of her marriage to Amos. And look where *Mamm* was now. In love! The shock of that thought ran all the way through Sandra.

Clyde must have taken her silence for permission as he leaned back in his chair and said, "You need to get some sun on that leg."

"If you'd move, I could," Sandra snapped.

Clyde didn't seem offended. He grinned instead and said, "If you stand up with your crutches, I'll move your chair."

Reluctantly, Sandra stood while Clyde moved her chair closer to the rails. Once he was done, she lowered herself back down.

"There, that's better," Clyde said. "Plenty of sunshine for a quick healing."

Silence settled between them, and Sandra moved her leg further into the sunlight. Warmth filled her cast.

Clyde's voice was gentle. "I'm actually glad you're not moving into the house with us."

"Oh?" Sandra couldn't hide her surprise.

Clyde nodded. "It means there's hope for us. If we take this slowly, you can start to see that the Lord has His hand on our relationship."

Sandra tried to breathe. What was she supposed to say? Protests obviously did no good.

"You should see how my *daett* and your *mamm* have fallen in love," Clyde continued. "It's embarrassing, in a way—like what your *mamm* said at the dinner table today. But on the other hand, great hope rises in my heart. The same thing could happen for us, Sandra."

"If you say so," Sandra finally said, with characteristic sarcasm.

Clyde chuckled, sounding almost like Amos. "You are a challenge, Sandra, but a beautiful challenge. Your spirit stirs my affections deeply."

"Please don't say that!" Sandra shot back.

His response was to softly lay his hand on Sandra's arm. To her surprise, she didn't shake it off.

"See?" Clyde finally said. "You do like me a little."

*What is the use?* Sandra thought. *He still doesn't get it.*

# Chapter Twenty

That Sunday afternoon after the service, Rosemary parted ways with her sister Ann outside the washroom door and walked toward Bishop Henry's barn. A few young boys were standing in the yard looking her way, but they paid her no further attention.

*Ezra is out here somewhere,* Rosemary told herself. Ezra had gone outside ten minutes ago, but his buggy was still in the barnyard. She hadn't dared to offer to serve the unmarried men's table today, even though she had wanted to. There were limits to her charm, and Ezra should be handled carefully like the valuable prize he was. But she had made progress since the wedding. Ezra was smiling at her much more than he used to—which was surely evidence of some change of attitude on his part.

So far no one other than Sandra and Lydia had taken her seriously as a contender for Ezra—if they noticed her at all. Her sister Ann hadn't said anything, and *Mamm* was too wrapped up with all the care of the younger children to notice what was going on right under her nose.

Rosemary paused before she entered the barn. A few steps later she found the stall where she had left her horse, Buster, before the morning service. Buster whinnied when Rosemary approached, and several other horses joined in.

"Your turn will come soon," Rosemary assured them, as she untied Buster's strap. "Everyone will be going home before long."

There was no sign of Ezra, but perhaps he would appear at the sound of her voice. Rosemary listened for a moment before she led Buster toward the barn door. She had to stop thinking about Ezra, but even if she succeeded for the moment, her resolution would only last until tonight at the hymn singing. She would see his handsome face, and her hopes to win him would start all over again.

Rosemary heard the sound of men laughing outside as they approached the barn. *Yah*, that was Ezra's voice mixed in with several other men's. Rosemary stepped aside from the barn door as the men made their way inside. Buster whinnied again, and they all turned to look at her.

"Rosemary!" Ezra exclaimed. "Let me help you hitch Buster to the buggy."

"You know my horse's name?" Rosemary didn't hide her astonishment.

"We know everything about girls," one of the other boys said.

They all laughed, and Ezra motioned them on with a wave. "Get going. I'm taking care of this one."

Rosemary found her voice again. "But Ann is out there waiting. She'll help me."

"*I'm* helping you." Ezra took the tie rope from Rosemary's hand.

"This is so nice of you," Rosemary cooed.

Ezra opened the barn door and motioned for Rosemary to go out first. "I've wanted a chance to speak to you in private," Ezra said, following her outside to the buggy.

Buster whinnied again, and Ezra stroked his neck. "Not you, silly."

Rosemary looked away, but Ezra must have seen the blush that leaped into her face. He surely knew how he affected her.

"I'd like to take you home from the hymn singing, Rosemary," Ezra said. "That is, if you will let me."

Rosemary tried to breathe. "You want to take *me* home from the hymn singing?"

"*Yah*, that's what I said." Ezra grinned. "If you can stand me."

Rosemary stood frozen in place. What was she to say? *Yah*? Or, *I'd love to*? Or, *I never dreamed this day would come*?

"A simple *yah* will do," Ezra said with a grin. "Unless you're trying to think of a nice way to say no."

Ezra knew *goot* and well that she wasn't going to say no. Rosemary let out a long breath. "The answer is *yah*, of course."

"*Goot*. Then why not tonight?" Ezra said.

"Tonight will be fine," Rosemary said.

"You had me worried there," Ezra teased.

Ezra had his hand on Buster's bridle as Ann approached the buggy.

"What have we here, if not the little sister?" Ezra teased Ann, who appeared nonplussed.

"Hi, Ezra," Ann said, as she promptly climbed in the buggy.

Rosemary stayed on the other side of Ezra while they hitched Buster to the buggy. When they finished, Ezra smiled and said, "I'll be seeing you, then." He went forward to hold Buster's bridle while Rosemary climbed in the buggy.

Ezra let go and waved as Buster dashed forward and the sisters whirled out of the Bishop Henry's lane. Near the main road Rosemary leaned out of the buggy for one final wave back at Ezra.

"What was that all about?" Ann asked.

"Ezra's taking me home from the hymn singing tonight." Rosemary almost sang the words.

Ann stared at her sister. "Ezra Wagler is bringing you home after the hymn singing?"

"That's what I said," Rosemary gushed.

"You should calm down a little bit," Ann advised. "Boys don't like excited females."

"Nothing else has worked with Ezra, so don't criticize my methods," Rosemary shot back.

"Does that mean you're kissing him on your first date?"

Rosemary felt the heat rush into her face. "Most certainly not. Ezra's not like that."

"Just making sure." Ann didn't appear convinced. "But hasn't that Johnny fellow written to you again?"

"No, I told him not to pursue the relationship." Rosemary shivered with delight all the way down to her shoes.

"Ezra," Ann mused. "I guess he'd make a decent brother-in-law. He's handsome enough."

"He's a man of unrivaled character and unblemished in all ways," Rosemary informed Ann. "That's more than handsome."

Ann laughed. "No wonder you snagged the man when others failed. You deserve Ezra. You'll make him a decent *frau*."

Rosemary glared at Ann. "Thanks for the ringing endorsement. But I don't think we're quite at that stage yet."

Ann laughed again. "Maybe not, but I'm serious. I hope it works out."

That was the problem, Rosemary thought. They were nowhere near a wedding date, so anything could happen to mess things up. But she mustn't let her mind go there. She'd stay upbeat and take each day at a time. Hadn't that attitude taken her over tremendous hurdles already? Who would have thought she would snag a date with Ezra when the Troyer cousins had failed?

Rosemary slowed for the home driveway. She turned in to stop beside the barn. Ann hopped down to help her unhitch Buster, then raced for the house while Rosemary led Buster into the barn. No doubt Ann was rushing in to inform *Mamm* about Ezra, but Rosemary didn't mind. *Mamm* wouldn't object, although *Mamm* likely wouldn't see the full extent of her accomplishment. Even a sweet smile from Ezra a few months ago had seemed unimaginable. And now today his face had glowed with happiness when he had asked to drive her home after the hymn singing. That she could bring joy to Ezra's life made her dizzy.

Rosemary left Buster in the stall and hugged herself with delight. The time until they had to leave for the hymn singing tonight must not be wasted, Rosemary told herself. There wasn't any special food in the house, but Ezra would need something extra when he brought her home. Cherry cheese cups would be just the ticket. She had time to prepare them if she hurried.

Rosemary raced across the yard to burst into the house. *Mamm* met her with a broad smile. "Ann just told me about Ezra. That's not bad, Rosemary. I guess you did tell me that when Johnny wrote to you. But are you sure?"

"*Yah*," Rosemary admitted. "You don't object, do you?"

"I guess not now that he's asked," *Mamm* assured her. "I like Ezra."

"Can I make cherry cheese cups for Ezra tonight?" Rosemary said, hugging herself again.

*Mamm* thought for a moment. "I suppose so." She glanced at the clock. "You'll have to hurry, though. And how is Ann going to get home? We can't have her driving Buster by herself."

Rosemary's face fell. "I hadn't thought of that. I guess there's more to this than I had imagined."

"There always is," *Mamm* allowed. "But that's all part of the joys of life. Responsibility goes with progress. Hurry along now, and we'll figure out some way of getting Ann home."

"She could ride with us," Rosemary suggested. "But that doesn't solve the problem of how to bring Buster home."

"We'll take both of you tonight, dear," *Mamm* said after a moment of thought. "That way we'll be along to celebrate your big night, but Ezra may have to pick both of you up after that."

Rosemary gave *Mamm* a long hug. She was speechless with joy.

"I heard all that," Ann hollered down the open stair door. "And just to let you both know, I can drive Buster by myself. I'm not a *bobbli*."

"I know you're not," *Mamm* called back to Ann. "But tonight we'll take both of you."

"Oh, *Mamm*, thank you," Rosemary managed before she hurried into the kitchen. She took down the recipe book from the top cupboard. Ten minutes later she was stirring the ingredients together and then dropping the dozen small cupcake holders into place. She soon had the oven fire stoked, and slid the plate of cakes onto the middle rack. She timed the minutes with a careful eye on the kitchen clock.

When she peeked in the oven door the first time, Rosemary whispered to herself, "Not quite. These have to be perfect for Ezra."

As Rosemary watched the clock, a sudden pain shot through her lower abdomen. Rosemary groaned and clutched with both hands. When the pain let up, a smile spread over her face. "I really must be nervous. Now who would have thought that?" she said to herself.

*Mamm* stuck her head in the kitchen doorway. "What did you say?"

Rosemary laughed. "Just talking to myself. I'm so happy."

"How's the dessert coming?"

Rosemary pulled open the oven door and retrieved the plate of cakes.

*Mamm* inspected the results over Rosemary's shoulder. "Not too bad for a girl in the throes of nervousness."

"Thank you," Rosemary whispered. "I'm too tense to tell what's *goot* or not. Will you taste one for me after they've cooled off?"

"Ann will," *Mamm* decided. "But you can't bring those anywhere close to the supper table or the children will eat all of them."

"I know," Rosemary agreed. She slid the plate onto a pad on the counter and stepped back. They were perfect. Now hopefully this nervousness would leave soon, or she'd have a stomachache every evening Ezra brought her home. And there *would* be other evenings. She had come too far to lose Ezra.

Rosemary bent low over the cakes to take a deep breath. The smell was delicious. This was the very thing she wanted on the first evening Ezra brought her home. They would sit in the living room and eat cherry cheese cups together, and she wouldn't be nervous any longer.

"Thank you, Ezra. And thank You, Lord, for this day," Rosemary sent a quick prayer toward the heavens.

# Chapter Twenty-One

Rosemary pinched herself that evening at the hymn singing as the first song number was given out. The singing began and the joyous notes matched her feelings exactly. She lifted her head and sang with all her heart. If someone noticed her extra effort, they would have assumed the song had stirred a religious fervor in her. They wouldn't have been far from wrong. Ezra stirred things long buried in her heart. She had never dared dream this would happen. Not to Rosemary Beiler. She was in love.

She would soon float away, Rosemary decided, as the song continued. She felt so close to heaven, it was as if she could reach out and touch a cloud. Now if this pain in her side would just go away. Nervousness, no doubt. Perhaps by her second or third date with Ezra she would no longer have this reaction. Until then she would ignore the pain and enjoy every minute of this evening.

No one among the young people had noticed anything different, even when the Beiler family had all arrived in the surrey. They were an ordinary family who didn't warrant any special attention. And she had managed to hide the joy in her heart until the first song had broken the dam. Now her face must glow with happiness, but she didn't care.

From across the room Ezra glanced her way and smiled. Rosemary lowered her head. This would not do. She had to act normal to some degree, and too many smiles from Ezra would bring out a deep flush in her face. Rosemary forced herself to concentrate as another song number was given out. This time the tune was slower and more reverent. Rosemary closed her eyes and sang along, her spirit drifting joyously upward as visions of the Lord and Ezra floated together through Rosemary's mind.

Was this how every girl in love felt? Surely it was. She would have to calm down, Rosemary told herself. Excitement seemed to make the pain in her side worse, which could be the Lord's way of keeping her from flying too high. She already held Ezra in the highest esteem, so the rebuke came as no surprise. Rosemary smiled as the song came to a close, and another was given out. She was content with whatever the Lord allowed. The chance to pursue Ezra for his affections had come as a total surprise, but the path had been opened for her. She would be thankful and accept what was given to her. With the roses came the thorns. Was that not how the Lord worked?

Rosemary kept her gaze away from Ezra's direction. Flirtations could wait for later in the evening. For now she focused on the words of the song. They spoke of the Lord's greatness and of the comfort He supplied to those who obeyed and trusted in Him. She wanted that comfort and guidance, and so did Ezra. That was part of the wonder of their relationship. They would travel through this evening and on to whatever lay ahead of them. If the Lord willed it, they would one day stand and say their marriage vows together, but she would not think of that now.

The songs continued, and Rosemary allowed herself a quick glance at Ezra once the clock crept toward nine o'clock. Ezra caught her look and smiled. Rosemary allowed the joy to rise all the way through her. With a final flourish the last song number was given out. When the song concluded, Rosemary gripped the edge of the bench as the conversations began around her. If someone spoke to her, she had no idea how she would speak. Her throat was too dry. Rosemary held perfectly still and listened to the conversation between Amy and Wanda, who were seated beside her.

"Emanuel's coming home on Wednesday from his trip to the old community," Amy was saying.

"On the Greyhound?" Wanda asked.

"*Yah*, there weren't enough people who wanted to visit to take a van," Amy said.

"Your cousin's wedding, wasn't it?" Wanda asked.

"Distant." Amy laughed. "Emanuel had his reasons, you know."

"I can imagine."

"What about you and this Johnny fellow, Rosemary? I heard some rumors from a little bird." Rosemary jumped when Amy addressed her.

"What about him?" Rosemary said.

"We heard that Johnny wrote to you," Amy said. "If you're writing him, you have kept an awfully *goot* secret."

"No, I'm not writing him," Rosemary said.

"But you don't seem surprised we asked," Amy persisted. "So Johnny must have written. Is there something in the future perhaps?"

"No," Rosemary managed. The rush of heat to her face gave both girls the wrong idea, but she couldn't help that. "We're not writing," Rosemary repeated.

"I guess things can get mixed up," Amy said. "All kinds of mis-understandings can happen with these long-distance relationships. That's why I want someone from the community."

"Like Clyde?" Wanda teased.

Amy sighed. "I think Clyde's got his heart set on Sandra Troyer. So that one's flown the coop."

They laughed again, and Rosemary forced herself to join in. But perhaps she should tell Ezra about Johnny if rumors were floating around the community. She mustn't let any misunderstanding arise between them.

Rosemary glanced around as several of the dating couples rose to their feet to walk out. Ezra was still deep in conversation with his cousin Joseph. He would soon walk out, though, and Rosemary would watch for it. The younger couples always waited until the steadies had gone, and most of those had left. Sure enough, after a few minutes, Ezra slipped out the front door. Rosemary waited for what seemed like a long time before she stood up. Amy and Wanda gave her strange looks, but Rosemary kept her head down and hurried to the washroom. Before Rosemary could find her shawl, Amy appeared in the doorway.

"Is this what it looks like, Rosemary?"

"*Yah*, if you must know," Rosemary answered.

"But Ezra Wagler? Well! I'm glad for you." Amy managed a smile. "I never would have thought this, as hard as the Troyer cousins worked on the man. But I suppose financial trouble can do this, and now that Clyde is making moves toward Sandra, the coast is clear."

Rosemary was in no mood to analyze the situation, but she must be polite. "Ezra's asking me home, and that's a great gift from the Lord. I am deeply thankful."

"The best to you, then." Amy's smile was more relaxed. "And congratulations."

"Thank you." Rosemary returned the smile.

She wrapped her shawl tightly over her shoulders and slipped out into the fallen darkness. The dim lights from the buggies lined up along the sidewalks cast a soft glow against the horizon. Rosemary spotted Ezra's buggy and hurried across the lawn. Ezra pushed open the door as she approached and Rosemary pulled herself up and settled onto the seat beside him.

Ezra's deep voice filled the buggy. "*Goot* evening."

"And a *goot* evening to you," Rosemary whispered.

Ezra let out the reins and his horse dashed forward. Rosemary hung on with both hands.

Ezra chuckled. "He's a little energetic after dark."

Rosemary took a deep breath. "What's his name?"

"Midnight. Do you like it?"

She would like any name that Ezra chose for his horse, but she probably shouldn't say so. "Sounds mysterious," Rosemary said instead.

Ezra laughed. "Only you would say that."

"Well, it does," Rosemary protested. "I know he's a black horse and that's probably why you named him Midnight, but that's still mysterious."

"What would you have named him?" Ezra leaned forward to check for traffic before he pulled out onto Route 15.

Rosemary thought for a moment. Why Ezra teased her she didn't know, but she might as well tell the truth. "I would have been happy with whatever you named your horse. I'm not that original."

Ezra grinned. "You're plenty original, Rosemary. Don't knock yourself."

Rosemary regarded Ezra for a moment. "Okay, if you say so."

"I do say so." Ezra let out the reins again.

When there was silence for a few moments, Ezra went on. "You'll have to give me a pass if I say something wrong…I'm kind of nervous, you know. I've never taken a girl home before."

"You're nervous?" Rosemary didn't hide her astonishment. "You have to be kidding."

"No, I'm not." Ezra had sobered. "Thanks for letting me take you home."

Rosemary nodded and clasped her hands on her lap. *He* was nervous? If only he knew how she felt… The pain in her side stabbed at her as a reminder.

"I see your parents left earlier with the rest of the family," Ezra said.

"*Yah*, that's how *Mamm* wanted things done tonight, what with Ann having to drive by herself otherwise."

Ezra smiled. "I had wondered about that, but I didn't want to say something this early in our relationship. I would have been glad to pick you up on the way to the singing too. It's not that far out of my way."

Rosemary kept her gaze on the road ahead. "Oh. Does that mean we might do this again?"

Ezra laughed. "Do you want to?"

The words rushed out. "You know I want to. You must know I'm misty-eyed and breathless just because you asked me home at all."

Ezra laughed again. "You underrate yourself, Rosemary, but perhaps that's what I like about you. You're unpretentious."

"I don't know what that means, but I think it must be a compliment."

"*Yah*, it's a compliment," Ezra assured her. "It means you don't pretend."

"I try not to," she said.

A mile later Ezra slowed Midnight for the Beilers' lane and turned in to stop at the hitching post. "Well, here we are. Home, sweet home."

Rosemary jumped down from her side of the buggy and Ezra climbed down to tie up Midnight. He called over his shoulder, "What have you got to eat inside?"

"Come." Rosemary took his arm when he finished with Midnight. "I'll show you what I've made, then you can decide for yourself if it's worth coming back again."

Rosemary's nerve faltered now that she had taken Ezra's arm, but she didn't dare let go. Ezra hadn't objected, but he must have been astonished at her boldness on their first date.

Rosemary paused at the front door to let go of his arm. "I should tell you something, Ezra. I thought to do so later, but now's better."

"More surprises?" he teased.

"I'm afraid so." Rosemary made a face. "I wouldn't have said anything, but Amy asked me about it at the singing tonight, and if she knows, it'll eventually get around to your ears."

"Okay, I'm waiting."

"Johnny Mast from the old community wrote me to ask if we could begin a writing relationship, and I told him I didn't want to begin something. That's really all there is to it. I said no, but Amy didn't know that, so word is getting out."

Ezra squeezed her hand. "Sounds like you're in great demand. See, don't underrate yourself."

Rosemary opened the door. Once they were inside, she motioned for him to sit on the couch, but he followed her into the kitchen instead.

"Now you're going to make me nervous again," Rosemary protested as another sharp pain shot through her abdomen.

Ezra must have noticed Rosemary's expression because concern flashed across his face. "Is something wrong?"

"Nothing that these can't fix." Rosemary forced a smile.

She opened the cupboard to bring out the plate of cherry cheese cups.

Ezra's face glowed. "That's food fit for a king, if you ask me."

"Then I made the right choice." Rosemary took a deep breath

as the pain eased in her side. She shooed Ezra back into the living room, where she set down the desserts and returned to the kitchen for plates and forks.

Ezra had his gaze fixed on the cherry cheese cups when she came back. "I think you've sealed this deal on your first evening," he said.

Rosemary laughed and handed him a plate and a fork. "You're a *goot* teaser, Ezra, but eat now."

"You try them first," Ezra insisted.

"I'll do nothing of the sort," Rosemary shot back.

"What if I die of poisoning?"

"Then I'll bury you by the moonlight in our garden."

Ezra threw his head back in laughter. "You are an original, Rosemary, and *yah*, we'll do this again."

Ezra bit into one of the cups.

"Excellent!" he proclaimed. "Absolutely excellent!"

Rosemary took one herself, and swallowed a bite. She wouldn't be able to eat more than one. Not the way her stomach felt.

Rosemary gave Ezra a warm smile as he took another cherry cheese cup and gulped it down in two bites.

# Chapter Twenty-Two

Two weeks later after the Sunday morning church service, Lydia waited toward the back of the kitchen until the girls serving the unmarried men's table had been assigned. At least Rosemary hadn't volunteered today. The girl had shown great discretion and wisdom in the past few weeks, so Lydia shouldn't be surprised. Rosemary had always been a decent girl, and ever since Ezra had taken Rosemary home from the hymn singing, the girl had blossomed like a rose.

Lydia forced herself to smile and stepped closer in the crowded kitchen to lay her hand on Rosemary's arm. "You look a little woozy. Did Ezra just walk past?" she teased.

A hint of a smile crossed Rosemary's face, while she fanned herself with both hands. "No, I'm just a little weak, that's all. Food—even the sight of it—seems to do that to me lately."

"Well, congratulations on your success with Ezra." Lydia pressed Rosemary's arm and turned to go.

Rosemary reached out to clutch Lydia's hand, and whispered in her ear, "Thanks for not being angry with me about Ezra. And I know Sandra isn't either. She just spoke with me today. The two of you couldn't be nicer about it."

"Hey, you caught him fair and square." Lydia forced another smile. "How can we complain?"

"Well, thanks anyway," Rosemary whispered as Lydia moved away.

Lydia stepped to the counter where Sandra was filling the peanut butter bowls. "Let me help you," Lydia suggested.

She took several bowls off the counter to set them on a tray before Sandra could answer. She hurried to the married women's table. Several of the women at the table smiled and nodded their thanks as she served them.

Once the tray was empty and Lydia had stepped back, Sandra said, "I figured you'd be down with the unmarried men, scrounging up prospects."

Lydia frowned and said, "What about yourself at the service today? Clyde would welcome your attentions, I'm sure."

A troubled look crossed Sandra's face. "Lydia, can I go home with you this afternoon and talk? I need someone to pour out my troubles to."

"Of course!" Lydia didn't hesitate. "The truth is, I need someone to talk to too!"

"What's wrong?" Sandra whispered.

"*Mamm* and *Daett* and Rudy."

Sandra squeezed Lydia's arm. "Then we must speak at the first opportunity."

Lydia left again with her arms loaded with bread and red beet bowls. When those had been delivered, they returned to the women's table with coffeepots, which were quickly emptied.

"It's cold weather today," Lena offered with an apologetic smile.

"We'll be right back with more," Lydia responded, and headed back to the kitchen for refills. She was soon at the table again pouring coffee until Bishop Henry called for another prayer of thanksgiving.

After the "amen" Lydia filled a final few cups while the older women lingered to visit. The younger girls arrived with their bowls of dishwater to clean the utensils for the next serving.

Lena chuckled as she and the others stood up without further objection. "Looks like we're getting chased right off the table." Lydia returned the coffeepots to the kitchen and brought Sandra with her on crutches to sit at a clean table. They had just seated themselves when Bishop Henry called for the prayer of thanks again.

Lydia bowed her head to whisper her own silent prayer. "Help us, dear Lord, through these dark times. And don't let our hearts stray from the truth."

She wanted to spill her heart right now, but the subject was too explosive to talk about here. She would have to wait until they were someplace more private—such as at home. But even at the house, privacy wasn't a sure thing. Emma and Rhoda would have their *Englisha* friends over this afternoon, and if the hints they had dropped all week were correct, Rudy would be with them. He hadn't made an appearance again since Thanksgiving Day, apparently to give her time to think. But the truth was, she had done everything *but* think. Mostly she worried. Thinking about Rudy got her nowhere. How she had gotten into this situation was beyond her. She should have shoved Rudy out of her mind, but while *Mamm* and *Daett* focused on Emma and Rhoda, they were missing the precipice she teetered on. But surely she wouldn't go over the edge. Not now! Not after the choice she had made to join the community.

"Don't look so somber," Sandra whispered. "The deacon's *frau* is coming our way."

Lydia gathered her scattered thoughts and pasted on a smile.

"So, how are the Troyer cousins this afternoon?" Ruth Ann asked.

"Perfect!" Sandra chirped.

"My condolences on Ezra," Ruth Ann said, patting Sandra's hand. "I must say, I was most surprised that both of you lost that race."

"Well, you never know," Sandra said in the same tone of voice.

Ruth Ann moved closer to whisper, "You seem to be taking it well, but maybe it's because you both lost together. That must make it easier."

"I suppose it does," Sandra allowed.

"Well, I'm sure neither of you will have much trouble securing decent Amish husbands," Ruth Ann said. "Just don't try for the same one next time!"

"Thanks for the advice," Lydia finally said as Ruth Ann walked off.

"Why did you have to say that?" Sandra asked.

"Because it's true," Lydia told her. "And we should take all the advice we can get."

"I'm sure she'd say I'm supposed to accept Clyde's attentions," Sandra mumbled, then fell silent until they finished the meal and Bishop Henry called for a prayer of thanks again.

"Go tell Mark where you're going," Lydia said as she got up from the table.

Sandra hobbled off, and Lydia found *Mamm* outside the kitchen doorway. "I'm taking Sandra home with me for the afternoon. Can you take Emma and Rhoda?"

"Sure," *Mamm* said at once. "I'm glad you two are getting together."

Lydia smiled her thanks and moved to the washroom. She had found her shawl by the time Sandra appeared, then Sandra dug in the pile to find her own. Together they walked across the lawn, where Sandra stayed by the buggy while Lydia went to bring her horse, Timber, from the barn. When she returned, Clyde was engaged in conversation with Sandra. Lydia hung back for a moment. But there was no sense in that, Lydia told herself. If Clyde wanted a private conversation with Sandra, he could have come out sooner or asked for a moment alone.

"Howdy," Clyde called when Lydia approached.

"Hi, yourself," Lydia responded, pausing with her hand on Timber's bridle.

"Well, I should be going," Clyde announced. "See you later, Sandra."

Lydia watched him leave before she turned to Sandra. "Is this what you wanted to speak of? His pestering?"

"*Yah*," Sandra responded. She helped hitch Timber to the buggy the best she could, with only a brief glance toward Clyde's retreating back. Lydia helped Sandra climb into the buggy, then she tossed Sandra the lines. Lydia pulled herself up to settle on the buggy seat.

"Get up," Lydia hollered out.

As they passed, Lydia saw *Daett* and Deacon Schrock leaning against *Daett*'s buggy, deep in conversation. Lydia motioned with her head toward the two. "That's my problem, or part of it."

"So it was true what you told me on Thanksgiving Day? I guess I was hoping things had changed by now."

Lydia turned onto Madrid Road before she answered. "I'm living in a daze, to tell you the truth. I can't believe half the time what's happening."

"Me too!" Sandra muttered. "Who would have thought Rosemary Beiler would win Ezra's affections?"

"So what about Clyde?" Lydia asked.

"Sometimes I think I'm starting to give in," Sandra sighed. "At least, that's how it seems. I ask myself why, but I honestly don't know. Is it because I'm scared of walking alone through life as an old maid? Is that it?"

"You're *not* going to end up an old maid!" Lydia said. "Somehow we'll both find husbands. Good husbands too!"

Sandra snorted. "After our disaster with Ezra we'd better think of a new strategy."

Lydia didn't answer as she turned Timber into the driveway. As Timber plodded toward the barn and came to an abrupt stop, Sandra noticed a car parked near the house. "You have visitors," she said.

Lydia rolled her eyes. "Emma and Rhoda's friends, and probably Rudy. They must be waiting for Emma and Rhoda to come home with *Daett* and *Mamm.*"

"You still care for Rudy, don't you?" Sandra asked as she climbed down to help unhitch Timber from one side of the buggy.

Lydia undid the tug on her side. "I wish I knew. But come with me for a short walk on your crutches if Rudy's here. That way I can avoid him."

"Just say you already have company. *Me.*"

"We'll see," Lydia said as she led Timber to the barn. Sandra hobbled toward the house, and by the time Lydia approached the porch, Sandra was chatting cheerfully with the group of *Englisha* young people who must have come outside to greet them. Rudy now stood with his back toward her.

Lydia took a deep breath. Both Avery and Julie had turned toward her, and Rudy followed their gaze, a broad smile spreading across his face. Lydia forced her feet forward. She had to face this problem.

"Everybody inside for popcorn," Lydia announced with forced cheerfulness. It was all she could think of.

"Hi, Lydia," Rudy said. "Good to see you again."

"And you too," Lydia managed. Her throat had gone dry as Rudy's blue eyes blazed in front of her.

Just then, *Daett's* buggy pulled in the driveway and Emma and Rhoda tumbled out. They raced across the yard to greet Avery, Julie,

Benny, and Jimmy. Rudy waited and stepped closer to Lydia, whispering, "I said I'd come back."

Lydia ignored him and announced again, "Everyone inside for popcorn, please."

Emma shushed her at once. "We'll take care of that. Rudy doesn't come that often, so why don't you take a few moments with him?"

"But Sandra's here for a visit," Lydia said.

"That I am." Sandra finally waved her hand in the air.

"We'll take care of Sandra," Emma ordered. "Now go, but don't be long."

Lydia looked at Sandra, who just shrugged her shoulders. Lydia could hardly refuse, even when *Mamm* came up the walk with disapproval on her face. Rudy settled the matter when he pulled on Lydia's dress sleeve and headed toward the pasture gate. Lydia followed in a daze. This was where they had come on Thanksgiving morning when Rudy had arrived so unexpectedly back in her life.

As they passed through the pasture gate, Rudy's hand slipped into hers. The touch of his fingers was so familiar and comforting. Lydia looked up at him. His smile still made her heart race. He was so handsome and kind. He was also a temptation.

Rudy paused to gaze across the field. He caught Lydia's glance moments later. "We really must find more decent ways to meet than in the field beyond your pasture gate."

Lydia laughed in spite of herself. "I see you're still the romantic at heart, Rudy."

"Oh, I am," Rudy assured her.

"But this is the Amish way."

"You're not really Amish, Lydia." Rudy's eyes seemed to pierce all the way through her.

Lydia found her voice to protest. "Oh, but I am."

"Trust me, you aren't," Rudy said. "Or else you wouldn't be out here with me now."

Lydia's head spun. She should tell Rudy to leave right now. He was clearly a threat to the decisions she had made about her life. Her *Amish* life.

"I *am* Amish," Lydia repeated. Couldn't the man understand?

Rudy chuckled. "We still have to find a better meeting place. Like in town somewhere. I'll pick you up sometime next week when it suits you."

"I can't." Lydia kept her voice steady.

"Let's not argue now," Rudy said. "We'll settle this later. Right now I want to walk with you and hold your hand. I still love you, Lydia. You know that, don't you? I've never stopped loving you."

Lydia dropped her eyes. In spite of herself, she clung to his hand. She didn't have the strength to resist. Perhaps the courage would come later, but from where? Her world was spinning out of control.

"We'd best not be too long," Lydia told him.

He smiled and shrugged. "As you wish."

# Chapter Twenty-Three

It was the Friday night before Christmas Eve. Lydia changed into her Sunday dress for her agreed-upon outing with Rudy. She could hear Emma and Rhoda giggling from their bedroom across the hallway. Her sisters were in high spirits tonight, but she couldn't say the same thing for herself. Why on earth had she agreed to this meeting?

Well, of course, it was the way Rudy had insisted that convinced her. And now, according to Rudy's plan, Lydia would ride along when Avery and Julie picked up her sisters for their planned Christmas lights tour. This arrangement was to make the evening's activities easier for *Mamm* and *Daett* to swallow.

Everyone would meet at the first stop in Rensselaer Falls, where Rudy would take her in his car. They would be alone, like in the old days of her *rumspringa* time, as if nothing had changed. But much had changed since those long-ago days. That was the truth. She wasn't the same person, so why was she acting as though she was? The past could not be recaptured, yet she had given in to Rudy's plan. She wanted to blame him, but the fault went deeper. She had no one to blame but herself. She was flirting with danger outright, but she had given her word and wouldn't change that now.

*Mamm* had told her this morning when they finished the break-fast dishes, "Deacon Schrock is coming over tonight."

Lydia hadn't responded, but *Mamm* knew she understood. The visit was with *Daett* but the deacon would eventually speak with her too. Especially if the deacon learned of Lydia's date with Rudy. So why was she taking the risk? Where could the relationship with Rudy lead? Nowhere but trouble. She knew she wouldn't leave the community. To stay Amish had been her choice two years ago, but she was baptized now, and had made promises on her knees to the Lord and the church. Rudy would never join the community, so the *bann* would be a certainty if she strayed. A shiver ran up Lydia's back.

Then again, a Christmas lights tour wouldn't decide the matter. Her behavior was even understandable, considering everything else the family had gone though. At least that's what she could tell Deacon Schrock if he asked. But maybe it wouldn't come to that. Deacon Schrock might succeed in his talk with *Daett* tonight, and her parents would clamp down on Emma and Rhoda's behavior. Not so long ago *Mamm* would have forbidden most of their antics, and if she had, Rudy would never have reappeared in Lydia's life.

Lydia shivered again. Across the hall Emma and Rhoda's bedroom door burst open, and her sisters spilled out into the hallway. They came across to pound on her door.

Emma hollered, "Hurry up, slowpoke. We have to get going."

Lydia had not heard a car in the driveway, so there was no real hurry. After a few minutes her sisters gave up and raced downstairs, filling the stairwell with giggles. Her sisters could be lighthearted about all this, but they didn't face the *bann* like she did. There the soul waited in darkness for the church to lift its disapproval. Bishop Henry had warned of this many times in his sermons. What the church bound on the earth, Bishop Henry said, heaven bound also, and a soul who could not live at peace with the community could not live at peace with the Lord.

Lydia put the last pin in her *kapp*, and glanced out the bedroom window. A car was visible in the distance, so Avery and Julie would be here any minute. She waited a moment before she opened the bedroom door and took the stairs in slow motion. Her sisters might race downstairs, but she wanted to act differently. Yet in her heart tonight she wouldn't be so different at all. She would be spending time with an *Englisha* boy just as her sisters often did. They would look at Christmas lights, and likely stop someplace for hamburgers. Rudy and she would no doubt do likewise.

The front door slammed as Lydia stepped out of the stairwell. The forms of Emma and Rhoda raced past the living room window. Lydia stopped at the kitchen doorway to say, "Good-bye, *Mamm*."

"Have a *goot* time." *Mamm*'s smile was weak.

Lydia grabbed her thick winter coat and slipped outside into the brisk winter air. Snow had fallen last night. The Christmas lights tour would be breathtaking…if only her heart could forget for a few hours the danger she was in and soar with the beauty around her.

Maybe that was the best approach, since she had committed to the evening. She had forgotten how enjoyable these Christmas tours used to be during her *rumspringa* days.

Lydia drew a deep breath and walked toward Avery and Julie's car. Maybe *Mamm* and *Daett* would make their peace with Deacon Schrock tonight, and she would find the strength to resist these temptations. Wouldn't that be a miracle?

"Hi, Lydia," Avery called out. "Ready to set off on the great adventure? Hop in the back seat. There's room for you there."

Lydia nodded and opened the door to squeeze in with her sisters. Avery turned the car around in the barnyard. Lydia took one last look at the house as they pulled out, before memories of her *rum-springa* time began flooding back. There had been long evenings spent in Heuvelton on the weekends, filled with laughter and light-heartedness—and Rudy, of course. But that was in the past, Lydia reminded herself. This was only a ride to see the Christmas lights. Lydia closed her eyes as Emma and Rhoda began a silly conversation with Avery and Julie.

Avery soon slowed the car as they approached the intersection in Rensselaer Falls. Off to the side three cars were parked in the gas station. The snowplow had turned around there and left several large spaces. Avery pulled in and parked. Emma and Rhoda looked at Lydia with big grins on their faces. "See you later."

"Rudy's in the green mustang," Avery said. "But I suppose you know that."

Lydia forced a smile. "Of course. And thanks for the ride." With a quick push of her hand Lydia opened the car door and hurried toward the green mustang.

As Lydia approached, the driver's window rolled down and Rudy called out. "Hi, Lydia. So glad to see you again, love."

Lydia choked back a response. No man had called her "love" ever before. Not even Rudy.

"Chilly tonight, isn't it?" Rudy said as she took her place in the passenger's seat.

Lydia took a quick wipe at her eyes. "*Yah*, and the wind stings a little bit. But it's warm in here." She pulled back her coat from her shoulders, revealing her simple blue dress.

"You used to wear…" Rudy let the sentence hang as his gaze traveled down her attire.

"I'm Amish now," she reminded him.

"I don't know how all that works," Rudy muttered. "But you're still Lydia to me, and I'm glad you're here."

"Did you think I wouldn't come?" Lydia tried to tease.

Rudy didn't laugh. "I feared you wouldn't, but here you are."

Lydia tried to keep her voice lighthearted. "Yep, here I am."

How was she to explain to Rudy what had transpired since her *rumspringa*? It wasn't possible. Rudy could never understand it all. Was she a fool to be here?

"The others are pulling out." Rudy motioned toward the several cars in the agreed-upon caravan. "Shall we follow…or go off on our own?"

"Whatever you wish," Lydia said. "I'm yours for the evening."

Rudy remained sober-faced. "Lydia, I know this must be hard for you. I don't know about your life as a…whatever you call it. Let's say, your life in the community."

"That's *goot* enough," Lydia allowed.

Rudy nodded. "I know that whatever you did to be with me tonight, must have caused some consternation. I wouldn't ask that of you, if I didn't think it was worth it. If I didn't want it badly, Lydia. See, I've never forgotten the times we had together. They shine in my heart, and they have never dimmed."

Lydia lowered her head and didn't answer. What was there to say? Her presence here was answer enough. Lydia waited, and finally Rudy started the car and followed the others. Only he drove slower and dropped his speed even further as they approached the edge of Ogdensburg. Bright lights glimmered in the front windows and strings of colored beads went everywhere in the yards. A huge sleigh and reindeer ran along the edge of several trees.

Lydia took a deep breath and forced herself to focus on the sights.

Rudy chuckled. "Looks like everyone is trying to outdo each other."

Which was exactly how everyone in the community tried *not* to live, Lydia thought, but she pushed the thought away. She was here with Rudy, and it wasn't right to bring things from her world into this moment.

Rudy didn't seem to notice Lydia's troubled thoughts as he pointed to another bright display. "How about that huge snowman? That's not a very original idea to anchor the lights that way, but it does work. Look at the streamer going all the way to the rooftop. That took some energy to climb up there!"

"I guess so," Lydia agreed.

She had to say something, but Rudy had no idea how she felt or what despair was gripping her deep inside. The thought of what they used to share had glowed in her heart while she had been at home, but out here, the memory seemed to have flown far away. Lydia glanced at Rudy's handsome face. This was the man she had once kissed, but he wasn't the same. Or rather, she was no longer the same. She shouldn't blame Rudy.

Lydia struggled for words as Rudy exclaimed over another display. "Splendid, absolutely splendid. Lydia, remember how we used to take this drive together?"

"*Yah*," Lydia managed. She did remember.

Rudy reached across the console to squeeze Lydia's hand. "You always were the shy one, while your cousin, what was her name, was so bold."

"Sandra." Lydia struggled with the name. Sandra might be bold, but she would never do something like this.

"Yep." Rudy laughed but didn't seem to notice her discomfort. "Could that woman ever chatter up a storm! It took a little effort to draw you out, but I succeeded eventually. I even got a kiss out of you. Remember? You were all the sweeter for the hard work involved." Rudy grinned and squeezed Lydia's hand again.

How could she forget? Lydia wondered.

"Can we get something to eat?" The question burst out of her.

Rudy seemed puzzled but shrugged. "Sure. But there's still plenty of lights to see. We can stop to get subs. Is that good enough?"

"*Yah*. It's perfect." Lydia tried to sound cheerful.

Rudy accelerated and moments later pulled into the Wendy's parking lot. The couple went inside and placed their orders.

"Shall we eat here?" Rudy suggested, motioning toward a table. "We can see the downtown lights from the windows."

Lydia nodded and followed Rudy to a seat. A feeling of loneliness swept over her. Lydia pressed back the tears, and this time Rudy noticed when he sat down with the tray of sandwiches and their drinks.

"This isn't working, is it?" he asked.

Lydia tried to smile. "I wanted to come out with you. It's not that. Rudy, I just have…" Lydia couldn't finish the sentence.

Rudy reached for Lydia's hand across the table. "I understand."

"It's not your fault." Lydia motioned with her hand in a wide circle that included the restaurant and the streets outside. "I've been away from this for so long…and I never planned to come back."

Rudy leaned forward. "But you *can* come back. I'll help you… anytime you're ready."

Lydia took a bite of her chicken sandwich, but it somehow didn't taste as good as she remembered it. She thought she might choke.

"Are you okay?" Rudy half stood to his feet.

Lydia motioned him to sit again. "I'm okay. I guess I'm not as hungry as I thought I was. I'm not feeling well."

Rudy stood up. "Then you're not okay. Come. Bring your sandwich and we'll leave. I'm sorry about this, Lydia. I didn't mean to rush things."

Lydia squeezed back the tears as she slid her sandwich into the bag. What a fool she was, caught between two worlds like this. How could she have been so stupid?

"Thank you for understanding," Lydia said as they left. "I'm so sorry."

"It's okay." Rudy took Lydia's hand to lead the way back to the car. "We'll try again some other time."

Lydia tried to protest, but the words stuck in her throat. They drove in silence back to Lydia's home.

# Chapter Twenty-Four

Barely half an hour later, Rudy pulled into the Troyers' lane. The gas lantern was burning in the living room window, casting a soft glow over Deacon Schrock's buggy. It was still parked beside the barn. At the moment, though, Lydia didn't care about Deacon Schrock. She was more concerned about how badly tonight had turned out. Rudy would have every justification to throw her out of his car at the end of the driveway. Instead he drove her all the way up to the sidewalk before he stopped.

"Good night," Rudy told her. His voice was kind.

"Thanks for tonight," she whispered. "I'm sorry..."

"It'll be okay," Rudy said. "We'll wait until..."

"I don't know what's wrong with me," Lydia whispered.

"I enjoyed the evening while it lasted." Rudy attempted a chuckle and reached over to touch her hand.

"I wish I hadn't..." Lydia's free hand didn't move on the handle. "Maybe we had best..."

Rudy stopped Lydia with a gentle squeeze on her hand. "We'll try this some other time, so don't say anything more tonight. I will wait a few weeks and call again."

Lydia nodded and pushed open the car door, then plunged into the night. She hurried up the walk as Rudy's headlights streamed across the snowy lawn. At the porch she turned for a wave, but his car was already out on Madrid Road. She stepped into the shadows of the porch to catch her breath. Her whole body felt numb. What a disaster she had created. With Rudy gone the reality sank in deeply. Deacon Schrock was still inside. Maybe she should hide in the barn until the deacon went home. Knowing Deacon Schrock, that could be a long time, and she was too cold to wait outside.

Lydia sighed and pushed open the front door to see *Daett* sitting on his rocker with his head bowed. *Mamm* was in the same posture, while Deacon Schrock was on the couch. He looked up when Lydia walked in.

"You're back," *Mamm* spoke first.

Lydia didn't answer. She wasn't expected to.

Deacon Schrock looked like he was carrying a great weight on his shoulders. "*Goot* evening, Lydia. Please have a seat. We've been waiting and praying that the Lord brings you home early."

Lydia caught her breath. Was that why her panic attack had happened? Because of Deacon Schrock's prayers?

"Please take a seat," Deacon Schrock repeated.

There was no getting away from this, Lydia decided, so she sat on the chair near the stove. Her knees trembled.

Deacon Schrock waited with his head lowered for a few minutes. He finally looked up and asked, "Would you mind explaining what you were doing tonight? Your *mamm* told me you went with your sisters and two of their *Englisha* friends to tour the Christmas lights. You know that's strictly a *rumspringa* activity, one that you promised to leave behind when you made vows to the Lord and His church."

Lydia kept her head down. She couldn't argue with the deacon's point. What he said was true.

"And yet you went?" Deacon Schrock continued to probe.

Lydia raised her head. "There's more to it than that." The deacon wouldn't be satisfied until he knew the truth, so she might as well confess.

"*Yah?*" Deacon Schrock waited.

"We met up with the two men Emma and Rhoda run around with, Benny and Jimmy." Lydia gathered her courage. "But that's not what it was all about. I met my old *Englisha* boyfriend, Rudy. He's the one who dropped me off right now."

Deacon Schrock stared. "What is wrong with this family? Have your *daett*'s sins affected everyone, Lydia? You know this cannot be. For this action alone you have sinned grievously. And this, after you promised to forsake the world and all that lies out there." Deacon Schrock's arm waved in the general area of the living room window. "Lydia, first your parents allow all kinds of mischief from their youngest daughters to happen right in their own home, and now *you?* Are we to lose all of this family to the world?" Deacon Schrock stopped to catch his breath. "I can believe none of this. There must be an explanation. Is this happening because of the sin your *daett* and his brother allowed into the community? If it is, I find myself at fault first. I should have recommended to the ministry that your *daett* be sternly disciplined for his financial sin. Instead, I figured the death of his brother would be enough of a rebuke from the Lord, but I see once more that the church must also do its part. In this we all seemed to have failed."

"You shouldn't blame yourself, nor should anyone else," *Daett* spoke up. "I take this blame upon myself."

Deacon Schrock glanced at *Daett.* "That is a start, but you still have a very long way to go, Ben. I think a knee confession is certainly called for. And I wouldn't be surprised if Bishop Henry received counsel to place all of you in the *bann* for six weeks."

"The *bann*?" *Mamm* gave a little gasp.

Lydia saw her *mamm*'s alarmed face. What had she expected?

Deacon Schrock addressed Lydia again. "What did you and your former boyfriend speak of tonight? And you had best tell me the truth, Lydia."

Lydia waited before she answered. "We did nothing evil, but I am tempted by the love we once had for each other. In this I admit my wrong."

A look of horror filled Deacon Schrock's face. "You spoke of love with your former *Englisha* boyfriend! But this sort of thing is from the world, Lydia. You have promised to forsake such things and leave behind all that is impure and to join yourself to the people of the Lord. This is worse than I imagined."

"I said I was tempted, that is all," Lydia protested.

Deacon Schrock thundered his response. "Lydia! Listen to yourself. These are not the words of the Lord. An *Englisha* man cannot love one of the daughters of the community. This is unspeakable. You must repent at once."

Lydia's head spun. "I cannot but speak the truth. Would you have me lie?"

Deacon Schrock stood to pace the floor. "Something must be done with you, Lydia. I will make a trip over to Harvey Miller's place first thing tomorrow morning and speak with him. Harvey lost his *frau* last year, and he still hasn't married. He needs to plan a quick wedding with you and get this all behind us."

Lydia tried to breathe. "You would match me up with Harvey Miller?" Visions of Harvey's face appeared in Lydia's mind. He certainly wasn't unattractive, but she had never entertained a romantic thought about the man in her life. Nor had Harvey had romantic thoughts about her. It was common knowledge that Harvey still mourned the death of his beloved *frau*, Leslie.

"It is the ministry's responsibility to make suggestions in cases like yours." Deacon Schrock was firm. "Your aunt Edna took my advice after the death of Emil, and the Lord has greatly blessed the match. I cannot see how things could turn out differently in this case. Harvey needs a *frau*, and you would be a very suitable match for the man. Your willful ways would be calmed down."

Lydia finally found her voice. "You cannot do this!"

"You will repent of your willful ways," Deacon Schrock ordered. "And the Lord will cleanse the rest of your soul. I will speak to the rest of the ministry about this matter, and after the Christmas holidays, we will speak further. Why trouble like this has to arise around the celebration of the Lord's birth is beyond me, but I suppose men have sins in their hearts at all times." Deacon Schrock stood up and moved toward the door. "Well, a good night to you, and may all of you find the Lord's blessing again—and soon."

The door slammed, and silence settled over the room.

"Aren't you going to see him off, Ben?" *Mamm* asked.

*Daett* groaned. "Like he wishes to see me right now. I have been a foolish man to allow my home to get to this state. Look what I have begotten—nothing but the whirlwind. I'm disgraced even further after my financial ruin, if such a thing is possible. And now Lydia is to be forced into a marriage she doesn't want."

"Will you be making the knee confession?" *Mamm* asked.

*Daett* groaned again, but didn't answer.

Lydia stood and headed to her room upstairs. She ran her hands along the wall in the darkness for guidance. There was nothing but confusion in the house at the moment. This was what happened when *Daett* wandered aimlessly, as he had of late. But why blame *Daett* instead of herself for this trouble? *Daett* was still hurting from the mistakes he had made. She ought to comfort him, but how? She was in a fix herself.

Deacon Schrock's threat was no idle chatter. The deacon would speak with Harvey Miller. She couldn't imagine Harvey cooperating the way Amos had with Aunt Edna, but there was an outside chance he might. If Harvey showed up at the Troyers' doorstep to see her, she'd deal with the matter then. She could at least be kind to Harvey even if she couldn't marry the man. In the meantime, Deacon Schrock wouldn't suggest any further discipline for her. Not unless she rejected Harvey outright. For that much she could give thanks.

Lydia entered her bedroom with hands outstretched. She found a match on the dresser and lit the kerosene lamp. As she watched the flicker of the flames on the bedroom walls, Lydia lowered herself onto the bed and sank into the soft quilt with a sigh. Besides Harvey and Deacon Schrock, there was still Rudy. He would be back, and he was still a temptation.

What confusion! Would anything ever be right again? Lydia slipped to the floor for a quick prayer, but no words came. She finally gave up and rose to her feet to gaze out the window at the star-swept heavens until a measure of peace filled her heart. Only then did she climb into bed and drift off to sleep.

# Chapter Twenty-Five

Early Christmas morning Sandra was sitting in the buggy with her cast propped up against the dashboard. Her hands were clasped tightly as Mark drove Dixie toward *Mamm* and Amos's place on Todd Road. Sandra's fingers dug into the palms of her hands until the pain made her cry out.

"What's wrong with you?" Mark gave Sandra a sideways glance, but he didn't wait for an answer. "It's your foot, isn't it?"

Sandra shook her head. "Just nerves, I guess."

Mark appeared skeptical. "You've been on pins and needles all morning, and we're only going to *Mamm*'s place. Are you sure that foot isn't bothering you worse than usual?"

"It's okay," Sandra said. "The truth is, what bothers me about going to *Mamm*'s is that we were only invited this past Sunday. You know *Mamm* plans her holidays much further in advance. This must be Amos's doing."

"You're still on Amos's case," Mark chided. "You need to accept the situation. Amos is our stepfather, and a decent one at that. Why can't you see that?"

Sandra gave Mark a glare. "Maybe I'll feel better once we're at *Mamm*'s for breakfast."

Mark said nothing but stared across the snowy landscape. Dixie's hooves beat a steady rhythm on the icy pavement. She had to stay calm, Sandra told herself. Even though something about the day made her nervous. Would Clyde take today's occasion to present a marriage proposal?

Finally, Mark broke into her thoughts. "You ought to stop worrying about what's happening in our family and think about Lydia and what's going on in that house. It's not *goot*."

Sandra didn't reply, but Mark was right. Though neither she nor Mark had been to the service on Sunday, they had heard the rumors. "Ben and Mary Troyer may be excommunicated along with Lydia," one of the older girls had declared. "They've all gone off with wild ideas. Ben's losing control of his family, and Lydia's seeing some *Englisha* man from her *rumspringa* days."

Chills had run all the way down Sandra's back at this public report. She didn't know about the excommunication, but there was truth to the rest of the story. Lydia had said so herself, and she had seen Lydia consorting with Rudy. On that subject she had kept silent, but word still leaked out. Such things couldn't be kept hushed in the tightly woven community. And Amos would not accept this state of affairs for long. Amos was known for his strong feelings against anyone who even threatened to jump the fence.

Sandra calmed herself as Mark began to whistle. They soon approached Amos and *Mamm*'s place. Sandra tried to listen to the tune and hoped some of Mark's cheerfulness would relax her nerves, but she was still tense when they pulled up beside Amos's barn. There were no other buggies present, but perhaps other guests would come later. She had to keep up her hope. Sandra waited until Mark came around the side of the buggy and gave her a hand to climb down.

She had her crutches out when Clyde appeared in the barn door and said, "*Goot* morning. Happy you came so early."

"*Goot* morning yourself," Mark responded.

Sandra managed to smile. Grouchiness would get her nowhere, and acting nervous around Clyde wouldn't either.

Clyde addressed Sandra directly from a few feet away. "How are you this morning?"

"I'm here." Sandra tried to answer calmly. "This foot isn't as sensitive anymore, and I expect *Mamm* will have a delicious meal prepared before long."

The diversion seemed to work, and Clyde grinned. "Well, I'm glad you're here. It gets right lonely around the house."

"Sandra's been talking about visiting you for a long time," Mark quipped.

Clyde laughed. "That's *goot* news indeed. I'm thrilled to hear it."

Sandra glared at both of them and they laughed even harder.

Clyde winked at Sandra. "I'll see you later in the house."

Still laughing, the two men headed into the barn with Dixie. Sandra gathered her courage and walked up to the front door and knocked, then poked her head in the door. "It's me!" she called. "Can I come in?"

*Mamm*'s voice called from the kitchen. "Of course you can. You know the door is always open for you."

Sandra took a deep breath and hobbled in. *Mamm* was alone in the kitchen as bacon fried on the stove. Several plates of pancakes, which were covered by cloths, were stacked on the table. Sandra pulled a chair out to support her knee and reached for the handle on the bacon pan.

*Mamm* refused to let go. "I've got things under control, Sandra. Sit down at the table and we can talk."

"Please," Sandra begged. "I want to help. You should have told me to come sooner, so I could have helped with the entire breakfast."

*Mamm* smiled. "That's some of your old spirit. But you have plenty of work at home in your condition. I'm the one who should be over at your new place on Johnson Road more often."

"We're doing fine," Sandra assured her. She settled into the kitchen chair. "Is anyone else coming?"

"No, just you and Mark." *Mamm* gave Sandra another warm smile. "It'll be so *goot* to have both of you here for Christmas breakfast."

Sandra grimaced. She didn't want to spoil their moment of togetherness with her complaints, so she said, "I'm glad you invited us. It gets a little lonely over at the house with just Mark."

*Mamm* reached over to give Sandra a quick hug. "Sorry, but with my own busy life I keep forgetting how things must be for you." Sandra didn't answer as *Mamm* chattered on. "All I can say is that Amos keeps things interesting around here. The man has more things going than you can shake a stick at. Not only does he run the farm, but also Amos and Clyde went over to help our *Englisha* neighbor with his leaky barn roof two days this week. Winter's hard enough on old Mr. Harrison without the upkeep on their place. He might sell in the spring, Mr. Harrison said, and Clyde's looking at the property. It would be an excellent start for a young couple."

Sandra kept her head down. "Did Amos put you up to this, *Mamm*?"

A hurt look crossed *Mamm*'s face. "I'm speaking from my heart, Sandra. Please don't take offense. Amos has made no secret about his opinion of Clyde and you. And Clyde would love it if you accepted his attentions. It was Amos who said we should have you and Mark over for Christmas breakfast. I was thoroughly ashamed that I hadn't thought of it myself. I'm sure I would have eventually, but things have been so confusing lately. And with the trouble Ben and Mary are in…" *Mamm* stopped to wipe her eyes. "All I can say is that I was glad Amos thought of the two of you, even before I did."

Sandra said nothing, so *Mamm* laid her hand on Sandra's arm. "Just open your heart to Amos, Sandra. The man cares about you, and Clyde loves you. I'm not Clyde's *mamm* by birth, but my affections have been touched deeply by Clyde's kindness and concern for me. They both know how difficult things have been since *Daett* passed. Listen to Amos today if he speaks to you, Sandra."

Sandra sighed and raised her cast higher on the chair for support. Oh, for the old days before *Daett* passed, when everything made sense and there was no pressure from an overbearing stepfather. And when there was no Clyde who wanted her attentions. Back then there had been only Ezra and her hopes of a married life with him. That chance was past now, of course. Ezra had taken Rosemary home from the hymn singing every Sunday night since their first date. Rosemary always seemed to be glowing with happiness, so things must be going well between them. There had been whispers this past Sunday that Rosemary had some sort of health problem, but no details had been given.

*Mamm* touched Sandra's hand again. "You've heard about Lydia and her family, haven't you?"

"*Yah*," Sandra replied.

A troubled look crossed *Mamm's* face. "I think that's one thing Amos wants to speak to us about. He takes these things quite seriously, as we all should. Being cast out of the church is a very grave matter, Sandra."

Sandra nodded. "I know."

Amos would have harsh things to say about the straying Troyer family. But *Mamm* wasn't the one to blame if Amos chose Christmas breakfast as the time to speak his words. *Daett* would never have spoiled such a precious time with the family, but *Daett* was gone now, and there was only Amos and Clyde. Maybe Mark was right. Maybe she should be more accepting of Amos…and Clyde.

*Mamm* lifted the bacon out of the pan and smiled. "Again, I'm so glad that you and Mark came over this morning."

"So am I," Sandra replied.

"Now stay seated while I call the men," *Mamm* said.

Sandra waited as *Mamm* called from the front door. She could almost imagine that this was a Christmas morning from years past, only it wasn't. She had to remind herself of that today. She had to move on, let go of the past. *Daett* was gone, and so were Ezra and his love. And before long, Lydia and the relationship they had always shared might be no more.

Sandra wiped her eyes as men's cheerful voices mingled with *Mamm*'s. She pasted on a smile as Amos appeared in the kitchen doorway.

"What a lovely maiden is sitting in my kitchen!" Amos boomed.

Sandra forced herself to laugh. That was not what *Daett* would have said, but *Daett* was gone.

"Cheerful and happy, I see," Amos continued. He beamed and pulled out his chair to sit down.

Mark grinned and sat down beside Clyde. Sandra chose to ignore them both.

"Shall we pray?" Amos said. "I can hardly wait to eat this *wunderbah* breakfast Edna has prepared for us."

"Oh, Amos," *Mamm* demurred.

Amos smiled at *Mamm*. "I'm so blessed of the Lord, I can't find words to express my feelings."

*Mamm* blushed as they bowed in prayer. Perhaps Sandra had been all wrong about Amos and Clyde, she thought with her eyes closed. Maybe this was the new life the Lord had laid out for their family. *Mamm* seemed to think so, and so did Mark. And Amos hadn't lectured her so far. At least he knew not to spoil breakfast with such things. What if this was the road that had been opened for her?

Sandra tried to grasp the idea. Could she actually become Clyde's *frau* someday? Could she ever love him? Only with the Lord's help, Sandra decided. She certainly couldn't by her own strength.

"Amen," Amos announced.

Sandra kept her head down for a few more seconds and made sure she avoided Clyde's glances as she helped pass the food around. Clyde as her husband? Who would have thought she'd even consider the idea?

# Chapter Twenty-Six

As Sandra finished the last of her pancakes, she looked across the table to see Amos's face beaming at her. "So when is this cast of yours coming off, Sandra? Here I've been doing all the talking this morning, and you haven't told us much about how things are going with you."

Sandra lowered her head. Amos sure had turned on the charm, but his interest seemed genuine enough. "I'm doing fine," she managed. "The doctor will take the cast off sometime after the first of the year."

Amos raised his eyebrows. "That's quite some time you've been in that thing. It happened at our wedding, and that's been..." Amos smiled at *Mamm*. "Not long enough."

*Mamm* turned red, and Sandra blushed as well. If Amos wanted to keep both of them off balance, he certainly knew how. *Yah*, he could be bossy, but he also had a way with words.

"The doctor wants to make sure the fracture heals," Sandra explained. "It's the part of the bone, the tibia, where only a few muscles are attached, so the blood supply is limited."

"I see." Amos smiled. "I hope all goes well. I still say that eight weeks does seem a little excessive to be in a cast. Six weeks is more normal, isn't it?"

Sandra shrugged. "I'd rather have things heal right than rush into a disaster."

Amos appeared pleased. "You are a woman of the Lord, Sandra. That is well-spoken." Amos laid down his fork, and a sober look crossed his face.

*Here comes the lecture,* Sandra thought. She stilled her mind to listen. Amos was her *daett* now, and he deserved some respect.

Amos glanced around the table before he continued. "I've been waiting to share what the Lord has laid on my heart. In fact, this is partly why I wanted only the immediate family here for Christmas breakfast." Amos paused to smile. "Although I do appreciate all of you, I don't get to see much of Mark and Sandra for reasons that I can understand. You have moved to a new place and all that. I know this is a time of adjustment for us. Part of that adjustment has to do with your Troyer relatives, Ben and Mary, and especially Lydia. I don't know how much you have heard, but let me assure you that things are not *goot* with that family. Ben has been confused ever since he became involved in that awful money scheme, and now Lydia…well, let's say the reports are troubling."

A sob escaped from *Mamm*, and Amos leaned over to slip his arm around her shoulders. "I know this is a tender subject with you, Edna, but it must be addressed."

Sandra looked away. A familiar stab of pain ran through her. Would tragedy never cease for their family?

Amos patted *Mamm* on the arm and continued. "I'm sorry for the price your *daett* had to pay for this matter, and I don't mean his passing. Edna has assured me that Emil was in ill health for some time. His death might have come sooner, triggered by the stress of the financial disaster, but what would have happened eventually, happened earlier. We can take comfort that the Lord has taken Emil into His hands, and will judge all things righteously. Emil died with repentance on his heart. Edna has assured me of this, and I believe Edna because she followed the path Emil laid out for her. Only a woman of the Lord would have turned her heart so quickly to a man like me who was hardly known to her. Not only has Edna accepted me fully, but she has loved me with her whole heart." Amos paused to wipe his eyes. "I'm moved deeply by this woman's love, and by the respect and reverence she expresses for the Lord's ways. A woman such as Edna has the power to change so much in the world for *goot*, and Edna has done so. She has not rebelled against the sorrow the Lord has allowed. Instead, she has brought healing and hope to her family by her acceptance of the Lord's will."

*Mamm* was sobbing openly now, hiding her face in her hands. "Come, dear," Amos admonished. "I did not mean to open the floodgates of grief and tears."

"I'm sorry." *Mamm* lifted her tearstained face to his. "I'll try to control myself better. But speak no more of my actions. You know I'm a sinner like all of us, and I know that Emil is safe in the hands of God. I only wish to see him again someday."

"That is well-spoken." Amos bowed his head for a moment.

Sandra stared at the two of them, unable to pull her gaze away. She had not seen *Mamm* so broken up since the funeral. Yet there was a difference this morning. The pain was less, the loss more distant. A touch of joy even rose with *Mamm*'s sobs. So this was why *Mamm* had married Amos? *Mamm* wanted to follow the road to repentance. And Sandra had argued with *Mamm*'s decision to her own shame.

Look what had happened in Sandra's life. She had lost Ezra, even with the best of her schemes, and *Mamm* had found happiness with

Amos. It was more than she could comprehend. And here was bossy Amos, in tears at the Christmas breakfast table.

Amos finally lifted his head. "I don't know how to continue, but this must be said. Your Uncle Ben and Aunt Mary are not following the path of repentance. I hear that Ben might do a church confession soon, but that is a small matter to me. What troubles my heart is what Ben has already done. Ben should have volunteered to confess even though Deacon Schrock did not demand it after Emil's passing. Not only has he failed to humble himself fully in front of the Lord and the church about the money scheme. But also, Ben has not restrained his family. A church confession won't change that. I say, the devil stands ready to take advantage of every opening we give him. Look what is happening in Ben's home. His youngest daughters are bringing their wild *Englisha* friends freely into his home, and Lydia has made contact with her former *Englisha* boyfriend. She has even gone out to see the Christmas lights with him. How could Ben not see where these things would lead? There is nothing in front of Ben except destruction—church confession or not."

Amos sounded like himself again, as he paused for breath. But his words didn't cut deeply, as Sandra had expected. *Perhaps Amos's earlier tears made the difference,* Sandra told herself.

Amos looked around at all of them before he continued. "This is what I want to request from all of you. If the Troyer family comes to the service on Sunday or any of the other gatherings of the community, then we must accept the decision of the church. Until I am satisfied that this sin is fully repented of, I want none of my family to make contact with the Troyer family other than for community-sanctioned activities. Is that understood?"

*Mamm* clung to Amos's arm and said nothing. A flash of anger rushed through Sandra, but she pushed it away. Amos had a right to his concern, and perhaps he was even correct. Look at the danger Lydia was in, flirting openly with jumping the fence.

"I can support this fully!" Mark proclaimed. His voice made Sandra jump.

"And you, Sandra?" Amos looked straight at her.

"I support your feelings," Sandra managed. "I will abide by them."

A smile spread over Amos's face. "Well, that's said now. And I'm sorry the subject had to be addressed on Christmas morning, but I did want to have all of you over for breakfast. So, shall we read the scripture now before the women clean up the kitchen?"

*Mamm* had already jumped to her feet to disappear into the living room. Moments later she came back with the huge family Bible. This was the same one *Daett* used to read. *Mamm* handed the book to Amos and sat down again.

Amos found his place and read with a strong voice the story of Christmas morning. Sandra listened to the familiar words and allowed the sound to soak all the way through her. This was what she wanted, Sandra told herself. Her rebellion and self-will were not gone completely, but she knew they would leave soon. This was the way back to what used to be. Strange as that sounded, it must be right. *Daett* would never come back, but what Amos had to offer replaced the old life with the familiar feel and sounds of home. *The Lord must be in this,* Sandra decided. Otherwise, how could what had happened between *Mamm* and Amos be explained?

After Amos finished, they knelt at the kitchen table to pray. Sandra's chair squeaked as she pushed it far enough away from the table to lower her cast to the floor. She listened as Amos's voice led out in the German prayer, and soon ended with a hearty "Amen."

Before Sandra could raise herself from her knees Clyde's hand reached over to hold the chair. Sandra balanced herself with both hands and smiled her thanks. Clyde nodded and left the kitchen with Mark. *Mamm* pulled one of the chairs up to the counter and motioned for Sandra to seat herself. "You can sit and wash dishes if you want to help, because you're not hobbling all around my kitchen this morning."

A big grin spread across Amos's face. "I see everything is taken care of here. So I'll see you later, Sandra."

She wanted to say something, but the words stuck in Sandra's throat. Amos had been quite decent this morning, and she should thank him, but he had already gone.

"Sit," *Mamm* said, as if she expected rebellion.

Tears stung Sandra's eyes. "I appreciate what Amos had to say this morning."

*Mamm* appeared a little surprised. "Really? Well, I'm happy to hear that."

"Do you think we can ever go back to what we used to have?" Sandra whispered.

*Mamm*'s disapproval showed. "You know that's not possible, Sandra. The past is past, and we must move on. And the future will come whether we choose the Lord's ways or not."

"I'm not trying to argue with you," Sandra objected. "I guess I didn't say it right. It seems to me that Amos is restoring what was lost, in a different way—but somehow, it feels the same. I'm sure that makes no sense to you, but that's how it feels to me."

"Oh, Sandra." *Mamm* gave her a hug. "I didn't dream I'd hear those words out of your mouth. And on Christmas morning. Has the Lord given us another touch of His hand?"

"I don't know." Sandra kept her head down. "I'm sure nothing changes too quickly."

*Mamm*'s touch on Sandra's shoulder was light. "Can I ask you this without you getting angry?"

"Please, *Mamm*, I'll not get angry."

*Mamm* appeared to proceed with caution. "Would you...? Could you...? How do I say this? Clyde loves you, Sandra. Why don't you open your heart to him? Just a little crack of the door is all that's needed. The Lord will do the rest, because He is in this thing— Amos and Clyde. This could happen to you, the way it did with me. We could be a whole family again."

Sandra's hand trembled. "But I've never loved the man, *Mamm*. How do you wed someone you haven't loved? Ezra had my affections, but he doesn't want them. I can't just change like that."

*Mamm* reached for Sandra's hand. "The heart is the Lord's doing. He alone knows how to turn it to the left or the right. Trust Him, Sandra. Or trust me. I didn't love Amos either. I didn't love him on our wedding day. There was still much of your *daett* in my heart, but you see what has happened. I don't know how to explain it otherwise."

"I understand." Sandra squeezed *Mamm*'s hand and took a deep breath. "Okay, I will open my heart to Clyde. I'll at least *try*." After a moment's pause, Sandra said, "You can tell Clyde if you wish."

"You should tell him yourself," *Mamm* said.

Sandra reached up to turn on the hot water in the sink. "I'm not going that far today, *Mamm*."

A smile played on *Mamm*'s face. "We should leave this in the Lord's hands, then. Perhaps that would be for the best."

"*Yah*, it would be," Sandra agreed.

Clyde would see soon enough that her attitude had changed toward him. The road still appeared rough, but she was ready to begin the journey. In the meantime she had to adjust her attitude and become used to the idea of Clyde as the man who might win her heart. That would take a long time—if indeed it could happen.

Clyde's voice interrupted Sandra's thoughts from the kitchen doorway. "Sandra, can I have a moment with you?"

"Of course," *Mamm* said at once. "I'll be right back." She hurried down the basement steps with a smile on her face.

"Was that necessary?" Sandra asked. "Chasing *Mamm* off?" She did not like Clyde's confidence.

Clyde ignored her comment. "Sandra, don't you think we could get to know each better? I don't think you know me very well."

Sandra found herself answering, "*Yah,* perhaps I don't. I'm willing."

Clyde looked surprised. "There is hope rising in my heart. Tell me I'm not mistaken, Sandra."

"You're not mistaken."

Clyde's face lightened. "Would you even allow me to take you home from the hymn singing sometime?"

"I didn't say that," Sandra teased, her face turned away from him.

There was silence for a moment before Clyde chuckled. "But you will? Am I not correct?"

Sandra peeked over her shoulder at him. His face was filled with happiness. She didn't feel any love in her heart yet, but she had the hope of it. And so she nodded to Clyde.

"See you in two Sunday evenings, then," he said, then she listened to his footsteps fading away. Sandra, despite her hesitancy, felt no remorse for her words. She was relieved in a way. *Yah,* she could wait on love. *If* it came.

# Chapter Twenty-Seven

Rosemary kept her face expressionless as the nurse escorted her and *Mamm* into Dr. Katz's office. She should never have submitted herself to this long series of tests, Rosemary told herself. The expense was reason enough to have refused. There was nothing wrong with her that a few days' rest wouldn't cure. But Ezra had insisted she see a doctor when she had hurried from the table at his parents' place on Christmas Day to throw up in the bathroom.

"I'm so sorry," Rosemary had told Ezra's *Mamm*, Rachel, who had followed her. "I'm nervous, I guess."

"It's okay," Rachel had assured her. "Don't feel bad about this."

She hadn't wanted to worry Ezra or his family, but these episodes also occurred when she wasn't around Ezra. Still, there was nothing wrong with her. There couldn't be.

"You're going to see a doctor," Ezra had ordered on the drive home. "I'll take no argument from you."

Now a week later, the tests were taken and the money was spent.

"Please have a seat, and Dr. Katz will be with you soon," the nurse said, before she left them.

*Mamm* sat on the chair closest to the big desk and motioned for Rosemary to take the other one. *Mamm*'s face was grim, which was understandable considering the huge medical bill that *Daett* would have to pay. She was now a burden to her parents instead of a blessing. And what if Deacon Schrock had to come over some Saturday and offer the community's help with the expenses? She would shrivel up from shame and be sick for sure.

The office door opened, and *Mamm* stood to her feet as Dr. Katz entered with a folder in his hand. He glanced at Rosemary and then at *Mamm*. "Please be seated, ma'am."

*Mamm* obeyed but her expression didn't change.

Dr. Katz paged through the folder before he met Rosemary's gaze. "I see you've taken the tests I requested, Ms. Beiler. I know you thought they were unnecessary, and I would have loved it if I'd been proven wrong. But my concerns were legitimate. I'm sorry to have to tell you that."

"Please, dear Lord, help us," *Mamm* prayed out loud.

"What's wrong with me?" Rosemary felt the first stabs of fear reach deep inside her. This couldn't be serious. How could it? She had Ezra in her life now. His love! The Lord had given her Ezra!

"It's pancreatic cancer," Dr. Katz said without mincing words. "This is rare for someone as young as you. And apparently the cancer has spread to the liver as well as to several other locations in your body. I wish we could have caught this sooner, but pancreatic cancer is one of the most undetectable cancers we deal with. I'm sorry again. I had hoped for better news."

"What does this mean?" *Mamm* had risen to her feet again. "Surely there is something we can do."

Dr. Katz cleared his throat. "I don't want to give false hope. We can do aggressive chemo. There are also some experimental treatments. But in either case, there are no guarantees."

*Mamm*'s voice was a whisper. "But Rosemary is so young, and she has only begun…" She clasped and unclasped her hands. "I don't understand how this can be. Why would the Lord allow such a thing?"

Dr. Katz's gaze was full of compassion. "I'm a medical doctor, Mrs. Beiler. But I'm sure there are answers, if not on this side then on the other side. And you are a people of great faith. Faith is a great asset with cancer patients."

*Mamm* appeared dazed. "Then there is nothing we can do? Nothing! And so suddenly? Why was there not more warning?"

"Please sit down," Dr. Katz told *Mamm* again. "The problem is that many of the symptoms—abdominal pain, weight loss, and digestive problems—are easily explained or ignored. And the weight loss is often welcomed in young patients. This cancer hides well, Mrs. Beiler. I'm sorry."

Rosemary focused on the wall above Dr. Katz's head. She had thought her symptoms had been caused by Ezra's affections. And *yah*, she had foolishly rejoiced over the pounds she'd shed these past few months. She was sure it had added to her attractiveness.

"How much will these experimental treatments cost?" *Mamm* asked.

Rosemary forced herself to speak. "There will be no treatments. We will trust in the Lord."

*Mamm* brushed her words aside. "I will not hear of that, Rosemary. We will speak with *Daett* and do what is possible."

Dr. Katz nodded. "They are expensive, I understand. I don't get involved on that end, but I do understand that you have no insurance."

Rosemary faced Dr. Katz. "How long do I have?"

"Without the treatments?" His face was sober. "Not long, I'm afraid."

"And with the treatments?" Rosemary kept her voice steady.

Dr. Katz waited a second. "Not much longer, unless one of them works."

Silence gripped the room. Rosemary stood to go, and pulled on *Mamm*'s arm. "Come. We're taking up his time."

"You don't have to hurry," Dr. Katz assured her.

Rosemary repeated, "Come, *Mamm*." Only then did she address Dr. Katz. "Thank you for everything you've done. You've been more than kind."

"I'm here to help." Dr. Katz was on his feet. "Let me know what you decide, and we will go from there."

*Mamm* trembled once she was on her feet. Rosemary held *Mamm*'s arm on the long walk back to the waiting room and out to the buggy. Rosemary helped *Mamm* inside before she untied Buster and gave *Mamm* the reins. Only then did she climb up herself and settle into the seat. She felt just fine, except for this bone-deep weariness. How could what the doctor had said be true? That she had cancer. That there was no cure. That she would die.

Rosemary gazed into the clear winter sky where a few wisps of clouds were hanging on the horizon. Soon the sun would set and they would be home. And soon, the sun of life would set on Rosemary's time on earth. She bit back the tears. This wasn't possible. There must be some mistake. She was terribly in love with Ezra, and she had accomplished the impossible when she gained his attentions. This was not the Lord's will. How could it be?

*Mamm* said nothing as she drove Buster out of the Canton Hospital parking lot and turned toward home.

"I'm so sorry about this, Rosemary," *Mamm* finally said, somewhere near the outskirts of town.

"It's not your fault," Rosemary said. "I'm the one who got cancer."

"And how are you to blame for this?" *Mamm* sat up straight. "Let's not go down the blame road. This is in the Lord's hands whether the treatment works or not."

"There will be no treatment," Rosemary repeated.

*Mamm* didn't argue, but this would not be the end of the matter. Rosemary was sure of that. Once they told *Daett*, he would have an opinion. *Daett* always did, and what *Daett* decided carried the day. She would have to submit, but she would still insist. She didn't want to leave this world with the knowledge that a huge debt was left behind that others would have to pay.

The miles on Route 68 rolled by in silence before they turned south on Old State Road, other than for an occasional sob from *Mamm. Why am I not crying?* Rosemary wondered. Perhaps because the reality of the verdict had not set in, or because hope died slowly. How could she give up Ezra and their future together? She couldn't. Dying was not an option, regardless of what Dr. Katz claimed was wrong with her.

Rosemary stilled her thoughts as *Mamm* turned into their home's driveway. *Daett* came out of the barn to wait. His lengthy beard flowed down over the front of his shirt, and for the first time the tears came. Rosemary pressed them back, but a sob still caught in her throat as *Mamm* brought the buggy to a stop.

*Daett* came up to hold Buster's bridle while they climbed down. "What did the doctor say?" he asked.

*Mamm* wailed and rushed over to throw herself in his arms. "Oh, *Daett*, pray for us. The storm has come into our home. Our eldest is at death's door."

*Daett* appeared puzzled. "How can this be? You look well, Rosemary."

Rosemary didn't answer. That was her feeling exactly. But if she was honest, her body spoke of other things. Only Ezra had made her pay attention. That was the cruel twist in all this. Ezra! The man she loved with all her heart.

"The doctor claims it's highly advanced," *Mamm* continued. "Pancreatic cancer is among the slyest ones, he says. And it crept up while we were busy with other things. Only chemo and experimental treatments are available, and they are very expensive. Oh *Daett*, this cannot be."

"Incurable," *Daett* muttered. He unhitched Buster and led the horse toward the barn without a backward glance.

"Come." *Mamm* took Rosemary's arm. "You come inside and rest."

Rosemary resisted. "I must tell Ezra."

*Mamm* shook her head. "Ezra will be here. He knows about your tests today, and in times like this...well, Ezra will know he's needed."

Rosemary gave in and allowed *Mamm* to lead her inside. But she refused to sit down, even though a great weakness flooded through her. This was only a case of nerves, Rosemary assured herself, but she had said that often enough in the past. Perhaps she had best admit that she had been wrong before and was wrong now. With a sigh, Rosemary settled on the couch.

Ann appeared in the kitchen doorway, and Rosemary tuned out the conversation between Ann and *Mamm*. She didn't want to hear the words again. Words that spelled such awful things. Words that said the world would soon not be her home. Only when Ann came to her with a tearstained face did Rosemary try to stand. Ann pushed her down and sat on the couch to embrace Rosemary with both arms. Great sobs racked Ann's body. *Why am I not the one in tears?* Rosemary wondered again. But already she was weary of questions that had no answers. If this was the way of the Lord, then she would rather travel the road quickly.

Now if only Ezra would come. But how could he? Ezra didn't
know. No one expected this would be the news. At the worst, Ezra
probably figured she had a mild flu or something equally benign.
Perhaps *Mamm* was right. Ezra would come tonight. She had only
to wait for him. Ezra had never held her in his arms before, but that
was what she wanted. The feel of his strength around her shoulders,
to hear the pounding of his heart against her ear. Ezra's health would
become hers. She would draw strength from him, as she had these
last weeks. Wasn't that what had kept her going this long? If Ezra
hadn't been in her life, she would have been to the doctor long ago.
*But even that would have been too late,* Rosemary told herself.

"You had best come up to your room." *Mamm's* concerned face
floated in front of Rosemary. "Come, we will help."

Ann appeared on the other side of Rosemary, and together they
walked her to the stair door. But only *Mamm* stayed with her on
the climb up.

"Now, lie down for a while, and we'll call you for supper," *Mamm*
said. She smoothed out the quilt and helped Rosemary onto the bed.

The room spun slowly even before *Mamm* left, and the soft click
on the bedroom door was a welcome sound. She wanted to drift off,
but she wanted Ezra worse. The desire to see him rose like a deep
thirst inside of her. Rosemary staggered to her feet and made it over
to the window before she slid to the floor.

Dreams of starry nights and dark clouds floated in front of her
mind, and when Rosemary woke, Ezra's face was just above hers.
*Mamm* was right beside Ezra.

"She must have fallen," *Mamm* said.

Rosemary felt a smile fill her face. "You have come," she whispered. "Hold me, Ezra. Hold me tight."

*Mamm* appeared more frightened than horrified at such plain
talk. *Mamm* stepped back, and Ezra lifted Rosemary in his strong

arms. Rosemary clung to his neck and pushed her face close to his chest. The steady beat of Ezra's heart pounded in her ears. *This is heaven,* Rosemary decided, *or the first taste of it.* These were the arms that would carry her through the rough waters ahead. She had been given Ezra for a reason, and now she knew why. Rosemary took a long breath as Ezra lowered her effortlessly onto the quilt-covered bed.

"Never let me go," she whispered in his ear.

But Ezra detached himself from her arms with a great gentleness.

"She's in shock," *Mamm* said.

Rosemary smiled and let herself drift off again. Ezra had held her, and that was enough for now. She would sleep until this dream came to an end.

# Chapter Twenty-Eight

Lydia sat unmoving on the long unmarried women's bench. The Sunday morning church service had begun over two hours ago. She had dreaded this time all week and for most of the week before. Ever since Deacon Schrock had paid his visit and *Daett* had been ordered to make a church confession. The shame the family was facing was an awful thing. *Daett* should never have allowed himself to get into this situation. If only he had dealt with Emma and Rhoda earlier or stayed out of that horrible money scheme. Now Emma and Rhoda were more committed than ever to never coming back from their *rumspringa* time. Both of her sisters had refused to attend the Sunday service this morning. They would jump the fence for sure. Lydia hadn't wanted to come herself, but that would only make matters worse. Thankfully Harvey Miller hadn't been by with a marriage proposal yet, but she was sure Deacon Schrock had spoken to him. Unless she planned to jump the fence along with her sisters, she had some tough decisions ahead of her.

Was she ready to leave for the love of Rudy? She had chosen the community's life, but that choice seemed distant and unreal right now. Her decision had been made in a time of dreamy happiness, when she had set out with Sandra to pursue Ezra. How silly they had both been, and how childish their actions. Yet those had been the times when she had felt the most loved by everyone. Now Ezra was dating Rosemary, and to make matters worse, Rosemary had taken ill. The news of Rosemary's diagnosis of pancreatic cancer had been on every woman's lips this morning.

"Poor girl, she was trying so hard."

"*Yah*, for Ezra's sake," they said.

"Love does strange things to people, that's all I know."

"Even keeps cancer at bay for a time."

"But all things are in the hands of the Lord."

Most of them had gathered around Rosemary's *Mamm* to comfort her and whisper short prayers with their heads bowed. The service had been delayed a few minutes until all the woman could come in from the kitchen where they had gathered to pray for Rosemary. The full compassion of the community was on display for the Beiler family—and on the very morning *Daett* must experience his humiliation. Rosemary might find healing for her sickness, but for years to come *Daett* would bear the shame for what he had allowed to happen in his house. Families from the community would point to the Troyers as an example of how their young people's *rumspringa* time should not be conducted.

Yet *Daett* had known the consequences, and had refused to stand up to his daughters. Now there would be no men gathered to comfort *Daett* after his confession. Not like the women who had supported Rosemary's *Mamm*. The community didn't show its sympathy for those who transgressed the *ordnung*. How could discipline be maintained if those who willfully transgressed were given support in any way?

Lydia shifted on the bench as Bishop Henry asked for testimonies and sat down. When those were finished, the bishop rose again and with slumped shoulders said, "Will all those who are members please remain seated? There is work that must be done in the Lord's vineyard today."

The soft rustle of small feet as they scurried off filled the house. Several girls were needed in the kitchen to begin lunch preparations for the smaller children, but Lydia had best not volunteer. The evasion would be obvious. And Sandra had already left the room along with several of the others. So Lydia settled down on the bench and pressed back the tears.

Sandra's words to her this morning in the washroom still stung. Sandra had whispered, "I won't be able to come over any longer, not until this whole thing blows over. And Clyde's taking me home next Sunday night from the hymn singing."

The sad meaning was plain enough. Lydia would be toxic until *Daett* proved himself worthy again of the community's confidence. Even Lydia herself was on trial. Sandra hadn't mentioned that, but they understood each other well enough to communicate without plain words.

What hurt most was the cut of the cords that had once bound Sandra to her. They were still cousins, but they would never again be lighthearted girls held together by their love and enjoyment of life. Now that Sandra had accepted a date from Clyde, it was clear that she would stay with the community's tradition, while she, Lydia, was still tempted to stray. She'd have to find her way now without Sandra's help.

Bishop Henry stood to his feet again, his voice trembling. "It is always a heavy thing when discipline in the Lord's vineyard must be exercised. Such is the case this morning with our brother Ben Troyer. He has been found lax in the management not only of his financial affairs but also more seriously of his family. Only after great failure and a sharp rebuke from brothers who care for his soul, has Ben repented. For this we are thankful. But since these two things followed each other so closely and are related, we believe measures must be taken to assure that full repentance is found. With that in mind, Ben has agreed to a church confession, and has also voluntarily offered six months' time of proving himself, during which he will attempt to restore our confidence in him. We rejoice and gladly accept this further sign of repentance. It will be *goot* for all of the church to see Ben humble himself before the Lord and before his brothers and sisters. So Ben, will you please leave us now? We will take the counsel of the church on this matter."

Lydia looked away as *Daett* rose to his feet. The front door opened and closed while Lydia kept her gaze on the floor. Long moments later, she saw Deacon Schrock move down the line of unmarried women to ask for their vote. The other two ministers were scattered throughout the rooms where the other members sat. When one finished his section, he took his seat again beside Bishop Henry. From the looks of things Deacon Schrock would be the last to finish.

Lydia whispered into Deacon Schrock's ear when he arrived, "I have no objection."

Deacon Schrock said nothing, but moved on to finish his section. When he was done, the deacon sat down again with his head bowed.

Bishop Henry addressed Deacon Schrock first. "So what did you find?"

"There were no objections among the women," Deacon Schrock told him.

The other two ministers reported similar results.

"You may call Ben in," Bishop Henry ordered.

Deacon Schrock slipped outside and returned moments later with *Daett* in tow. *Daett* took a seat across from Bishop Henry.

"The vote has passed to accept your confession," Bishop Henry told *Daett*. "You may kneel now before the Lord and the church and confess your sin."

Lydia slipped to her knees herself as *Daett* did likewise. She couldn't bear the sight. A quiet sob came from the married women's section. That would be *Mamm*. Lydia wasn't about to cry out, but perhaps a quiet time spent in prayer while *Daett* was humiliated would steady her spirit.

Lydia heard *Daett*'s voice rise and fall as he mumbled the prescribed words. "I confess my faults and sins before the Lord and before the church. I beg your forgiveness for my great weakness and ask for restoration in the name of the Lord."

"Your confession is accepted," Bishop Henry spoke clearly. "Please stand, Ben, and go forth into a better life than you have lived the past few months. And the service is now dismissed."

There was a shuffle of feet, and Lydia eased herself back onto the bench. No one looked her way. They likely took her kneeling as a sign of her repentant spirit. *If only I had one,* Lydia thought. The battle with her heart was far from over. Rudy hadn't made contact with her after that embarrassing episode when they toured the Christmas lights in Ogdensburg, but he would. Even if *Daett* no longer allowed Emma and Rhoda's *Englisha* friends on the farm, *Daett* had waited too long to prevent this temptation from taking root.

Lydia stood with the line of girls as they moved toward the kitchen. She didn't stop to help, but continued on to the washroom. She had insisted this morning before they left home that she would not stay for lunch. But to leave early she needed her own buggy. *Mamm* had objected at first, but Lydia had calmly harnessed Timber in the barn by herself. *Daett* had stayed out of sight, while Emma and Rhoda giggled behind their hands at the fuss. *Mamm* had said nothing more about the matter.

Lydia paused as a step came up behind her in the washroom.

She turned around when Sandra whispered, "Lydia, please stay for lunch. We have to talk, and I can't come over to your place."

Lydia shook her head. "We had best just leave things alone. My heart is much troubled. But you can help me hitch Timber to the buggy."

Sandra's face fell. "I can't do that. Amos had a very strong warning for us all, and I want to take his words to heart. And you would benefit yourself from what Amos has to say."

"Maybe." Lydia reached for her shawl and pulled it tight around her shoulders. "You can pray for me, Sandra. That's about all that can help right now."

"Oh, Lydia," Sandra sighed. "I wish we could get together again like we used to."

Lydia hesitated. "Sandra, we can never be what we were before. I'm not competing anymore, with you or anyone. My heart has been too torn. I don't know what will happen to me."

Sandra's smile faded. "Just don't do something foolish, Lydia. Don't jump the fence. We've already been through too much. You and I were baptized together. We have to make this together."

"I want nothing more," Lydia said. "And I won't do anything crazy."

"Like go out with Rudy? Please tell me you won't," Sandra begged as Lydia slipped out of the washroom door.

"I'll see you later," Lydia called over her shoulder. She hurried across the yard and entered the open barn door. Several younger boys were standing nearby, and one of them asked, "Do you need help with your horse?"

"No, but thanks," Lydia said, attempting to smile.

The boy nodded and returned her smile. She found Timber in his stall and slipped on the horse's bridle. A soft man's voice stopped Lydia cold. "I thought perhaps I could help."

Lydia spun around. It was Harvey Miller.

"I couldn't help but notice you leaving early." Harvey's words were gentle. "I...ah...I'm sorry about your *daett*. Can I take Timber for you?"

Lydia let go of the bridle as Harvey reached out. He hadn't waited for an answer, but simply stepped in to do what needed doing. Lydia's gaze lingered on Harvey as she followed him outside. He was thin. His pants hung heavy on him, and his beard blew over his shoulder when a gust of wind rushed through the barn door.

Harvey didn't look back as he led Timber to Lydia's buggy. He seemed to know where she had parked, and he had known her horse's name. Lydia hurried ahead and held the shafts up for him. Harvey didn't look at her as she helped him hitch Timber to the buggy. But Harvey had a ghost of a smile on his face when he handed Lydia the lines. "I hope you can stay next Sunday for the meal," he said, then stepped back from the buggy.

Lydia hesitated. Was that all the man wished to say? Surely he had more, but Harvey just stood there with a hint of a smile on his face.

"Thank you," she said with a nod, then called to Timber to "Get up."

Harvey was either a strange man or still quite grief-stricken, Lydia decided. And what would she have said if Harvey had asked for a date? She had no idea. And that troubled her. What had happened to her in these past few months? Had the loss of Ezra cut so deeply that she no longer cared about anything or anyone? If that was true, this was an awful state to be in.

Lydia shivered and hung on tightly to Timber's reins as he plodded along in his usual fashion. Lydia jiggled the reins, but Timber paid her no mind at all. She settled back into the buggy seat and let the tears flow freely.

# Chapter Twenty-Nine

Timber shook his head in objection as Lydia turned to the west at Rensselaer Falls instead of north toward the Troyer home on Madrid Road. The house would be empty and she wasn't ready to go home. The solution was a visit to see Rosemary. Why shouldn't it be? Rosemary was ill and a good friend.

Lydia jiggled the reins, and Timber soon settled back into his steady pace.

Rosemary's younger sister Ann also hadn't been at the service today. Ann must have stayed home with Rosemary. Hopefully that didn't mean Rosemary was too ill to have visitors. If so, she would leave at once. The last thing Lydia wanted was to cast a greater burden on Rosemary's shoulders. The load of sickness was already too much to carry. It didn't seem possible that Rosemary had fallen so seriously ill, but if Lydia had learned anything of late, it was to expect the unexpected.

Certainly Rosemary was learning that too. How could the joy Rosemary had found with Ezra be so cruelly ripped from her grasp? It seemed harsh of the Lord to allow such a thing. But if that did happen, *Daett's* humiliation today was a small matter compared to the pain Rosemary was facing. Perhaps that's why Lydia wanted to visit this afternoon. She might not be much comfort to Rosemary, but she could try. She held no grudge against Rosemary for having won where she and Sandra had lost. Rosemary deserved Ezra if she could win his affections.

A mile later Lydia pulled on the reins and turned into the Beilers' driveway. She parked the buggy by the barn and climbed down to tie Timber to the hitching post, then she made her way up the sidewalk.

"Is Rosemary up for a visit?" Lydia asked when Ann opened the door at her knock.

"Oh, *yah*." Ann smiled and stepped back. "Rosemary is up in her room. *Mamm* wanted to fix a bed down here where Rosemary could be around the family, but she'd have no peace and quiet."

"How is Rosemary doing?"

Ann shrugged and led the way toward the stairs. "They don't tell me much, and I suppose no one really knows, but I've never seen Rosemary down like this. She hasn't worked around the house since they came home from the doctor's office last week."

"Then it must be bad," Lydia agreed. She followed Ann as they tiptoed up the stairs.

Ann knocked on the bedroom door and waited until Rosemary called out, "Come in."

Ann opened the door. Rosemary was propped up on the bed with pillows and held a book in her hand. She looked up and exclaimed, "Lydia! You came up the stairs so quietly I didn't know anyone was around but Ann." Rosemary struggled to swing her legs over the edge of the bed.

"No, please," Lydia protested. "Don't make yourself uncomfortable."

Rosemary tried to laugh. "I'm not this helpless. It just looks so. I can't work—that's the worst of it. Every time I've tried I get tired in a few minutes, and now *Mamm* won't hear of me trying."

"I'm going back downstairs," Ann interrupted. "Call me if you need anything."

"Thank you for staying home today," Rosemary called after Ann. "I'm so unworthy of all this kindness."

"You just get better and I'll be happy." Ann lingered by the bedroom door for a moment before she retreated down the stairs.

"Sit," Rosemary ordered, and motioned toward the only chair in the room.

Lydia sat down and clasped her hands in front of her. Rosemary was a little thinner than the last time she had seen her, but otherwise she seemed as normal as ever. Lydia cleared her throat and said, "I'm so very sorry to hear about all this. Everyone is. We're all praying for you."

"Thanks," Rosemary said with a solemn face. "It's the Lord's will, and who are we to argue with Him?"

Lydia unclasped her hands. "Surely there must be treatments for you. The *Englisha* doctors always have them."

Rosemary looked away. "None that I want to take a chance on. They would leave the family in terrible debt."

"But the community…" Lydia protested.

Rosemary shrugged. "The treatments will do no *goot*. I can feel it in my bones for sure."

"But you don't know before you try," Lydia pressed on. "Do your *mamm* and *daett* agree with this plan of taking no treatment?"

"*Mamm* will be back to see Dr. Katz this week, but I'm sure there won't be much that can be done. But I do have Ezra." A thin smile spread over Rosemary's face. "He comes over every other evening or so. I think the Lord gave him to me for this time of trouble. Nothing else makes any sense. Why else would Ezra ever have paid me any attention?"

Lydia leaned forward to take Rosemary's hand. "Ezra loves you. That's why. You must not say these things in your dark hour. And I rejoice that you have Ezra's love." Lydia forced a smile. "Clyde is taking Sandra home next Sunday evening. And you're going to get better, and live to have many *kinner* with Ezra. You must not give up, even when the road is hard."

The faint smile flitted on Rosemary's face again. "Thank you for your kind words, Lydia. But life feels pretty dim to me right now. Never have I been this weak for this long and not been able to work. It feels as if the lights are going out in my life. Only Ezra's love comforts me. I get on my knees every night and thank the Lord for Ezra, but before long I won't even be able to get out of bed for my prayers. I guess I'll whisper them to the ceiling, which I suppose the Lord understands."

"I'm sure He does."

"How are *you* doing?" Rosemary asked.

Lydia gave a little sigh. "Troubles and trials, but I won't weary you with them."

"They're not a weariness to me," Rosemary said. "You've always been my friend, you and Sandra. Even when I stole Ezra from the two of you."

"We were too astonished to complain," Lydia joked.

Rosemary laughed, then sobered. "When I came home from Dr. Katz's office and passed out up here, I awoke up to see Ezra leaning over me. He lifted me in his arms, Lydia. I floated almost up to the heavens, or so it seemed. He was so strong and handsome, and I thought the Lord had taken me up Himself. How I love the man, as I have never loved anyone. Do you think that was my sin, Lydia? Did I love Ezra more than the Lord?"

"You have not sinned," Lydia said softly. "You must not say so, Rosemary. We were made as women to lose ourselves in the love of a man. There's no sin in that. Your love for Ezra may well be what carries you through this dark time to a healing. Do not doubt what the Lord has given."

Rosemary smiled again. "Your words are too kind, Lydia, and I'm thankful for what the Lord has given. I believe He wanted me to know what His own arms would feel like when He carries me over the river. Why else would I get to lie in Ezra's arms when I haven't said the wedding vows with him?" A shadow crossed Rosemary's face. "But I'll never get to see him with his beard once he's wed. He'll be so handsome, Lydia." Rosemary wiped away the tears. "But I must be happy with what I have been given. It's already more than I'm worthy of."

Lydia squeezed Rosemary's hand and waited for a moment before she could speak. "I don't know what to say, Rosemary. You are a saint, but you must not give up. We need you in the community. We really do. I don't want to lose you."

"That's what Ezra says." Rosemary brightened again. "You speak the things I need to hear, but we must leave it all in the Lord's hands." Rosemary laid her head back on the pillow, her face pale.

"I'm going to leave now." Lydia got to her feet. "I don't want to weary you."

"Thanks for coming. You're such a joy," Rosemary said. "You've always been—you and Sandra. But I do think I must sleep."

Lydia nodded and retreated out of the bedroom, closing the door softly behind her to tiptoe down the stairs.

Ann met Lydia at the kitchen doorway with a sandwich in her hand. "I've made you something to eat."

"You didn't have to do that," Lydia said, taking the sandwich. "But thank you."

"Rosemary treasures your friendship," Ann said. "Thank you for being here for her."

Ann held open the front door and was still standing there when Lydia had Timber untied and turned around in the driveway.

A great sorrow swept over Lydia on the drive home. In spite of Rosemary's brave words, the woman was very ill. Lydia wasn't a doctor, but the matter was plain enough to see. If something wasn't done, Rosemary wouldn't last long—unless Ezra's love could pull Rosemary through. Lydia hoped with all her heart that Ezra would accomplish the task. Rosemary would make an outstanding *frau* for Ezra. He deserved all the love and adoration Rosemary could give him.

Lydia pulled the reins to the right and turned Timber into their driveway. *Mamm* and *Daett*'s buggy wasn't in the barnyard, so they were still at church. Maybe *Daett* had received more comfort from the other men than she expected he would. Why else would *Daett* have stayed? Lydia's breath came sharply when she caught sight of an *Englisha* automobile behind the barn. Rudy's car. She would have recognized it anywhere. She had feared this moment, and now it had arrived.

Lydia parked beside the barn and unhitched Timber. As she led Timber to the barn, the car door opened and Rudy climbed out. Lydia waved to him but didn't stop walking. She would rather speak with Rudy inside the barn than outside, where anyone who passed by on the road could see them. And Rudy would have to leave before *Daett* came home, that was for sure.

Lydia had the stall door closed when Rudy's light step came up behind her. He greeted her with, "Lydia, I've been waiting for you."

"You can't stay long," Lydia said. "*Daett* can no longer have any of Emma and Rhoda's friends here."

"But I'm *your* friend." Rudy reached out to touch her arm. "Am I not?"

Lydia dropped her gaze. "All the more reason to leave quickly."

"What's wrong?" Rudy asked. "You seem troubled."

Lydia looked up at him. "I just came from visiting a friend who's quite ill. Now isn't a good time for you and me to speak."

Rudy sobered. "I'm sorry to hear that. Will she be well soon?"

"It's in the Lord's hands," Lydia said. "It doesn't look good."

Rudy persisted. "We need to talk. About you and me."

"Rudy, you know I have feelings for you. You are a temptation to me…but that's all you can ever be. Can't you see that? What we had was in the past."

Rudy's gaze bore into her. His hands reached for hers and he pulled her close. "Is this in the past?" He gave her a gentle kiss and whispered in her ear, "Have you forgotten how good we were together? I was young and foolish back then, and I thought the world was full of girls like you. But I was very wrong, Lydia. There's only you."

Lydia pulled away. "No, Rudy. We can't." Her head was swimming from the kiss.

"But Lydia," he insisted, "nothing has changed. That's what I'm trying to show you."

Lydia took a breath. "Rudy, please. You have to go. Everything has changed. Everything!"

"Lydia, I said I'd wait, and I still will." Rudy touched her face with his hand. "I'll go, but I'll be back. I'm not giving up on us."

With that, Rudy turned and disappeared. Lydia waited until his car had left the driveway before she splashed her flaming cheeks with cold water from the horse's trough.

Before she could reach the house, *Mamm* and *Daett's* buggy came down the lane. Lydia hurried on. *Daett* could unhitch the horse by himself. She wanted to wash her face once more before anyone saw her. Now that *Daett* had repented, she couldn't let him know Rudy had been anywhere near the farm. And if Deacon Schrock found out she had seen Rudy again, even involuntarily, his prescribed grace period for her would end at once. Of that she was certain.

# Chapter Thirty

The following Sunday Clyde pulled his horse to a stop beside the barn on Johnson Road, where Sandra and Mark now lived. Sandra pushed open the buggy door and gingerly lowered herself to the ground. The cast had come off over two weeks ago, but she still had to take precautions and not overdo herself.

Tonight had been her first date with Clyde—a drive home from the hymn singing. And so far, to Sandra's amazement, it had gone well—with no uncomfortable moments or awkward silences between them.

Clyde tied his horse to the ring on the barn and teased, "I see you still know how to get down from a buggy unassisted."

Sandra gave him a glare. "I didn't forget everything while I was stuck in my cast."

Clyde came around the buggy to take Sandra's arm. "Still, I'm sure this isn't easy. Now come. Shall I walk you to the house?"

"In case I stumble and fall?" Sandra looked up at him.

Clyde didn't answer, but he grinned. She actually enjoyed his light banter, Sandra thought to herself as they walked toward the house. Was this the charm Amos had used to capture *Mamm*'s heart? If so, she could see why *Mamm* had fallen for the man.

Sandra opened the front door, and Clyde waited while she lit the gas lantern. "Still looks the same," Clyde quipped, once light flooded the living room.

"What did you expect?" she teased back. "That I would remodel the house to entertain you?"

They laughed together, until Clyde took Sandra's hand. "Sandra, I want to say I'm honored to be here, I really am. At times, I thought this day would never come."

Sandra lowered her head. "Now you're making me nervous. Sit on the couch while I get some donuts and milk from the kitchen. You must be hungry."

"My hunger flees far away when I'm with you," Clyde said.

Sandra ignored Clyde and hurried into the kitchen, where she lit the kerosene lamp. She took the donuts from the cupboard and put several on a plate. Sandra balanced the plate and two glasses of milk on a tray and returned to the living room.

Clyde looked up with a gleam in his eyes. "What a treat! Now I do think I'm hungry."

"Men are *always* hungry," Sandra reminded him.

Clyde still had a smile on his face when the front door opened and Mark came in with his girlfriend Marie. Sandra jumped to her feet. "Oh, I forgot that you two were coming! I was so caught up in the evening. How stupid of me! Clyde and I can go upstairs so the two of you can have the living room. There are still plenty of donuts in the kitchen."

"Whoa," Mark said. "Not so fast. I'm fine with going upstairs."

"No, you're not." Sandra stood her ground. "You're already going out of your way to help me, Mark. I can entertain Clyde in my room. Marie will be more comfortable in the living room of a strange house."

Clyde spoke up. "Do I have any say in this?"

"No, you don't." Sandra tugged on his hand and motioned with the other. "Grab the plate and I'll bring the kerosene lamp from the kitchen. There's another one in the washroom you can use, Mark." She hurried Clyde up the stairs. "I'm sorry for not mentioning anything on the way home about Mark and Marie, but I forgot."

"It's okay," Clyde answered.

"Thanks for understanding." Sandra opened the bedroom door. "There. We'll have to make do with my room, I'm afraid."

"I'm being given a smaller and smaller place in the house as the evening progresses, I see," Clyde teased.

Sandra ignored him and placed the lamp on the dresser. She pointed toward the chair. "You can sit there. I'll take the bed."

Clyde set the plate he had carried beside his chair, then took a donut. "It's nice up here…but next Sunday night, I'll take you home to our place."

Sandra nodded. Clyde sounded like his *daett* now, decisive and firm. He hadn't asked whether she would go home with him again, but Clyde presumed he knew the answer.

"You should have consulted me or your *mamm* about tonight," Clyde continued. "Mark has your best interest in mind, but he doesn't always think things through. It's not that I don't like this—being up here—but if the community found out that we had a practice of dating in your bedroom, that could be just as indecent as being alone in the house together."

"I'm sorry," Sandra said. "I guess I should have asked *Mamm*, but I didn't. I was…"

"It's okay," Clyde said with a smile. "We won't stay up here long. I can't stay late anyway. Next time we'll take care of this the proper way. And I must say, I'm glad to see you accept correction so well. That's important in a *frau*. I'm also glad to see that you're heeding *Daett*'s request to stay away from your cousin Lydia. I know that's difficult and that Ben made his confession in church, but until his time of proving is over, you should follow *Daett's* decision."

"I agree," Sandra said. "I only spoke to Lydia at the service this morning. I couldn't make it to the youth gathering last week, so I don't know what happened there." Sandra tried to sound cheerful. "Did you go ice-skating with the others?"

Clyde smiled. "I went, and I missed you. But you should try to come whenever possible now that your cast is off. We don't have too much time together before…" Clyde looked away and let the sentence hang.

Sandra felt the heat rise up her neck. Apparently a girl blushed even if she wasn't in love. At least she didn't feel a stab of fear or panic. *Yah*, Clyde was bossy like his *daett*, but he also had a gentle side.

"You will see more of me after tonight, won't you?" Clyde asked. He stood up to pace the floor.

Sandra nodded. "If you wish."

"I wish it very much," Clyde answered. He stopped pacing to sit down again. "I have admired you ever since we moved here, Sandra. Even before *Daett* asked your *mamm* to marry him, I prayed that the Lord would open your heart to me, as mine had been opened to you."

"You did?" Sandra's voice croaked.

Clyde remained sober-faced. "I know that dreams sometimes are of our own doing, so I wasn't sure if my heart had strayed, or if this was from the Lord. But I knew I had feelings for you, Sandra. The Lord has since seen fit to bless those feelings. All signs point in that direction. The biggest one is the change in your heart. You have allowed me to bring you home."

"*Yah*," Sandra admitted, looking downward.

"You will wed me, then?" Clyde asked. He reached over to lift Sandra's chin with his hand.

Sandra met his gaze. With only a moment's hesitation, she said, "I will if you wish it so."

His fingers tightened for a moment. "You know I do." Clyde stood to pace the floor again. "If you agree, I want the wedding date set quickly. Perhaps you could speak to your *mamm* and see how soon it can happen."

"Before the next wedding season?" Sandra's voice squeaked.

His smile was kind. "Surely you don't expect us to wait all that time?"

Sandra gathered herself together. "I guess, not really. I mean, *yah*, I agree, but it is kind of sudden."

His eyes met hers. "We're in extraordinary circumstances, and the community will understand." He came closer and sat in the chair in front of her.

Sandra reached out to take his hands in hers. "I have to be honest. I don't think I love you yet, Clyde. But I can live with that, if you can. Love will come when the Lord grants it, just as it did for *Mamm*. I only ask that you love me, and that you lead our home in the ways of the Lord. I don't have any desire to follow my cousin Lydia in her flirtations with the world."

Clyde's eyes moistened. "What can I say, Sandra? You are…"

"Don't say anything," Sandra whispered. "It's *goot* enough the way it is."

His hand reached over to play with a strand of her hair that hung loose from under her *kapp*. "You're an angel, Sandra. You must have come straight from heaven to walk with me in this world. How can I ever say I love you often enough?"

"You just need to take it slowly," she said. "My heart needs time to catch up."

Clyde's Adam's apple bobbed as he said, "*Yah*, of course. I will always love you, Sandra. You can rest assured of that."

"And I will be the best *frau* I can be," Sandra said through moist eyes. "But you must also understand me."

A smile played on his face and he stood to his feet again. "That's fair enough."

Sandra dropped her head to say, "Thank you for being so kind, Clyde. There already must be a seed of love for you in my heart, or I wouldn't have agreed to marry you."

Clyde's face glowed. "You must have learned this wisdom during your time of trouble."

Sandra hesitated. "You could say that I fell and broke my foot so the Lord could get my attention away from Ezra—and onto you."

Clyde laughed and the sound filled the room. "I would not be so bold, but perhaps the Lord was kind and helped me out a little. Sandra, thank you for accepting my request for marriage tonight. You will be a better *frau* than I deserve…but you know I will still expect obedience on your part."

"You would have to say that at this moment," Sandra said. "It's not very romantic, you know."

Clyde chuckled. "That's why I'm saying it. It's an important part of marriage."

"So is romance," Sandra shot back.

Clyde laughed again. "There will be plenty of that! And *yah*, you will have to get used to some of my ways…my bossy ways, I suppose."

Sandra grinned. *Yah*, that much about marriage to an Amish man she knew. He wasn't that different from other Amish men, but then again, wasn't that what she wanted?

Clyde reached over for Sandra's hand. "Let me assure you that if there is any failure in our marriage it will be on my part. I ask your forgiveness ahead of time. In fact, I know you're already overlooking many of my faults. And I know I'm unworthy of such love."

With that, Clyde rose to his feet and said, "I think I had best be going."

He took Sandra's hand to lead the way down the stairs. At the last moment, before they stepped into the living room, Clyde let go—but not without one final gentle squeeze.

# Chapter Thirty-One

Sandra pulled on her thick winter coat before she ventured out into the late afternoon snow squall. Mark had hitched Dixie to the buggy earlier, and the horse was patiently waiting for her at the hitching rack. Sandra patted him on the nose and pulled off his blanket. She climbed in the buggy to drive out of the lane. Along the road's ditches, snowdrifts formed and shifted with each blast of the wind. Surely the squall would end soon, Sandra hoped. January could bring bitter blasts of weather in upstate New York, but so far the winter had been mild. This must be the blessing of the Lord. How could she organize her wedding in the middle of a blizzard?

Clyde had asked on Sunday evening, "Have you and your *mamm* decided on a date yet?"

"We're working on it," Sandra had assured him. She teasingly had added, "You're not buying the farm until spring, are you?"

Clyde had grinned. He was impatient, but in the end he understood. They needed time to enjoy each other's company and become better acquainted before the wedding. An engagement on the first date was unusual, but she didn't have any regrets. The community would understand the short courtship. She could tell when Deacon Schrock shook hands with her at the last Sunday service that he was thankful Amos and Clyde had saved her side of the Troyer family from the trouble Lydia and her parents were in.

Sandra's face clouded. She hadn't spoken with Lydia or Aunt Mary since before Christmas. Lydia, being the sensible person she usually was, hadn't pushed the matter in their brief greetings at the meetings. Why Lydia couldn't see the truth about Rudy was beyond her. But Lydia appeared withdrawn and preoccupied when she showed up for the community gatherings, so apparently Lydia still hadn't made up her mind. Surely her cousin wouldn't allow this situation to continue for long. Everyone knew something was wrong, and the whispers abounded.

"She might be ill like Rosemary but doesn't know it yet," someone guessed this past Sunday.

"No, it's something else," another girl ventured.

Sandra kept her mouth shut. Before long everyone would know. She knew what was wrong, and so did some of the other women. Those were the ones who said the least. They knew that with her head, Lydia was committed to the community…but with her heart, she continually brooded over the possibility of a life with Rudy. A jump over the fence into his arms seemed more and more a possibility.

Sandra shivered. How could Lydia do such a thing? How had they drifted so far apart? Lydia had always done everything with her. They had shared their school years, their *rumspringa* time, and had been baptized together. The pursuit of Ezra had been the last thing they had done together. And they had both lost him. That should have drawn them together, but it hadn't. *I must pray for Lydia,* Sandra decided. *Lydia must be saved from an awful mistake.* Lydia couldn't leave the community and be placed in the *bann*. If Lydia jumped the fence, it would be a tragedy no one could begin to comprehend.

Sandra held onto the reins as the wind picked up and the buggy leaned sideways. Surely this buggy ride wasn't a mistake, was it? Maybe she should have waited to ride with Mark. He would arrive later to the supper *Mamm* had invited them to. But Sandra had wanted to visit Rosemary, and this had seemed like the right time. She had best see Rosemary soon. From the sound of the report Ann gave her at the last Sunday meeting, Rosemary wouldn't live much longer on this earth.

Sandra let out the reins so Dixie could increase his speed. The horse shook her head when another blast of snow blew over them. They were almost to Rosemary's place now, so Sandra couldn't turn even if she wanted to. She pulled the buggy blanket higher over her knees. The warmth crept over her, but Sandra still shivered. That Rosemary was so ill still seemed impossible to imagine. How quickly it had all happened. As had all the tragedies of the recent months— *Daett* and Uncle Ben falling suddenly into financial ruin, then *Daett* passing unexpectedly. If Amos and Clyde hadn't shown up when they did, who knows what would have become of *Mamm* and her. She had been so wrong about Amos and Clyde from the beginning. That showed how much *goot* sense she had, or rather didn't have. How quickly things changed.

Happiness had arrived for her just as suddenly. That didn't seem fair when Lydia wasn't happy. How could Sandra look forward to a husband and a farm with *kinner* in the future, while Lydia contemplated leaving the community? And Rosemary's situation was even worse. Rosemary might soon lose everything in this world. All while Sandra felt so blessed. Maybe she shouldn't have come to see Rosemary. What comfort could she be to a person on her deathbed when things were going so well in her own life? Sandra's hands tightened on the reins for a moment. But no, she would go on. She was Rosemary's friend, and friends comforted each other whatever the situation.

A mile later Sandra pulled back on the reins and turned into the Beilers' driveway on Old State Raod. She stopped at the hitching post and climbed down carefully on the slippery buggy step to tie up Dixie. Sandra retrieved a blanket from under the backseat of the buggy and fastened the blanket securely on Dixie's back, to protect him from the continual wind blasts. He should be okay for the short visit she planned. Rosemary shouldn't be kept up too long, even for a visit with an old friend.

Sandra made her way slowly up the icy walk and knocked on the door. Ann answered a moment later, an apron tied around her waist. "What a surprise, Sandra! How nice of you to come." Several of the smaller children behind Ann peered out of the kitchen at their visitor.

Sandra smiled at them and asked, "So it's okay to visit Rosemary?"

"Oh, she would love to see you," Ann said. "She's upstairs. *Mamm* would bring her down so she wouldn't be by herself so much, but Rosemary insists on staying in her own room."

Sandra hesitated. "Is it okay if I just go up?"

"*Yah.* Just knock on the door." Ann waved Sandra on.

Sandra tousled several of the smaller boys' heads as she passed them. They grinned and retreated into the kitchen.

Sandra tiptoed up the stairs and knocked on Rosemary's bedroom door.

"Come in," Rosemary's weak voice called out.

Sandra opened the door to find Rosemary under the quilt on the bed. Her face appeared pale and thin.

"Rosemary!" Sandra cried out. She rushed over to kneel in front of the bed and grasp both of Rosemary's hands. "This cannot be! You must become well again."

Rosemary's smile was weak. "It's in the Lord hands, Sandra. He decides these things, and there's nothing any of us can do. I find peace in the comfort I have been given. Ezra comes over almost every evening now. What a gift the man is. I can't believe I've been given such a love to see me over to the other side."

"But Rosemary," Sandra protested, "is there not something that can be done?"

Rosemary shook her head. "Dr. Katz has been kind enough to get me into an experimental treatment. I objected, since *Daett* doesn't have the money, but Ezra talked me into it. That, and Deacon Schrock came by personally. I think Ezra put him up to it. Deacon Schrock said he spoke with Dr. Katz and they worked out a reduced rate, which the community will help pay. I still don't like it, but I finish with the final treatment this week."

"And there is no difference yet?" Sandra's hands tightened on Rosemary's.

Rosemary winced. "I'm afraid not, but I have to trust it was all for some reason. Perhaps it will give me a few more weeks."

"You poor dear." Sandra stroked Rosemary's forehead. "I am so very sorry. I wish there was something I could do, but I feel so helpless."

"You came to visit." Rosemary attempted another smile. "And there is something you can do for me."

"Oh?" Sandra didn't hide her surprise.

Rosemary nodded. "*Yah*, there is. You will think me crazy, but I've prayed about this and I know it's the right thing to do. Will you agree?"

"Agree to what?" Sandra asked.

"I won't tell you unless you agree first," Rosemary said, her smile wider and slyer now.

Sandra hesitated, then said, "I agree."

Rosemary's smile changed to one of gratitude. "Sandra, I want you to encourage Lydia to open her heart to Ezra once I'm gone."

"Rosemary!" Sandra scolded. "I will not speak of such a thing."

"But you promised—and I insist," Rosemary said. "I was never a decent match for Ezra to begin with. I'm sure he was given to me only as a comfort on this journey to the other side. And I heard that you have agreed to wed Clyde, so surely you don't still want Ezra for yourself."

Sandra tried to breathe. "Rosemary, please. No, I don't want Ezra. He chose you, and I will not even think of such a thing as speaking with Lydia about this matter."

Rosemary touched Sandra's arm. "Are you offended by the thought that you didn't get Ezra?"

Sandra rushed the words. "No, it's not that. I'm going to marry Clyde. I wouldn't think of going back to all that before…and besides, Ezra didn't want me. It's just not the will of the Lord—me and Ezra."

"So it's settled, then." Rosemary was matter-of-fact. "You don't have an interest in Ezra while Lydia still does. If you encourage her, maybe Lydia can be saved from making an awful mistake."

Sandra let out her breath. "So you've heard about Rudy?"

"*Yah*, Ann told me." Rosemary tried to sit up. "You will do this for me? Remember, you agreed!"

"But you're the one to talk to Lydia about this, not me," Sandra insisted.

Rosemary sighed. "I will speak to Ezra, and he will understand. You speak to Lydia."

"What bothers me about this," Sandra went on, "is that you seem to be giving up. But maybe the treatment will work yet. Or maybe they can try something else. You can't give up!"

Rosemary lay back on the pillow. "I'm not giving up. But I need to be realistic. Pancreatic cancer is one of the worst. Even if the treatment works, it's probably only a short-term solution. Sandra, I'm tired. Let's leave it at that. I will speak to Ezra, and you'll speak to Lydia, okay?"

Sandra pressed back the tears. "You're such a dear, Rosemary. I'm still going to pray your life is spared. May the Lord be with you."

"He is." Rosemary tried to sit again, but failed. "He has already comforted me greatly."

Sandra squeezed Rosemary's hand and slipped out of the bedroom. Rosemary had her eyes closed and looked exhausted, so Sandra closed the door quietly and tiptoed down the stairs. What a self-sacrificing girl Rosemary was, but she would not speak to Lydia about Ezra until she knew for sure…she couldn't bring herself to think the awful thought.

Sandra stepped out of the stairwell and peeked into the kitchen. Ann was still there with flour dough all over her apron and with several of her smaller siblings gathered about. They seemed more interested in sneaking small bits of crumbs than in any help they could give.

"I'm going now," Sandra whispered.

Ann glanced up with a smile. "Thanks for coming. *Mamm*'s in town right now, but she'll be back soon. I'll tell her you were here."

"Behave yourselves, now." Sandra wagged her finger at the little fellows on the chairs.

They grinned but said nothing.

Once outside, Sandra pulled the buggy blanket off Dixie's back and turned him around before she climbed in. The snow still had not let up. She had been too distracted to notice at first. The sight of Rosemary sick in bed gripped her. How shamed she should be for her own selfishness. Even in her illness Rosemary spent time in thanksgiving for what life had given her, and in considering the well-being of others. What a lesson Rosemary was for Sandra. Thankfully she had done one thing right, by choosing what the Lord had given her in Clyde. That had been a big step in the right direction. Maybe that was why the Lord placed people like Rosemary on this earth, so they could leave behind a godly example for others to follow.

Sandra rubbed her hand across her cheek as the wind whipped through the cracks in the buggy door. Stray snowflakes stung her face. She was trying hard to love and accept Clyde, but now she would redouble her efforts. If Rosemary could display such grace in her life while facing a terminal illness, she should get down on her knees and thank the Lord each day for the blessing He was sending her way in Clyde.

Sandra pulled back on the reins again as she approached *Mamm* and Amos's place on Todd Road. She turned in to stop near the barn. She'd better unhitch this time. Dixie would be warmer inside the barn. The extra effort was worth the horse's comfort. She climbed down the buggy step again as the barn door burst open to reveal Clyde hurrying toward her.

Clyde greeted Sandra with delight. "You're early!"

Sandra, remembering her encounter with Rosemary, smiled at him. "How could I not be early with such a handsome and caring man waiting for me?"

Clyde glowed with happiness, and Sandra slipped off her glove to brush his cheek. "Thanks for coming out to help me unhitch."

"Wow!" Clyde shook his head. "What a welcome!"

"Just be thankful," Sandra told him. "That's the lesson I've been learning."

# Chapter Thirty-Two

Rosemary sat on the edge of the bed with a glass of water on the chair beside her. *Mamm* had told her a few moments earlier that Ezra was due to arrive soon.

Ezra hadn't been over since Sunday afternoon. A great longing to see him had gripped her since yesterday. She wanted to hold his hand again. She wanted to feel the strength in his fingers. Ezra was strong where she was weak. Ezra exuded health and vigor as her body gave out more and more each day.

*I must not give in to dark thoughts about my increasing weakness,* Rosemary reminded herself. She had felt better this past week, and tonight she could sit up. Maybe the experimental medicine had begun to work. Was there hope after all? Rosemary pushed the thought away. She must prepare for the worst, and her talk with Sandra last week had been the first step. Now she must encourage Ezra to pursue a relationship with Lydia if she was taken in death. She should have brought up the subject with Ezra on Sunday, but weariness had overtaken her. And she couldn't bring herself to say the words while Ezra had been sitting so close to her. What if she really did become well? What if they could go on?

The thought made Rosemary dizzy, and she lay down again. Would she be Ezra's *frau* someday? It seemed so impossible after the ravages the disease had caused in her body, but hope knocked on the door. She couldn't deny the fact. Soon Ezra would come through the door and notice that she looked much better—because she did. Both *Mamm* and Ann had said so today.

Manly footsteps came up the stairs, and Rosemary sat up again. Ezra only knocked once and came in before she said anything.

"Rosemary?" he said, coming to a stop a foot away. He appeared to study her.

*Do I look better?* The words wanted to leap from her lips, as she gazed up at him.

"You're looking *goot*," Ezra finally said, hope in his voice. "And you're sitting up."

Rosemary reached for his hand and held it while Ezra sat down beside her. "I was hoping you'd say so," she whispered. "*Mamm* and Ann said the same thing."

A smile formed on Ezra's face. "You *are* much better." Ezra's arm slipped around Rosemary's shoulder.

Rosemary leaned against him. "Do you really think so? Oh, I hope so!"

"The Lord does work miracles," Ezra assured her. "We must not doubt that. We must think happy thoughts of the future." Ezra held both of Rosemary's hands. "We must speak of the day you are well and all this sickness is driven from your body. And pray, of course, that the Lord will continue to use the medicine to accomplish His will."

"His will, then, is that I get well?" Rosemary clung to him. "Can I hope for such a thing?"

Ezra's face grew solemn. "We must follow the signs the Lord

gives, and if you are feeling better, then perhaps this is His will. But that's up to the Lord. It's not our best thinking that He listens to, but to His own wisdom."

"But I will believe." Rosemary gathered her strength to sit up further. "I will allow hope to live."

Ezra brushed Rosemary's face with his fingers. "I will also cling to hope with all my heart. We will always love each other."

Tears stung Rosemary's eyes. "You know I will always be yours while there is breath in my body, even though I'm so unworthy of you. Yet you have been given to me by the Lord."

"Hush now," Ezra scolded. "Don't talk like—" Ezra stopped when a knock came on the door.

*Mamm* opened the door to look in. "Anyone hungry?"

Rosemary didn't hesitate. "I'd like to go downstairs for supper. It would do me *goot*."

Alarm filled *Mamm*'s face. "But should you? It might do you harm now that there is some improvement."

"But I'm getting better." Rosemary's face glowed. "Take me downstairs please, *Mamm*, even if I have to sit on the couch with a plate in front of me."

"Should we?" *Mamm* directed her question to Ezra.

Ezra thought for a moment. "If she wishes, we should."

"Then let's go." *Mamm* came over to stand on one side of Rosemary. "I'll support one arm, and we'll see how it goes."

Rosemary steadied herself on the bedpost with one hand, and reached for *Mamm*'s arm with the other. She pushed upward and tottered to her feet. The room moved in circles before her eyes, but soon settled down. "Take my other hand," Rosemary whispered to Ezra.

With slow steps the three made their way down the stairs.

"She is stronger, isn't she?" *Mamm*'s voice was tinged with hope.

"*Yah*, she is," Ezra said. "But we must continue to pray."

Once in the living room Rosemary settled onto the couch slowly. She sat still and took deep breaths with a smile on her face.

*Mamm* peered down at her. "Are you okay?"

"I'm so happy," Rosemary told her, "And oh, Ezra, you're here to enjoy this victory with me."

"I wouldn't have missed it for the world," he replied, sitting down beside her. "I'll stay for supper, and we can eat together."

*Mamm* hurried off, but quickly returned with a small quilt in her hand. She wrapped it around Rosemary's thin shoulders. "I wouldn't want you catching a chill right when you're showing the first signs of improvement."

"I'll be okay," Rosemary assured her, but the warmth of the quilt did feel *goot*. Rosemary pulled it tight around herself.

Ezra stroked Rosemary's arm. "The day you walk again by yourself will be a day of great joy for all of us. It can't come too soon for me."

"Oh, Ezra." Rosemary leaned against him again. "It's so *goot* that you're here tonight."

"Okay, lovebirds, that's enough," Ann scolded from the kitchen doorway. She held two plates in her hands. "Now, aren't you two special, eating in the living room."

"Every moment I spend with Rosemary is special," Ezra said.

Ann laughed. "Okay, I've heard enough sweet talk. I'm gone." Ann set down the plates and hurried off again.

"I don't think she likes me," Ezra teased.

Rosemary pressed back the tears as Ezra reached for her plate. She had so much happiness inside of her right now. Was this the turning point of her sickness, or had the Lord given her a respite to enjoy Ezra for an evening? Right now, she didn't want to think of the answer. It was enough that Ezra was close and that he loved her.

"Eat," Ezra said, holding out a spoonful of food.

Rosemary looked up at him. "You would feed me like a *bobbli*?"

"Hush," Ezra ordered. "*Yah*, because I love you."

Rosemary said nothing. This was simply too *wunderbah* to endure for long. She opened her mouth and Ezra placed the spoonful of soup inside. The coolness of the steel brushed her lips, and his fingers touched the edge of her chin.

"Does it taste better this way?" Ezra teased.

"Everything tastes better when you're here." Rosemary pressed back the tears.

"See, you're even getting your hunger back," Ezra encouraged.

She wasn't going to argue with him, and he was right on that point. She must keep her spirits up. After Ezra left tonight there would be plenty of time to cry. She needed to drink in every moment the Lord gave her with this *wunderbah* man.

"Are you drifting off to sleep?" Ezra teased again.

"Just like a *bobbli*," Rosemary said. They laughed softly together.

Ezra continued to feed her for several minutes until Ann reappeared. "Ready for dessert?"

Ezra grinned. "*Yah*. Let's try some."

"I'll be right back," Ann said.

When she returned a minute later, she was carrying two slices of apple pie heaped with scoops of homemade pecan ice cream.

Rosemary stared and exclaimed. "You made this special for tonight!"

Ann nodded, sober-faced. "We weren't sure, but we took a chance you'd be up for dessert tonight."

"Oh, Ann, thank you." Rosemary leaned forward to give her sister a hug.

"Anything is worth making you happy," Ann whispered. She wiped her eyes and fled back to the kitchen.

Even Ezra's eyes seemed to get a bit misty. "This is a very happy evening," he said.

Rosemary didn't respond as she took the first bite of ice cream. The cool sweetness melted in her mouth, and the taste tingled all through her body. She was touched that her family had made pecan ice cream especially for her. Maybe she was on her way to better health. But a deep weariness had already crept over her body. She would hang on until she had eaten all of the ice cream. She must not allow the illness to steal these last moments of the evening from her. Not with Ezra by her side.

"Like it?" Ezra glanced at her.

"Nothing tastes like homemade pecan ice cream," Rosemary said with great content.

"We must have this every time I'm here." Ezra squeezed Rosemary's arm with his free hand.

"Homemade pecan ice cream and you…" Rosemary let the words hang in the air. Ezra understood. His arm slipped around her and pulled her close. She wished Ezra could carry her upstairs, holding her in his arms as he had that night she passed out by the window—but that wouldn't be decent. She must be thankful for what had been given to her.

"This is great ice cream," Ezra pronounced. "I could eat another bowl if it was *goot* for me."

"Ann will get you more," Rosemary offered.

"Thanks, but I'd better not," he said. "Too much of a *goot* thing isn't right."

Rosemary took a deep breath. There was her answer. The Lord provided direction even before she asked. She didn't like the answer, but Ezra was right. If he carried her upstairs in his arms, that would be too much of a *goot* thing for one evening. But surely the Lord would allow her the joy of lying in Ezra's arms again before she left this earth. If she lived and wed Ezra, there would be plenty of those moments, but…

"Should you go back upstairs now?" Ezra asked. "You look…"

A small bite of mostly melted ice cream remained in her bowl, and Rosemary slipped it into her mouth before she answered. "I'm ready if *Mamm* will help you."

"I'll call her." Ezra rose to his feet.

*Mamm* appeared at once, and they maneuvered Rosemary up the stairs and into her bed. With a sigh she looked up at both of them. "Thank you so much, and Ezra especially. This has been a very *wunderbah* evening."

Ezra reached down to take her hand. "All I can say, Rosemary, is let there be many more."

*Mamm* averted her face and hurried from the room without a backward glance.

"Hold me, Ezra, for just a little bit," Rosemary whispered.

Ezra knelt down in front of her and wrapped his arms around her. He pulled her close and whispered in Rosemary's ear. "Get better, dear. I'll be praying for you."

"Thank you," Rosemary whispered back. "I'll try."

Ezra held on for a long time before he let go. Then he caressed Rosemary's pale cheek. "I love you, darling. Good night."

"Good night." She held on to his hand until he was out of reach, and listened to Ezra's footsteps on the stairs until they faded away.

"Thank You, Lord, for this evening," Rosemary whispered toward the darkened window. "You have been so good to me."

# Chapter Thirty-Three

The following week Lydia was sitting on the living room couch with *Mamm* beside her and *Daett* ensconced in his rocker. She squirmed under the steady gaze of Deacon Schrock. She had known this moment would arrive, but she had pushed the dread into the recesses of her mind. No doubt if she had been able to return Harvey Miller's affections when he offered to help her the other Sunday, this wouldn't be happening. She hadn't been unkind to Harvey, but Harvey had understood. She wouldn't have accepted his offer to drive her home even if he had asked. And so now, in Deacon Schrock's world, she was to blame for rejecting Harvey's overtures.

Deacon Schrock cleared his throat. "This is a most uncomfortable thing to speak of, Lydia. We as the ministry don't choose life partners for our members, but we do have evidence that the ministry possesses considerable wisdom in these matters. Your cousin Sandra and your Aunt Edna are certainly proof of that. Edna is happily married after the ministry suggested she accept Amos's offer, and Sandra has come into a *wunderbah* love of her own after following our advice. Do you think you're better than either your aunt and cousin?"

"Of course not!" Lydia exclaimed. "But don't you think a man and a woman should feel love for each other before they think of marriage?"

Deacon Schrock offered a thin smile. "I'm not sure what you mean, Lydia, but if this has anything to do with that *Englisha* man, you know what my answer will be. Yet I'll try to be patient and talk this through with you."

Lydia groaned under her breath. Why did she even try to argue with Deacon Schrock?

"I don't love Harvey Miller," she said. "Nor does he love me. Is that plain enough?"

*Mamm* jumped into the conversation. "But love for him can grow! It has happened before, and like Deacon Schrock said, both Edna and Sandra are *goot* examples."

"Well, I guess I don't have the faith it will happen," Lydia said. "Can't you understand that? I am not like Sandra or Aunt Edna. And neither is Harvey like them. Why do you insist on pushing us together?"

*Mamm* spoke up again. "But the deacon is right. This worked for both Sandra and Edna, and I know that Edna was in love with Emil while he lived on this earth. Her love for Amos came later... but it did come."

Lydia sighed. There was no use, so she might as well be silent. If she promised never to see Rudy again, they might leave her in peace, but it was clear Deacon Schrock didn't trust her, and *Daett* was still in his proving time with the community. The deacon must have serious doubts about this family and feel he needed solid evidence and not just promises.

Deacon Schrock stared intently at Lydia. "Please pay attention, Lydia. Listen to your *mamm*. I know these examples don't fit you exactly, but it's still true that you could learn to love Harvey. And he is willing to open his heart to affections for you. He told me so himself."

"Perhaps he is," Lydia allowed. "But I am not."

"Lydia!" *Mamm* moaned. "How can you say that? You know that Rudy isn't *goot* for you. The man has thrown his web of deceit around you, and now you can't see straight."

Deacon Schrock dropped his gaze to the living room floor. "None of this comes as a surprise to me. Yet I'm disappointed in you, Lydia, and in you, Ben." Deacon Schrock paused to give *Daett* a sharp look. "Why are you still allowing these things to happen on your place? And this after you've made a confession in front of the church."

"It's not *Daett*'s fault," Lydia said.

Deacon Schrock shook his head and sighed. "I can't believe things have gotten so out of control in this house. You are a member of the community, Lydia, as are your parents. It is disgraceful behavior to consider an *Englisha* man as a marriage partner. The church has tried to exercise patience, but this has gone far enough. I am completely ashamed of myself that I've been so soft with your family. I'm sure Bishop Henry will share my feelings when I tell him of this. Both of us understand that we are partly to blame for letting our compassion get the best of us, so this has to stop." Deacon Schrock gave Lydia a sharp look. "Or have you already promised this *Englisha* man that you will marry him?"

"No, of course not!" Lydia exclaimed. She then calmed herself for a second. "And I know that I am to blame for this. I want to make that clear."

Deacon Schrock shrugged. "All I can say is, this is entirely unacceptable. If you know what is *goot* for you, you will show some affection to Harvey and allow him to bring you home from the hymn singing when he asks permission. And you will never see this *Englisha* man again."

*Mamm* reached over to clutch Lydia's arm. "Please, Lydia. Listen to Deacon Schrock's advice."

"Harvey hasn't even asked me," Lydia objected. "And I don't think he will, even if I promise to return his affections…which I cannot do."

*Mamm*'s fingers dug into Lydia's arm. "Do what Deacon Schrock says. He knows what's best. I'm sure Harvey has made his desires known to Deacon Schrock."

Lydia faced all of them. "This will not work, and I cannot agree to it. I'm sorry, but I can't."

Deacon Schrock stood to his feet, and his words were brisk. "I will not argue with you anymore, Lydia. You are a woman, and it's time you realize that. Your emotions will not be catered to. I think I can get Harvey to ask you home for a date or two. He has that much interest at least, and you should be thankful the man even considers you as a possible *frau* in spite of the circumstances your family is in— to say nothing of your own thoughts about *Englisha* men. That is an abomination, Lydia, and I will have no part in it. We have other things to work on in this community, and our patience has run out. Either you will accept a date with Harvey, or Bishop Henry will speak of the *bann* with the congregation at the next Sunday service."

Lydia held her breath. The *bann*? For her? She tried one last desperate plea. "What if I promise not to see Rudy again?"

Deacon Schrock paced the floor. "And you would keep your promise?"

Lydia hesitated. "*Yah*, but I must at least tell him good-bye in person and explain why I can't see him anymore."

Deacon Schrock faced her again and thought for a second, then said, "*Yah*, you can tell your *Englisha* fellow good-bye sometime this week, and after that you must put your life in order. I'm not saying you have to marry Harvey, but you have to give him six months at least, and open your heart to what the Lord's will is for the two of you. Either you get in Harvey's buggy on Sunday evening, or we as a ministry will take further steps."

Lydia found nothing more to say. How could she get in Harvey's buggy on Sunday evening? Harvey didn't have feelings for her. She was sure of that.

"Good night to all of you." Deacon Schrock picked his hat up from the living room floor and went out the front door.

*Daett* didn't make any effort to see him off, which would have been customary. Beside Lydia, *Mamm* moaned. "The Lord has smitten us mightily. My head will hang in shame among the community people over what my family has become. First, Ben, you have shamed us, and now Lydia."

*Daett* still didn't say anything, but he got up and left for the barn without a backward glance. As Deacon Schrock's buggy drove out of the lane, *Mamm* wept softy and Lydia slipped an arm around her shoulder. What could she say? She was part of the problem. When *Mamm* didn't look up or stop her tears, Lydia stood to her feet. She might as well go upstairs and cry herself to sleep. That, and figure out what she must do. She would have to make up her mind about Harvey, and she would have to abandon Rudy.

Lydia passed the kitchen and glanced in. Both of her sisters were seated at the table. Clearly they had overheard every word spoken in the living room. Emma and Rhoda didn't appear guilty in the least. They both stood and tiptoed behind Lydia up the stairs. When they reached the top, Emma whispered, "That was awful, Lydia! Absolutely awful! I will never be baptized now. Not if Deacon Schrock can order me around like that, and tell me who to marry."

"I agree," Rhoda echoed.

"He's not telling me who to marry," Lydia objected.

"I can't believe you're defending the man!" Emma exploded.

"Calm down," Lydia said. "The two of you were on your way over the fence before this, so don't blame the deacon. You can blame me and *Daett* perhaps, but not him. The deacon's a decent and humble man. When the community's values come into question, he must be firm."

"Firm?" Emma exploded again. "He's harsh and cruel! That's more like it!"

"Don't say that," Lydia said.

"You're still defending him!" Rhoda exclaimed. "Surely you're not coming home with that horrible Harvey Miller on Sunday evening?"

Lydia turned on her sister. "Rhoda, watch your mouth. Harvey's a kind and gentle man."

"We're telling Rudy everything we heard," Emma said. "Then maybe he can catch you in town and talk some sense into your head."

"Fine," Lydia said. "Tell Rudy what you will, but also ask him if he wants me to meet him somewhere so I can tell him the true story, rather than your mangled version of it."

Lydia didn't wait for an answer but turned to enter her bedroom. She walked over to the window to look out. She didn't like Deacon Schrock's dictates, but breaking her vows wasn't an option either. She had known for some time that it would come down to this. *Yah*, she must tell Rudy the truth from her own lips. With a groan, Lydia knelt by the window and looked up into the cloudy heavens for a long time, until peace came.

# Chapter Thirty-Four

On Sunday afternoon, Lydia kept her head down low in the back of the car. Avery Coon had picked her and her sisters up, and together they drove toward Avery's house, where Lydia was to meet Rudy.

Lydia had known all along she could never leave the community, not even for Rudy. But her earlier willingness to see Rudy had sent him the wrong message. That was her fault entirely, and now she must undo the damage…if she could.

Lydia held back the tears as Avery pulled into her parents' driveway. Lydia was *Daett*'s daughter at heart—afraid to face things. *Daett* set out on journeys he couldn't complete, but she did not want to be like that. *Daett* had ruined the family's finances and destroyed their reputation in the community. The least she could do would be to tell Rudy the truth and be done with it.

"Here we are," Avery announced. "And Rudy's already here, I see."

*Of course,* Lydia wanted to say. Rudy was always on time. Rudy was decent and proper and thoughtful. That's why she had loved him once. Lydia wiped her eyes and opened the car door.

"Take courage," Emma whispered in Lydia's ear as they walked up to the house. "I heard you stand up to Deacon Schrock the other night. You have it in you."

Lydia didn't answer as they made their way up the porch steps. Julie was waiting at the open front door.

"Where's Rudy?" Avery asked.

"In the dining room," Julie said. "We're to leave until Rudy calls us on his cell. He wants some privacy with Lydia."

Everyone glanced at Lydia, and she lowered her head. "Thanks for bringing me," Lydia managed before she hurried down the hall, following Julie. Lydia slowed when she saw Rudy waiting for her just beyond the wall. She forced herself to move forward.

Rudy's eyes shone when he looked up. "I knew you would come."

"*Yah*, I had to," Lydia said as she reached out to receive his embrace.

Rudy held her for a long moment. He let go to take a seat, then motioned to Lydia with one hand. "Sit. We have to talk."

"*Yah*. And I suspect you already know what I am going to tell you, don't you?"

Rudy shrugged. "Well, Emma told me all about your brave stand against that deacon of yours, but…"

Lydia nodded. "I'm sorry about all of this. If I've led you on by seeing you again, I regret that. All along I've tried to tell you that I can never be part of your world, even as my own heart betrayed me. I can't keep trying to convince myself we could somehow live happily ever after. That can never be, Rudy."

Rudy didn't answer at once. He slowly reached over and took both of Lydia's hands in his. "I had to try, Lydia. And we did once love each other. I guess I hoped against hope there might still be a chance for us. Would you rather I had stayed away?"

"No," Lydia cried. "I don't know. Nothing makes sense right now. When you come out to the farm it's like you blend in with what I am, but when I get away from home—out in your world—it's not the same. You saw how I reacted on our Christmas lights tour. So no matter what we may have felt in the past or think we feel now, we can never be a couple, Rudy. Not ever. That's what I came to tell you. Not very well, I'm sure…but I so very much hope you understand."

Rudy reached over to tuck loose strands of hair back under Lydia's *kapp*. "You're beautiful as ever, Lydia. Even through a veil of tears. Do you know that?"

"Hush," Lydia scolded. "That doesn't help."

A trace of a smile flitted on Rudy's face. "I'm not sorry that I said it. I meant every word…and more. You know that."

Lydia stood to her feet. "Don't make this harder than it is. I need to go, Rudy. Good-bye."

Rudy reached for her hand again. "If we must, then, good-bye. Have a wonderful life, Lydia. I'll never forget you."

Lydia pulled away. "Nor I you, Rudy. You will find someone who can love you and be fully part of your world. In a way, I'm envious of her…but I'm not her."

Rudy nodded and reached for his phone. He dialed a number and waited. "I'm ready. Come back."

Lydia paced the dining room floor. "I so wish you could understand," she pled.

Rudy looked up at her. "I do understand, Lydia. You're an Amish girl now. Our worlds are different. I regret that it must be that way, but I will let things lie."

"Thank you," Lydia whispered as Avery's car pulled into the driveway.

Rudy stood to his feet and walked with Lydia out to the car. Emma rolled down her window and asked, "So, did you get everything straightened out?"

"It's really none of your business," Lydia answered with a glare.

"It's all fine," Rudy offered. "As fine as possible."

Rudy helped Lydia into the car and closed the door.

"So, what happened?" Avery asked after she had backed the car out of the driveway.

"We have things straight now," Lydia said.

"That's all?" Avery asked. "We don't get the whole story?"

"*Yah*, that's all," Lydia said. She had no words anyway. How did one explain such a thing? She mourned the past but was happy to be beyond it at the same time.

"Don't try to figure her out," Emma told Avery. "I've about given up myself."

"So what now?" Rhoda asked. "Harvey Miller?"

Lydia shook her head but said nothing.

"Lydia wants the boring life of the community, and she can have it," Emma explained to Avery. "Can you imagine?"

"Be careful," Rhoda scolded. "She's still our sister, much as she makes bad choices."

Avery turned into the Troyers' driveway. As Lydia got out, she said, "Thank you, Avery. You've been a big help to me." Her sisters stayed in the car, and Avery had turned the car around and sped out of the lane by the time Lydia reached the front door. *Mamm* met her with open arms and wrapped Lydia in a hug.

When *Mamm* let go she held Lydia at arm's length. "All of us have loved and lost. It's life, Lydia. You did the right thing. I'm sorry I doubted you these past months, but I thought for sure I had lost my daughter to the world. And that would be worse than death, Lydia. Thank the Lord He has guided your thoughts and led you safely back to us."

"What is to become of me?" Lydia asked.

"You will fall in love with Harvey," *Mamm* said, "and Deacon Schrock will be proven right once more."

Lydia shook her head. "That won't happen, but at least I can be nice to Harvey. He deserves that much."

"You leave that in the Lord's hands. You'll be okay." *Mamm* patted Lydia's arm.

But she wouldn't, Lydia knew. She wouldn't be okay for a very long time.

# Chapter Thirty-Five

L ater that evening, Lydia sat beside Sandra on the front bench for the hymn singing. Sandra gave Lydia a sharp sideways glance now that they were seated. In times past, the girls would have chatted all evening about the blessings and trials in their lives, but that was no more. Tonight they had spoken a few words of greeting, but there had been no action that could have been deemed a public display of closeness. Their lost friendship was a pain that stirred deep inside both of them.

Moments later the front door opened, and the line of unmarried men filed in. Amid the shuffle of feet as the men settled in, Lydia leaned over to whisper in Sandra's ear, "You can stop ignoring me now. I'm going home tonight with Harvey. That should make things all right again."

Sandra gave a little gasp, and several of the men looked their way. Sandra covered her exclamation with a smile as a man hollered out the opening song number from the back of the room.

"Is this really true?" Sandra whispered out of the side of her mouth.

"Don't you see Harvey sitting back there?" Lydia motioned with her head.

Sandra craned her head. Harvey was indeed seated on the back bench. As a widower, his presence at the evening hymn singing wasn't expected, but no one would see the significance if they didn't think twice. But Lydia, and now Sandra, knew the reason Harvey was here.

She whispered in Lydia's ear, "You really did it."

"Shhh…" Lydia whispered back.

This was almost like old times, when they used to giggle together after Ezra smiled at them. But that was in the past. Ezra wasn't even at the singing, which meant he was with Rosemary, who must have had a rough day.

Lydia blinked and focused on the page of the songbook as the young people's voices rose and fell around them. She noticed Sandra in particular singing with vim and vigor. Her wedding date would be announced soon, if one could judge from the flurry of activity at Aunt Edna's place. Lydia's side of the family had been left out of the planning, but that might change with her actions tonight. Perhaps Sandra would even feel free to invite her to serve as a table waiter… unless Amos objected. But Sandra would have her way and Amos would come around. Maybe not overnight, but Amos would be impressed when he heard that Harvey Miller had taken Lydia home from the hymn singing.

Sandra's face was still glowing when Lydia glanced again in her direction. At least the problem with Rudy was solved once and for all. Rudy must have known all along that their love couldn't be brought back to life. In the troubles of life he had hoped that such a thing was possible—as she also had. But that wasn't possible. And one couldn't make the heart obey on command. Thankfully even Harvey in his simple ways knew that. He had obviously been wise enough not to try his affections on her until Deacon Schrock put on the pressure.

Lydia sighed. They would enjoy the evening together as friends perhaps. After all, Harvey must be lonely. That must be why he had agreed to drive her home tonight. But Harvey surely knew that loneliness wasn't enough to build a relationship upon. He must still pine for his *frau*, Leslie, as Lydia still mourned for having lost Ezra to Rosemary. Lydia might as well be honest about the fact that she and Harvey would be two broken hearts riding home in a buggy tonight.

Lydia tried to focus again as another song was given out. Joyous voices rose all around her, as young voices sang the praises of the Lord. She would try to look happy at least when she climbed in Harvey's buggy later in the evening. The man knew she didn't love him, but then Amos had known Edna didn't love him at first either. The problem was, in her heart of hearts, she still had feelings for Ezra. Still, Rosemary had played fair and square, while Sandra and Lydia had been distracted by their family troubles. Rosemary had earned the right to fall in love with Ezra.

Lydia tried to even her breathing and at least move her mouth to the sound of the singing. The truth was, Ezra deserved a *frau* like Rosemary who lived her life with an open heart. Instead, Lydia and Sandra had relied upon artful maneuvers in order to catch his attention.

So what if she never felt love for a man again? Maybe Harvey was a man who wouldn't care. Maybe he wasn't looking for love in his second marriage. Maybe that's why Deacon Schrock had been able to persuade Harvey to drive her home from the hymn singing. They were alike in their pain, at least. She could comfort Harvey, but she could never love him the way she had loved Ezra—or Rudy. Nor would Harvey ever love her the way he had loved Leslie. Perhaps they could come to terms with each other. It was an awful thought, but her soul was floating near the bottom of the ocean at the moment, and anything seemed possible. Even Harvey Miller.

The songs continued as the minutes ticked past. Lydia pinched herself several times when thoughts of Ezra and Rosemary returned. She would not think of the couple as they shared moments together in Rosemary's sickroom. She must think of Harvey and the evening ahead of them.

Sandra jiggled the songbook in Lydia's hand and whispered, "Sing. You've been spaced out all evening."

Had she been that obvious? Lydia forced herself to glance up at Sandra and mouth the words. "I'm sorry. I'll do better."

Sandra smiled before she looked away. But Lydia knew there would be no sympathy from Sandra on Harvey or Ezra. She ought to stop this pity party herself and grow up. Life was what it was. She had made her bed, as the old people said, and she must lie in it.

Lydia coughed into her handkerchief, and Sandra squeezed her arm. At least Sandra had that much sympathy for her. Lydia stole a quick peek at Harvey. He had his head down and seemed absorbed in his songbook. She forced herself to focus again as another song was given out. Twenty minutes later, the parting song was sung— "God be with you till we meet again."

As the last notes ended Sandra was all smiles, but she made no further effort to speak to Lydia. Clyde got to his feet at once and Sandra bounced up to follow him. They likely had plenty of things to talk about with their wedding plans in the forefront of their minds. Thankfully Harvey waited a decent amount of time until he rose to his feet, giving Lydia a brief glance on his way out.

"Be happy, Deacon Schrock," Lydia muttered under her breath as she got up to follow Harvey. The steady couples had left the driveway by the time Lydia slipped into the washroom. She finally found her shawl under several others. Some girls came in behind her and whispered together, but they didn't pay Lydia any attention. All of them would go home with their brothers unless one of them had a date, which wasn't likely. From the sound of their giggles they enjoyed spending time in each other's company before the evening ended—the way she and Sandra used to, before the troubles of life intervened.

Lydia hurried outside and found Harvey's buggy on the first glance. He had pulled off to the side of the lane and was waiting with his buggy lights on low. The buggy door remained closed as Lydia approached, but she paused for a moment. What if she was wrong, and this wasn't Harvey's buggy? After another quick look around, Lydia reached up and pushed the buggy door open.

Harvey was sitting on the seat with a nervous grin. "Sorry about that. I should have waited outside the buggy. I wasn't thinking, I guess. But *goot* evening."

"And *goot* evening to you," Lydia said, climbing in to settle on the buggy seat.

"Get up," Harvey hollered to his horse, and they were off down the lane.

After a few minutes of silence, Lydia finally asked, "So, how are you doing?" She made a point to look straight up at him.

Harvey's chuckle was still nervous. "Okay, I guess. I'm not used to being with a nice woman like you. I hope you understand that."

"That's kind of you to say. Don't be nervous, though," Lydia offered. "I'm…happy to spend time with you. You don't have to feel out of place at all."

Harvey didn't look persuaded as he turned onto Madrid Road. The silence inside the buggy was broken only by the steady beat of his horse's hooves. Searching for a subject that should put Harvey at ease, Lydia asked, "What's your horse's name?"

"Roger Boy," Harvey said, a smile filling his face.

"Did you come up with that yourself?" Lydia asked. "I've never heard such a name."

Harvey gave her a brief glance. "The sale barn called him that name when I purchased the horse, and I thought it was *goot* enough. And Leslie did too, and…" Harvey's voice trailed off into silence.

"Well, it's a nice name," Lydia said, shifting on the buggy seat. Now she had made the poor man uncomfortable for sure, and with such an innocent question. Still, she was on the subject now, so Lydia took a deep breath. "Do you still miss her?"

"*Yah*, a lot," Harvey responded. "It feels like I've lost part of myself." He searched for words. "Or like my heart is torn out, yet my body goes on living."

Lydia reached over to touch his arm. "I'm so sorry. But I think I can understand that. At least a little."

"You can?" Harvey stared at her in the darkness.

Lydia nodded. "I've never lost a loved one to death. Not a husband at least, but everyone has their sorrows. Enough that we can sympathize with others, I suppose."

"I guess," Harvey grunted, but he didn't look convinced.

Lydia brushed an imaginary wrinkle out of her dress. "Did Deacon Schrock tell you about me? About my sins?" She hadn't thought of this angle of conversation yet. What if Harvey knew she had seen her old *Englisha* boyfriend Rudy this very afternoon?

A slight smile played on his face. "No, the deacon said we should get acquainted and that I would like you eventually."

Lydia made a face in the darkness. "That's what he told me too."

"Well, he was right in that you seem nice enough," Harvey said.

"Thanks for saying so," Lydia responded. "I'm sorry we're both in this situation. I really am. If I would have employed better wisdom in my choices the past few months, this wouldn't have happened."

"But then you wouldn't be riding home in my buggy," Harvey said. "I'm glad you're here."

"You're a very nice man," Lydia said. "I just mean that I'm sorry we're together because of our sad circumstances."

"*Yah*," Harvey agreed. "I suppose I could do better by not spending so much time thinking about the past, or what might have been under different circumstances. Had Leslie not been taken from me."

"At least we have that in common—sad circumstances."

His face had grown sober. "I hope you understand when I say that being with you seems like a safe place. I'm not good with words."

"Oh, you are, dear," Lydia said. "You're very good with words. I haven't had anyone say nice things about me in a long time."

"But they are things that should be said," Harvey mused. "We all need to speak well of each other and not say things that hurt."

"Perhaps Deacon Schrock needs to hear that."

His chuckle filled the buggy. "So what is your big secret? If you don't mind me asking."

Lydia stared out into the night. She saw Rudy's handsome face this afternoon and felt his strong arms wrapped around her.

"Let's just say that I've made some wrong choices," Lydia finally said. "I'm sure you've heard some of the stories about me. Mostly true, I'm afraid."

"Everyone makes wrong choices," Harvey responded.

"Again, you know the right words to say. Thank you. I have to admit I wasn't sure how this would turn out…but I'm glad you brought me home, Harvey."

"And you were more than kind to allow me the opportunity," Harvey said as he slowed down for the Troyers' driveway. He turned in and swung the buggy around at the end of the walk.

"You're not coming in?"

"No, this is far enough." Harvey's nervous grin was back.

Lydia tried to smile. "But I have brownies and pecan pie ready."

"No, Lydia." His voice was firm. "It's best if I go. But I'll see you next Sunday evening, if you'll let me drive you home again."

"*Yah*, of course." Lydia hesitated at the buggy door. "You won't be telling Deacon Schrock that I sent you off early?"

Harvey laughed. "I'll tell the deacon you were a very charming host and had pecan pie and brownies ready for me."

"Thank you, Harvey. You're very kind." Lydia climbed down and stepped back from the buggy.

Harvey clucked to Roger Boy and took off into the night. Lydia watched the buggy lights until they disappeared into the distance. Her first date with Harvey had been easy enough, and not that unpleasant, but still…

*One day at a time,* Lydia told herself as she walked toward the house. *Only one day at a time.*

# Chapter Thirty-Six

Sandra pulled the buggy out of her driveway and headed toward Lydia's house on Johnson Raod to pick her up.

For a few Sundays in a row now, Harvey Miller had taken Lydia home after the evening hymn singing—and the Troyer family seemed to be back in the *goot* graces of the community. Ben Troyer still had some weeks' worth of proving left, but even Amos Helmuth had approved of Sandra resuming her friendship with Lydia. "You can visit your cousins again," he had told her. "Especially since your wedding is coming up soon."

That she would be exchanging wedding vows with Clyde, the man she had once written off entirely, was still mind-boggling to Sandra. Her heart actually beat faster at the thought of their upcoming marriage. Clyde hadn't kissed her yet, but of course he would after the wedding. Clyde loved her. She could tell from the look in his eyes when he gazed at her, and from his kind words about her beauty and her worthiness to be a *frau*. What girl's heart wouldn't beat faster at such attentions?

"You are the best thing to ever happen to me," Clyde had told her last Sunday evening.

The couple would set up housekeeping at the new farm Clyde had purchased next to his *daett*'s place. He'd spoken with the *Englisha* owners and explained their wedding plans, and the owners had already closed and vacated the house. Today Lydia had agreed to help Sandra begin to clean the place. But beforehand, the two girls would stop in for a visit at Rosemary's house on Old State Road. The reports on Rosemary's health were *goot* one week and down the next. Lydia had suggested the visit, now that her relationship with the community had been patched up. Sandra had agreed, especially since Rosemary was their friend, and they'd always regret a missed visit if Rosemary's health took a turn for the worse.

Sandra slowed for Aunt Mary's driveway and pulled to a stop at the end of the sidewalk. She pushed the buggy door open and leaned out to call, "I'm here!"

Lydia opened the front door at once. "I'm coming. Just a minute!" she yelled back.

Things were almost back to how they used to be, though Sandra's time was now mostly taken up with Clyde. Soon she'd likely have *kinner* to fill a big house, while Lydia had announced no wedding plans with Harvey.

Lydia had been firm on the point the last time Sandra had asked. "We're just friends," Lydia had said. Sandra couldn't envision what lay ahead for Lydia, but she could easily imagine her own future. Before long there would be the pitter-patter of little feet on the long hardwood floor hallways of the big house. All of Clyde's *kinner* would be handsome like he was, she was sure.

Just then Lydia raced from the house, down the porch steps, and toward the buggy. Sandra leaned out and said, "You don't have to hurry. We have all day."

Lydia waved her hand and deposited the mop and rags in the

back of the buggy before she answered. "I'm always in a hurry, you know. And we're stopping in at Rosemary's place, aren't we?"

"*Yah*," Sandra said. "We have plenty of time. We won't finish the house today because there's too much to be done."

"That's okay. We have time before the wedding."

"Speaking of weddings," Sandra said with a wry smile, "how are things going with Harvey?"

"Fine. He brings me home. I serve him food. We talk," Lydia deadpanned.

Sandra laughed. "Maybe it'll happen suddenly to you the way it did to me. But you don't have to worry, it will happen. Soon your days of trouble will be over and you'll be looking forward to a wedding this fall yourself."

Lydia shrugged. "Let's not talk about me and Harvey. Deacon Schrock's happy, and Harvey's a pleasant friend. Let's leave it at that."

"Okay, but have you asked Harvey whether he'll be a table waiter at our wedding?"

"Yep," Lydia replied. "Harvey said that he most certainly would, that he would be honored."

"*Goot!*" Sandra said as they pulled into Rosemary's driveway fifteen minutes later. "Should we tie up?"

"We're not staying that long," Lydia said as she climbed down from the buggy.

As the two approached the house, Rosemary's *mamm* opened the front door before they knocked. She had a tired smile on her face.

"Is Rosemary awake?" Sandra asked.

"*Yah*, she woke up an hour ago," Rosemary's *mamm* said. "And she will be glad to see you both. She's still upstairs in her bedroom. You can go on up."

Sandra led the way up the stairs and peeked into the open

bedroom door. Rosemary was propped up on several pillows, and her face broke into a big smile when she saw her friends. "Come in, both of you. This is such a treat." Rosemary motioned toward two chairs in the room.

Sandra stepped up to the bed to give Rosemary a hug. "How are you doing?"

Lydia did the same, as tears moistened her cheek.

Rosemary managed another smile. "I'm okay. The Lord has His reasons and His ways. He doesn't always explain them to us."

"But are you doing any better?" Sandra inquired.

"Good days and bad days, I guess." Rosemary sat up straighter on her pillows. "I've had another of Dr. Katz's experimental treatments this week. It's different from the last one. This one makes me sleepier. Of course, neither *Mamm* nor Deacon Schrock will say how much this all costs, but that will be the end now. No more expensive treatments if this doesn't work."

Lydia reached over to hold Rosemary's hand. "I can't imagine what you must be going through."

"At least I have Ezra." Rosemary grinned. "He's such a blessing, but you both already know that. How are you doing with Harvey Miller, Lydia?"

"We're friends, but that's all."

"That's all so far," Sandra interjected. "With God all things are possible. Look at me and Clyde if you have any doubts."

"Have you told Lydia about Ezra, like you promised?" Rosemary gave Sandra a long look.

Sandra gasped. "No. And I'm not going to."

"What on earth are you talking about?" Lydia asked.

"I asked Sandra to talk to you about Ezra," Rosemary said.

"What about Ezra?" Lydia asked, casting a wary glance at Sandra.

"Rosemary, don't…" Sandra begged.

"If you won't, I have to," Rosemary said. She turned to Lydia. "I don't have much time left…I just feel it in my bones. I want you and Ezra to look after each other when I'm gone."

"Rosemary!" Lydia gasped. "How can you say that? Ezra is yours."

"He's mine while I'm here," Rosemary agreed. "But he won't be mine when I'm in heaven."

"Oh, Rosemary! You don't know what you're asking!" Lydia said.

Rosemary ignored Lydia's outburst. "You will, won't you, Lydia? Ezra has been the most *wunderbah* man I could have had by my side all these long months. I know he loves me, but I also know he was given to me for a reason and for a time. That time is almost over. And when I'm gone, I want Ezra to have the best *frau* possible."

"Rosemary!" Lydia scolded again. "Stop talking like that. I will not hear it. You are going to get well, and Ezra will wed you, not me."

Rosemary lay back on her pillows. "Will you at least promise not to turn him away if he comes to you after I'm gone? Will you promise me that?"

Sandra held her breath. Lydia didn't say anything as she stared at the bedroom wall.

"Promise me?" Rosemary repeated. "Promise for my sake?"

Lydia broke her silence and squeezed Rosemary's hand. "Look, Rosemary, I would love to say whatever brings you comfort, but I can't make promises about such matters. You must think about getting better, and not about Ezra and me. I once pursued Ezra, but that's in the past. Sandra did, too, but now she has Clyde. I'm seeing Harvey, Rosemary. You know that."

Rosemary reached up to touch Lydia's face. "You have a heart of gold, Lydia. I know you're the one for Ezra, but I also understand your situation. Remember, though, what I told you when I'm gone. Be kind to Ezra. He's a man with a tender heart."

Sandra cleared her throat. "Maybe we'd best go now, Rosemary. We must have already tired you by now."

Rosemary tried to sit up but fell back on the pillows. "You have lightened my load considerably now that you know this, Lydia. I love Ezra so much and he has been so kind to me. He will be here again tonight."

Lydia reached down to squeeze Rosemary's arm. "You let Ezra help you get better."

Sandra gave Rosemary another hug before the cousins slipped out of the room.

After they had climbed into the buggy, Lydia whispered to Sandra, "I was so embarrassed by that conversation."

"I know. I would be too," Sandra said. "Rosemary asked me to tell you earlier, and I told her I expected her to pull through. I said I would only say something if she didn't make it. I also told her she should be the one to tell Ezra."

"Ezra!" Lydia exploded. "Would she really say such a thing to Ezra? Oh, now I feel like crawling in a hole and covering myself up with dirt."

Sandra gave Lydia a sharp look. "Ezra might consider Rosemary's advice, you know. What would you do then?"

"It won't happen. She's not dying." Lydia was firm. "Rosemary will get well."

"You have no argument with me on wishing for that," Sandra agreed.

Lydia was quiet for the rest of the ride until Sandra pulled into the driveway of the farm Clyde had purchased beside his *daett*'s place on Todd Road.

Lydia took a long breath at the sight of the huge house. "Sandra, this is what you have always dreamed of."

"I know." Sandra laughed as she pulled Dixie to a stop by the barn. "I never really thought it possible. I was just, well, dreaming."

But Lydia wasn't listening. She had climbed out of the buggy to gaze at the house. "Sandra! This is delightful! I'm so happy for you!"

Sandra tied Dixie to the barn wall and returned to gaze at the house alongside Lydia. Sandra finally exclaimed, "Someday I will rejoice with you, Lydia, as you are rejoicing with me! We will all be whole again!"

Lydia didn't answer as tears trickled down her cheek. "I'm just happy for you, Sandra."

# Chapter Thirty-Seven

The morning sunlight flooded the upstairs hallway where Sandra held Clyde's hand. Today was their wedding day…at last. Sandra looked up into his face and declared, "You're so handsome this morning in your new black suit, Clyde. I could—"

Standing beside them, Mark chuckled. "Um, the rest of the wedding party is here, you know."

"Surely I can tell my almost-husband that he's *goot*-looking," Sandra retorted. "You can plug your ears if you don't want to listen. And if I kiss him right here and now, feel free to look the other way."

"The bride's feisty this morning," Clyde's cousin Dennis commented.

"Okay, enough out of you two," Clyde said. "Anything my bride says at this moment is fine with me—in public or in private."

Sandra giggled and gave Clyde a quick hug. Mark and Dennis shook their heads in mock horror.

Finally Mark glanced at his watch and said, "It's time to go now. Besides, I can't take much more of this."

Sandra clung to Clyde's arm and whispered in his ear, "I'm so happy this morning. And you are so very…"

Mark glared at Sandra. "You're not going to hang on his arm as you go downstairs, I hope. The family will never live down that embarrassment."

"I know how to behave myself," Sandra replied. "But I'm happy today, and I'll show it however I want."

"Do they always fight like this?" Dennis quipped.

"At least she doesn't quarrel with me," Clyde said with a smile. "She likes me."

Mark hid his smirk. "That's because she hasn't had time to fight with you yet."

"I'm going to get you for that remark." Sandra took a step toward Mark.

Dennis pretended to tremble with fear. "She *is* feisty! Soon she'll come after me."

"You two stop!" Clyde ordered, but he glowed with happiness himself. "Who would have thought I'd have clowns for witnesses on my wedding day?"

"Ignore them," Sandra decreed. She brushed the front of her dark blue wedding dress one last time before she took Clyde's arm and marched toward the stairs.

Sandra took a deep breath as Clyde opened the stair door and they stepped out into the living room. The minister's bench was set up to the right of the stairwell, and Bishop Henry's smiling face looked up at them. Deacon Schrock was seated at the end of the bench, and he also appeared pleased. Sandra followed Clyde to the special chairs set up near the bedroom door. She had placed them there herself early in the morning, well before daylight. She had stepped back in the light of the kerosene lamp to imagine how they would look seated across from each other, with the two witness couples on either side of them. Now she didn't have to imagine it—the moment had arrived.

Sandra waited until Clyde sat before taking her own seat. She pinched herself to think that by afternoon, Clyde would be her husband.

A song number was given out, and from across the room Amos's broad smile caught her attention. Sandra forced herself to smile back. He was still demanding at times, but the man had paid for her wedding. He had allowed her to plan the day as she wished. Amos had insisted on one thing, though—that her dress be made of a dark blue material. That was a tradition in their family, he had said.

"You'll look *goot* in anything, dear," Amos had assured her. *Mamm*, too, had married Amos in a dark blue dress. That was fine with Sandra—sort of fine. She didn't look her best in dark blue, but Clyde had seemed impressed this morning when he saw the dress for the first time. So it wasn't worth a battle.

Sandra focused on Clyde as Bishop Henry rose to his feet. He led the line of ministers up the stairs, and Sandra followed Clyde's lead when he stood to follow them. The two witness couples stayed behind. This would be a time of final instructions given to the wedding couple before they said the marriage vows. She already knew how to keep house, can food, wash clothes, and cook. She also already loved Clyde. Still, there were doubtless things she could learn. She'd pay close attention this morning. A teachable spirit was highly valued in the community, and she would be a *goot frau* for Clyde. On that, she was determined.

Bishop Henry had seated himself when Sandra entered the largest upstairs bedroom with Clyde a step in front of her. Mark had helped her move the bed yesterday in preparation of this moment. They had set chairs for the ministers on one side of the room and two on the opposite wall for Clyde and herself.

"We'd best practice," Mark had teased.

"This can't be that difficult," Sandra said.

Mark had chuckled and seated himself on Clyde's chair. "The simplest things are what trip you up."

She had given in and seated herself beside Mark to stare at the line of empty chairs. She had descended into giggles, and Mark joined her with laughter of his own.

"Thankfully the ministers don't see us now," Mark had quipped. "They'd declare you unfit to be wed."

"No they wouldn't," Sandra had shot back. "They'd know I'm just happy."

A smile lingered on her face as Sandra remembered the moment. She glanced across the room at the line of ministers and sobered at once. They wouldn't know why she was smiling, and she wasn't about to explain.

Bishop Henry gave them both a brief glance before he opened the session. "Let's have prayer and remember our young couple before the Lord," he said. "As you all know, we are very thankful for this moment and for the testimony they both bring to the community. But we know the enemy lies ready to destroy and to steal. Also, we can remember Rosemary on this our day of joy. As the Lord sometimes wills it, sorrow and happiness walk close together."

"Amen," several of the ministers said, and they all bowed their heads.

Bishop Henry led out with the words from a psalm. "O LORD, our LORD, how excellent is thy name in all the earth! who hast set thy glory above the heavens."

Sandra sent up her own prayer. *Dear Father, remember Rosemary today in her suffering. Let Rosemary become well, if it's not against Your will, perhaps even on my wedding day. If not, then comfort Rosemary's heart and give her joy during her suffering. And help us all today. Let me not be overcome with my happiness, but let me remember that life has sorrows ahead for Clyde and me. Help us to endure and finish our journey together with faithfulness and commitment to each other.*

Bishop Henry finished his prayer with an "Amen." Sandra kept her head bowed for a moment.

"And now for the instructions for our young couple," Bishop Henry said. "I don't have much to say myself, really. Both of you have manifested a spirit of humility and submissiveness in your life. Sandra, you have been through a difficult valley with the death of your *daett* last year. But you and your *mamm* have made wise choices since then, and the Lord has clearly blessed your efforts. For that we give much thanks. As to further instructions for the bride, I've tasted of her mother Edna's cooking, and have been greatly blessed. I'm sure, Sandra, you have learned to work equally well in the kitchen from a *mamm* who is such an excellent cook."

"She won't be starving Clyde, that's for sure," Deacon Schrock quipped.

The line of ministers joined in the laughter.

"Have you instructions for our young couple?" Bishop Henry asked the deacon.

"I've given plenty already," Deacon Schrock deadpanned. "Perhaps we'd best leave the floor to the others this morning. We don't want to stay up here all day."

"Are you saying that you're long-winded or that we are?" one of the other ministers asked.

Deacon Schrock laughed. "I was referring to myself, of course. Sometimes I don't get home from my Saturday rounds until after the cows come home."

This produced another round of laughter, and even Clyde joined in. Sandra didn't, though, because it might not be proper. She could laugh in the presence of the other women, but a smile was sufficient at present. These were all ministers, after all, even if they indulged in a lighthearted attitude this morning.

"I think I'll follow Deacon Schrock's excellent example this morning and keep my thoughts brief," the first minister said. "I have been married now for ten years to Melissa. The Lord has blessed us with six children in that time. If there is one thing I would wish to say, it's to Clyde. Be the man in your home, and lead your children in the fear of the Lord. Be careful to discipline your children for their disobedience, and bring their will under the Lord's order. This will save much trouble for you and for them later. And to Sandra, I say support your husband. Stand by his side always when you have differences with the children. Speak to him in private, and Clyde, when she does, consider her thoughts. You are the head of the home and must make the final decision, but your *frau* will have important things to say. As one wise man once told me, 'Your *frau* is often right, but it's difficult to accept it when it happens.'"

Another round of laughter went up and down the line.

"I thought you were keeping your thoughts brief," Bishop Henry teased.

"I couldn't resist that line," the minister said, with a chuckle.

"Okay, let's keep moving," Bishop Henry instructed. "Those were all wise words, so Clyde and Sandra, consider them."

Fifteen minutes later the last minister finished his remarks. He said, "Be strong in the Lord, both of you. Keep a teachable spirit about yourselves. Listen to each other and raise your *kinner* in the fear of the Lord. On our part we will remember you in prayer, and wish you the Lord's fullest and complete blessing."

"Okay, thank you all for that," Bishop Henry concluded. "You can go now, Clyde and Sandra. We'll be down in a bit. That is, after we've figured out who can preach the shortest sermon on your important day."

Clyde joined their laughter and stood up to lead the way out of the room. "They were awful nice to us," Clyde whispered on the way down the stairs.

"*Yah*, and my heart is overflowing with happiness," Sandra whispered back. "Because soon you will be my husband."

Clyde's face glowed. He paused long enough on the stairs to give Sandra a quick hug. "I'd kiss you now, but they'd see our red faces," he said.

Sandra suppressed her giggle and clung to Clyde's arm until the moment before he opened the stair door.

Clyde seated himself, and within a few minutes the ministers came down the stairs. They still had smiles on their faces, so Deacon Schrock must have made a few more jokes since they left the upstairs room. Sandra forced herself to pay attention as the first sermon began. The words were all *goot* and helpful as the time drifted past. Lydia caught her eye during the second sermon, and sent a warm smile her way. Sandra smiled back as the joy of the day flooded all the way through her.

Finally the moment arrived. The clock on the living room wall read a quarter to twelve. Bishop Henry rose to his feet when the last sermon was concluded and turned to face them. "If the two of you are still willing to enter into the holy state of matrimony," he said, "you may rise to your feet."

Sandra knew the back of her dress shook as she stood before the community. She said "*yah*" over and over again to the questions. After the last one, Clyde's familiar hand was placed in hers by Bishop Henry.

The bishop's voice echoed through the house. "By the power invested in me by the state of New York and the Lord as a minister of the gospel, I declare you man and wife. May the God of Abraham and Isaac and Jacob bless your union and give you many happy years together. Amen."

The room went in circles as Sandra sat down. She clung to the sides of the chair with both hands until Clyde's handsome face slowly came into focus again. Someone gave out the song number and the singing began. Sandra wanted to jump up and hug Clyde and kiss him right there in front of everyone, but that wasn't how things were done. She held still and allowed the thought to sweep over her.

She was Clyde's *frau* now.

# Chapter Thirty-Eight

I t was a Wednesday night, as the last shadows of the evening
stretched across the Beilers' lawn. Rosemary, her bed now set up
in the living room, tried to raise her arm to reach for the glass of
water beside her bed but failed. As Rosemary drooped over the edge
of the bed, *Mamm* and *Daett* both hurried to their daughter's side.
Rosemary sighed, but allowed *Mamm* to lift her head to take a small
sip before Rosemary closed her eyes again.

*Mamm*'s voice reached Rosemary through the fog. "Ann has
gone for Ezra."

Rosemary formed the words with effort. "Don't bother him
tonight. He was here only last night."

"Nevertheless, he's coming." *Mamm*'s voice was firm. "You need
him."

Rosemary opened her eyes. "Am I dying, *Mamm*? Is it tonight?"

"Ezra is coming," *Mamm* repeated, then hurried away toward
the kitchen.

Yah, *this must be dying*, Rosemary told herself. She had avoided
the truth even as she felt the strength seeping from her body these
past few days. Each evening found her weaker than the night before,
and each morning brought a little less relief from the long dark

hours. Was her battle nearly over? Perhaps this was for the best. The experimental treatment had obviously failed, and even the pain medication Dr. Katz had given her only dulled the pain to a bearable ache. This was not living. Though hope still knocked on the door, the sound was dim—and grew dimmer tonight. Her road on this earth was near its end, and she was afraid. She didn't want to fear death, but the truth was the truth. She was very afraid.

"*Mamm*," Rosemary called out, but the sound came out in a cough, faint and distant.

*Mamm* appeared in the kitchen doorway. "*Yah*, Rosemary?"

"Perhaps I do need Ezra tonight."

"He's coming, dear." *Mamm* came near to stroke Rosemary's forehead. "And Bishop Henry and Deacon Schrock are also coming along with their wives. Ann is stopping in at their places on the way back with Ezra."

Fear again filled Rosemary's face. "They shouldn't be bothered."

*Mamm* didn't answer as a tear trickled down her face. Rosemary looked away. She knew what that meant. Bishop Henry and Deacon Schrock wouldn't be on their way if it wasn't going to be her last night on this earth. Rosemary tried to sit up, but her head didn't leave the pillow.

"Lie still," *Mamm* chided. "They'll soon be here."

Rosemary stared out the living room window. *Daett* stood near her bed, silent, with his head bowed. Her life was over, and she had only lived a few years. The pain medication couldn't remove the sting of that truth. She had given herself up to the Lord's will many times, but she still wanted to live. Leaving this earth meant that she had to leave behind the *wunderbah* gift of Ezra's love. Yet, hadn't that gift been given to help her through this time? There seemed no other explanation. Yet, what if she could have lived and become Ezra's *frau*? What would it have been like to say the wedding vows with him? If there had been time to wed Ezra, she could have borne him a child before she left this earth. Other women were allowed to see the faces of their *kinner*. Shouldn't she be allowed to see one of her own?

*Mamm*'s voice broke through Rosemary's thoughts. "Ezra's here now."

Rosemary forced a smile as the front door burst open and Ezra rushed in with Ann close behind him. Worry lines were deep across his face. *Daett* nodded to him and left to put away Timber. Rosemary managed to lift her arms to Ezra, and they embraced. *Mamm* hurried off again to the kitchen, but Rosemary didn't care who saw her embrace Ezra. She loved the man more than words could ever say.

Ezra's hand slowly stroked her face. "How are you tonight, dear? Ann came and said I should come."

"You look so tired," Rosemary whispered. "I wish…"

Ezra shook his head. "Don't say anything. I was glad to come."

"I think the time has come," Rosemary said. "I've tried not to be afraid, but I am."

Ezra wrapped his arm around her again and pulled Rosemary's thin frame close to his strong one. "We must pray and beseech the Lord," he said. "While there is breath, there is hope."

"Just comfort me," Rosemary whispered. "Pray that I have strength for the journey. The waters look so dark."

Ezra choked and didn't speak for a long time.

"I haven't told you this before," said Rosemary, "but I must speak the words before I go. Lydia—"

"No! You must not!" Ezra ordered. "You must rest your mind."

"I must say what I have to say," Rosemary insisted. "You have been kind to me, Ezra. You have loved me when I am so unworthy of your love. I know you were sent by the Lord to see me through this moment. I know that with all my heart, so don't tell me otherwise. Only the Lord could have filled your heart with the tender love you've shown me, but that will soon be over. You must move on with life. That's what I want to say. When I'm gone, you must open your heart to Lydia. She's not in love with Harvey Miller, because she's always been in love with you. And don't protest. After I'm gone, remember my words. You were meant for each other from the beginning, Ezra. Lydia is the *frau* who can walk by your side through life. Lydia can bring you the honor you deserve."

Ezra released Rosemary back onto the bed, and she laid her head back and tried to breathe. All her strength seemed to have gone into the words. Maybe she could go now, right at this moment when she had done her duty. Would the Lord not honor her heart once she was gone? Ezra would have to listen. "You must," Rosemary added out loud.

Ezra didn't answer as he held Rosemary's hand.

*Mamm* reappeared from the kitchen. "You'd better take your medicines," *Mamm* interrupted. "Bishop Henry and Deacon Schrock have just pulled in the driveway. *Daett* is helping them put their horses away."

Rosemary shook her head. "I don't want any medications. Ezra is here."

*Mamm* hesitated, but Ezra spoke up. "You can always take them later if it's necessary."

"I want a clear head," Rosemary whispered, "while I have Ezra here." Things were hazy enough without the medicines. She wanted to experience fully her last moments with Ezra—if that's what this was. And from the look on *Mamm*'s face, it was.

*Mamm* hurried to the front door. "Hello," *Mamm* said to the arriving guests. Ezra's hand left Rosemary's when the voices came closer. He greeted the visitors with a smile and a nod.

Bishop Henry looked pleased to see Ezra, and worried at the

same time. He turned to Rosemary and asked, "How are you feeling, dear?"

"Weak and dizzy," Rosemary managed. "But you didn't have to come."

"We wanted to, Rosemary," Deacon Schrock said. "We are here to help where we can."

Both ministers' wives, Lena and Ruth Ann, came to stand beside Rosemary with *Mamm*, *Daett*, and Ann behind them. Ezra stepped sideways to make room. They all stood in silence until Deacon Schrock said, "Let's pray."

They all bowed their heads as Deacon Schrock led out, "Dear Father in heaven, the merciful one, we ask for Your presence this evening and in the night ahead of us. Have compassion on us all as we confess our sins and seek Your guiding hand in this time of trouble."

Rosemary closed her eyes until Deacon Schrock said "Amen."

Bishop Henry broke the silence that followed. "We should have communion."

Deacon Schrock nodded. "There's no reason why we can't break holy bread with Rosemary."

A sob escaped *Mamm* before she hurried off again. Moments later she returned with a small loaf of bread and a glass of wine, which she handed to Deacon Schrock. Bishop Henry held one hand over the bread and wine and the other over Rosemary's forehead. Softly he prayed, "We give You thanks, oh Lord of heaven and earth, for Rosemary and the life she has lived with us. Rosemary has been a great gift to us, and she has loved You as an obedient and faithful child. Bless this food that we take in remembrance of Your death, and bless Rosemary, whatever Your plan is for her life. Keep Rosemary through this night, and take her spirit into Your hands in life or in death. For we know that those who believe in You shall never really die. Amen."

"Amen," echoed Deacon Schrock.

Ezra said nothing, but his hands clasped Rosemary's tightly. Rosemary clung to him as Bishop Henry broke off pieces of bread and passed them around. He placed one in Rosemary's mouth with a gentle touch. Rosemary closed her eyes as silence filled the room. Ezra soon lifted Rosemary's head so Bishop Henry could place the glass of wine to her lips. Rosemary took a small sip and swallowed, and the others took their turn with the cup.

"And now to the God who has redeemed us, be all the praise, honor, and thanks," Bishop Henry intoned. "May His name be exalted in all the earth and in our humble lives. Let His glory fill the whole world and receive now our unworthy praise and the feeble utterances of our lips. Amen."

"Amen," Deacon Schrock echoed.

"Let us sing now," Bishop Henry said. Rosemary listened to their voices rise and fall, and drifted off to sleep. She awoke and slept again as the time passed. She couldn't see the clock in the times she was awake. But what did it matter? Ezra was still by her bedside. The other faces faded in and out.

Lydia and Sandra arrived with Clyde. Lydia, overtaken with grief, turned to Ezra and cried on his shoulder. Rosemary smiled at the sight. It was to her a holy sight. Now the Lord had everything under control. Why else were her last hours so peaceful? And the singing went on—voices raised in the familiar songs she had grown up with. Now the voices sang with sorrow and weariness, but also joy.

"You must be tired of singing," Rosemary muttered once.

"Hush," Ezra ordered. And she didn't argue. There was no strength if she had wanted to.

Sandra bent low to kiss Rosemary on the cheek.

"I'm sorry I couldn't make it to your wedding," Rosemary said.

Sandra wrapped Rosemary in a tight hug and hushed her. "Don't you say a word. We're the ones who are so very sorry."

*Mamm* brought another blanket and wrapped it around Rosemary's shoulders. She was cold, but she hadn't noticed that, either.

"Do you think this is it?" Sandra whispered from somewhere off in the distance.

"She'll leave us with the dawn," Ezra said. "Let us pray for strength."

*The dawn,* Rosemary thought. What did that mean? The room was dark. It had been dark for a very long time. What would the dawn look like? Would she see it? Another dawn. The thought was pleasant…and yet…

Rosemary drifted off to the soft singing still in the room. Bishop Henry and his *frau* left sometime in the night, as did Deacon Schrock and Ruth Ann. Lydia, Sandra, and Clyde stayed awhile longer, but they too left as Rosemary slept. She awoke to silence and to still forms seated around her. She stirred, and Ezra's hand was on her forehead at once. The dim kerosene lamp cast faint shadows on his tired face. When Rosemary managed to reach up to touch him, the stubble on his chin bristled under her hand. How she loved the man.

"Is it morning?" Rosemary asked.

He didn't answer.

"Is it?" Rosemary insisted.

"The dawn is breaking," Ezra admitted. His gaze shifted to the living room window where the first streaks of light stirred the horizon.

"Hold me," Rosemary whispered.

Ezra's strong arms lifted her out of bed, as the others stirred around them. The soft murmur of voices was silenced by Ezra's order. "Be still, everyone."

Silence fell, and Rosemary allowed herself to sink into Ezra's strength. He was distant now and fading away. He seemed to lift her higher, but Ezra hadn't moved. Sounds reached her, at first distant, but beautiful until they filled the room. Songs she had never heard.

"Are they singing again?" Rosemary asked.

"No," Ezra said.

"But they are singing," Rosemary insisted.

"They must be angels," said a voice.

Rosemary struggled to sit up, but she sank back into Ezra's arms. It was the strangest feeling. Try as she might to reach upward, only one hand would raise up before it fell back on Ezra's knee. Yet she was lifted from within, drawn upward with a pull of a mighty force. A light more brilliant than the sun rose through the living room window, and yet she could look straight at it.

"The dawn," Rosemary whispered. "It has come."

Ezra held her in his arms. She could feel him, and then…

"She's gone," Ezra said after long moments had passed. He laid the body tenderly back on the bed. "Rosemary has left us with the dawn."

He stood for several moments with a bowed head. Then he walked out of the house to look toward the east, where he shielded his eyes against the bright rays of the blossoming sunrise.

# Chapter Thirty-Nine

I n the early afternoon, on the day of Rosemary's funeral, Lydia stood among the crowd of people huddled in the graveyard. *Mamm* and *Daett* stood a short distance behind her. Ezra was with the immediate Beiler family, his head bowed, as the casket was lowered into the ground. Emma and Rhoda had attended the service at the Beilers' house, but they hadn't come to the graveside service.

"I've seen enough sorrow for one day," Emma had whispered before she left with Rhoda.

And Emma was correct. There had been much sorrow today, but there was also an undercurrent of joy. On the morning of Rosemary's passing, Deacon Schrock had brought word to the Troyer home and had spoken about his final evening with Rosemary. He said the presence of the Lord seemed to be in the room, and that Rosemary's sister Ann had reported, "We all heard the angels singing when she passed."

Emma and Rhoda had been skeptical of that report. "Anyone can hear anything at those moments," Rhoda declared, and Emma had agreed.

But Lydia realized her sisters just didn't want to open their hearts to any divine comfort, for fear they would be drawn away from their determination to leave the Amish faith. Neither Emma nor Rhoda had been a friend to Rosemary, so they hadn't understood the depth of Rosemary's suffering or the loss Lydia and Sandra had felt.

Lydia had certainly felt the loss deeply. In her grief, she even had embraced Ezra at Rosemary's bedside—and without hesitation or embarrassment. Somehow it had seemed right that Ezra had embraced her right there in front of Bishop Henry and Deacon Schrock—and even Rosemary herself.

Ezra's face was steadfast today as he stood with Rosemary's family. That was Ezra's rightful place. He had been Rosemary's boyfriend, and had been with her until the end—even holding her in his arms as she passed over. They gathered now around the open grave as the casket was lowered.

"I'm so glad Ezra was there to help Rosemary cross over," Ann had said. "And the singing was beautiful at the end. It was so faint, but Rosemary heard clearly. You could tell by the look on her face."

Lydia glanced over at *Mamm* as a song was begun at the gravesite. *Mamm*'s head was uplifted, and tears filled her eyes. The beautiful words of the German song rose and fell in the stillness of the open air. "Oh, great are the works of our God, He gives life and He receives it unto Himself again. Each morning His face is lifted with mercies anew, and each evening finds us again in the hollow of His hand..."

Lydia caught sight of Harvey Miller among the mourners. She should be at his side as his girlfriend, but theirs was a strange relationship. They saw each other every Sunday night, but Harvey still went home early most of the time. Not infrequently he simply dropped her off at the end of the sidewalk and said good night. She was comfortable with the arrangement since it kept any questions Deacon Schrock might ask at bay. Harvey must know about the six-month mandate, but he never mentioned it. If Harvey intended to woo her, he still hadn't made the effort. Maybe she was just pleasant company in his dreary life and nothing more. Strange as their situation was, she had no energy or inclination to break the reverie before the six months were complete.

What would happen afterward, she had no idea. Her heart still mourned Ezra, but she had no right to the man, despite what Rosemary had said. That whole thing was unthinkable. It felt as confusing and meaningless as Rosemary's illness and passing.

Lydia brought her attention back to the present. The third song had ended, and silence filled the graveyard. Faint sounds of dirt being shoveled came from the graveside. Men came forward with bowed heads to offer their help. Ezra, his face focused and serious, was one of the first to take his turn with a shovel. Lydia watched him lift each shovel of dirt with ease and drop it carefully into the grave. When he finished his turn, Ezra handed the shovel to the next man, straightened his back, and gazed off toward the east and the open blue sky. He seemed to be remembering something.

What had Ezra seen in those last moments when he held Rosemary in his arms? He must have seen something, because Ezra was changed. He had always carried about him a happy-go-lucky attitude. Now that part of him seemed buried under the surface. Ezra had a seriousness about him, an intensity she had never noticed before. Ezra seemed to have made up his mind.

Lydia looked away as the last of the dirt was tossed into the grave. The crowd began to mill around her, and people began to whisper to each other.

"There was something so comforting about the day," someone said. "We sorrowed but we also rejoiced."

Lydia smiled. *Yah*, that was how it was today.

"*Yah*, there was such a testimony at the deathbed, they said. I know I was comforted in my heart when I heard," someone replied. "It's such a great sorrow when a young person passes, especially when it's a girl like Rosemary who had such promise. She had even won the love of young Ezra Wagler. I do so hope the Lord comforts his heart in his loss."

"Ezra loved her greatly," another voice answered. "Rosemary died in his arms, they say."

Lydia moved away. In the distance, by the graveyard fence, she saw Ezra and Harvey speaking together. They seemed caught up in an intense conversation. Lydia sighed and turned away. What could Ezra and Harvey possibly have to say to each other? Especially today? The answer wasn't so difficult to fathom. On the day of Rosemary's funeral, there was no connection between the two of them but herself.

Lydia pushed the thought away. She would think no more about this. Thankfully *Mamm* stood near their buggy, so *Daett* must be about ready to leave. Lydia pressed through the crowd, nodding and shaking hands with several people. No one engaged her in a long conversation on this somber day.

Lydia paused to catch her breath when she arrived at the buggy. "Are we ready to go?" she asked *Mamm*.

"*Yah*." *Mamm* glanced around. "*Daett* was just here."

Lydia felt a soft touch on her elbow and turned to find Harvey Miller behind her. He appeared flustered. "Can I drive you back?" His voice was a little above a whisper.

*Mamm* must have heard and turned to Harvey with a smile. "Harvey. It's good to see you. Of course you can drive Lydia home."

Harvey's head bobbed. "I need to speak with Lydia. I'll take her back to the Beilers' place for the meal. Is that where you're going?"

"*Yah*, we are." *Mamm* still smiled. "We'll see you there."

Lydia followed Harvey toward his buggy, where he untied Roger Boy. She climbed in the familiar buggy and Harvey gave her the lines, then he climbed in without making eye contact.

"Get up," Harvey called to the horse. The buggy slowly pulled out onto the main road.

Lydia decided to let Harvey take his time in broaching whatever had prompted this ride to the Beilers'. She waited for a long time as Harvey stared off into the distance, but he finally spoke.

"Lydia, I want to say that I appreciate your efforts over these past months. You've put up with me and my loneliness without complaint. All along I knew you could never love me, or me you, but that was okay. I didn't expect much out of the relationship. I also knew why you agreed to allow me to take you home, and I knew I should spend time with a woman again. I also knew that a serious relationship with someone would have been too much for me. So I want to tell you, Lydia, that I appreciate what you have done for me these past months. You have helped me move on with life without making me feel like I had to be someone I'm not. Thank you for that."

Lydia lowered her head. Harvey had never spoken this many words before. Sometimes he had never spoken so many words in one evening.

Harvey continued, "You have been kind to me, Lydia. I know you could have scorned me silently, but you didn't. You showed me the tender side of yourself, and your joy. You were considerate of my strange ways. You stuck with me without a bitter attitude, and you even made me smile when I thought I wouldn't smile again. You probably think you didn't give me anything these past weeks, but I know differently. You gave me your best, and for that I will always thank the Lord."

Lydia searched for words. "I don't understand. Why are you telling me this? And what does Ezra…?"

"Ezra will be taking you home on Sunday evening instead of me."
Harvey hesitated a moment, then offered a lopsided smile. "I don't
suppose you object."

Lydia drew a long breath. "I don't know what to say…or think.
Are you sure?"

"I believe this is what was always supposed to be," Harvey said.
"The story is going around that at the end, Rosemary claimed God
sent Ezra into her life for the purpose of loving her during her final
battle. I think He sent you to me for a similar reason—except in my
case, He sent you so that I could begin to live again."

Lydia felt her face blushing at his praise. "I…I…had no idea,
Harvey. I don't know what to say."

"There's no need to say anything, Lydia. Besides, here we are.
Whoa!" Harvey called out to Roger Boy. Harvey stopped the buggy
along the back barn fence.

"Thanks again," Harvey said, as they both climbed down from
the buggy. "I really do appreciate what you did for me."

"You're welcome," Lydia managed. To say "welcome" felt strange.
She ought to thank Harvey, but that didn't seem right. Instead, she
looked around and seeing no one, she reached over and gave Harvey
a brief hug, then quickly backed away and hurried toward the house.

Out of the corner of her eye, she saw another buggy pull in.
Ezra's buggy. At the sight her heart began to beat faster.

How wise and considerate Ezra had been to allow Harvey to
explain himself before speaking with Lydia—if indeed he intended
to speak with her. The very notion that it might happen took her
breath away.

# Chapter Forty

Lydia slipped out of the washroom door the following Sunday evening after the hymn singing. None of the other girls gathered around gave her a second glance. There was no reason anyone should think she wasn't on her way to Harvey's buggy as usual. They didn't have to know until the news leaked out tomorrow morning. She had told *Mamm* about the change in plans, but no one else. *Yah*, there was still sorrow over Rosemary's death, but it was subdued by the knowledge that Rosemary was in a much better place. Besides, Rosemary had wanted this very evening to happen. "Open your heart when the time comes," Rosemary had told her.

The thought had seemed indecent back then. She would not have pursued Ezra again. Yet Ezra had been firm with his decision to take her home tonight. Otherwise, she would not be headed toward his buggy instead of Harvey's. Ezra's change of heart was what eased her conscience. She had noticed the lift of his head in the services today and his occasional glances her way. *Yah*, much had changed. She would ride home with Ezra tonight and they'd take it from there. The thought that Rosemary's wish for them might come true made her dizzy. Deacon Schrock could certainly find no wrong if Ezra took her home from the hymn singing. What could he say?

Lydia found Ezra at his buggy just as he was fastening the last tug.

"*Goot* evening," Lydia greeted him, still feeling a bit awkward, but also excited.

Ezra was matter-of-fact. "*Goot* evening to you. Climb in."

Lydia pulled herself up and settled on the buggy seat.

Ezra climbed in and clucked to his horse, and they whirled out of the driveway.

Just as she had let Harvey speak first, so too would Lydia remain silent now and let Ezra take the lead.

His face was sober as he began to speak. "I know this is awkward, Lydia. But I think we both need to find out if what Rosemary wanted for us is also what we want for us. Beginning with me taking you home tonight."

"*Yah*, I agree," Lydia offered. "But you need to know I've not exactly behaved myself in the past few months. Just ask Deacon Schrock." Lydia gave him a quick sideways glance. "That's why I was going home with Harvey, not because—"

"I know all about it," Ezra interrupted. "But that's past. Now we have to believe the Lord works things out for the best. I spoke with Deacon Schrock this afternoon, and he agrees with me that you have made your intentions clear about staying in the community. I have his blessing to take you home."

Lydia clutched the side of the buggy door and tried to breathe evenly.

Ezra smiled. "So there will be no dropping you off at the end of the sidewalk tonight."

"You sound pretty sure of yourself," Lydia chided.

"I am sure of myself," he said. "But more than that, we have to be sure of the Lord in all this."

"We have all changed, haven't we? We used to be so silly," Lydia said. "Sandra and I. You've certainly changed. I'm not sure I deserve you, Ezra."

"It's not a question of deserving, but of love." He gently reached over to touch her arm with his free hand. "Can we find love together? I believe we can. Life has touched us deeply with sorrow and left us better for it. At least, I believe that of you."

"Of me?" Lydia croaked. "I still feel like I have such a long way to go. You, on the other hand—oh, Ezra, I can't say more or I'll cry for sure."

"Go ahead and cry. I'll understand," Ezra assured her. "After all you've been through, you've only become better."

Lydia's voice trembled. "Did you know that I backed away from pursuing you so Sandra could have you to herself?"

Ezra looked a little grim. "You two were the limit, but *yah*, I knew. I suppose Sandra asked for that after her *daett* passed?"

"*Yah*." Lydia didn't dare look at him. "But then Rosemary captured your heart."

"And this Rudy fellow captured your heart again."

Lydia forced her hand to touch his arm. "*Yah*, and that was my mistake. You need to know the truth, Ezra. I did love Rudy once, back in our *rumspringa* time, and *yah*, I was tempted to return to that love, but I realized it could never happen. If my having loved Rudy changes your mind about me, you can drop me off at the end of the sidewalk and I won't blame you at all."

"I wouldn't do that, Lydia." Ezra's voice was tender. "I'm not that perfect a saint myself. You loved Rudy. I loved Rosemary. I would have married her if she hadn't passed. Can you live with that? Knowing I loved her and would have married her?"

"I could never hold such a thing against you, Ezra…if you will really and truly love me now."

"*Yah*, and that's what this time together must be. For each of us to know for sure that we share the kind of love that is from God. And that we are meant to be together," Ezra said. He took the turn into the Troyers' driveway. "Shall I come in then?"

"You know you can," Lydia said. "I have apple pie ready, or perhaps only the half that Emma and Rhoda didn't eat."

Lydia waited beside the buggy while Ezra tied Midnight to the hitching post. She took his arm and led the way to the house. At the front door Ezra stayed a step behind until she held it open for him.

"The couch, I suppose?" Ezra pointed.

"You can come to the kitchen with me," Lydia suggested.

"Did Harvey come into the kitchen with you?" Ezra's gaze pierced her.

"No," Lydia said. "Remember, we were just friends. There were never romantic feelings on either side. He is a decent man and much in need of a *frau*. I hope he finds someone…soon."

"I do too, then," Ezra said. "And about Rosemary…I loved her, but in God's plan, it wasn't meant to be forever. Maybe Rosemary was right all along. Maybe we were given something for a time, something for a reason, something that wouldn't have happened any other way, or at any other time, something…"

"*Yah*," Lydia agreed. "It was God's way of comforting Rosemary… and Harvey."

"Perhaps we had best leave these things to the Lord. I am here and you are here, and we have apple pie to eat."

"Just like a man!" Lydia teased. "It always comes back to his stomach!"

As she turned to slice the pie, soft footsteps came up behind her and Ezra's arm slipped around her shoulder. She turned back to him to bury her face in his chest, and the embrace of his arms closed around her. This seemed so right and yet so long in coming. Lydia started to cry. "It'll be okay," Ezra whispered into her hair. After a moment, he released his embrace.

Lydia gathered herself together and continued cutting the pie, then poured them each a glass of milk.

Ezra took Lydia by the arm and both plates with the other. "Come. The couch is more comfortable."

Lydia brought the milk glasses in both hands.

Ezra seated himself and took the first bite. "This is quite *goot*."

"See, I can cook." Lydia gave him a triumphant look.

Ezra laughed. "I never had my doubts."

When they had finished, Ezra said, "So, now one important question remains."

"*Yah?*"

"Can I come again next Sunday evening?" he said, flashing a grin.

"You can." Lydia looked deep into his eyes. "I would be pleased, very pleased."

# Chapter Forty-One

Lydia was hanging out the wash on a Monday morning. Ezra had said he would stop by later to pick her up for a drive over to a small farm he had his eye on. Ezra wanted to know whether she liked the house, and would consider…

"I'm sure I'll like it," Lydia had assured Ezra on Sunday evening. "Whatever you like, I'll like."

"I still want you to see it," Ezra had insisted.

More than anything, Ezra probably just wanted to spend time with her. He still hadn't formally asked her to be his *frau*, but that was where things were headed. They had both known this would be the eventual outcome ever since Ezra first brought her home from a Sunday night hymn singing.

Occasionally guilt niggled at Lydia with the thought that she had stolen Rosemary's boyfriend, but Ezra's presence always comforted her. Ezra knew where he wanted to go in life, and he wanted her along. Maybe that made everything right enough to say the marriage vows together. Many a woman had married a widower, and she would be doing no worse. She must open her heart fully to the joy of Ezra's love. How long had she waited for this to come into her life? Too long.

Lydia hung a shirt on the line. The pinned laundry had begun to move as the breeze stirred. *Yah,* life moved on, and she must move with it. She was in love with Ezra and Ezra loved her. There was no shame in that. The Lord had made a man to love a woman, and a woman to respond to his attentions. She would say the vows with Ezra this fall.

Lydia reached into the hamper again, holding the clothespins in her mouth as she struggled with a long dress. Her reputation in the community was back to where it had been before *Daett's* financial mess. There was nothing to prevent her wedding day.

Ezra's strength since Rosemary's passing comforted her. Not only his physical strength, but also an inner strength that he had not previously possessed. When Ezra held Rosemary in his arms that dawn, he had seen more of the other side of the river than he admitted. Lydia would have to dig the memories out of him sometime, but she hadn't dared so far. The matter seemed too sacred to approach yet. Perhaps after their wedding vows, she would ask him.

Ezra was changed, that she knew, and for the better. Of course she had undergone her own adjustments. Ezra would no longer be impressed with the silly girl she had once been. Neither was she capable of further childish stunts, like the ones Sandra and she used to pull.

Lydia hung the last piece of laundry on the line and hurried toward the house. Emma was in the kitchen with her apron on and flour all over the table. There was a tidier way to make bread than this, but Lydia held her tongue. Emma had already made up her mind to jump the fence after her *rumspringa* time was up. But *Mamm* still hoped to change both of her youngest daughters' minds. She must not interfere or make things difficult for them.

"You don't have to get that look on your face," Emma snapped. "I know I'm not like you when it comes to baking bread, but neither do I have to be. I'm leaving for a world where they have bread-making machines, or you just buy the stuff at the store." A look of bliss filled Emma's face.

Lydia kept silent as Emma continued. "You could have had the same thing, you know, instead of this boring life we lead. Rudy would take you back gladly."

"You should think about coming back yourself," Lydia told her. "Back to where you belong."

"Not a chance!" Emma said.

"You should join the baptismal class this fall," Lydia said. "Become a church member and settle down."

"No way," Emma replied as she measured flour into the bowl. "I'd have to learn how to bake bread properly, and put up with an Amish husband who would work me half to death."

"Sometimes the hard things lead to the best end," Lydia said. Emma made a face at her sister and added milk to the bowl, then stirred the contents. "Think about it," Lydia added as she heard Ezra's buggy pull in the driveway.

Lydia washed her hands, grabbed her shawl, and went out to greet Ezra's waiting buggy.

"What's the big smile for this morning?" Ezra teased as Lydia climbed in the buggy.

"Just glad to get away from washing," Lydia teased back. "And from trouble-bound sisters!"

"So you just want to get away," Ezra said. "It's not about me." His boyish grin appeared.

"Okay," Lydia admitted. "I was thinking of being with you."

Ezra chuckled. "Well, that's better. Did your *mamm* object that I took you away from the housework this morning?"

"Nope. She's glad I'm with you," Lydia said.

"Then your *mamm* approves of me?" Ezra raised his eyebrows in mock surprise. "Of me? Just think about that!"

"You are so full of yourself this morning," Lydia teased.

"No, I'm just happy that I'm with you and that we're on our way to look at a lovely farm—our future farm."

Lydia gave Ezra a shy look. "Did I miss something? If you're taking me to see a farm that you might buy for *us*…shouldn't we do something formal about…*us*?"

Ezra grinned. "I think I've been plain enough about my intentions."

Lydia faked a glare. "I think we should…like, maybe…"

Ezra's laughter filled the buggy. "Okay, I give up."

"I mean, we do still have to say the wedding vows, so we still should…" Lydia stopped.

Right now she wanted nothing more than for Ezra to take her in his arms and kiss her…but he wouldn't do that. Not yet.

Ezra kept a grin on his face as the miles rolled under the buggy wheels. Lydia leaned back and closed her eyes. Ezra would ask the question eventually. And then she would begin to plan the wedding. What a day that would be!

A mile later Ezra pulled back on the reins and turned into the driveway of a well-kept farm on River Road. The trimmed white house stood back from the road, with small bushes and a rail fence. The porch went all the way around the side and was wide enough for a front porch swing. There was no swing there now, but Ezra would add one right away, Lydia was sure.

"Here it is," Ezra proclaimed. "Do you like it?"

"Oh yes! But I'd like to see the inside," she said, still thinking about the unasked question that would settle whether she would live in this house. Ezra was a German-stubborn man, but surely he would ask the question soon.

Lydia jumped down to get a better look. They'd have to make a lot of changes to the place. The power pole would have to go, of course. And all the signs of electric power. *The hitching post will go right here,* Lydia decided. She could see their guests arriving already. Sandra would tie up her horse and run toward the house while Lydia rushed outside to greet her. Sandra would have her *bobbli* along, because she was already showing at the last Sunday meeting. Such things were all hush-hush in the community, but the obvious was the obvious. Sandra had giggled when she caught Lydia's eye. That was all the answer she needed. Sandra was happy with Clyde, and Lydia would also be happy here in this place. She already knew that. Ezra would be here, and that would be enough.

"I'm glad you like it," Ezra whispered in her ear.

"You still haven't asked the question," Lydia reminded him.

Ezra laughed. "No, I guess I haven't, have I?"

Lydia rolled her eyes. He was obviously teasing her. She wondered if he realized women had a limit when it came to teasing about marriage.

"There's no one home," Ezra said, "and I have the keys. Let's look inside."

Lydia relaxed and allowed the stillness of the farm to wrap itself around her as they walked up the porch steps.

Ezra paused to unlock the front door, and stepped back to motion her inside.

Lydia caught her breath. The house had appeared small from the outside, but the look had been deceptive. The living room was open and spread back toward the kitchen. They could easily have the church service inside the house. That was always a plus, since houses large enough to hold winter services were growing scarcer each year. She could hold her head high and announce that Ezra's house was ready to take its place among the best. She could already see Bishop Henry standing at the kitchen entry to preach the closing Sunday message. They would spread the tables out afterward, and the married men could eat at one end and the married women at the other. There was also a basement. She had seen the outside entrance on the way in.

"Like it?" Ezra asked.

"I love it." Lydia's gaze swept the living room again.

Ezra's hold on her hand tightened. "Will you, then? Marry me, Lydia? And live in this house? With me and our *kinner*, if the Lord gives us any?"

Lydia struggled to breathe. He had asked so suddenly, yet *not* so suddenly. The moment had been a long time coming, but now it was here.

"Well, will you?" Ezra repeated. "I want you to be my *frau*, Lydia."

"Oh, Ezra. *Yah!* Of course I will! Oh, you've finally asked. Can I hug you?"

As an answer, he wrapped his arms around her and Lydia buried her face in his chest. The sweet smell of straw and of the haymow filled her senses.

"You wanted more, didn't you?" he whispered in her ear.

Lydia closed her eyes and lifted her face to his. For a long moment he didn't move. Then he kissed her gently. When he drew back, Lydia opened her eyes to gaze into his. "Ezra, I'm so very happy!"

"You deserve happiness," he said, wrapping her in another tight hug. He let go and said, "Now that you've had your wish, shall we look at the rest of the house?"

"I already like it," she said, "but your desire is my command."

He took her hand in his. "I do desire it."

"Then so shall it be." Lydia smiled up at him, and they walked on toward the kitchen together.

# Chapter Forty-Two

Lydia trembled as Ezra held her hand on the short walk to the pole barn. The time for the evening meal on her wedding day had arrived. The warm Indian summer days of a late October sky hung over their heads. She had never trembled before at Ezra's touch, but Ezra had never been her husband until today. Bishop Henry had declared them man and wife this morning, and she still hadn't gotten her breath back. Ezra wasn't supposed to hold her hand. Not with all the community people gathered in the yard around them. But of late, Ezra did what he wanted. Deacon Schrock stood beside the pole barn door and smiled as they approached. Ezra would get away with his capers as usual.

Ezra let go when they entered the pole barn, where they slid behind the corner table again. Their two witness couples came in from either side with big grins on their faces. Emma had been persuaded to serve for her side of the family, along with Marlon, the younger son of Deacon Schrock. They seemed to have gotten along well today, but you couldn't always tell with Emma. Lydia wouldn't get her hopes up. Emma likely wouldn't go any further with the relationship. She had her heart set firmly on jumping the fence. Besides, Marlon was likely not interested in Emma.

"Penny for your thoughts?" Ezra teased in Lydia's ear.

"Just thinking about Emma and Marlon," Lydia whispered back.

Ezra sobered. "*Yah*, there might be hope there. We must pray, I suppose."

As usual, Ezra understood perfectly and without much explanation. Lydia had noticed that quality about him this summer as their relationship progressed. Likely Ezra had always been that way, but she had failed to notice.

The other witness couple was Ezra's younger brother, Levi, and his girlfriend, Nancy. At the moment Levi was leaning around Nancy to whisper to Ezra. They both laughed at whatever Levi said. Ezra turned to Lydia and explained, "Levi was just reminding me of Uncle Elmo's wedding story. At the evening meal, the older serving couple was so exhausted from the day's events that the woman let the whole bowl of potato salad slip into Uncle Elmo's lap. He had to go and change, and the hymn singing started without him."

Ezra waved to his uncle, and Lydia chuckled. Uncle Elmo must have figured out what all the commotion was about because he headed their way with his *frau*, Thelma, at his side.

"Now stop laughing," the man ordered his nephews. "I know what's being said. My infamous wedding story."

"At least things turned out well," Ezra teased. "You're still married."

"And happily married even with the potato salad in his lap," Thelma added.

"Just think how much you would have missed in life without that potato salad story," Levi said amid the laughter. "It's been the icebreaker at many a family gathering, so what a blessing that potato salad has turned out to be."

"Yep," Uncle Elmo agreed. "I haven't regretted a moment."

The laughter continued between them, until Uncle Elmo and

Thelma moved along. Uncle Elmo turned around to quip, "Now, watch that potato salad bowl when it arrives."

"I will," Ezra promised.

The chuckles continued until Bishop Henry called for prayer. With the amen said, the meal began in earnest. Levi burst into laughter when the evening servers, who were none other than Lena and Bishop Henry himself, appeared with the first course of meat, potatoes, gravy, and potato salad.

"What's so funny?" Bishop Henry demanded. "Did I botch the prayer that badly, or is my suit coat stained with gravy? You can't expect too much from an old man, you know."

Ezra chuckled. "It's an old family joke. Uncle Elmo's servers let fly the potato salad bowl, and it ended up in his lap. The poor fellow had to go change and missed out on the opening of his own evening wedding meal."

Bishop Henry smiled, but said, "You know how those tales grow with the telling. I remember that wedding, and there was a spoonful of potato salad involved. It dropped from your Uncle Elmo's plate and onto the tabletop. He got a little splattered—that's all."

"Isn't that something?" Ezra grinned. "Here we have been told a tall tale all these years."

"Now don't quote me on that." Bishop Henry smiled. "I'm getting old, you know, and my memory often drifts at times."

"Just don't drop the potato salad," Ezra told him, and everyone laughed again.

"That's quite a treat, having the bishop serve us tonight," Lydia said once things had quieted down.

"He likes you." Ezra glanced at Lydia out of the corner of his eye.

Lydia punched him in the ribs. "The bishop likes *you*. That's the reason he's serving our table."

"I'm glad you know what a *goot* catch I am," Ezra deadpanned.

Lydia faked a horrified look. "You have become so conceited. I should tell the bishop."

Ezra laughed and said nothing more. He knew she liked his confident ways. Lydia was now married to the man of her dreams, and she would wake up tomorrow morning with Ezra in the house. She would fix breakfast for him, and they would say their first morning prayers together. She would have Ezra to herself all day. No longer would Ezra leave each Sunday evening or after he dropped her off at the house on a weeknight.

Lydia focused her attention on Marlon, who was seated to her right. He had leaned over to whisper something to Emma, and the two laughed. Lydia waited until silence had fallen before she told Marlon, "Congratulations on your sister's wedding announcement this past Sunday. I figured that was coming, but you never know."

"*Yah.*" Marlon smiled. "It's been busy around the house all summer, but I guess that's the way it goes."

"She's getting a *goot* husband—a Troyer," Lydia said.

"Now look who's conceited," Ezra said. "Besides, you're not a Troyer anymore. You're a Wagler now."

"Oh, that's right,' Lydia said. "I forgot. I'm now Lydia Wagler."

"And don't you forget it!" Ezra warned.

"Ha! As if you'll let me," Lydia teased.

Ezra gave Marlon a look. "See what you're in for when you marry? Only married a few hours and she's onto me."

Just then Bishop Henry and Lena reappeared with their arms filled with dessert bowls. "What have I missed?" the bishop demanded to know. "You'd best tell me, or there will be church trouble."

"Their first argument," Marlon said. "Better sign them up for marriage counseling!"

Ezra pretended to give Marlon a glare, and the bishop joined in their laughter. He set down his dessert bowls and Lena did likewise. "*Goot* to see you all having such fun tonight." The bishop nodded his head to both Ezra and Lydia. "Both of you have come a long way, and have much to thank the Lord for."

"That we do," Ezra agreed.

"*Yah*, we do," Lydia managed.

Tears stung Lydia's eyes at the bishop's unexpected reminder. Indeed, how *wunderbah* the Lord had been to her. His blessings rose higher than she had imagined possible. She would not have experienced this if she had left the community with Rudy. Somehow, in some mysterious way, she had captured the affections of Ezra Wagler and was now his wife. She was at peace with her family and the community. There was also that *wunderbah* homeplace Ezra had purchased for them on River Road. She deserved none of these blessings. Not one of them.

Ezra must have noticed the train of Lydia's thoughts because he reached under the table to squeeze her hand. Lydia gave him the best smile she could muster. Thankfully Ezra didn't make a further display of his affection where everyone could see them. He settled for a grin, and Lydia leaned against his shoulder for a moment. They finished their dessert in silence until Bishop Henry and Lena reappeared to remove the plates.

"A blessing to you all!" Bishop Henry pronounced on them in parting.

Lena added with a smile, "Welcome to the world of married life, Ezra and Lydia."

"Thank you," Lydia replied. "That means so much to me coming from you."

Ezra confirmed the sentiment. "*Yah*, it does. We're honored that you served us tonight."

"I wouldn't have missed the chance." Bishop Henry grinned and left with Lena close by his side.

The singing began within minutes, and Lydia joined in. She couldn't keep her gaze off of Ezra's face, though. And he seemed to have the same problem with her. Their hands often found each other under the table, and Lydia hoped her face didn't flush too much. Emma noticed, though, and smiled, which gave Lydia an idea.

"Hold her hand," Lydia whispered sideways to Marlon.

He appeared startled, but moments later Emma's face colored. Maybe Emma would fall in love with Marlon. Wouldn't that be a decent accomplishment on her wedding day—along with saying the vows with Ezra?

The songs continued, as did the glances between Ezra and Lydia. Lydia finally looked away and kept her gaze on the songbook. There was a limit to the attention even married couples could pay each other at their wedding supper. Time dragged, and slowly the clock on the pole barn wall crept toward nine o'clock.

The parting song was given out on the dot of nine, as if everyone was ready to leave. But that didn't happen once the song ended. The young people made their exit quickly enough, but the older people and the visitors from out of state lingered around the pole barn in deep conversation. One by one, people came by to shake the newly-weds' hands and offer their blessings on the marriage.

"You can leave if you want," Ezra told the two witness couples around ten o'clock.

"I've been enjoying myself too much," Levi quipped, but he was the first to jump to his feet. The others followed him outside. Emma turned and gave a little wave of her hand, but Lydia saw that Emma's other hand was still in Marlon's. Lydia gave her sister a knowing grin.

"You saw that too?" Ezra chuckled when Emma and Marlon had disappeared. "We must continue to pray for them."

Lydia took a deep breath. "*Yah*, and for Rhoda." Her younger sister had served as a table waiter today and had left earlier, but *Mamm* and *Daett* had stayed to take Emma home. *Mamm* was still in conversation with Ruth Ann Schrock, so Emma would have a few moments to talk with Marlon in private. She hoped the conversation went well. Very well indeed!

Ezra smiled and took Lydia's hand under the table again. No one had come by for some time, and the pole barn was almost empty. They waited and waited until at last, Bishop Henry appeared and shooed the last stragglers out the door. He turned out most of the gas lanterns, but left one above their heads.

"To show you the way out." Bishop Henry grinned. "Your horse is ready, Ezra."

Ezra stood to take Lydia's hand and lead the way to the buggy. Midnight pawed the ground as if he'd waited much too long. Lydia climbed in while Ezra went to check on his horse. Ezra patted Midnight's neck for a moment and whispered something. The horse calmed down, and Ezra came back to climb in the buggy.

"Off we go," Ezra said as he took up the lines. "To our new home, and our new life together."

Midnight dashed out of the driveway, and Ezra laughed as he held the lines tightly. The moon had risen above the horizon and hung on the tree line. Overhead the stars twinkled in the darkened sky. Lydia leaned against Ezra, and his arm draped around her shoulder.

"Ezra, what did you see that morning you held Rosemary in your arms?" Lydia whispered.

Ezra didn't answer for a few moments. Lydia raised her head, and he finally spoke. "I saw glory shining in the sky, and I heard a little of what Rosemary must have heard. And I saw this—you and me, our life together."

"Would you have seen it otherwise?" Lydia sat up straight, but Ezra's arm didn't leave her shoulder.

His voice was hushed. "I have always loved you, Lydia. You know that."

Lydia laid her head back on Ezra's shoulder. "Somehow I understand." No other words came, but no words were needed. Ezra clucked to Midnight, and they raced through the night with the beat of horse's hooves and the whirl of buggy wheels beneath them.

# Discussion Questions

1. What is your first impression of the rivalry between Lydia and Susan?

2. What is your opinion of Rosemary's decision to pursue Ezra while the cousins are occupied with their family's financial problems? What was your first assumption as to where her dreams would lead?

3. If you had been in Edna Troyer's circumstances after Emil's death, would you have accepted Amos Helmuth's marriage proposal?

4. What would you have done with Lydia's rambunctious sisters, Emma and Rhoda?

5. At the time Rosemary received the letter from Johnny Mast, the future was still unknown. Where did Rosemary find the

strength to turn down Johnny for her seemingly useless pursuit of Ezra?

6. Do Sandra's strong negative reactions to both Amos and Clyde give any indications of her future acquiescence to both of their charms?

7. What are Rudy's real motives in his renewed pursuit of Lydia's affections? How would you have responded to them in Lydia's situation?

8. Could you tolerate the degree of interference Amish ministers exert over their members? Do you think there is any degree of benefit in this level of oversight?

9. What grade would you give Ezra in his handling of Rosemary? Do you think Ezra would have married Rosemary if she had not passed away? Would that match have worked?

10. Do you have any observations on the evening and night of Rosemary's passing?

# About the Author

**Jerry Eicher's** Amish fiction has sold more than 700,000 books. After a traditional Amish childhood, Jerry taught for two terms in Amish and Mennonite schools in Ohio and Illinois. Since then he's been involved in church renewal, preaching, and teaching Bible studies. Jerry lives with his wife, Tina, in Virginia.

# More Books by Jerry Eicher

### The Adams County Trilogy
Rebecca's Promise
Rebecca's Return
Rebecca's Choice

### Hannah's Heart
A Dream for Hannah
A Hope for Hannah
A Baby for Hannah

### Little Valley Series
A Wedding Quilt for Ella
Ella's Wish
Ella Finds Love Again

### Fields of Home Series
Missing Your Smile
Following Your Heart
Where Love Grows

### Emma Raber's Daughter
Katie Opens Her Heart
Katie's Journey to Love
Katie's Forever Promise

### The Beiler Sisters
Holding a Tender Heart
Seeing Your Face Again
Finding Love at Home

**Land of Promise Series**
Miriam's Secret
A Blessing for Miriam
Miriam and the Stranger

**The St. Lawrence County Amish Series**
A Heart Once Broken

My Dearest Naomi
Susanna's Christmas Wish

**Nonfiction**
The Amish Family Cookbook (with Tina Eicher)
My Amish Childhood

To learn more about Harvest House books and
to read sample chapters, visit our website:

**www.harvesthousepublishers.com**